THE DRAGON KING

THE BLESSED OF THE DRAGON

Book Three

Patrik Martinet

www.patrikmartinet.com

CONTENTS

ACKNOWLEDGMENTS

Thank you, Barrett. For some reason you agreed to read the early drafts of chapters as I wrote them. I feel as though I should apologize for letting you do that. I hope that you find the story much improved.

Thank you, Elayne Morgan, for your amazing editing skills. Thank you, Jake, of J Caleb Design, for once again making an amazing cover. And thank you, Zach Bodenner, for bringing Dradonia to life with your wonderful map.

A list of acknowledgements wouldn't be complete without also thanking all those who have helped me one way or another along the way. To each of you, I say thank you.

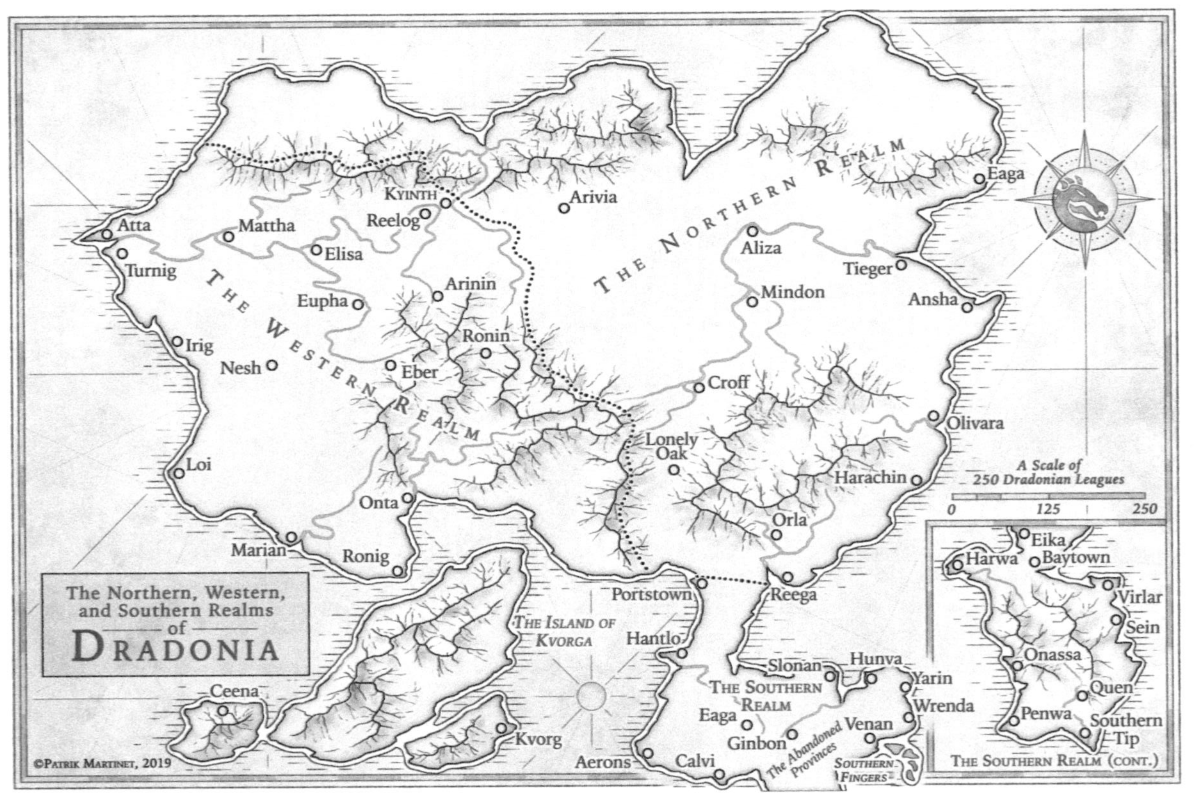
THE NORTHERN REALM
Eaga
Arivia
KYINTH
Reelog
Aliza
Tieger
Mindon
Ansha
Atta
Mattha
Elisa
Turnig
Eupha
Arinin
THE WESTERN REALM
Irig
Nesh
Ronin
Eber
Croff
Olivara
Loi
Lonely Oak
Harachin
Onta
Orla
Marian
Ronig
Portstown
Reega
THE ISLAND OF KVORGA
Hantlo
Slonan
Hunva
Yarin
Wrenda
THE SOUTHERN REALM
Eaga
Venan
Ginbon
The Abandoned Provinces
SOUTHERN FINGERS
Ceena
Kvorg
Aerons
Calvi
A Scale of
250 Dradonian Leagues
0   125   250
Eika
Harwa
Baytown
Virlar
Sein
Onassa
Quen
Penwa
Southern Tip
THE SOUTHERN REALM (CONT.)
The Northern, Western,
and Southern Realms
of
DRADONIA
©Patrik Martinet, 2019

THE DRAGON KING

BEFORE

389 United Era

Orwyn stood in the burning tavern, Harachin sword in hand. He anxiously watched the wall of flames inch closer. As he waited for Jax to return from the kitchen, he looked down at the two bodies clad in black leather at his feet and considered his options. He couldn't check the exit in the kitchen himself, so he'd sent Jax. He needed to maintain mental acumen at this crucial moment, and he knew the sight of Elen would shatter his concentration.

I should have sent her away with the boys.

The moment the entire front wall of the tavern erupted in flames, he'd known they were in trouble. The true extent of their peril became apparent when the flames began to creep unnaturally across the floor.

Draego's Fire.

Jax returned from the kitchen gripping the tattered cuff of his cloak in his hand. "The door's jammed. A trap?"

Orwyn nodded. With one less option to consider, he watched the flames creep closer and made up his mind. "They have us boxed in."

"Then let's fight our way out!"

"Jax, you know as well as I that the Sodality is out there in force. And they do not underestimate those they're sent to eliminate. The moment we attempt to open that door"—Orwyn looked from the unnatural flames moving toward them to the kitchen door—"they will attack us with everything they have. We wouldn't make it two steps out of this building, and you know it."

"What do you suggest, then? That we stay here and die?"

"Our only hope is that they don't know you're here as well."

"I'm not leaving you here, Orwyn."

"It's our only option, Jax. I'm getting you out of here."

"No!"

"There's no other choice."

"We should've left when we had the chance."

"I know," Orwyn acknowledged. His decision had cost him his wife. He didn't know if he could ever forgive himself. She didn't deserve this. "But I'm tired of hiding."

"Orwyn, no matter what, we're in this together. I'm not abandoning you here."

Orwyn forced himself to look away from the assassins. They'd killed his wife. He looked intently at his friend. "If you stay here, we're both dead. And I won't permit it."

"Then I'll stay," Jax said.

"No. You know they're here for me."

"Orwyn, if I had brought you—"

"Jax!" Orwyn shouted. "This isn't about that! The Regency's wanted me dead since the war. Now listen to me. *Please.* Go upstairs and position yourself by the window in my room. I'll create a distraction to draw them in. Wait until I strike. When you see them close in on the back door, flee out the window."

"Orwyn—"

"I'll catch up with you in the Mindons."

Jax hesitated. He stroked his beard and looked intently at Orwyn. Then he put his hand on Orwyn's shoulder and squeezed it tightly. "See you in the Mindons."

Orwyn knew when he said it that it was a lie.

He walked calmly into the kitchen as Jax positioned himself upstairs. He looked down at his wife lying in a pool of blood. He knelt beside Elen and moved a strand of hair so he could see her face one last time. He tried to hold back the tears welling in his eyes, but when he blinked, he set them free.

Orwyn took a deep, shuddering breath and stood. He drew deeply from the Harachin sword. Using Synthesis, he forced the door open.

When the first black-clad soldier appeared through the opening, he acted.

The kitchen wall exploded and sent bodies flying.

CHAPTER 1

410 United Era

The sun crept over the troubled sea, reflecting brilliantly off the water. Its light illuminated the remains of a once-dense forest. The fire-blackened trunks stood guard over the eastern shore of the Southern Realm, warning any who might come from the east of impending death. However, no one ever came; the ever-present cyclones swirling in the distance barred the way.

Empty cities stood abandoned, surrounded by leagues of failed crops, browned and withered by the sun's growing oppressiveness. Mansions that had once housed those worshipped by the masses now gathered dust, ignored even by those who had chosen to remain once their stores were picked clean.

As the sun's light raced west, the destruction became less evident. Cities and towns gradually became inhabited. Crops survived, but with diminished yield. Empty lakes gave way to lakes with deep water lines, and dry riverbeds began to flow. By the time the growing light illuminated the nearly identical palaces of Hantlo, all except the nearly continuous wagon train moving north appeared normal.

Hadie stood before the familiar mirror in Sonja's room. Her room. The feeling of disbelief at how easily her plan had worked still overwhelmed her. None of the women who worked for Sonja owed Hadie anything, and yet they had unanimously pledged their loyalty to her, knowing what she intended to do.

She examined herself in the mirror while Ursella selected her clothing for the day from the armoire. She decided that if she was going to do this—be a madam—she would not pretend to be someone she was not. She would not alter her being simply for the sake of pretending to be someone the Blessed desired.

"Dorlan and the other regents aren't nearly as picky as Drenan," Ursella said.

"Yes, but what if he returns?"

"It will not be done at his palace, so if he wishes to participate in Dorlan's revelries, he will have to partake of what Dorlan provides."

She'd had Ursella get rid of all the corsets with pockets for the water-filled pouches made from sheep stomach. They were used to alter the appearance of one's breasts, and she wouldn't permit any of her whores to use them. They were who they were and wouldn't pretend otherwise.

Ursella selected a yellow corset with flowers embroidered on it, and slipped it around Hadie's chest. While Ursella cinched it up, Hadie wondered whether she was still pretending to be someone she wasn't. Never in the time she worked with Sonja had she felt as though she was being true to who she was. She wasn't a whore. She'd gotten pretty good at pretending to be one, but it wasn't who she was. She wasn't a madam either.

"What is it?" Ursella said with a look of concern.

"I'm just wondering—"

"You are who you decide to be," Ursella said.

And I have decided that I am Madam Sheena.

"Thank you, Ursella," Hadie said. She took as deep a breath as was possible in a corset. "I couldn't do this without you, you know."

Ursella smiled up at Hadie. She finished cinching the corset, then retrieved a pleated skirt from the armoire.

When the skirt was in place, Hadie admired her new self. She held her hand out, and Ursella handed her her knife. She had decided to keep the knife she'd bought in Portstown instead of Sonja's slender blade. She slipped the blade into the sheath Ursella had sewn to the inside of her corset, bottom left side. Satisfied, she turned and walked out of the room. Ursella followed close on her heels.

Hadie walked each hallway as she made her way down to the lobby, and knocked on every door. At the beaded lobby entrance, she turned to address the crowded hallway. "Today is a big day," she began. "Word has reached the blessed ears of His Highness that Sonja has retired. Word has also reached the blessed ears that there's a new madam: Madam Sheena."

The women's eyes lit up in excitement, and they began to talk excitedly with each other.

While Hadie waited for them to quiet down, she thought about the visit she'd received last night from Dorlan's servant Sethlan. "We have been summoned to His Highness' court today, so please—"

Another murmur overtook them.

"Girls! Girls!" Hadie shouted. "Please!" The women quieted down. "So, please, don your finest."

The women dispersed back into their rooms. Hadie parted the beaded curtain with her hand and walked over to the chair in the back corner of the lobby, where Sonja used to supervise the goings-on of her brothel, and sat.

Ursella had already ordered the carriages that would take them all to the palace, so while she waited, she reflected over the past few days. She really couldn't have done any of it without Ursella. She had gracefully taken up her old position as Sonja's aide and served at Hadie's side. When she wasn't tending to Hadie's needs, which weren't many, she was tending to the patrons, serving them wine and lowering their inhibitions.

"Can I get you anything while you wait, Madam?" Ursella said.

"Some tea would be great."

While patrons moved in and out of the lobby throughout the evenings, Hadie sat in her chair, sipped wine, and studied each patron carefully. When Sonja had made her prepare the guests, she didn't want to know the least bit about them; she'd barely wanted to look at them. Now, she needed to know whom she served. She needed to know who it was that could afford to solicit the most elite of brothels in the entire Southern Realm. When Ursella had lulls in her work and came to stand beside Hadie, Hadie asked her about those who particularly piqued her interest. If they were successful in killing the Blessed, someone would need to rise and replace them. As much as she hated the idea, those best qualified to lead the people—at least initially— were her clients. They at least had the means.

Last night, after Sethlan's visit, she had overdone it with the wine. Ursella handed her a hot cup of tea, and she took a sip, hoping her headache would abate before she had to stand before the chancellor.

"Does the chancellor know you?" Ursella said.

Hadie shook her head from behind the cup poised at her lips.

"Then why are you so nervous?"

"I guess…" Hadie began. "I guess it's because it's not every day one gets summoned by the Chancellor of the Southern Realm."

"Relax," Ursella said. "It'll be fine."

Hadie sipped her tea, hoping Ursella was right.

* * *

Sethlan sat at his desk at the top of the dais in Dorlan's throne room, mindlessly recording another transaction. He scratched his head, trying to remember how he knew the woman who referred to herself as Madam Sheena. He knew he recognized her, but couldn't quite place her.

With Dorlan's mind preoccupied with his crumbling realm, he had barely reacted to the news of Sonja's sudden retirement.

However, it had shocked Sethlan. Drenan would not be pleased when he returned from Onta. But what had shocked Sethlan more than Sonja retiring was Sheena's sudden rise. All proprietors were required to present themselves for the blessing of their province's regent, and even though that didn't typically fall under Dorlan's responsibilities, Sethlan still heard about them. It was his job to know what was happening, not only in the Hantlo province, but in the whole realm. However, in his experience, it typically took months before he heard about new businesses. With Sheena, it had taken only days.

Which made him even more curious about who she was.

"Madam Sheena!" he called out.

A group of women wearing orange corsets—sensual attire from the Northern Realm—led by a woman wearing a yellow one walked forward from the back of the throne room.

The absence of Drenan had placed a heavy burden on Dorlan—and on himself, as Dorlan's servant and scribe—but for the first time since Drenan left, Sethlan didn't mind. Sheena's identity had been bothering him since Dorlan had sent him to visit her last night.

The whores sauntered to the front of the throne room and stopped at the foot of the dais. They spread out side to side with Sheena in the middle, giving Dorlan a view of them all. *An excellent view*, Sethlan thought to himself, looking down at them.

Sheena bowed deeply, along with all the other whores, then said, "It's a pleasure to stand before you, Your Highness."

"The pleasure is all mine," Dorlan said.

"I'm sure you've heard of the great void left in Hantlo by the sudden retirement of Madam Sonja," Sheena said, "I know how much respect she earned from years of dedicated service to the Regency. If it pleases you, Your Highness," Sheena said with a bow, "I request the privilege of filling that void. As you can see," she said, gesturing to her left and right, "I have under my employ the very same whores who faithfully served Sonja."

Sethlan's eyes lit up. Not because of her offer, but because he had remembered who she was. He didn't know her name, but she was the woman traveling with the man who'd attacked Drenan.

What is she doing here?

"Despite whom you may have under your employ," Dorlan said, "respect must be earned. Prove yourself a loyal subject of His Blessed Highness, Drakonias Irigwin Draeko Drake, Emperor of the United Realms, as well as to myself as Chancellor of the Southern Realm and the Regent of Hantlo, and I will consider your offer."

Sethlan watched the woman flinch slightly at the mention of the Regent of Hantlo. He looked over at Dorlan, who looked to have missed it.

"Yes, Your Highness," Sheena said with a bow. "I am but the most faithful of subjects, and it is my pleasure to meet whatever needs you might have. Thank you for your time." Sheena bowed again, as did the other whores, then turned to leave.

Sethlan made some notes in the ledger, then filed the other piece of information away in his mind for future consideration. It might be worth something to his true employer, Jorgan, at some point.

He looked at the list of the day's petitioners—they were only about halfway through them—and called out, "Walton Brythe!"

Yet another travel-worn man separated himself from the crowd with his equally ragged family and approached the dais.

* * *

Ursella shut the door to Hadie's room, and Hadie plopped into her plush chair.

"How do you think it went?" Hadie said.

"I thought it went well, Madam."

"He seemed… hesitant."

"Well, what did you expect? For him to give you the same treatment as Sonja without ever having heard of you before?"

"Yes, you're right."

"I think he will warm to you quickly, Madam. And who knows, your name might be on the list for entertainment when next he plans a gala."

"That's another thing I'm worried about," Hadie said. "One doesn't have to be Blessed to know things aren't right. I have a hard time believing the Regency would continue their debauched ways when the realm is falling apart around them."

"I don't think you have to worry about that. Their debauchery has no end."

"I hope you're right," Hadie said.

She had done what she needed to do with Dorlan. There was nothing more to be done except wait to be summoned for services, so she turned her attention to other matters that needed tending to; namely, she needed to procure more of the poison that was on the pin she was going to use to kill Drenan. And since she didn't know how to make it, she would need to buy it. She doubted buying poison was cheap, so before she even thought about where she might buy the poison, she needed to have an idea of how much money she had at her disposal. At her desk, she flipped open the ledgers that Ursella filled out daily and looked them over.

Hadie pointed at a figure and said, "Is this right?"

Ursella walked around the desk and looked at where Hadie pointed. "Yes, Madam."

Hadie added up the numbers in her head again. "We made nine hundred drakes the first night we were open?"

"You made nine hundred drakes, Madam. It went up to twelve hundred the second night and fourteen hundred the third."

Hadie was beside herself. "That's unbelievable!"

Procuring more poison was not going to be a problem.

"Where is it?" Hadie said.

"Madam Sonja always kept the gold at one of the depositories in the city. I opened a new account there the morning after we opened. It's not safe to keep that much gold here."

"Thanks," Hadie said, still in shock at how much money the brothel brought in nightly.

"Do you require anything else, Madam?"

"Not at the moment," Hadie said. "Thank you." When Ursella turned to leave, she added, "If you have the time later, I'd like to review the client list for the night."

"Yes, Madam. I'll return before they begin to arrive." Ursella curtsied and walked out.

When the door closed, Hadie opened the top left drawer of the desk and removed the poisoned hairpin. A small flower adorned it, made from tiny yellow and red gems. She turned it over, looking for clues as to who might have made it, but didn't find anything. She returned the pin to the drawer and shut it. Her plan would be worthless if she couldn't get several more of them.

Still recovering from too much wine the night before, she went over to her bed and lay down. A good nap would be the perfect thing after a stressful morning before the chancellor while nursing a throbbing head. She closed her eyes, and while she waited for sleep to overcome her, she thought about who Sonja knew in Hantlo who sold poison. It didn't take long for sleep to arrive.

* * *

"Madam," Ursella said, shaking Hadie gently by the shoulder. "It's time."

Hadie sat up on the bed and rubbed her eyes. Thankfully, the throbbing had stopped. She went over to the washbasin and used the cool water to wash her face and under her arms. Then she sat in her seat and listened to Ursella review the list of clients who would be visiting tonight.

"Stop there," Hadie said when Ursella read the name Phenor Morrigan. "I don't need to know any more about him."

Ursella looked at her askance. "Madam?"

"I already know everything I need to know about him."

"You know Phenor?"

"I do," Hadie said.

"How? Next to Drenan, he's probably the wealthiest man in Hantlo."

"Because he's my father."

Ursella stared at Hadie with a blank face. "Your father is—"

"Yes."

"What in Draego's Fire are you doing here?"

"It's a long story that's not important. What *is* important," Hadie said, suddenly realizing what she was going to do to replace the Regency once they were gone, "is what sort of influence I might still have with him."

"What do you mean?"

"Let's just say that when he sees me, he won't be pleased. Now, let's get downstairs."

Hadie stood and led the way out of her room and down the stairs. "What time is he supposed to be here?" she asked as they walked through the beaded curtain.

"Ten, Madam."

"And who is he coming to see?" Hadie asked, taking her place in the corner.

"Ylonna."

Ylonna? Hadie thought with a shake of her head. She did *not* want to think about the women her father was bedding. "Good," she said. "Please have her come see me."

"Yes, Madam."

Ursella brought her a glass of wine, then disappeared through the beads. While she was gone, Hadie moved to a couch and thought about what she was going to say to her father when he arrived.

Ylonna appeared through the beads before she could formulate any thought. Ylonna curtseyed and said, "You wanted to see me, Madam?"

Hadie gestured next to her and said, "Have a seat."

Ylonna sat.

"Tonight, you're going to have a particular guest. And when he arrives, this is what you're going to do…"

Hadie took the next few minutes to explain what she wanted Ylonna to do. When she finished, Ylonna curtsied again and returned to her room. Hadie looked at the clock on the wall. She had plenty of time to contemplate what she was going to say.

The night wore on, and her mind remained blank. She could think of nothing to say to her father except to yell at him for bedding women behind her mother's back. When the hour arrived and a familiar face walked through the front door, Hadie watched the middle-aged man dressed in a trim brown suit walk over to a vacant couch. He unbuttoned his coat, which was probably stifling to wear in the prevalent wet heat of the south, and sat down with his back to her. A spike of fear surged through her veins, and she knew she couldn't confront him. She gestured to Ursella to come to her.

"What?" Ursella whispered.

"When you take him back, please inform Ylonna I've changed my mind," she whispered back.

Ursella nodded then quickly retrieved a glass of wine.

Hadie watched Ursella saunter over to her father and hand him the glass. When Ursella leaned in as she had once taught Hadie to do, Hadie watched through clenched teeth as Ursella prepared him for Ylonna. She took a deep breath and breathed out slowly when Ursella led him through the beads.

Ursella returned all too quickly and said, "What happened?"

"I wasn't ready."

"You won't be able to do that the day we go to the palace, you know."

"I know," Hadie said. Feeling angry with herself for letting fear control her, she said, "And don't speak to me with such impudence again."

"Yes, Madam," Ursella said with a curtsy. "I'm sorry."

CHAPTER 2

Fire rained from the sky. It flowed from the towers guarding Onta's east gate like a flood over the bridge spanning the Onta river. Merchants abandoned their wagons, and farmers left their empty carts behind as they fled. People pushed and shoved as they tried to move faster. A mother carrying a crying baby in her arms screamed when the fleeing mass separated her from her husband. Jax wanted to help her, but he couldn't risk taking his attention away from the flow of air he was using to keep the fire from burning them all alive. He gestured with the Harachin sword and shouted, "Deborah!"

Deborah ran over to the woman and put a reassuring arm around her. She guided the young mother toward Jax and Deanna as they slowly backed off the bridge.

The crowd spread out on the road after it passed the last abandoned wagon and began moving faster. Those who were able to run, ran. Jax, Deborah, and Deanna kept to the rear of the crowd and moved with those unable to run. Once everyone was safely off the bridge, Jax stopped the flow of Energy from the Harachin sword into his Core. The air he controlled returned to its normal patterns, and the river of fire crashed down to the bridge. A wave of heat washed over them.

Jax shook his head. *I've failed you,* he thought. For the first time since Orwyn's death, he was powerless to protect Orwyn's children. Through clenched teeth, he said, "*Draego's Fire.*"

Deborah reunited the crying mother with her husband, and they all moved as quickly as they could away from the bridge.

A thunderous roar from behind them overpowered the sounds of the fleeing crowd. Jax, Deborah, and Deanna all turned around. From the towers now hidden by the high-arching span, fire continued to rain down, illuminating the night.

"What was that?" Deborah said. She took a step toward the city.

Jax grabbed her by the arm to stop her. He knew the mother in her wanted desperately to run back to the city, tear down the walls, and get Kaylan back.

"Deth," Deanna said.

Jax looked over at Deanna. "I thought he wasn't going to leave the mountain?"

"He must have changed his mind," Deanna said.

The downpour of fire abruptly stopped, replaced by the screams of dying men.

Deborah gasped when a giant silhouette glided overhead. They watched the shadowed beast climb higher into the sky. They pivoted around, following Deth as he flew overhead. Jax heard the beating of his wings over the sounds of the fleeing crowd. He stared in amazement until the shadow disappeared into the night sky.

Deborah turned back toward the city. "We need to go back for them."

"No," Deanna said.

"I agree," Jax added.

"We can't just leave them!" Deborah shouted. "Kaylan's in there!"

"I have a feeling that they're all right," Deanna said, looking up at the night sky.

"I agree," Jax said again.

"What, then?" Deborah said hesitantly.

"We find the dragon," Deanna said.

CHAPTER 3

*I*t's a trap!"

Jax's words echoed in Yolken's mind as he hung helplessly in the dragon's claw. Onta grew smaller by the second as Deth carried Yolken away—away from the city, away from Kaylan, away from Javen. The rushing wind quickly dried the tears streaming from his eyes. The pain of losing Kaylan and Javen's betrayal reverberated along with Jax's words, all tearing him in different directions.

He knew running into Onta by himself had been foolish. How could it not have been a trap? Of all the people leaving the city on foot, the rider on horseback had randomly singled out Kaylan? No. It was no coincidence. And yet he had foolishly gone after her. Jax had tried to stop him, but as he'd done when the bandits accosted Kaylan, he'd ignored Jax. But just as he couldn't stand helplessly and watch Issa die, he couldn't just stand there on the bridge and watch Kaylan be carried away on horseback by a stranger. His instinct had called him to action, and he had acted before he'd had time to think through what was going on. He couldn't lose Kaylan to the Regency like he'd lost Javen.

Javen was in Onta! He'd finally found him.

"Join the Regency, as your brother has done."

Javen joined the Regency? The words were as astonishing when he thought them as they had been when Devin Drake, the Regent of Onta, had spoken them. Javen was lazy, impulsive, often selfish, but he wasn't foolish. And he would certainly never betray Yolken. Had he helped Devin lure Yolken back into Onta by suggesting they steal Kaylan from him? Javen would never do such a thing. Would he? *"I'm so glad it worked,"* Javen had said.

Now Yolken wasn't so sure. Why would Javen betray him? What lies had the Regency been telling Javen?

And now Deth was carrying him away from both of them. He'd lost the two people who meant the most to him. No… they'd been stolen. "Draego's Fire!" he yelled at the top of his lungs. He could barely hear his voice over the rushing wind. Since the day he'd healed Issa, all he had wanted was to find Javen and free him from the Regency's clutches. He'd gone all the way to the Island of Kvorga in search of help. And now that he knew where Javen was, Deth was carrying him away. Well, he was not leaving them behind in the hands of the Regency.

"I love her!" he yelled at Deth. "Why didn't you help me?"

His words went unanswered. Either Deth ignored him, or he couldn't hear him.

Relief lurked behind his anger and fear. As much as he hated that Deth was carrying him away from the fiery inferno in the streets of Onta, he was relieved that Deth had decided to leave his cave. Running into Onta without help—and without the Harachin sword—had been foolish, he now realized. He had never faced a regent before—he'd barely survived facing Drenan's bastard son at the top of the Mindon Falls—and then he found himself confronted by what looked like at least a dozen of them, all standing on the steps of the Onta palace, dressed in violet and blue armor. Worse still, dozens of armored men had surrounded him, preventing his escape.

"It's a trap!"

He must have allowed Deth's revelations back on the island to inflate his ego. He was the Blessed of the Dragon. The *only*

Blessed of the Dragon. Everyone else who could Synthesize, both in the Order and the Regency, were just the lucky recipients of a gift given by an errant dragon—Deth. It didn't belong to them. They didn't deserve it. That wasn't true with him, though. He could do what no one else could: He could store Energy in his bones. But did that make him stronger than them? Deth had said his strength rivaled that of the dragons. And at that moment, he must have believed Deth—else why would he have done something so incredibly stupid? It was because he loved Kaylan. He couldn't stand losing her like he'd lost Javen. But she was gone. Because of his stupidity, she was gone.

"You should have helped me!" Yolken shouted. "Not rescued me!"

As Deth silently carried Yolken into the night, the nearly full moon rose and illuminated the ground far below. The Onta River snaked by below, brightly reflecting the moon's light. The river split; one fork snaked off to the left, and Deth followed the fork to the right.

Yolken watched the river as it passed silently by. When a cloud moved over the moon and hid the river from view, he closed his eyes and tried to will the undoing of what had just occurred. He couldn't imagine continuing without Kaylan at his side. Her calming presence was a strength he hadn't known he needed. With every beat of Deth's wings, he felt her wrenching absence.

Yolken's breath caught—he felt like he was plummeting to the ground. It was the same sensation as when he had gone over the Mindon Falls. Deth's grip was still firm around him, but he was definitely falling. With the moon hidden, he couldn't see anything. Deth's wings opened with a loud flutter, causing Yolken to feel like he weighed twice as much as he did. The odd sensation replaced that of falling. Deth beat his wings rapidly, and the strange heavy sensation slowly decreased until Yolken felt his normal weight again. Deth settled to the ground with his right hind foot, then unfurled the enormous claws of his back-left foot, the one gripping Yolken, and lowered Yolken to the ground.

Yolken crawled out from underneath the dragon and looked around. It was pitch black, so he used the small amount of Energy remaining in his bones to light a small fire. He held the flames up high but couldn't see much. It looked like they might be in the middle of a meadow.

Deth folded his wings along his body. His long tail wrapped along his body and legs like a cat, then he gracefully lay on the ground.

Yolken wanted to yell at Deth again for rescuing him instead of helping him, but Deth's piercing, reptilian gaze melted the urge away. Instead, he said, "How did you know where to find me?"

"Dragons sense one another," Deth said. "And I sensed you were in danger."

"I'm not a dragon."

"You are the Dragon King."

The moon came out from behind the cloud. Its light made Deth's scales shimmer.

"You have discovered your abilities," Deth said.

"My bones…" Yolken said pensively.

"Yes, you possess all you need to accomplish your task." Deth took a deep, rumbling breath. "Your fight is not with the humans, Dragon King."

"They stole Kaylan!" Yolken shouted. The anger that had been melted by Deth's gaze now surged back to life. "You should have helped me!"

"You would trade the lives of every living thing for that of your mate?" Deth said. His voice rumbled calmly.

"I love her!" Yolken screamed, near hysteria. He turned in circles, wanting to boost his strength with Energy and sprint back to Onta, but he could tell his bones were nearly depleted and he didn't know how long his Energy store would last.

"As I loved my mate."

"You hid when your mate was taken from you," Yolken said. Deth's head twitched. Yolken knew his words stung the dragon, but he couldn't leave Kaylan behind. "I'm not going to do that. I *have* to get her back. Please help me! Take me back."

Yolken felt a calming presence push into him like a gentle caress. It was the same feeling as when Deth had, at their first meeting, tested his strength in Synthesis. It had been a gentle touch with Energy, unlike Deanna's Energy probe that nearly burned him to death from the inside out. He took a deep, shuddering breath and let it out slowly. He needed to think through his options logically, not react impulsively.

Deth withdrew his presence from Yolken and said, "Dragons were not meant to die. With the gift of Regeneration, we were created to live eternally. The connections we made with other dragons were not meant to be severed. My relationship with my mate was infinitely more intertwined than anything possible with you short-lived humans."

"You're saying my relationship with Kaylan doesn't matter because I'm not as old as you are?"

"You must accomplish your task, or the life of your mate will not matter."

How could he possibly think about anything else when he knew Kaylan was now a prisoner of the Regency like Javen? Kaylan consumed his thoughts when he was with her, and now that she was gone… it was much worse now than when she'd left him in the Mindons to train with Jax.

And Javen—was he even a prisoner anymore?

"I'm so glad it worked."

"I had to get you away from them."

"They're the enemy, Yolken."

"They've told me the truth."

"This time you're the one who's wrong."

"I'm not leaving."

Javen's words echoed in his head. Each one cut Yolken worse than any of their childhood fights ever had. Javen had willingly stayed—refused to leave with Yolken. Refused to help him with Kaylan.

"You must restore balance," Deth said.

Where Yolken's mind was running around frantically like a cornered animal, Deth remained resolute. He focused his thoughts and tried to understand what Deth meant. It didn't make sense. Restore balance? "I have no idea what that means."

"Solarian is the source of Energy," Deth said. "It is dying because your war disrupted its balance."

"Whatever you think I'm supposed to do about it is no clearer now than when you said it back in your cave," Yolken said. He was one simple man, barely learning how to Synthesize. How was *he* supposed to undo damage to the sun?

"Balance must be restored."

Yolken was lost. When it came to ale, he'd learned to balance its flavor by how much of the special flower he used in it. If he used too much, the ale was bitter, and if he didn't use enough, it was too sweet. It had taken experimentation to figure out exactly how much of the flower was enough—to keep the ale in balance. He understood balance, but he had no idea how it applied to the sun, or what he was supposed to do about it. "Yes, but how?"

"What was taken must be replaced."

Yolken snorted as he stared dumbfounded at Deth. What Deth suggested was impossible. "Replace the sun's Energy?"

"Yes."

"I *use* Energy, Deth. I can't replace it." He might be a new Synthesizer with much still to learn, but he knew what Deth was suggesting was impossible. "That's not how Synthesis works."

"Dragons *create* Energy," Deth said.

"They... you do?"

Deth snorted, almost as though he were chuckling. "How else could I Synthesize in the belly of a mountain?"

"I... I don't know," Yolken said. "I thought maybe you had it stored in your bones."

"For four hundred years?"

Yolken didn't know how to answer.

"Dragons were made to be like Solarian."

"If you can create Energy, then why don't *you* restore the sun's Energy?"

"Because I cannot."

"Why not?"

"I have not the strength," Deth said. "But you do."

Now it was Yolken's turn to chuckle. The very thought was ludicrous. "I can't create Energy."

"Yes, you can."

Deth spoke so matter-of-factly. But Yolken knew what Deth was saying couldn't possibly be true. At no point since he'd started learning to Synthesize had he ever felt as though he could create Energy. He couldn't even access it if he wasn't either in direct sight of the sun or holding a dragon bone. Even after the change since visiting Deth—his ability to store Energy in his bones—he Synthesized the same as he always had. He shook his head. "No, I can't."

"Dragons don't simply store Energy, but also create it."

"I'm not a dragon!" Yolken repeated.

"All you need to do is ignite the flame."

Yolken looked up at the flame hovering over his head.

"The flame within," Deth said.

"What flame?" Yolken said.

"All dragons are born with the ability to Synthesize. However, the flame within hatchlings must first be ignited."

"And how do you do that?" Yolken said sarcastically.

"Hatchlings begin growing their Core as soon as they are born. When they are strong enough, the Assembly gathers to celebrate. Together, they pour Energy into the hatchling until its flame ignites."

When Yolken had visited Deth in his cave, Deth spoke about the Assembly and how they refused to intervene in the human wars. He also spoke of how he had gone against the Assembly's decision when he decided to give Synthesis to the man who would become known as the Dragon King, and how he was wrong and they were right. He'd said the Assembly disapproved of his actions.

"The Assembly were your rulers," Yolken said, as a statement more so than a question.

"Not just rulers, but the first of the dragons. Draego created Dimras first. Draego blessed him and named him Dragon King. Next, Draego created Dimras' mate Devrith. Together they hatched six eggs. All subsequent generations of dragons came from the six, but the eight of them became the Assembly."

"And now the Assembly's gone," Yolken said. Yolken's ancestors had killed all the dragons—except Deth—and turned them into weapons and armor. "Without them, who will ignite the flame in me? You?"

"Only the Assembly had the strength."

"What about the Council?" *Did Deth even know what the Council was?* Yolken wondered.

Deth snorted. That answered Yolken's question: Somehow, he did know. "Their combined strength wouldn't amount even to mine—and I am many generations removed from Dimras."

"But you gave Draeko the gift."

"I simply sparked to life that which was dormant."

"Meaning what?"

"That all creatures have the gift within them whether they use it or not."

"So what am I supposed to do?" Yolken asked. "Convince the Regency to join with the Order and try to light a fire for me?"

The dragon breathed deeply. Yolken felt hot air stream from his nostrils each time he exhaled. "You must ignite the flame within yourself," Deth said.

Yolken exhaled in exasperation. "Are you saying I have the strength of the Assembly of dragons?"

"You are the Dragon King," the dragon boomed.

Yolken stood silently before Deth. The dragon's words reverberated in his head. He considered the impossible task that the dragon had put upon him. "Why are you telling me all this now and not when I came to see you in the mountain?"

"Because I often forget the limitations of human knowledge."

"I had no idea dragons could create Energy," Yolken said. "I don't think anyone did." Neither Jax nor Deanna had ever mentioned anything about it.

The dragon breathed deeply but did not speak.

"If you won't take me back to Onta, will you take me to Kyinth? Perhaps together we could put an end to the conflict with the Regency. Perhaps together—"

"Your fight is not with the humans, Dragon King," Deth repeated. "And neither is mine."

Without warning, Deth pushed himself to his feet and launched into the air. He quickly flew out of the light Yolken was using to illuminate his surroundings, and disappeared into the night.

CHAPTER 4

Hadie stood in the dark, out of the reach of the lanterns illuminating the road. She kept her hands in the pockets of the black coat she wore over her corset. With her left hand, she toyed with the corner of an envelope folded in the pocket as she studied the long, tree-lined entrance behind an ornate gate. Her childhood home loomed at the end of the entryway—at least it had been her home before she'd decided to leave behind the life of privilege she had once lived.

She had watched her father leave her brothel, still buttoning his suit coat on his way out, then had gone to her room and penned him a letter detailing her vision for the south. Leaving Ursella in charge, she'd made her way here. He was a powerful Silk, and her best chance of convincing the other Silks that her plan was in the south's best interest.

She fingered the envelope again. She did *not* want to see her father. She hated everything he represented. That was part of the reason why she'd left Hantlo in the first place: She no longer wanted to be a part of the society that defined his life. The only reason she now stood at his doorstep was that she hated the Regency more. She didn't like the idea of putting people like her father in power, but she needed to stop the Regency.

But now she hesitated to ring the bell that would summon

the guards to the gate. It wasn't just her father she didn't want to see. She didn't want to face either of her parents. Her mother had been heartbroken when Hadie had announced that she was leaving, and she knew if she looked her mother in the eyes, she would likely lose all her resolve.

Hadie continued to toy with the corner of the envelope. It wasn't just not wanting to see her parents that prevented her from ringing the bell. She knew a letter was not the way. It was too risky. She knew her father would highly suspect the authenticity of a letter from his daughter suggesting he organize a rebellion.

She crumpled the letter in her pocket and turned away. But something inside the gate caught her eye, causing her to pause. Large decorative pots lined the entrance. They contained a familiar flower—a flower she had seen in only two other places in the city.

Now she knew who made the poison.

But before she did something stupid, she decided she needed to be sure. She returned to the brothel and took her place in the corner. After the last patron left for the night, she left Ursella to close up and went to her room. She opened the blinds of the eastern-facing window and went to bed.

* * *

The rising sun woke Hadie. She dressed quickly and left before any of the girls woke. She waited outside the shop nearest to the brothel that sold plants. The moment they opened their doors, she inspected their flowers. Not finding what she was looking for, she went to the next shop and the next.

Hadie spent the entire day visiting dozens of shops all across the city, but didn't find a single shop that sold the flowers planted in the pots at her parents' house. She also visited other mansions in the city and found that some of them had the same flower growing in their gardens or planters as well. Someone was selling the Silks a flower that no local seemed to sell. And she thought she knew who it was.

Satisfied that the flower growing in the pots at her parents' mansion was not widely sold in Hantlo, she made her way to Lyoll's.

"Hadie!" Lyoll said excitedly when he opened the door and saw her. "Or should I say 'Madam'?"

"You heard?" Hadie said, surprised.

"I thought it curious when I heard someone took over at Sonja's, so I did a little investigating."

Hadie stepped into the house and said, "I did a little investigating myself, Lyoll."

"What are you talking about?"

Hadie walked through the house to the kitchen and picked up the potted flower on the table. She held it up toward Lyoll, who had followed close behind her, and said, "This."

"What about it?"

"You're selling it to the Silks."

"Sorry, lass, I'm not."

"You're not? I was sure. I spent all day looking for this flower, all over the city. I went to practically every shop that sells plants, and not a single one of them sold this flower. Most of them hadn't even heard of it when I described it to them."

"Sorry, lass, I don't know the first thing about flowers."

"Then who?"

Lyoll let out a chuckle.

"What?"

"Well, your investigation wasn't completely off base."

"What do you mean?"

Lyoll grinned broadly. "I think the one you're looking for is Ganip."

"Ganip?" Hadie said, surprised. She had always assumed he was just a dumb lad who followed Lyoll around because he didn't know any better.

"Yes, Madam."

"Is... is he here? I have something to ask him."

"Not at the moment, no." Lyoll looked at Hadie, furrowed

his brow, and asked, "What interest do you have with this flower?"

Hadie set the pot back on the table and reached into her pocket. She pulled out the pin and held it up. "This."

"I see," Lyoll said grimly. "He should be back soon. In the meantime, why don't you catch me up on what it is you're doing."

"Do you have any whiskey?"

"Always."

Hadie sipped Lyoll's whiskey while she updated him on her plans. Before taking a seat on the couch, she'd moved the potted flower to the short table in the sitting room.

"You know this plan of yours is insane, right, lass?" Lyoll said.

"It's not. And it'll work."

"I can understand your wanting to kill Drenan, but the whole of the southern Regency?"

"Most of them are already in Hantlo. If I wait for the right opportunity, it'll work."

"But why?"

"Because. What year is it? Four ten? They've ruled for over four hundred years, and other than themselves, only a fraction of southerners are prosperous."

"And you think replacing rich people with more rich people will change anything?" Lyoll said.

"It'd be different."

"How?"

"Because they only rule because people think the Great Dragon blessed them."

"You don't think they're blessed?"

"Not any more than the rest of us."

The door opened, and Ganip walked in. "Hadie!" he exclaimed when he saw her sitting on the couch.

"Hi Ganip," Hadie said.

"What are you doin' here? Lyoll said you took up whoring."

"I didn't say that," Lyoll said. "I said she was running a brothel."

"What's the difference?"

"I'm not a whore," Hadie said. "I *manage* whores."

"Wha' you wanna do that for?"

"Because I need the money."

"I figured you'd head north again," Ganip said.

"I have something I need to do first."

"What?"

Hadie held up the pin with a flower on it and said, "I need more of these."

"I—"

"I know you make them, Ganip."

Ganip looked at the flower on the table then over at Lyoll, trying to resist the urge to pick at a blemish on his chin.

"What? She figured it out on her own," Lyoll said.

Hadie picked up the pot. "Where's this thing come from, anyway? I searched the city over and couldn't find anyone that sold it."

"I... I found it in a field while we were traveling back from Tieger several years back. My ma always liked flowers so I thought I'd bring it back for her. Only, by the time we returned, she'd died."

"I'm sorry," Hadie said.

"It's okay. She'd been sick for a long time, so I was sort of expectin' it. She always liked gardenin', so when she couldn't tend to hers no more, I did it for her. Thought that flower'd look nice with the others."

"Well, that explains why nobody here recognized it," Hadie said. "It's not local."

"Since my ma had died, I planted it out back here. They started growin' 'em out back and a few years ago thought I'd see if I could sell 'em. Turns out them rich peoples were willin' to pay good money for 'em."

"And how did you learn about the flower's other...

attributes?" Hadie said. Ganip looked at her hesitantly as she took a sip of her whiskey.

"That's a secret best kept close," Lyoll said for Ganip.

"Fair enough," Hadie said. You heard about people being poisoned in folk tales, but not in real life. She wondered how often it happened. She knew at least Sonja'd had use for it from time to time. It had to occur more than was let on—probably another thing the Regency kept hidden from the people. Hadie held the pin up again. "As I said, the reason I'm here is because I need more of these."

"How many do you need?" Ganip said.

Hadie counted silently to herself and said, "Is the poison on this one still good?"

Ganip nodded. "So long as it doesn't get washed off, it'll last forever."

The pin had never been wet, but there was no guarantee her sweat hadn't washed it off while she carried it around in her pocket. She didn't want to take any chances, so she said, "Twenty-two."

Ganip's eyes went wide. "W-what in Draego's Fire do you need with twenty-two poisoned pins?"

"That's a secret best kept close," Hadie said with a wink.

CHAPTER 5

Hadie left after Ganip agreed to make her more poisonous pins. Never having needed to buy an illicit item like that before, she was shocked to hear how much each one would cost, but assured him she had the money. He said he would need several days to make them, so she returned to the brothel, determined to be ready.

It took another four days for her father to return to the brothel, but this time she was ready. She'd put a lot of thought into what she would say to him. No matter how much or how little she said, she was putting herself at risk. She was learning to live with it, though. Ever since she had first set foot in the brothel and told Sonja her original plan, she'd been putting herself at risk. So to help safeguard herself, she wrote Lyoll a message—a message he would deliver to her mother should anything befall her.

Hadie hid in the closet in Ylonna's bedroom just before her father's scheduled appointment. She toyed with the hilt of the knife tucked under her corset while she waited. Ylonna stood in the corner, sipping wine. Hadie took a deep breath and held it when the door to the bedroom finally opened.

"I've missed you, Phen," Ylonna said seductively.

Hadie cringed at the sound of the name. It was what she'd

grown up hearing her mother call her father. She slid the knife from its sheath. Through the crack in the sliding door, she watched as her father took the glass of wine from Ylonna and upended it into his mouth. Ylonna pushed him roughly onto the bed, then straddled him and engaged him in a sensual kiss.

Hadie eased the door open and slid out of the closet. She knelt on the bed behind her father, who was completely unaware of her presence, and slipped the knife against his throat. Ylonna broke off the kiss and stood back up.

"What the—" Phenor blurted.

"Don't move," Hadie whispered into her father's ear. "Or I'll open your throat."

"Wha… what is this?"

Hadie nodded to Ylonna, and Ylonna walked around the bed. She climbed onto the down mattress and placed her hand over Hadie's, taking hold of the blade. Hadie slipped her hand free, leaving Ylonna holding the blade against her father's neck. Hadie stood, took a deep breath, and walked around the bed.

"Hadie?" Phenor said. "What are you doing here?"

"I could ask you the same thing," Hadie said. "But I won't."

"I thought you went north."

"What you thought isn't important. What is important is what you're going to do if you want to walk out of here alive."

"I—" Phenor started, but stopped when he tried to sit up and the blade Ylonna held bit into his neck.

"You won't speak," Hadie said. "You'll only listen to what I have to say."

Phenor nodded.

Hadie hesitated a moment before speaking, knowing that what she was about to say was treason. She didn't know if she could trust her father, but she also couldn't continue with her plan if there wasn't something to at least temporarily fill the void she was about to create. "A time is coming very soon when the Regency will be no more," Hadie began. "When that time comes, the people of the south will need someone to lead them. Not to rule over them, but to help them transition to a life without the Regency."

"What are you—"

Hadie held up a finger, silencing her father. "Your whole life has been one of privilege. Not because you earned it, but because the Regency gave it to you." Hadie leaned in close, applying the techniques Ursella had taught her to help lower the inhibitions of Sonja's clients. She wasn't doing it to entice her father, but to make him uncomfortable. When he turned his head, she knew it was working. "I am going to kill every last regent in the south," she whispered into his ear. "And when I do, you will do your part to ensure a fair system takes its place." She stood back up and poured herself a glass of wine from Ylonna's personal supply.

"And if I don't?" Phenor said.

Hadie sipped her wine, then said, "Then I will bring your world down around you."

"And how do you propose doing that?"

"Easy. Look around you, Pap. The chancellor is barely maintaining control of the realm. Were I to speak to Ma about this," she said, gesturing around the room, "your… empire… would become as precarious as Dorlan's."

"You don't think she already knows?" Phenor said.

"I know that Ma would never permit such behavior," Hadie said.

"And how could you possibly know that?"

"Because it is not she who needs you, Pap."

Phenor's eyes widened.

"What? Don't act surprised. Did you think that Ma wouldn't ever tell me that it wasn't her who married up?" Hadie took a drink of her wine.

"What do you want me to do?" Phenor said after a moment.

"I simply want you to do the right thing for the people when the time comes," Hadie said.

"And when will that be?"

"Soon." Hadie gestured to Ylonna, and Ylonna removed the blade from Phenor's neck. She handed the blade back to Hadie, and Hadie slid it back into its sheath.

Phenor rubbed his neck and said, "You know this won't work. And you know how the chancellor will respond if he finds out."

"He won't. Because if he does, you'll lose everything. And I know you're too selfish to let that happen." She walked over to the door. "Feel free to finish if you wish. It's on the house. Only, after tonight, never come here again."

CHAPTER 6

Do you think he'll go to Dorlan?" Ursella asked.

"No," Hadie said.

"How can you be sure?"

"Because he loves his wealth too much to throw it away."

"What do you mean?"

"I told him if Dorlan found out, my mother would learn of his indiscretions. He might stop what we're doing, but he'll lose everything in the process."

"You don't think she already knows?" Ursella asked. "The majority of the Salts have multiple lovers. Draego knows even your mother probably has a lover on the side."

Hadie shook her head. "Not my parents. At least, not my mother."

"Hadie… I mean, Madam, with all due respect, with all of our lives at risk here, I just don't see why your mother would be any different. I don't see how this threat you've hung over your father's head has any validity."

"That's because you don't know my mother. You don't know that their wealth is hers—not my father's. He became wealthy only because the Regency arranged it."

"So he's unlikely to betray them—or permit you to betray them."

"I believe he's more afraid of losing his wealth; plus, he stands to gain great power from this. That, and my mother has no patience for further infidelity."

"What do you mean?" Ursella said.

"When I was younger, I had to watch my mother discover my father bedding another woman—one of my mother's closest friends. She was devastated, Ursella. And even though she forgave him, she swore to him that if he ever bedded another woman, her family would take their wealth back."

"I hope you're right, Madam."

"Me too, Ursella. It's a risk, I know, but our whole plan is fraught with it."

The next few days proved to be very tedious. Hadie spent the nights sitting in her corner, half-expecting soldiers to burst through the door and arrest her for treason. But each night came and went with no soldiers. When someone from the palace *did* come, it was a messenger. She maintained a confident and cool composure while she accepted the rolled-up parchment with its wax seal. When she finished reading it, she was unable to stop herself from trembling.

"What does it say, Madam?" Ursella said.

Hadie looked up at Ursella, a smile growing on her face.

"What?"

"It's from Ronlar."

"Regent of the Slonan province—well, what's left of it. What does he want?"

"He's sending for a whore," Hadie said with a big smile.

"It's working," Ursella said with a smile of her own.

"It is," Hadie agreed. "Call a meeting with the girls."

"Yes, Madam."

* * *

Ursella continued to prove herself invaluable to Hadie. Daily, she helped her learn the clients who frequented the brothel. And now, she helped her make sense of which regent preferred which girl, how often, and the nuances of their inclinations.

"Ronlar is one of the more docile," Ursella said.

"But still," Hadie said, looking over his sheet, "why can't they bed women normally, like other men?"

"Because they've been bedding women for centuries," Ursella said. "It's like the wine you drink in the evenings. The more often you drink it, the more you *can* drink, and the more it takes to get you drunk. The same is true with bedding needs. They've been bedding women for so long that in many cases, normal bedding no longer satisfies them."

"All right," Hadie conceded, "but I still don't understand why some of them have to hurt the girls."

"I don't understand it either," Ursella said. "Let's go; they're assembled."

Hadie and Ursella entered the lounge, which was crowded with the girls. Before she sent Delori, Ronlar's preferred whore, she wanted to make sure they were actually willing to bed them. "We've received our first invitation from a regent," she said.

The girls clapped.

That surprised her. She hadn't thought they would be *that* enthusiastic about the idea of bedding regents again. But then, they probably understood that it was necessary for their plan to succeed.

"But before I send any of you to them, I want to make absolutely sure that you're willing. You're all intimately aware of the regents' peculiarities when it comes to their bedding needs, and I don't want you to go to them unless you want to. Especially with those who can be abusive." She paused a moment to let her words sink in with each girl before she continued. "If you're willing to endure a little longer in the name of ending the Regency's tyranny on the south, raise your hand."

Every hand in the room went up.

"Good," Hadie said.

Delori went and returned without incident. It took another day, but the invitations started coming regularly.

The girls expertly played their double roles; at every

appointment they satisfied the regents they went to visit, as well as prying from them information that they reported to Hadie.

Even though they provided her with information on many different things, she didn't get the specific information she wanted. She knew it could take time, so she waited patiently. She did, however, learn that Drenan had gone to Onta, and that Dorlan had been cross ever since he left. She wondered if it had something to do with Javen. She hoped he was all right. She missed him, but couldn't think about him right now.

Edill was the first to return with bruises. Her client was Metra, the displaced regent of the abandoned Onassa province. Hadie felt an overwhelming desire to rush to his mansion and bury her blade in him, but Edill pleaded with her not to. She said making trouble would compromise their mission. In that moment, Hadie realized the dedication of the girls. They all supported Edill, and agreed they would take the occasional beating if it meant the eventual downfall of the realm.

"Fine," Hadie said. "But I won't permit what happened to Panny and Kitt to happen to any of you." If her father talked to Dorlan, she would likely end up dead—that, she accepted—but she wouldn't allow her whores to suffer because of her ambition. "If any of you suspect anything, let me know."

A few days later, the front door of the brothel opened, and a messenger entered. Hadie exchanged the rolled-up parchment for a coin, then unrolled the parchment. All it contained was a simple sketch of a flower.

* * *

Hadie slung her satchel over her shoulder and left the brothel. She held it against her body with her arm as she walked so it wouldn't bang against her body. She didn't want it to be too obvious that it was full of coins. Lyoll had offered to come and escort her to their house, but thinking it might look suspicious to have someone escort her from her own brothel, she opted against the idea. She didn't want to draw any more attention to herself than she needed to.

When she knocked on the door, Lyoll opened it immediately, and shut it behind her as soon as she stepped inside. He gestured with his hand toward the kitchen, so she walked back and stood by the table. The pot with the flower in it was gone.

"Are you sure you want to do this?" Lyoll asked.

Hadie lifted her satchel over her head and set it on the table with a heavy clunk. "I'm sure."

"I'll go get him." Lyoll trotted up the stairs, taking them three at a time with his long legs.

Hadie sat at the table while she waited.

Lyoll returned a few minutes later with Ganip in tow. He carried a small wooden box.

Hadie looked at Ganip with a different eye as he sat across from her at the table. He was no longer the gangly lad full of innocence she had presumed he was. She saw past his lankiness, and wondered how many people he'd helped murder. She was still curious about how he knew how to make poison out of a simple flower, and what he did with all his money.

Ganip sat the box on the table.

"They're all there?" she asked.

Ganip nodded.

She turned her satchel so the top faced her on the table and unclasped the two buckles that held it closed. She lifted the flap and pulled a heavy bag of gold coins out. She set it on the table next to the box, reached into the satchel again, and pulled out another equally heavy bag.

Ganip reached out with his thin arms and pulled the two bags toward himself.

Hadie picked up the box, lifted the lid, and looked in. She counted. Twenty-two pins lined the inside, with matching yellow and red gems creating a little flower on each one. Each pin was secured by a small string loop. She closed the lid and placed the box into her satchel. "Thank you," she said.

Ganip nodded.

"I'm not just talking about this," Hadie said. "You two were the only ones who treated Javen and me like normal people back in the caravan. I really enjoyed the time I got to spend with you."

"You're talkin' like this is goodbye," Lyoll said.

"Isn't it?"

"Not if you don't want it to be."

Hadie looked at Lyoll, confused.

"Your plan might be foolish, but a rebellion's been brewing in the south for some time now. This may just be the catalyst those who lurk in the shadows have needed to spur them into action."

"I… I didn't realize…"

"You know what I say is true. You've seen it yourself, though you may not have known it for what it was, else you wouldn't have left."

"What are you saying, Lyoll? I thought you said you enjoyed working for the Regency because the money was good."

"What I said was that I did it for the money. I never said anything about enjoying it. I owe the scales no loyalty," Lyoll said. "And neither does the lad. We've both been around 'em long enough to know their true nature. And besides, it's not as though they're actually ruling anymore. Just living better. Which is what you're hoping to improve from this, no?"

Hadie nodded. "So if an uprising should occur, you'd support it? Even if it's foolish?"

"When the time comes, lass, you needn't fear. I'll be on the proper side."

"And you?" Hadie asked Ganip.

Ganip nodded.

CHAPTER 7

Reago looked at the enormous black skull. Red ribbons flickered in the lantern light. It sat a pace above the floor, supported by four marble legs—one under each side of the jawbone and two at the rear. It was as big as a horse. The eye sockets accused him of crimes he fully accepted committing and had trouble keeping buried. He'd accepted the position of Chancellor of the Western Realm because Drakonias asked him to, but he did so with a guilty conscience. And now, seeing a dragon swoop in and rescue Danavin's son had caused emotions long-buried to rise to the surface.

He stepped close to the skull and placed his hand on the tip of the long snout. A flood of Energy pulsed toward him, threatening to flood his Core. He closed his eyes and remembered watching the red dragon fall from the sky, pierced through with a giant metal arrow. They had been hunting the yellow dragon, but couldn't bring it down before it escaped. But they had been able to inflict a wound on its mate—the red— before the beasts had taken flight, and had successfully brought it down.

He allowed a trickle of Energy to flow into his Core, then walked around the skull to the desk in the corner. Using Synthesis, he blew the dust collected from a century of disuse into the air. He swirled it into a small cyclone and deposited it neatly in the wastebasket beside the desk.

He sat at the desk and slid the black key he held into a keyhole on the front of the desk. He turned it, then used what Energy remained in his Core to activate the mechanism in the desk. When the lock clicked, he pushed the curved wooden cover up. It rolled up and into the upper shelf as he lifted. From one of several horizontal slats on the upper right side of the desk, he pulled out a stack of parchment. He thumbed through the pages, not reading a single word on any of them—he already knew what the astronomer's report said, and the conclusions it predicted.

Drakonias had killed both Drashon and the astronomer to protect what the report revealed, he knew; but what the emperor didn't know was that he had a copy, and so did the Order. Reago remembered suspecting something wasn't right when their father had unexpectedly surrendered. The astronomer's report had confirmed his suspicions. He understood his brother's reasons for wanting to rebel. He sympathized enough to join in his cause—if begrudgingly—and even though it frustrated him, he understood why Drakonias had executed their father and his sympathizers instead of trying to win them to their cause. But what frustrated him most was that even though Drakonias had known the toll their war had taken on the sun for over a hundred and fifty years, he had chosen to do nothing. And with the reemergence of Deanna—along with a dragon—Reago could no longer sit by and do nothing. If he was going to act, he would not do it alone and risk the same fate as Drashon.

Reago reached into an inner pocket of his coat and pulled out an ink jar and three more pieces of fresh parchment. He removed the stopper, set it on the desk, and grabbed a pen— made from the feather of a condor—and began to write. He made three copies of the letter, one for each of the other realms' chancellors: Dorlan, Sheal, and Thena. He knew the letter destined for Thena wouldn't make it to the east, but he wrote it anyway.

Dorlan didn't know what was happening—other than that the weather conditions were growing steadily worse, making much of the Southern Realm uninhabitable—and he had only just returned to the south after another failed attempt to solicit help from Drakonias. So he knew Dorlan would join him; the threat of losing complete control of the south was very real.

Sheal's realm, on the other hand, was not suffering like Dorlan's. But Sheal, Reago knew, still harbored resentment of their brother for not originally naming him Chancellor of the Northern Realm. He hoped that when Sheal found out that the sun was dying and what really happened to Drashon, he would be willing to join Reago as well.

He doubted either of them would be able to join him in Kyinth, though Sheal *did* still possess an Auto, but he hoped they would at least pen letters of their own to the emperor demanding something, at last, be done.

Reago touched the strip of black bone inlaid in the surface of the desk and siphoned a little Energy from it. He used it to dry the ink on the three pieces of parchment, then pulled three bone cylinders from round cubbies on the left side of the desk. One by one, he rolled each parchment and slipped it into a cylinder. Then he returned the copy of the astronomer's report to its spot.

He slid the curved cover of the desk back down and turned the black key in the opposite direction. He drew Energy from the figurine made in his likeness in his pocket and locked the desk. Clutching the three cylinders, he walked back to the front of the skull. He considered it again, what they'd done, then closed his eyes. He took a deep breath and exhaled just as deeply. Even if it meant the emperor labeling him a traitor, he would no longer be complicit to the downfall of the empire, and more importantly, the downfall of all Dradonia.

He turned from the skull and walked out of the room, locking the door behind him. He strode swiftly to his private aviary—where messages too sensitive for a messenger to handle came in and went out. There was a condor-filled cage for each major city in the empire. The cage that housed condors bound for Thena—the capital of the Eastern Realm, which his sister had named after herself—contained only one condor. After word had arrived that no one had heard from the east in several months, he'd sent several messages to Thena. None were answered. He hadn't heard from Thena now for seventy years.

He opened the cage, and the large black bird with white patches on the underside of its wings hopped toward the opening. It was the last condor in Onta trained to fly to Thena. He was sending it to its death, he knew, but it was only alive now because the astronomer's prediction was not the only treasonous knowledge he possessed. He still traveled to Kyinth when required for Regeneration, but what Drakonias didn't know was that he knew the secret, and used it to keep the hope alive that one day he would establish contact with Thena.

Reago secured the black tube to the condor's spindly leg, then held his arm out. The condor climbed onto his forearm, and he lifted it through the open door. He held his arm up high until the bird opened its large wings and took flight. The message would not arrive at its destination, but he sent it nonetheless.

He repeated the process with a condor trained to fly to Hantlo. Before lifting it out of its cage, he hesitated. Allowing this bird to take flight, with the message he'd written attached to its leg, would be treason. He would be sharing the emperor's secret—one that he'd kept to himself for far too long. Taking another deep breath, he lifted the bird out of the cage and held his arm up. The bird took flight.

After releasing the condor bound for Tieger, Reago left the aviary and returned to his quarters. "Please send Devin, Drenan, and Javen here as quickly as possible," he said to his servant.

"Yes, Your Highness," the servant said. She bowed and hastily left.

Reago returned to his balcony and lit his pipe. He had nothing to do but wait for the regents and Javen to arrive, when he would set in motion another treasonous act.

CHAPTER 8

Javen trembled as he climbed the spiraling stairs, resisting the urge to vomit. He stepped around chunks of marble as he passed Devin and Karina's floor and looked up at the hole in the spiral. He didn't want to think about what had just happened, but just as when Drenan had killed Astora, it kept replaying in his head.

The whole plan made him nervous. He'd had a hard time concentrating in the days prior to Yolken and Kaylan returning to Onta. He attended the planning meetings, but hardly paid attention to what Devin and Drenan discussed. The first portion of his role was relatively simple: greet Kaylan to reassure her that she was safe. That had gone as well as it could have. Kaylan wasn't happy—he had known she wouldn't be—but she was safe from the fighting. The second part was what roiled his stomach for days, making it so he could hardly eat: confront Yolken. The moments immediately before Yolken arrived in the roundabout were the worst, but when he'd arrived and Javen approached him, a calm overcame him. He did what he could to talk some sense into Yolken—but then Yolken had attacked him! His brother!

Yolken and Javen had had their fights growing up, but never in his life had he thought Yolken would actually hurt him. And now that they both possessed the gift of Synthesis, Yolken had used it to attack Javen. Javen had hoped that Yolken had resisted the rebels' lies, but now he knew that Yolken was completely corrupted.

He'd been unable to participate in the ensuing fight. Despite knowing that Yolken was lost to him—no longer his brother—he couldn't bring himself to return Yolken's attack. He didn't want Yolken to die any more than he wanted Kaylan's mother or uncle to die. Instead, he'd lain there on the ground, at the foot of the palace steps, and watched, in horror, what was likely his brother's final moment of life. Yolken had fought back against several regents—something Javen still couldn't believe—but Javen had known the regents would eventually overpower him. He was one against many, and the regents had centuries more experience with Synthesis. When Yolken stumbled on a broken piece of marble, he knew Yolken was losing. Like a coward, Javen had looked away. He couldn't watch his brother die.

But then he'd heard a deep, booming roar overhead. He'd looked up and couldn't believe his eyes when he saw a dragon diving toward the roundabout. The dragon had crashed to the ground amid the fiery maelstrom, then carried Yolken away.

When cleanup in the roundabout began, he'd heard about casualties on the east bridge. As Devin made his way back into the palace, Javen asked permission to go inspect the bridge, and Devin had granted it. Javen needed to know what had happened to Kaylan's mother and uncle. The sight of the first burned bodies was more than he could bear. The anxiety that had been building over the last several days finally erupted in him, causing him to double over and vomit. He wiped his mouth on his sleeve, then forced himself to inspect every single corpse. Fortunately, he didn't see anyone he recognized. *They survived,* he had convinced himself.

When Javen arrived at the final landing, Reago's floor, it was blocked by a dozen guards. Standing behind the guards, Reago's modestly dressed servant said something that made them part.

"Right this way, Master Javen," the girl said.

Javen still trembled as he followed her down the hallway. When she opened the door leading into Reago's quarters, shouting from within greeted them. He paused a moment before entering, but after taking a deep, shuddering breath, he proceeded.

"I insist we give chase!" Drenan shouted as Javen stepped through the door.

"I said no," Reago said, through teeth clenched on his pipe. His hands were in his pockets.

"They attacked Onta! They've never done anything so brazen!"

Javen stood by the door and observed the scene. Instead of meeting on the balcony, which seemed to be their preferred place of gathering, they were in the sitting room, the first room within Reago's quarters. *Are they afraid of being outside?*

Drenan and Reago stood on opposite sides of a chaise, and Devin sat about five feet away on a couch. When the door closed behind Javen, the two regents and chancellor turned to look at him. Drenan sneered before returning his attention to Reago.

Reago took the pipe out of his mouth and said, "I permitted you to undertake your fool plan, and you failed. Besides, it seems we aren't simply dealing with a few weak rebels." He replaced his pipe, and it spontaneously started smoking. Javen figured Reago had a dragon bone in his pocket.

"So they found a dragon and convinced it to fight on their side," Drenan said. "We've dealt with them before. We destroyed them. I'm not worried about one dragon."

Reago removed the pipe once again. "We don't have the Machinery to deal with a dragon in Onta. By your report, it killed two dozen guards at the east gate. Besides, the dragon is not what worries me."

"What, then?"

"Deanna has aligned herself with them."

"Deanna?" Drenan said. "Deanna is dead."

"That was certainly the story Drakonias propagated," Reago said.

"It's treason to suggest that the emperor lied."

"It's not treason if it's the truth," Reago said. "The *truth* is that she disappeared, and Sheal was unable to track her down."

"How do you know it was her who attacked the gate?"

"That's what Javen's brother said."

"He was probably lying," Drenan said.

"What other reason would the Order have for going to Kvorga?" Reago said.

"K-Kaylan said they went there to find her," Javen said.

Drenan's eyes twitched toward Javen, who hadn't moved from the door, then back to Reago, who stood firm, not budging. Then he looked over at Devin, and Devin nodded. Drenan shifted his stance. "So, let me see if I understand you correctly," he said. "Deanna assaults your city, damages the east gate, the boy attacks you on the steps of your palace, killing dozens of guards in the process, the dragon kills dozens more, and you're going to simply let them go?"

Reago remained fixed like a statue. "I've made my choice."

"You're afraid of them," Drenan said derisively.

"Drenan," Devin interjected from the couch, "we must accept defeat when it has been dealt. We need to regroup and consult with Father."

"That's exactly what I was thinking," Reago said.

"So you're conceding defeat to the rebels?" Drenan said. "If this had happened in Hantlo I would have—"

"It didn't happen in Hantlo, though, did it?" Reago said. "And yes, I'm conceding defeat. You said there were several casualties—not only in the tower but on the bridge as well. And *none* of the casualties were rebels. Only guards under my authority and innocent bystanders."

"The rebels have never—"

"Haven't they, Drenan? How's your wife? What about your daughter?"

Drenan stepped toward Reago and said, "How dare you! Never speak of them!"

Devin stood and moved between Drenan and Reago. "You were assaulted by Deanna, Drenan; Father's sister. And the boy was much stronger than we anticipated. Not to mention that he has somehow figured out how to Synthesize without dragon bones." After a pause, he added, "And... Draego's Fire... they have a dragon!"

Drenan shook his head and stepped back. "I refuse to accept defeat. They assaulted the city, so we must give chase!"

"You assaulted them!" Reago shouted. "They were merely passing through, and *you* assaulted *them*. In *my* city."

"It doesn't mat—"

"Enough!" Reago shouted.

Javen hugged the door, wishing he could pass through it.

"I have had enough of your insolence, Drenan," Reago spat. "You will do as I say, or you can return to Hantlo."

Drenan stood rigid. "What is it that you propose, *Uncle*?"

"We will go to Kyinth and consult with Drakonias."

"We?"

"Myself, Devin, the boy," Reago said. He gestured toward Javen with his pipe. "And you, if you lose the insolence."

Drenan glared toward Javen then turned back toward Reago. "Consult with him about what?"

"I believe what is transpiring is much larger than killing the son of a dead rebel against whom you have a vendetta," Reago said. "It's time to put behind us the policies of a war that we never should have fought. As evidenced by what transpired tonight, we are still experiencing the fallout of what we did four hundred years ago. We must at last face the ramifications of what we've done."

"Again, you speak treasonously," Drenan said.

"As I said, it's not treason if it's the truth. On the morrow, we will travel to the capital. And, because of the urgency of this... situation, we will use a Train."

"That *is* treason," Drenan said.

"Stay behind if you wish," Reago said, "but Devin, Javen, and I will leave at first light. Now leave me be. I intend to spend the remainder of the night in peace."

Devin and Drenan moved toward the door. Drenan eyed Javen icily as he approached and shoved the door open.

When they were gone, Reago said, "See you at first light, Javen."

Javen nodded, and followed Devin and Drenan out of Reago's quarters.

CHAPTER 9

Javen anxiously made his way back to his quarters, where he knew Kaylan would be waiting for him. He'd sat briefly with her in the carriage, but their conversation was short and did not go as planned. He'd hoped that Yolken and the rebels would turn themselves in—he didn't want anything to happen to Kaylan's mother or uncle—but they had resisted. If her mother had died, she would never forgive him. Ever since they had been making these plans, he'd been looking forward to having the opportunity to sit down with Kaylan and discuss everything that had occurred over the last few months. More importantly, he was hoping to finally explain to her how he felt about her. Now he was afraid the night's events had messed all that up.

When Javen opened the door, he found Kaylan sitting stiffly on the edge of a couch. She was staring at an untouched glass of wine sitting on a short table in front of her. When she saw him, she jumped to her feet, knocking the glass of wine over, and ran over to him. She started pounding him on the chest with her fists until he pulled her in and hugged her tightly. She began sobbing uncontrollably.

"What... have... you... done?" Kaylan sobbed.

"Kaylan..."

She stepped back from Javen and shoved him in the chest,

making him take a couple of steps back. "You killed my mammy!"

"No!" Javen said. "I didn't. I mean, they're not dead."

"She's… she's not?" Kaylan sniffed and wiped her nose.

Javen shook his head.

"But you said…"

"Because I went and looked."

"What do you mean?"

"I mean, after the… after everything settled down, I went out to the east bridge and looked. They weren't among the dead."

"And Yolken?"

Javen gestured toward the couches. "Please, Kaylan, sit, and I'll explain everything." He walked over toward the couch where Oshie was now cleaning up the spilled wine. He turned, but Kaylan was still standing by the door. After a moment, she reluctantly came and sat stiffly on the couch, her back straight. Javen sat on the couch opposite her and studied her. He'd always thought she was beautiful. She wore her hair in a braid as always, but her usually beaming face was absent. Instead, her vivid green eyes glistened.

He spent the next while explaining to Kaylan the events of the last three months.

Kaylan gasped and covered her mouth when he got to the part about what Drenan had done to Astora. "Poor Astora," Kaylan said. "She was a sweet lass who didn't deserve that. Her poor mammy and pappy."

Javen agreed, and wondered if Astora's parents knew what happened to her. How could they? And as protective as her father was of her, they had to be worried sick about her whereabouts. He considered whether he should send them a letter, but then decided that was no way to be told that their daughter was dead. He would have to do something. And Drenan needed to be held accountable.

Javen gently set the thought of Astora aside and continued

his story. In the moment, he decided to omit any reference to Hadie. Now that he was with Kaylan—the woman he truly wanted—he figured there was no sense talking about her. And he certainly didn't discuss Lannary or any of the other women Karina sent to him. Lastly, he explained what took place in the roundabout, how he'd tried to talk sense into Yolken but Yolken refused. "Kaylan, I thought they were going to kill him, but then a dragon came out of nowhere and rescued him! A dragon!"

"Deth rescued him?" Kaylan said.

"*Deth?* You know about the dragon?"

Kaylan nodded. "Yolken met him when we were on Kvorga."

"He…" Javen was beside himself. Yolken met the dragon?

"How could you let this happen?" Kaylan said.

"I didn't want any of this to happen!" Javen exclaimed. "I certainly didn't want them to hurt Yolken. This whole plan was to *prevent* him from getting hurt. But then he attacked us. Devin planned to convince him to join the Regency."

"He never would. Not after what he learned what they did to your parents."

"They were rebels. At least our father—"

"Javen…"

The look on Kaylan's face was one of pure sadness.

"If anyone's to blame for what happened, it's Yolken," Javen said, shifting from talk of their parents. "He started all this when he—"

"No! You're not blaming this on Yolken!"

"Kaylan, we'd all still be in Lonely Oak if he hadn't healed Issa."

Kaylan turned her head and toyed with the ring on her finger. "Ever since he healed Issa, all he has wanted is to find you," Kaylan said, looking back at Javen. "He doesn't care about any of this—not the Regency or the Order. He has done nothing but look for you, Javen."

"And get married," Javen blurted. He crossed his arms

across his chest.

Kaylan looked down at the ring on her left hand then back up at Javen. "We aren't married. It was just a disguise."

"But you love each other?"

"Yes," Kaylan said.

Javen looked away from her. He could have any woman Karina offered him, but he didn't want them.

"And we *do* want to get married. Jax and Mammy thought we should get married right away, but Yolken wanted to wait until we rescued you because he wanted you to be there."

Javen looked back at her. His eyes drifted down to the ring on her finger. "I don't *need* rescuing," he said. He gestured for Oshie to bring him some wine. He should have had some the moment he got to his quarters, to help calm his nerves.

Oshie offered wine to Kaylan first. Kaylan avoided looking at Oshie's nakedness as she accepted it. Javen took a healthy gulp when Oshie handed him a glass, then he sighed with relief.

"What happened to your hands?" Kaylan said.

Javen looked down at his pale forearms and hands. The itching was gone, but the memory of what took place that day wasn't. And he didn't want to talk about it. "Nothing."

"It doesn't look like nothing."

"I don't want to discuss it," he snapped. Regretting it instantly, he said in a gentler tone, "I don't want to talk about it, okay?"

Kaylan nodded. "What now?"

Javen took a deep breath, looking at Kaylan. She hadn't touched her wine. "Kaylan, all this can be yours if you want it."

"What do you mean? All what?"

Javen gestured around the room. "This."

"I don't understand."

"Tomorrow, we're going to Kyinth. Devin says that the emperor wants to make me a regent."

"A regent! Javen—"

"Afterward, he could send me anywhere. But wherever it is,

it will come with riches we could never have imagined living back in Lonely Oak."

"And what does that have to do with me?" Kaylan said.

Javen hesitated. Thoughts of Lannary wormed into his mind. He hadn't seen her since the day he'd gotten angry with her for trying to coerce him into discussing things he wasn't comfortable sharing with her, and that had been three weeks ago. She evoked passionate feelings in him. She was very beautiful, and he enjoyed bedding her, but that was it. It was only physical. He didn't love her. Then he thought of Hadie. In the time he'd spent with her, he'd developed feelings for her far greater than physical ones. He didn't know if he loved her, but he felt something for her, especially since he knew he had no chance with Kaylan. He had hoped that Devin would be able to find Hadie, but he'd been unsuccessful—that or he was deliberately keeping her from him. Either way, there was no way for him to know if he would ever see her again. However, despite how he felt about Hadie, he couldn't pass up the opportunity to be with the woman he'd realized a few months ago that he loved—and that woman was sitting across from him now. The opportunity he'd hoped to have on the night of the festival in Lonely Oak was now. If he was going to make that happen, if he was going to win Kaylan's heart away from Yolken, he needed to tell her how he felt.

"Did you know that the only thing I wanted to do at the festival that night Dorlan stayed in Lonely Oak was to spend it with you?" he said.

"*Me?*"

"I looked all over the square for you. I circled the crowds twice trying to find you. I even talked with your mammy a couple times, but she didn't know where you were."

"Why me?"

Javen fidgeted with the rim of the glass in his hand. He shoved thoughts of Lannary, Hadie, and every other woman he'd ever bedded as far away as possible. This was his moment.

"Because… I love you."

Kaylan pursed her lips. "So that's why you asked to spend the festival with me that morning in the bakery?"

"Yes," Javen said. "The first thing I thought about when I found out there was going to be a festival was that I wanted to spend it with you."

"Javen…"

"Maybe I didn't realize it until recently, but ever since we were little, I've liked you. I remember when your uncle used to tell us stories around the hearth, I always wanted to sit next to you. I didn't want them to end because then you'd return to the bakery. My feelings for you only grew as we got older."

"Javen," Kaylan started again, "I love Yolken."

Javen pictured Yolken sitting under the oak tree with Kaylan. He turned his head and drank the rest of his wine, trying to suppress the anger he felt brewing. Turning back to Kaylan, he said, "I realize that, but I truly think that if you can love him, you can love me as well." He set his empty glass down and joined Kaylan on her couch. He took her by the hand and said, "Kaylan, Yolken can't offer you what I can."

"Which is what? He loves me. That's all I need—or want."

"I love you, too. Besides that, if you're with me, you'll be counted among the Blessed. Wherever we go, people will admire and love us."

"Javen…"

"Yes?" Javen said hopefully, looking into Kaylan's gorgeous green eyes.

"Please, can we leave?" Kaylan pleaded. "I want to go to Yolken, to Mammy. I want to make sure they're okay."

"No," Javen said tersely. "That's not going to happen."

Kaylan pulled her hand out of his. "Why not?"

"Because we're going to Kyinth."

"Go if you must, but I don't want to go, Javen. I don't want anything to do with the Regency. I mean, did you hear yourself? They *murdered* Astora, a beautiful young woman who I know you had feelings for. And they almost killed Yolken, and Mammy, and Jax! All the people you care about."

Javen stared at Kaylan's untouched glass of wine, seething. He stood abruptly and said, "You're going."

"So I'm your prisoner?" Kaylan said, looking up at him.

"Only if you choose to be," Javen said.

Kaylan stood, her hands clasped before her. "No one *chooses* to be a prisoner, Javen. I want to leave. Please."

"No," he said. "It's late, and we leave at first light, so we need to get some sleep. You can join me in my bed or sleep here. Your choice."

Javen started toward the door separating the sitting room from the dining room, but Kaylan didn't move. He waited for a moment, but when she just stared at him with her arms crossed, he turned and proceeded to his room. He slammed the door behind him.

CHAPTER 10

Javen waited in the palace atrium with Kaylan as instructed. He tried to stand next to her, but each time he moved closer to her, she glared at him and stepped away. He knew she was mad at him, so he gave up. She didn't try to fight him or refuse to come with him when it was time for them to meet downstairs, but she was making it known that she didn't want to be there.

Devin and Karina were the next to arrive at the base of the stairs. They both wore blue traveling clothes, and Karina's were as revealing as always. Javen groaned when he realized she was going to be coming on their journey; her presence would make it harder for him to win Kaylan's heart. He turned his head slightly so as not to look directly at her as they approached, but she walked over to him and, standing up onto her toes, pulled Javen's head down and kissed him on the lips. He pulled away from the kiss and removed Karina's hands from his cheeks. He took a step back and gestured toward Devin and Karina, saying, "Kaylan, this is Devin Drake, the Regent of Onta, and his wife, Karina." Kaylan looked at him with wide eyes. "Devin, Karina, this is Kaylan."

"This isn't the one you had Devin looking for in Hantlo, is it?" Karina asked.

Javen turned red in the face and shook his head.

"A new girl, then?"

"Kaylan and I grew up together."

"Ah," Karina said. "Was she part of the debacle last night that wrecked my city?"

"Devin didn't tell you about her?" Javen asked.

"He knows not to bore me with such details. And you fancy this girl as you did that other?" Karina asked. "What was her name again?"

"Hadie," Javen said, his face growing even redder. "And yes."

"Tsk, tsk."

"What?" Javen said.

"Lannary will not be pleased to hear this. Tell me again why you've been neglecting her?"

"Who is she talking about?" Kaylan said.

Javen clenched his jaw. "Lannary... doesn't need to know," he said.

"Now Javen, you wouldn't have me lying for you, now would you?" Karina said. "Three women?" She gave him a wink. "You are well on your way to having your own volume of *Lovers*."

If Karina was intentionally trying to embarrass him, she succeeded.

"No," Javen said. "Only one. Kaylan." He glanced over at Kaylan, who stared icily at Karina.

The sound of boots on the marble stairs caused Javen to look up. Drenan descended with two women, one on each arm. Javen groaned again when he saw that one of them was Lannary. Her long blond hair was curled into ringlets. It was the first time he'd seen her since he got angry with her. They were on the way to the docks to go sailing when they'd passed the empty lot where the beggars gathered. Seeing it largely empty, he'd questioned one of the beggars and learned that someone had healed them. The beggar insisted it wasn't a regent. Instead of sailing, they returned to the palace. Lannary had been annoyed that they hadn't gone sailing and wanted to know why, but he didn't want to talk about it with her and yelled at her.

Hearing his reaction, Karina looked up. "Looks like Lannary has found someone else to warm her bed," she said. "Perhaps she won't mind if you take another lover after all."

Lannary and the second woman were dressed alike, each wearing a blue dress with a deep, wide cut down the center that extended well below the navel. The other woman, whom Javen didn't recognize, was equally as buxom as Lannary. Whereas Lannary had pale skin and blue eyes, the other woman was olive-skinned like Karina, with brown hair and eyes. Drenan greeted Devin and Karina but ignored Javen and Kaylan. Lannary bowed slightly toward Devin and kissed Karina's hand. She shot a quick glare at Javen, then embraced Kaylan in a hug while Kaylan stood stiffly with her arms at her sides. Lannary whispered something in her ear, making Kaylan's eyes go wide.

Javen welcomed the sight of Reago descending the stairs— at the sight of Karina and Lannary, he had known the journey was not going to go as he'd hoped. Reago wore a suit similar to Devin and Drenan's, but it was a dull orange. Unlike Devin and Drenan, Reago's face was etched with age and his hair was peppered with gray. At the bottom of the stairs, he turned left and walked past them without acknowledgment. Devin followed him, and the rest fell into step. They passed through a door at the back left corner of the atrium and entered a long hallway.

"You can't seriously be planning to use a Train?" Devin said. His voice echoed in the corridor. "Last night, I assumed you were jesting."

"What would make you think that?" Reago said.

"Because you know what will happen when you show up in Kyinth in it."

"We are in perilous times, so I am authorizing its use."

"Because of last night?"

"For too long we've sat idly by while blindly marching toward death."

"You're rambling, Uncle."

"You're as blind as Drakonias, *nephew*."

"Enlighten me, then."

"You'll find out soon enough."

"What's a Train?" Kaylan whispered to Javen.

"I have no idea," Javen said. The question lightened his mood. It was the first Kaylan had spoken to him since their conversation had ended the night before.

The group followed Reago as he walked down corridor after corridor, each of them eerily illuminated by flickering lamps mounted on sconces. They descended several flights of stairs and followed progressively danker hallways. Finally, they arrived at a metal door at the end of a dimly lit corridor. Reago produced a black key from his pocket. He inserted it into the door and reached into a pocket with his other hand. Javen heard loud noises clanging inside the door, then the door swung open.

The group filed through the door and entered a cavernous chamber with a high arching roof. Javen stared in awe at the unfamiliar Machine in front of them. The Train resembled four long, rectangular carriages with rounded tops. They reminded him of the carriages he had traveled in from Lonely Oak to Portstown. Curtained windows lined three of the four carriages—if that was indeed what they were—but the one on the right, the smallest of the four, didn't have any. Each of them had four sets of metal wheels, two sets at the front of the carriage and two at the back. A thick metal bar linked the wheels of the farthest right carriage.

"What is that?" Javen asked, even though he knew it had to be the Train.

"Father will not be pleased when we arrive in this," Devin said.

"You're free to stay here if you wish," Reago said. He walked over to a set of stairs at the middle of the second carriage.

The door at the top of the six steps opened, and several servants, including Oshie, filed out. Javen also recognized Devin and Karina's servant. Instead of their revealing palace garb, they wore trimly cut black and white clothing. Frilly white scarves were wrapped around the women's necks, and white ties extended halfway down the men's stomachs. Oshie's raven-black hair perfectly matched her clothes.

"And what are we supposed to do with them once we arrive in Kyinth?" Devin said.

"That's not your concern," Reago said.

Four servants fanned out from the others. One walked over to Reago, one to Devin and Karina, another to Drenan and the two women with him, and Oshie approached Javen and Kaylan. She bowed slightly and said, "Might I show you to your quarters, Master Javen?"

Javen nodded. They waited for the others to climb into the carriage, then Oshie led them up the steps. Inside, a hallway stretched the length of the carriage. There were two doors on the right and windows on the left. Devin and Karina entered the farthest door down.

Oshie gestured to the first door and said, "This is the dining hall. I'll show you to your quarters. Once we're underway, I'll bring you back so you may have breakfast."

Oshie started down the hallway, behind Reago, Drenan, Lannary, and the second woman. They followed them through the door at the end of the hallway, out onto a narrow metal walkway connecting the two carriages. As he followed Oshie toward the door to the next carriage, Javen looked over the handrail and saw a thick metal bar connecting the Train's carriages.

They stepped into another hallway just as Drenan entered a doorway on the right. Reago went through a door at the opposite end of the hallway. Oshie led Javen and Kaylan past the door Drenan and his two guests entered, then opened the next door and gestured for them to enter.

They stepped into a large sitting room. There were two couches separated by a small table, three plush chairs, as well as a serving table in one corner. The wall opposite the door had a large window that stretched the length of the room. There was a door on the left leading into another room. Javen walked over to the door and looked in. It was the bedroom, featuring a large bed, a long built-in armoire, and a tub in the back left corner.

"I'll return when it's time to eat," Oshie said.

Javen nodded and Oshie left the room, shutting the door behind her.

Kaylan sat on a couch stiffly, just as Javen had found her in his quarters the previous night.

"There's only one bed," Javen said. "You're welcome to it if you want it."

"Thank you," Kaylan said.

The carriage lurched, causing Javen to fall back. He braced himself on the wall then stumbled his way to the couch opposite Kaylan. The light outside the windows disappeared, and the windows went black. A single dim lamp on the wall was all that lit the room.

"Have you ever seen anything like this before?" Javen said.

Kaylan shook her head. Javen could barely see her.

"Me either," he said. "When I left Lonely Oak, we traveled in large horse-drawn carriages similar to this, but this is much bigger. And I didn't see any horses."

Javen wondered how the thing moved. He didn't think horses could pull something so big anyway. Then he remembered the Cannon Devin had shown him when they were sailing to Onta from Portstown. "It's got to be a Machine powered by Synthesis," he said. "I'm sure Reago or Devin can tell us more when we meet for breakfast."

"I'm not going," Kaylan said.

"What?" Javen looked crossly at Kaylan.

"I have no desire to dine with someone who tried to kill my family. *Or* with someone who killed your parents and aunt."

"You have to eat," Javen said tersely.

"I'm not eating with them."

Javen had come to terms with what had happened to his

aunt. She was a rebel. He loved her and hated what had happened to her, but she had openly defied a regent, even if it was Drenan. He wanted to explain to Kaylan that the same was true with her mother and uncle, but knew it would only make her angrier. Instead, he sat silently as the carriage rumbled along.

"Devin's wife was awfully forward when she greeted you earlier," Kaylan eventually said.

Javen felt his face warm. He was glad for the dim light, hoping it hid his embarrassment. "Western customs are different than what we're used to."

Kaylan nodded. "I know."

"You get used to it… sort of," Javen said.

"Used to it? You mean you enjoy kissing another man's wife?"

"N-no," Javen said with a cringe. "What did Lannary say to you?"

Kaylan's face went red. "Your aunt would be ashamed if she knew what you've been doing here."

Javen clenched his jaw. Unable to hold back, he said, "Selena's not my aunt."

"Maybe not, but she raised you, Javen. She raised you to be a better person than that."

"She also raised us not to lie," Javen retorted, "but everything she taught us was a lie."

"Not everything," Kaylan said. "Who was Karina talking about back there?"

He'd thought maybe he was going to have the opportunity to have a heart-to-heart conversation with Kaylan about what had happened. If she was ever going to love him, she needed to understand the truth of who his father, his aunt, and her mother were, but the abrupt shift in subject threw Javen off guard. "What do you mean?"

"She mentioned something about Devin looking for someone in Hantlo."

Javen leaned back on the couch, not wanting to answer the

question. Now that Kaylan was here, it didn't matter what he'd previously asked Devin to do, but he knew Kaylan wouldn't be satisfied with him saying nothing. "Her name is Hadie. I met her in Lonely Oak the night of the festival."

"I thought you said you were looking for me that night," Kaylan said.

"I was, but I couldn't find you. Then I bumped into Hadie near the dance floor, and I spent the evening with her."

"You mean you bedded her?"

"What do you want me to say? We danced. We ate. We drank. She said she had a room at the Oak and could get me in to see Dorlan, so I went with her."

"You bedded her."

"I spent the night with her, yes."

"Why was Devin looking for her?"

"The next day when Drenan picked me up from the tavern—"

"After murdering your aunt," Kaylan interjected.

"Selena attacked Drenan and—"

"You're defending Drenan?"

Javen was quickly growing frustrated with the conversation. "You asked me what Karina was talking about," Javen said, deciding to ignore the path Kaylan was trying to take the conversation. "Drenan took me from the tavern. They must've somehow known where I spent the night because they picked up Hadie as well. We spent the next couple of weeks traveling together on our way to Hantlo. In that time, I began to develop feelings for her... feelings I never felt for anyone except..."

"So you love her?"

"I... I don't know," Javen said. "That night, when I saw you with Yolken, I realized you loved someone else."

"You saw us together?"

"Under the oak tree." Javen sat silently for a moment. "Seeing you together made me... I wanted so badly to spend the festival with you. I looked all over for you, and then to see you with him…"

"I'm sorry, Javen," Kaylan said. "But I *do* love him. I love him with all my heart and want to marry him. He wants to marry me too. And we want you to be there."

"That's not going to happen," Javen said tersely.

Kaylan stared at Javen intently, and he stared back. She rose to her feet and said, "I didn't sleep last night, so I'm going to go lie down." She felt her way around the couch Javen was sitting on and made her way to the adjoining bedroom. The door shut with an audible click.

CHAPTER 11

Javen sat on the couch and stared at the dark window. The conversation had left him in a sour mood. He didn't like having to talk to Kaylan about Hadie and was relieved that she hadn't asked about Lannary. *What did she say to her?* He felt like screaming in frustration. But that wasn't all that frustrated him about their conversation.

Javen felt the Train picking up speed. After a moment, the sensation disappeared, and the motion of the Train smoothed out. He stood and walked over to the lamp by the bedroom door. He turned the small knob at the bottom and increased the light in the room. He stared at the lamp, realizing that there was no oil, and the light wasn't from a flame. It was coming from inside a small glass ball instead of a wick. He turned the knob back and forth, watching the light inside the ball grow brighter and dimmer.

The black window burst into light and overpowered the lamp. Javen walked over to the window, swaying slightly to the motion of the rapidly moving Train, and looked out. Vineyards stretched as far as he could see, undulating on small hills. He watched them go by until he heard a knock. He crossed the room and opened the door.

Oshie greeted him with a smile. "It's time to eat."

"Thanks," Javen replied. His stomach answered as well, with a growl. He'd been largely unable to eat yesterday because of the plan to rescue Yolken from the rebels. Anxiety about what was happening caused his stomach to churn from the moment he woke until he had fallen asleep last night. He looked over at the bedroom door and thought about knocking on it, but he followed Oshie out into the hallway instead.

Oshie led Javen back up the hall the way they had come earlier. Javen looked out the windows stretching the length of the hall as they went. The scenery on this side of the carriage was the same—more vineyards. They passed the entrance to Drenan's suite and exited the carriage through the door at the end of the hallway. The sound of metal screeching on metal greeted them. Javen hesitantly stepped onto the narrow metal walkway connecting the two carriages. He looked over the railing at the ground moving rapidly beneath him. Vertigo crashed into him, causing him to grip the rails tighter. The carriages were moving along some sort of metal track.

Despite his trepidation, he exclaimed, "This is incredible!"

"It really is!" Oshie shouted back.

"I've never imagined anything like this before!"

"Me either!"

"You mean you didn't know about this thing, either?"

Oshie shook her head and pulled Javen into the next carriage. Inside, where it was quieter, she said, "I was called to a servants' meeting early this morning, and when I arrived, His Highness was there. I thought I'd done something wrong, and by the looks on the faces of the others there, they all thought the same thing. We were all surprised when he told us we were going to Kyinth. Even more so when he led us down to the Train and showed us around. He told us there had been an edict banning its use, and we were the first people to see it since then."

"You all seem to know your way around it pretty well," Javen said.

"It's not all that different than serving on the carriages, only bigger."

"And faster," Javen said. He looked over at the rolling hills passing by and asked, "Do you know how fast we're going?"

Oshie shook her head. "Come on; we'd best be going."

They passed the first door on the left—Devin and Karina's quarters—and made their way down the hall to the second door.

Javen pointed to the door at the far end of the hallway and asked, "Where does that door lead?"

"To the kitchen and preparations area. Beyond that is the Engine Car."

"What's that?"

"I don't know," Oshie said. "We're not allowed in there." She opened the door to the dining hall and ushered Javen in.

The room was the same size as the sitting room of Javen's suite. A large, intricately carved wooden table sat in the middle, with place settings enough for a dozen people. There was a large serving table on the far side of the room filled with steaming pans of food. Everyone else except Reago was already at the table eating. Devin and Karina sat at one end—Devin on the end and Karina with her back to Javen, next to the door. When she noticed him, she rose to her feet and greeted him with a kiss. Drenan, sitting at the other end of the table with a woman on either side, ignored him. Lannary glared at Javen, and the unknown woman smiled.

"Sit anywhere you like," Oshie said, "and I'll bring you some food."

Javen chose to sit with Devin and Karina. He thought about sitting next to Karina so he could see out the window but didn't want to sit within reach of her. He was afraid she would start pawing at him, and he didn't want Kaylan to see if she decided to come eat. Instead, he sat across from her, next to Devin.

Oshie set a plate of food in front of him, and he hungrily devoured a warm biscuit. He washed it down with tea, then said, "This Train is amazing!"

"And requires a lot of Energy to operate," Devin said.

"When you're finished eating, I'll show you what your task will be until we arrive in Kyinth."

Javen nodded as he filled his mouth with savory ham. Before he could swallow, Lannary said, "Where's your friend?"

Javen looked over at her. She stared at him, her arms folded under her breasts so that they almost spilled out of her plunging neckline. He averted his eyes and said, "She went to bed."

"Alone?"

"Yes," Javen said. "She didn't sleep last night."

"I don't remember you ever keeping *me* up all night," Lannary said.

Javen ignored her and returned his attention to his food.

"Tsk, tsk," Karina whispered from across the table.

Javen set his fork down and said, "What?"

"Have you forgotten so quickly what you learned in *Lovers?*"

With all that had happened since he'd first discovered Yolken was in Onta, Javen had forgotten that he was practically living in the books that Hadie liked to read. "I haven't read them."

Still whispering, Karina continued, "It never ends well for those who scorn their lovers."

Javen ignored the flirtatious looks Karina gave him. He shook his head and shoveled more food into his mouth.

"Let him eat," Devin said. "He has work to do."

"Well," Karina said, "if your lady-friend continues to scorn your affec—I mean, finds herself tired, you can always come visit me."

Javen stared at his plate, unable to prevent himself from blushing. After that, Karina let Javen finish his meal in peace. He set his fork down after his second helping then finished his tea.

Devin stood and said, "Let me show you your task."

Javen stood and followed Devin toward the door. As he rounded the table, Karina picked up her cup of wine and went to sit next to Lannary. Out of the corner of his eye, he saw them both look in his direction.

Devin turned left in the hallway and walked to the door at the front of the carriage. Javen looked out the window at the vineyards as he followed and wondered how far they went. Devin opened the door, and they stepped into a large, windowless kitchen. A clear path led from the door to another one on the opposite end of the kitchen. The rest of the area contained the necessary implements to see to the dining and drinking needs of the regents. Wine racks stretched from the floor to the ceiling of the entire wall on one end. Two barrels of ale sat in the corner next to the wine racks. Sinks, stoves, and three large rectangular metal boxes lined the wall. Several tables occupied the space in the middle of the room. A few servants worked busily as they passed through.

Devin went through the second door, which led to a small room with a dozen beds built into the wall. The only other thing in the room was a few chairs and a washbasin in the corner. Another door took them out onto a second metal walkway, connecting them to what Oshie had referred to as the Engine Car. The sound of the wheels turning on the metal rails below was deafening. Devin held the next door open for Javen, and Javen stepped into the Engine Car.

Javen stared in amazement at the giant segments of interlocking black bones that greeted him. Metal braces held them in place. The smallest segment of bone protruded from the ceiling at the back of the room. From there, the segments curved down and forward, each segment larger than the previous, to the floor.

"Is it a spine?" Javen asked.

"Yes," Devin replied.

Javen walked slowly around the bones, taking them in. Red ribbons were woven throughout the black vertebrae. The only other thing in the room was a small spiral staircase in the corner.

"After the war," Devin said, "we used the new technology to greatly improve civilization. The dragon bones that once powered our weapons then powered new Machines that improved the overall quality of life for everyone. In the first two hundred years of the United Era, the empire took on a completely different shape than what you're familiar with today. Trains such as this one crisscrossed the empire. They dramatically reduced the time it took to travel from city to city. They moved everything from people to trade goods. Except in cities and small towns, horse-drawn wagons became obsolete. There were many different types of Machines, all designed to perform any number of different functions."

"Like what?"

"Well, for instance"—Devin pointed back toward the door they just came through—"there are three Machines in the kitchen called Iceboxes, that keep food fresh and cool."

"Is that what those rectangular things are?"

Devin nodded. "That simple Machine revolutionized how we ate and stored food."

"And the lamps?" Javen asked, thinking of the strange lights in his sitting room.

"Are powered by Energy."

"I thought those little glass balls looked odd."

"They're called Bulbs. Don't ask me how they work, because I never could understand it. All I know is that they use Energy and somehow make light without a flame."

"I've never even heard of things like this," Javen said. "I mean, not until you showed me that Cannon on your ship."

"Because their existence is kept secret. Which is why Reago deciding to use this Train is so troubling."

"What happened? I mean, why aren't Machines used anymore?"

"The emperor banned them. He undid nearly three hundred years of advancement with one stroke of his pen. Those Machines that couldn't be cached were dismantled and destroyed."

"Why wasn't this Train destroyed? Or your Cannon?"

"Drakonias let us keep them. Everybody got to keep something, sort of like a keepsake. But we were forbidden to use them."

"Why were they banned?"

"Good question."

"You don't know?"

"The emperor didn't say, and we didn't ask."

"Why not?"

"Because it is not our place to question the emperor."

It seemed to Javen that something of such magnitude should *have* to be explained, but before he could ask any more questions, Devin walked past the bone, rubbing his hand along the segments as he went, and opened another door.

"This is where the operator works," Devin said.

Javen stepped into a cramped room with a large window at the front. A bearded man sat on an affixed seat in front of a series of levers. He stared straight ahead, adjusting a lever from time to time.

"This is where the Train is controlled," Devin said.

Javen looked out the window. The western range of the Ontali mountains loomed ahead. Metal rails stretched out ahead as far as he could see. Crossbeams supporting the rails zipped beneath the Train at a dizzying speed.

"How fast are we moving?" Javen said.

"Roughly ten times faster than the fastest merchant wagons." Javen's eyes lit up in amazement. "Once we reach the mountains, we'll slow down significantly," Devin continued, "but it'll still take us a fraction of the time to reach Kyinth that it would take a merchant. Even more so than if we used our painfully slow carriages."

"How long will it take?" Javen wondered aloud. He'd enjoyed learning about the empire as a child, even if the lessons their aunt routinely gave them were, at times, excruciating. But one thing he'd learned since leaving Lonely Oak—traveling in Dorlan's caravan, sailing in Devin's ship, and now riding in this

Train—was that looking at maps and experiencing the empire were two entirely different things. He was coming to realize he had no appreciation for how large the empire was.

"It's about four hundred and seventy-five leagues from Onta to Kyinth. It takes a month for merchants to make the journey—in part because the roads have to circumvent the Ontalis. But these tracks take us right through them, which cuts down the distance some. And even though the Train has to slow down because of the grades and curves, we'll make the journey in just over two days."

"Two days!" Javen exclaimed.

"Merchants have to stop, sleep, and rest their horses. A Machine doesn't need to rest. The Train doesn't need to stop, so long as the dragon bone remains charged. Which brings us to your task."

Devin stepped out of the operator's room and back into the room with the black spine. "Your task," Devin said when Javen joined him, "is to keep this thing charged. I'm going to warn you, it's no easy task, as a Train of this size uses an incredible amount of Energy."

"All right," Javen said, feeling overwhelmed. Devin had had him practice Synthesizing by stretching his Core and charging dragon bones. He knew how tedious a job that was.

"Normally we bring a team of Synthesizers, but since the chancellor didn't see fit to do so, the task is left to us. Well, you. And unfortunately, charging these bones will require the better part of the day to ensure there's enough Energy to make it through the night." Devin gestured toward the spiraling stairs in the corner and said, "Up here, you have access to both the bone and the sun. With all the *distractions* Karina sent your way it'll be good for you to do more conditioning."

Javen nodded.

Devin moved toward the exit of the Engine Car. "Well, have at it. Ensure they're full by sunset." He stepped through the door, leaving Javen standing alone with the backbone of a bygone dragon.

He walked around the bone that divided the room in two and climbed the spiral steps. He emerged on a small, circular platform, open to the sky. The roof of the Train circled all around, creating the feeling that he stood in a waist-deep hole. There was a small bench built into the wall. The end of the bone extended up into the center of the platform.

Javen sat on the bench and felt the heat of the sun on his face. He opened himself to the Energy beating down on him, then placed his hand on the bone and transferred the Energy into it. As the Energy flowed into the bone, he could tell how much it contained. It was mostly full. He transferred Energy until it wouldn't hold any more.

He took a moment to look at the scenery passing by. They were still mostly surrounded by vineyards, but mountains loomed ahead. With a feeling of optimism about where he was and where he was going, he descended the stairs and made his way back to his quarters, hoping to begin breaking down the wall separating him from the woman he loved.

CHAPTER 12

Javen knocked lightly on the door separating the sitting room of his quarters from the bedroom. He waited for a reply, then cracked the door. "Kaylan?" he said softly. Not hearing anything, he pushed the door open and looked in. Kaylan was asleep on the bed. She hadn't even taken the time to turn the sheets down. It looked as though she had just lain on the bed and fallen instantly asleep. He unfolded a blanket from the foot of the bed and slid it over her. It wasn't cold enough to need covering, but he always slept better with something over him, so he thought the same might be true with her.

Javen knew Kaylan had had a rough night, so he left the room and quietly shut the door. He wished that events could have been different. The idea of kidnapping Kaylan from Yolken didn't sit well with him, but there was no alternative. Had he not gotten her away from Yolken and the others with him, she could have died. He didn't want any of them to get hurt, certainly not Kaylan. And Devin and Drenan didn't seem to care if she was a rebel or not—association with rebels was the same as being a rebel to them—but she wasn't involved with the rebels, he knew. It wasn't her fault her mother was a rebel and had dragged Kaylan into it. In the end, Javen had gone with the only option he had. Kidnapping her was the only way he could ensure no harm came to her.

He sat on one of the couches and thought about lying down. He hadn't slept the previous night either, but his mind was racing with excitement. Instead, he looked out the window, still in awe at the Machine that was quickly carrying them toward the capital of the empire.

He heard noises coming from the adjoining room and rolled his eyes. Not wanting to listen to Drenan bedding women, he left the room. The closeness of the two doors leading into their respective quarters led Javen to believe that Drenan wasn't using the bed to do his bedding. He knew Drenan was in the sitting room. *Does he want me to hear?* The very thought of Lannary bedding Drenan made him feel sick. Why would anyone want to bed him? He was every bit as vile as Hadie had warned him he was. He should have listened to her from the very beginning. But then if he had, he wouldn't be where he was now. He decided that Lannary had no choice in the matter. He couldn't imagine she would bed him voluntarily.

He returned to the dining room in the second carriage. Devin, Karina, and the other woman he had yet to meet were still there. *So he is bedding Lannary.* Devin was reading a folded piece of parchment, and Karina conversed quietly with the woman sitting next to her. He walked around the table and picked up a pitcher of wine and a glass.

A servant rushed over to him and said, "I'll pour it for you, Master Javen."

"I got it," he said. He filled his glass almost to the brim, then sat at the table a few chairs down from Devin, and took a big drink.

"Trouble with your lady?" Karina said.

"She's in bed," Javen said from behind his glass.

"*Alone?*"

"She's sleeping." He looked at the woman sitting next to Karina. Just like every woman who found herself in Karina's presence, she was quite beautiful. She had dark skin, silky black hair, and deep brown eyes. "Hello," he said.

"Hello," the woman said with a smile.

"I don't think we've met." Javen held out a hand. "I'm Javen."

The woman took Javen's hand and said, "Leena."

"It's a pleasure to meet you, Leena. Why aren't you with Drenan?"

Leena flushed slightly. "Because he wished to be alone with Lannary."

"Ah," Javen said. He knew then that he was right about what Drenan was trying to do. He took another gulp of wine.

Karina watched Javen drink his wine and said, "Does that bother you?"

"Should it?" Javen said.

"It's just… Lannary spoke so highly of you. I figured you'd think more of her, is all."

"Karina, I enjoyed the time I spent with her, but I really want things to work with Kaylan."

"If you want things to work," Karina said, "you *make* things work. Soon you'll be a regent. Do you think Lannary wants to be with Drenan?"

"How should I know?"

"Women rarely *want* to bed him," Karina said. "He has a horrible reputation because of how he treats them. But it's not up to them, or her. Regents get what they want. So if you want that woman you brought with you, then take her. She is yours."

"Is that how it is with you two?"

"Of course not. All I'm trying to say is that if you want her so bad, as a regent, you have that choice."

Javen upended his glass and said, "I don't want to force anyone to love me. Certainly not like Drenan."

Devin folded the parchment he was reading and placed it in the open envelope on the table. He picked up the nearly empty glass of wine that sat before him and took a drink.

"Has Reago told you why we needed to go to Kyinth with

such urgency?" Karina asked Devin. "It can't possibly be because of what happened last night, can it?"

Devin took another drink of wine. He looked at Javen and said, "How's the bone?"

"Good," Javen said. "It was already mostly charged."

"Don't leave it unattended for long. If you get too far behind, you'll never be able to catch up before it gets dark."

Javen nodded.

"Keep in mind that once we get to the mountains, they'll block the sun in the mornings and evenings."

"I won't fall behind," Javen said. He surely didn't want to disappoint Devin. He didn't want to do anything that might ruin his opportunity to become a regent. His mind turned to a thought that had been bugging him since they'd emerged from the tunnel. "How did Reago keep this thing a secret?"

"It was hidden deep beneath the palace where no one knew about it," Devin said.

"What about the rails it moves on?"

"Tracks, you mean."

Javen nodded.

"Look outside. What do you see?"

Javen turned in his chair and looked at the large windows behind him. The scenery had not changed all morning. "Vineyards."

"I own them," Devin said. "No one sees the tracks except those I permit to."

"You mean those who work the vineyards?"

"Yes."

"They never talk about it?"

"They do not."

Javen thought that was hard to believe. "Surely someone has said something at some point. I mean, it's been, what… over a hundred years since you said the emperor banned the use of Trains?"

"Those who chose to betray me have met their

recompense," Devin said. "They and all those they told. Consequently, no one has said anything for quite some time. The same is true in the other provinces we'll pass through.

"As a regent, Javen, you will learn to govern. You must teach your subjects to both respect you and fear you. They may even grow to love you, as they have Karina and myself. However, you must not desire their love. If you do, you will fail. And even though my subjects love me—such as those who work my vineyards—they know not to betray me."

"Wouldn't it have been easier to remove the tracks than worry about people talking?"

"It wasn't my decision." Devin finished his wine. "Now, you'd better go check on the bones."

"Already?" Javen said.

"The Train consumes a lot of Energy. Remember, everything from the lights to the Iceboxes to the Engine uses it."

Javen got up and returned to the Engine Car. He was surprised when he placed his hand on the dragon bone and realized how much Energy had been consumed in the short time he was gone. In that moment, he realized he would be spending much of his time here. It wouldn't take him long to replenish what had been used since he'd charged it the first time, but if the Train ran all night, it would take considerably longer to fill it up the next morning.

For the remainder of the day, Javen alternated between charging the bone and checking in on Kaylan. She slept until mid-afternoon. He only knew she was awake because when he knocked on the door, she shouted, "Go away!" Javen cracked the door to the bedroom and, without looking in, he asked, "Would you like to join me in the dining room for a meal? You haven't eaten since you've been with me."

"I said, go away!" Kaylan shouted.

Javen sighed and shut the door. He wasn't hungry, but she needed to eat, so he went to the dining hall to get her some food. They were in between meals and there was nothing on the serving table except water and wine, so he went to the kitchen. When he got there, all the servants were sitting around a table eating. They stood to greet him.

"Can we get you something, Master Javen?" Oshie said.

He hated bothering them while they ate. He knew they spent almost every moment of their waking hours catering to the needs of the regents, and now himself, but Kaylan needed to eat. "Something for Kaylan to eat."

"Yes, Master Javen, of course," Oshie said. "What would she like?"

"I don't know. Whatever's easiest."

"Yes, Master Javen. I'll take something to her right away."

"I'd like to take it if you don't mind."

Oshie looked surprised, but said, "Yes, Master Javen."

Javen waited while she put food, water, and wine on a tray. The other servants stood around the table while she worked, making Javen feel awkward. He still wasn't used to their behavior. When Oshie brought the tray to him, he took it and thanked her, then quickly left the kitchen.

Back in his quarters, he knocked on the door to Kaylan's room. He heard nothing in reply, so he knocked again. When the response continued to be nothing but silence, he cracked the door and said, "I've brought you something to eat."

"I'm not hungry," Kaylan said.

"You have to eat." Javen waited patiently for her to come to the door and take the tray from him, but when he realized she wasn't going to, he said, "I'll leave it out here should you get hungry." He closed the door then set the tray on the table between the couches. He considered waiting for her to come out, but figured there was a better chance of her eating if he wasn't there. So he left, shutting the door firmly so Kaylan knew he was gone.

He slowly walked the length of the connected carriages, except for the last one—Reago's quarters. He'd tried the door at the end of the hallway earlier but found it locked. As excited as he was to be going to Kyinth and becoming a regent, he wasn't in the mood to be around any of them now. The one person he wanted to be with would barely speak to him, let alone spend time with him. Before long, he found himself standing in the operator's room, staring out the window.

They had traveled past the vineyards bordering either side of the tracks and were now in a completely uninhabited region. As the Train moved into the growing hills at the foot of the looming mountains, the tracks drew up alongside the north fork of the Ontali River. Javen stared out the window as the terrain passed by and the operator occasionally adjusted the levers.

The afternoon began to grow late, and he knew he would likely need to use what sun remained to charge the partial dragon spine. He turned to leave but stopped short when the operator spoke quietly, saying something he didn't quite hear. Javen looked over at the man and said, "What did you say?"

The operator looked Javen briefly in the eyes but quickly averted them, looking back at the track ahead. "N-nothing, Master Javen. I should not have spoken."

"No," Javen said. "I want to know what you said... something about love?"

The operator looked back at Javen and, after a brief hesitation, said, "I... only that you can't force love, Master Javen."

"And what do you know about love?" Javen said. He stared intently at the man and waited for a reply, but the man didn't offer one. The operator held Javen's gaze initially but then looked back out the window.

Javen continued to study the man. The longer Javen looked at him, the more he thought he knew him. There was something familiar about him.

"Do I know you?" he finally asked.

"What?" the man said with another quick look at Javen. "No, Master Javen, I-I don't believe I have ever had the pleasure of meeting you."

"Hmm," Javen said. He continued to look at the man, hoping to jog his memory as to why he seemed familiar.

"I'm sorry I spoke, Master Javen. I was out of place."

"It's all right," Javen said. "What's your name?"

"My... uh... my name?"

"Yeah."

"My... my name is... I shouldn't have spoken. I was out of place."

"You're not in trouble," Javen said. "I just like to know what people's names are, is all."

"Oh," the operator said. "My name is Norin."

"*Norin?*" Javen looked closer at the operator. Maybe *that* was why he looked familiar. He did sort of remind him of Norin in Lonely Oak. He realized he missed bantering with Norin when he went to pick up goods for the tavern at his warehouse. "Huh."

"What is it, Master Javen?"

"It's just... you remind me of someone back home."

"Oh?"

Javen nodded. "Well, I better go." He turned from the operator and said, "See ya, Norin."

In the next room, Javen placed his hand on the spine to check its capacity. Just as Devin had indicated, it was already partially depleted. He climbed the stairs and sat on the bench facing the sun. With a sigh, he placed his hand on the bone and began to fill it anew.

As the afternoon passed, while he worked to replenish the interconnecting bones, he thought about what Norin said. He didn't want to force Kaylan to love him. He wanted her to love him voluntarily. The question he faced was what to do if she refused. He knew he couldn't let her go back to Yolken—at least not while he was still associated with the rebels. Whether she came to love Javen or not, he didn't want her to get hurt.

Javen finished charging the bone just before the sun dipped behind the hills. He stayed until the sun set, then descended the spiral stairs. Someone had come along and turned on the strange lanterns in the room, casting an eerie glow on the bones.

The afternoon of Synthesizing left Javen hungry, so he stopped in the dining room to eat. The others were gathered together at one end of the table, and a servant busily cleared empty dishes from around them. Javen looked briefly at Lannary, who sat on Drenan's lap, then sat a few chairs away from them. Thankfully they let him eat in silence. He stayed only long enough to eat, trying his best to ignore Drenan as the regent fondled Lannary. When he finished, he stood up and moved for the door.

"Where are you going?" Karina asked.

"To bed."

"So early?"

"I haven't slept in two days, and I spent all day Synthesizing—"

"I really wish you'd stay."

"Let him rest, love," Devin said. "He has a lot of work ahead of him tomorrow."

"All right," Karina acquiesced. "If you find yourself having trouble sleeping, you know where to find me."

Javen left before they could see him blushing. He returned to his quarters, hoping to find Kaylan in the sitting room. She was not. His only greeting was an empty food tray. The water pitcher was missing, but the wine remained untouched. Javen sat on the couch with a sigh and poured himself a glass. When it was empty, he dimmed the lamp. He thought about knocking on the bedroom door but decided against it. Instead, he lay down on the couch and promptly fell asleep.

CHAPTER 13

Dorlan rubbed his temple as he made his way back to his quarters. He was beyond tired of tending to Drenan's affairs. The influx of southerners fleeing the southern and western provinces was straining Hantlo, and Drenan was off chasing after the son of a long-dead rebel. His actions were directly inhibiting Dorlan from seeing to the greater needs of the realm.

He needed a glass of wine. Probably several.

In his bedchamber, Dorlan walked around the long couch positioned in front of the floor-to-ceiling windows overlooking the Kvorgan Sea. He graciously accepted the glass of chilled wine Sethlan had prepared for him and sat on the couch. He took a sip of it, closed his eyes, and felt its coolness descend to his stomach. He opened his eyes again and looked down at the crowded balcony a floor below. He needed some time to himself before he joined in the daily gathering of regents, Silks, and other aristocrats from around the empire.

He turned at the sound of a knock on the door. Sethlan swiftly answered it, and returned with a message stuffed into a cylindrical black tube. He handed the tube to Dorlan and said, "From Onta, Your Highness."

Dorlan set his glass of wine down on the table at the end of the couch and said, "It's about time Drenan sends word." He tapped the end of the tube on his palm, making the parchment slide out, and unrolled it.

He recognized the handwriting immediately.

It wasn't from Drenan.

Blessed Nephew,

For too long, I have kept quiet about the danger that threatens us all, but recent events make it such that my silence will no longer contain what HBH has kept hidden for over a century.

What I write will no doubt be considered treason, but fear not; you will have no obligation to report me to HBH as I am going to Kyinth in my Train to face him personally.

A few months ago, through no fault of your own, you set in motion events that have resulted in my penning of this letter. Your healing of a cripple in a small town called Lonely Oak, and her subsequent injury, was the catalyst causing a Synthesizer to use the gift for the first time. As I'm sure you are aware, Drenan's investigation revealed that the Synthesizer was a boy by the name of Yolken Thornhill, son of Orwyn Thornhill. Danavin.

As you know, Drenan sent his bastard to apprehend Yolken, but he was unsuccessful. HBH then directed you to instruct Danavin's second son, Javen, in the ways of the gift. Devin tells me Javen's training did not go well and that Drenan used Father's unconventional method to force him to Synthesize. I am shaking my head at Drenan's continued lack of self-control.

Events with Danavin's eldest continue to unfurl despite our efforts. A little over a month ago, someone healed multiple beggars in Onta. With Javen's help, we were able to determine it was Yolken. He was traveling with three others, one of whom is a known rebel— the man who nearly killed Drenan in his very quarters. The others were likely rebels as well, helping Yolken for reasons we, at the time, knew not. We were further able to learn that they bought passage on a ship to Ronig, and that while at sea, they convinced the captain to take them to Kvorga. Why they went there, we did not know.

Devin and Drenan organized a trap for their return. They managed to separate Yolken from his group and had him surrounded and outnumbered. Devin spoke to him and learned that they had found Deanna and that she was now working with them. Despite Devin's efforts, the boy refused to surrender. Then, a most perplexing event occurred when Devin moved to apprehend him. With the sun already set and without the aid of dragon bones, the boy somehow Synthesized and thwarted the trap. Do you understand what I am saying? He Synthesized in

Despite this impossible display of power, Yolken was enormously outnumbered. However, before he ran completely out of Energy, a DRAGON rescued him. It flew down, snatched him in its claw, and flew away, killing dozens of men in the process.

This is the single most humiliating defeat the rebels have inflicted upon the Regency. Ever.

As I sit here, pen in hand, I hesitate to continue. But I have made up my mind. You, of all people, know we can no longer sit idly by and do nothing. And I am _not_ talking about the rebels. It has been seventy years since anyone last heard from Thena, and you are on the verge of losing your realm—I've heard the latest reports. And yet HBH refuses to act. He refuses to even admit that there's a problem. Well, there _is_ a problem. And I know what it is.

Dorlan lowered the letter. So many thoughts swirled in his head. *Deanna's alive? A Dragon? I thought we'd... Reago knows what's happening? How?* He took a drink of wine then continued reading.

As near as I can tell, HBH first learned about the problem in 245. At that time, he issued the first of two edicts for which he would give no explanation. He banned the art of astronomy. Moreover, he ordered Drashon to silently dispose of every *individual known to have practiced the art, except one: an astronomer in Tieger named Vashon.*

HBH commissioned Vashon to study the sun. He blessed him with Regeneration and Vashon spent the next fifty years, under Drashon's supervision, quietly discovering that HBH's war had a price much larger than any of us could have ever imagined. His war—our war—has somehow initiated a change in the sun. I don't know why, but it is now, without a doubt, marching steadily toward death. I don't begin to understand how it's even possible for the sun to die, but that doesn't make it not so. For some reason, it's changing. The change is slow and nearly imperceptible, but its change has magnified the cyclones plaguing the East Sea in both intensity and frequency. Its change is also causing the conditions plaguing your realm.

HBH knows this. But rather than take action, he chose to keep the astronomer's discovery a secret, and had Drashon murder Vashon instead. Then HBH murdered Drashon.

Dorlan lowered the letter again. What Reago was saying made no sense. He stared out the panoramic windows at the setting sun. *It's changing?* He studied the sun closely. The sun looked like the sun. Who ever looked at the sun and pondered what it looked like? With it hovering on the horizon, it didn't hurt to stare. Reago said it was changing, so he closed his eyes and searched his memory. He'd watched it set countless times over the centuries from this very room. With his eyes closed, he thought specifically about the evening he became the Chancellor of the Southern Realm. It was so monumental that the memory was still clear in his mind. He focused his memory on the sun then opened his eyes. He gazed at the sun, closed his eyes again for a moment, then opened them.

It *was* different.

Dorlan gasped.

How could I have been so blind?

They had all been blind.

And their father had deliberately kept them in the dark.

I was just there, and he lied to me.

Dorlan stood, glass of wine in hand, and threw it against the window. The glass shattered, sending shards flying. Red wine splattered on the window. It blended with the setting sun and the band of red water known as the blood river.

He sat heavily back on the couch and continued to read.

> *Now, you might be wondering how I know all this. I'm not going to hide it from you any longer: The rebels managed to obtain a copy of the report Vashon wrote for HBH, and they shared that report with me. It shames me to admit that I've known about the astronomer's report and have done nothing about it. Well, that ends with this letter.*
>
> *I don't know what's to be done about the sun. Nobody does. However, I intend to go to HBH and convince him that something <u>needs</u> to be done. If we continue doing nothing, then Dradonia is doomed. The sun has reached a point where its march toward*

Dorlan stared, dumfounded, at the letter. He saw Sethlan approach with a broom and a towel out of the corner of his eye. "Leave it," he commanded.

"Yes, Your Highness," Sethlan said with a bow.

"Leave me and ensure no one disturbs me."

Dorlan stood and looked out the window at the blazing half-disc still above the horizon.

"I need time to think."

CHAPTER 14

Phenor Morrigan leaned against the balcony, toying with the rim of his glass with his thumb. He looked away from the crowd awaiting the chancellor's arrival, out over the water.

"Phenor," a female voice behind him said.

He turned and saw a woman approaching, her long brown hair braided down to the small of her back. She was wearing a light blue robe, cinched at the waist.

"Hello, Lady Dreanna," he said.

"You don't seem your normally jovial self."

He wasn't. Ever since that night at Sheena's brothel, he had struggled with what to do. He was furious with Hadie for presuming she could put him in such a position after abandoning her mother when she'd decided to flee the south. She was forcing him to choose between taking part in a rebellion or his daughter's life.

"I've got something on my mind," he said.

A waiter walked by, and Dreanna scooped a glass of wine off his tray and took a sip. "What?"

"A difficult decision I need to make."

"Care to discuss it?"

"No offense, Your Ladyship, but no."

"I'm not unfamiliar with making difficult decisions, you

know."

She spoke the truth. The drought and fires five years ago had gotten so bad that she'd had to order the abandonment of the Southern Fingers. In his opinion, with its once-clear blue water and sandy beaches, it had been one of the most picturesque provinces in the whole realm. His decision did affect her, but he wanted to speak to the chancellor first. He looked over her head at the panoramic window a floor above them. He'd glimpsed the chancellor up there earlier, but now all he saw was what looked like something running down the glass.

He was no fool. He knew how the Regency responded to rebels. History was rife with failed rebellions. He looked out over the water again at the blood river. If it ever became known that he had foreknowledge of a rebellion and hadn't done his part to thwart it, he would forfeit everything he had worked for, including his life.

"Would you excuse me, please?" he said with a slight bow toward Dreanna.

Dreanna nodded her head and turned, immediately taking up conversation with someone else.

Phenor gulped down his wine and set the glass on the tray of the first waiter he passed. He picked his way through the crowd and back through the open double-doors to the banquet hall inside. People crowded it as well.

He wound through the crowd, offering a brief reply to those who spoke to him, and made his way to the stairs on the left side of the hall. He took them two at a time, to Dorlan's private gathering hall. Only the most respected of society's members were ever permitted up here, and he was not about to lose that right—not even for his daughter.

The door to Dorlan's private quarters opened, and his personal servant, Sethlan, stepped out. "Excuse me," he said, addressing Sethlan, "but I need a word with His Highness."

Sethlan walked past him, saying, "He's presently unavailable."

Phenor grabbed the servant by the arm, forcing him to turn. "It's of the *utmost* importance."

"What is it?"

"It's… sensitive in nature."

"If it's that important, then you can tell me, and I'll ensure he's informed the moment he opens the doors."

"Might I wait?" Phenor said.

"I'm afraid he won't be available for some time."

Sethlan turned to leave.

"Fine," Phenor said, "But understand that what I need to tell him is *extremely* sensitive."

"I handle all of His Highness' matters, Phenor," Sethlan said.

"R-right, right." He handed Sethlan a letter.

"I'll be sure His Highness gets it," Sethlan said.

"Y-yes, yes. Thank you."

* * *

So that's what she's up to, Sethlan thought. His mind swam. The girl was plotting a rebellion. And she was somehow associated with the Order of the Dragon. After ensuring Phenor he would inform the chancellor of the news at the first opportunity and sending him on his way, Sethlan went to his quarters on the opposite end of Dorlan's private gathering hall. Even without knowing what was in the letter from Onta, which had evoked a rare display of emotion in the chancellor, Sethlan possessed valuable information. It was something his true employer would want to know.

In his room, he turned up the lantern over his small writing desk and sat. First, he lit a red candle sitting on the desk, then removed the cork from his inkwell. He dipped his pen into it and began to write. When he finished, he capped his ink jar and stuck the pen in its holder. He blew on the parchment until the ink was dry, rolled it up, and sealed it with a wax seal, then stuffed it into a pocket inside his tunic and left his room.

Sethlan made his way to the aviary and handed the sealed letter to the attendant.

"Where to, Sethlan?" the attendant asked.

"Croff," Sethlan said. He handed the attendant a gold drake and said, "It's urgent."

The attendant nodded, and Sethlan left.

He'd considered waiting to see if he could learn the contents of the letter that had been sent to Dorlan, but knew the information about the girl was valuable in and of itself. It wasn't every day he learned about an impending rebellion. The Order *loved* news about rebellions. There was also no harm in sending another message if he managed to learn what the letter said—Draego knew there were enough condors trained to Croff. He made sure of that. And the more messages he sent, the more loyal the attendant became.

CHAPTER 15

Javen quickly lost the enthusiasm he'd felt when they first boarded the Train in Onta. The journey, as quickly as it was passing, was not what he had hoped it would be. Before Reago had taken them into the depths of the palace and revealed his plans for their journey, Javen had counted on having at least a month to win Kaylan's heart. In the end, he had a fraction of that time. Even if Kaylan had decided to come out of the bedroom—which she didn't—he wouldn't have been able to spend much time with her, since he spent most of the journey charging the Train's dragon bones.

Beginning with the dawning of the sun on the second day of their journey, Javen settled into a routine. He hastily ate breakfast, left instructions with Oshie to take food to Kaylan, and then went straight to begin charging the nearly-spent dragon bones. The moment he placed his hand on the bone at the top of the platform, he knew it would require the majority of the morning. He worked until the sun stood high in the sky, and only quit because he'd grown hungry and thirsty.

He climbed down the stairs with slightly shaky legs and proceeded to the dining room. A servant tended to the others who, unlike him, were enjoying the journey. Seeing him come in, the servant fixed him a plate of food while Javen walked over to the serving table and poured himself a glass of water. He drank it down quickly and poured another, which he drank just as quickly. After a third glass, he sat at the table and devoured the food on the plate set before him.

"Any of you want to take a turn?" he asked. "The bones still need more charging."

Devin and Drenan both looked at Javen, and Drenan chuckled.

"What?" Javen said. "It's a valid question. Someone has to charge the bones, right?"

"That sort of work is beneath a regent," Drenan said.

"So neither of you are going to help me?"

"You need the conditioning," Devin said.

Javen sighed and rose from the table. He poured himself another glass of water to take with him. On his way out, he stole a glance at Lannary and noticed the side of her face looked bruised. He hesitated and thought about punching Drenan in the face, but thought better of it. He didn't want to get into any sort of fight—physical *or* Synthesis-fueled—as tired as he was. And not until he was better trained. Instead, he clenched his jaw and left.

He returned to his post and set the glass of water down next to him. Unable to do anything presently about Lannary, he pushed the thought of her from his mind and set himself to finish his task.

The scenery had changed dramatically since the previous day. The Train now wound its way through the western range of the Ontalis. The terrain rose sharply to the west and dropped just as sharply to the east. The tracks were about halfway up the side of the rocky mountainside and curved to follow the ever-changing landscape. By mid-afternoon, just as Javen finished charging the bones, the sun dipped below the peaks. He was glad the next day would be the last.

The Train finished its journey through the Ontalis and passed well east of Arinin while he slept. By the time he ate breakfast and settled in to recharge the dragon bones they were surrounded by endless plains.

Excitement filled Javen when the towering buildings of Kyinth came into view. They were both majestic and foreign. He removed his hand from the dragon bone, cut himself off from the Energy flowing from the sun, and watched as they approached a city that, three months ago, he would never have imagined he'd ever see. The capital of the empire grew quickly. He watched for several minutes, then descended the stairs in hopes of convincing Kaylan to come look.

Javen knocked on the bedroom door and, not hearing a reply, called, "Kaylan! Come and watch as we approach Kyinth!"

"No!" Kaylan shouted through the door.

Not wanting to keep shouting, Javen cracked the door and said, "You have to come see it. It's incredible."

"I said no."

The door pushed closed against Javen's face. He clenched his fists and barely kept himself from punching the door. "Stay in there if you want. However, when we get there, you *will* come out!" he shouted. He stormed out of the room and slammed the door shut.

This was *not* how he'd wanted this to go. He had hoped that by the time they arrived in Kyinth, Kaylan would have changed her mind about him. However, with their arrival imminent, it didn't look as though that was going to happen. If she refused to come with him when they arrived, then, as much as he hated the thought, he would have to force her.

CHAPTER 16

Sheal stared at the parchment in his hand. He had to hold it open with both hands to prevent it from rolling back up into a tight coil. It had been some time since he'd received correspondence in the familiar flowing script, and the words written were hardly believable.

Deanna, he thought. Her disappearance had caused him much grief. In the years after the war, it had been his responsibility to find and eliminate those who'd fought against Drakonias. After all the others were apprehended, and subsequently eliminated, only Deanna had remained. It had cost him the southern chancellorship, he was sure of it. Drakonias never came out and admitted it, but that was the only thing that made sense. Instead, Drakonias made Dorlan Chancellor of the Southern Realm and him Regent of Hantlo. It wasn't until after Drashon's mysterious death that the emperor had made him Chancellor of the Northern Realm. And now, four hundred years later, Deanna had returned. Somehow that boy—the son of Danavin whom he'd only recently heard about—had accomplished what he had been unable to do; he'd found her. If the reason Drakonias had refused him a chancellorship *was* that he'd failed to apprehend Deanna, Sheal wondered how he was going to respond when he inevitably found out about her return.

A dragon? They'd killed every one of them. They were extinct. This belief was so entrenched within the minds of his brother and siblings that when cities had been restored after the war ended, they'd made no defenses against possible retaliation. Some argued that they should set up the Machines designed to bring dragons down in the capitals to protect against inevitable attacks, but Drakonias thought otherwise. After the campaign against the dragons ended, no one had ever seen a dragon again. And now, with the re-emergence of his sister, came the report that a dragon assaulted Onta? *Impossible.* And somehow, this was also connected with the boy. He read the part about the dragon rescuing the boy again, still in disbelief. The dragons were known to never interfere in the affairs of man. None of it made sense.

Even given the incredibleness of these two revelations, it was the third that gave Sheal pause. *The sun is dying*, he read in his brother's flowing script. *A secret HBH has kept from us.* And now Reago was going to confront Drakonias? *Is he insane?* But it was written right here on the parchment—the only reason he was Chancellor of the Northern Realm was that Drakonias had killed Drashon to protect his secret. *You know how this will end for me, blessed brother. It is why I am imploring you to join me in Kyinth. But time is short. I am taking my Train; by the time you read this letter, I will have arrived. I will delay my confrontation as long as I can, but if you wish to join me, you must make haste.*

Sheal let go of one end of the parchment, letting it roll back up. He stared into the distance and considered Reago's message carefully. What he wrote was treasonous, but Reago admitted as much. But if what he said about Drashon was true, then wasn't what Drakonias did treason as well? He was emperor, but that didn't permit him to act with impunity. Did it?

He didn't have a Train at his disposal as Reago did. Even if he did, the tracks were long since dismantled. Besides, they would have been in full view of all those traveling the highway connecting Tieger and Kyinth. He did, however, have one of Drashon's Autos.

Joining Reago in treason aside, he wondered if the empire could survive such a rift within the Regency. It was already unraveling as it was; the east was completely lost, and the south was crumbling. Add in the ongoing uprisings in the Turnig province out west, and Sheal was sure it would collapse. But did it even matter? If what Reago also said about the sun was true, then none of it mattered. He didn't know if what Reago said was happening could cause the cyclones separating the east from the rest of the empire, or cause what was troubling the south, but something bad *was* happening. Regardless, the empire was slowly imploding, and whether Reago was right or not, unless they all came together and did something, there wouldn't be an empire to commit treason *against*.

He squeezed the rolled-up parchment in his fist tightly, hating the position he unexpectedly found himself in.

CHAPTER 17

A feeling of despair washed over Yolken when darkness enveloped Deth. He'd been so close to rescuing both Kaylan *and* Javen, but he'd failed. And there was nothing he could do. He couldn't go back alone, horribly outnumbered as he was, and he doubted even Deanna, Jax, and Deborah would be able to help him fight his way back into Onta. He felt inadequate fighting with Synthesis, even with his strength and new ability to store Energy in his bones. He needed more time to learn to fight, but he didn't *have* time.

He sank to the ground and let the fire hovering over him go out.

He was helpless and alone.

Overhead, the Great Dragon constellation was climbing into the sky.

He loved Kaylan. And she was gone.

The promise he'd made to her when the bandits accosted her in the Karin Valley echoed in his mind: *I promise I'll never let anything happen to you. Ever.*

He curled up on his side and cried, his failure haunting him until he fell asleep.

He groaned when he woke. His body was stiff from the cool air and hard ground.

The sun had yet to rise, but there was enough early morning light for him to assess his surroundings. He was in the middle of a large meadow. There was no way he could be sure, but he figured he was somewhere in the southern Ontali range. He remembered Deth had followed the river east when it split, and he didn't think Deth had flown long enough to carry him to the northern range. There was no way for him to be sure, though. Making the best guess he could, he turned north and started walking.

Soon after entering the woods, streams of light pierced through the trees and warmed the side of his face. He absorbed the sun's Energy and used some of it to make his aches go away. The rest he pushed into his bones. The feeling was incredible. The implications were enormous: So long as he kept his bones charged, he would never have to depend on dragon bones again.

Yolken walked until the sun warmed his left side. Just as it was about to set, the trees gave way. He was on a ridge looking down on the Karin Valley, bathed in shadow. He saw two villages—easily identifiable by the smoke rising from chimneys—one to his left and the other to his right. As high as he was, there was no way he could reach either of them before nightfall.

The problem he faced was the same as when he and Jax had arrived at the Mindon Falls. Determined not to spend another night out under the stars, he made up his mind. He drew the last vestiges of Energy from the setting sun into his Core. He filled it until it began to stretch, then reached out in all directions with thousands of Energy threads. He collected air around himself, compressing it until he felt the pressure all around him.

The ridge didn't drop very far before the ground began to slope out again, so Yolken walked back away from the ridge. After taking a couple of dozen paces, he turned and faced the ridge. He launched himself into a sprint, sending Energy into his legs to boost his speed. He leaped at the ledge, and dove headfirst toward the village to the left.

Remembering the techniques Jax taught him, Yolken adjusted the air around his body to slow his fall. His descent toward the trees turned into more of a glide. He continued to gather more air, using most of it to keep himself from crashing down into the trees. The rest he pushed rearward, causing him to race faster and faster toward the village.

He kept his eyes on the village and could tell he was going to reach the treetops before he reached the valley floor. To prevent it, he added more air below him, along his chest, and decreased the air along his back. His descent slowed. He was now moving almost as far laterally as he was downward. As the village approached, he applied Jax's instructions on how to land—but his shifting of the air around his body sent him tumbling head over heels backward. The world spun around him.

"Draego's Fire," he cursed. That wasn't what he intended.

Each time he spun and looked down at the ground, it was a little closer. He estimated he would only spin a few more times before he hit the ground, but he wasn't sure how to make the spinning stop. With no time to fiddle with the air pressure around him in search of a solution, he let go of the air altogether. The spinning slowed, leaving him looking down at the rapidly approaching ground. He desperately collected air around him again and pushed all of it down.

Dust blew out and away from the area directly below him. He flinched in preparation for impact. When it didn't come, he opened his eyes. He was hovering about a pace above the ground. Smiling, he released the air and fell the remaining distance. He grunted when he hit the ground.

Yolken rolled onto his back. "Well, that'll need some practice."

He didn't have any more room in his bones for the remaining Energy in his Core, so he discharged it into the ground. He pushed himself to his feet, dusted himself off, then looked around. Hopefully, no one had seen him. Seeing how close he was to the village, he realized how foolish his stunt had been.

He set off toward the small village, which looked to be about half the size of Lonely Oak, and realized he had a problem. As he'd spent the day walking through the woods, he'd decided that his best chance of joining back up with Jax, Deborah, and Deanna was to wait for them somewhere. He figured they'd most likely go back to Croff, so he had planned on finding an inn along the road they'd taken to Onta. But now that he had found a village, he realized he didn't have anything with him. He'd shrugged off the pack he'd made with his cloak when Jax tried to stop him from going after Kaylan, and he'd dropped his satchel on the bridge as well.

He figured he could sleep in a hayloft if he needed to, but he was reserving that as his last option. He walked between two buildings and stopped on the dirt road. He looked at the mix of brick, stone, and wood buildings lining the road, and remembered staying at an inn here on their way to Onta. He walked down the road toward the inn.

The inside of the inn was not all that different than his tavern. Selena had told him his father originally built it to be a small inn, with the tavern on the bottom and the rooms above. Their father had intended the tavern to be a temporary home until he could build a house on their plot in the maple grove outside of town, but he never got around to it. Leanne's, however, looked as though the inn had been an afterthought. The building looked like it was built upside down.

The first level was a square brick building, which he remembered was a pub. Two more levels—the rooms—were built above the pub, out of wood. They hung off both sides and the rear of the brick building by a good two paces on each side. A few wooden support beams extended from the corners of the wooden structure to the ground.

Yolken opened the door and stepped into the pub. It was bustling with patrons eating their evening meal. He negotiated around the tables to the bar in the back of the room and waited for Leanne to address him. She was a middle-aged woman with three almost-grown children—one who worked in the kitchen, one who worked the pub, and the third tending to the horses of those spending the night.

"What'll it be?" Leanne said when she had a moment between filling mugs of ale.

"I need a place to stay for a few days," Yolken said. "Only thing is…"

"Out with it, lad. I haven't all night."

"I don't have any money."

"No money?" Leanne said, her voice rising a notch in pitch. "How you reckon on payin'?"

"Well, actually, I was hoping you'd recognize me."

"Why would I?"

"I was here not long ago. I stayed the night with my wife, her mother, and uncle." It felt weird to refer to Kaylan as his wife. Probably because it was a lie. He wanted to marry her more than anything else in the world, but he'd decided to wait until after they rescued Javen. He was all the family Yolken had left, so he couldn't get married without Javen present. But before they set off from Croff to the Island of Kvorga, Jax had convinced him that they needed to at least pretend to be married. Apparently, a young man traveling with an attractive— unmarried—woman would have been too suspicious. Sleeping next to her without bedding her had been one of the hardest things he'd ever had to do.

Leanne looked around the pub. "And where are they now?"

Yolken hesitated. "We got separated."

"Sorry, lad. If you don't have any money, I can't help you." She turned to fill three mugs with ale. "This ain't a charity, you know," she added over her shoulder.

Yolken took a chance, remembering the look of familiarity Leanne had given Jax when they'd entered the pub before. "I'm here to meet a man named Jax," he said. He didn't know if she was a member of the Order, or even whether she could Synthesize, but he wasn't worried either way.

Leanne closed the barrel spigot and turned to look at him. "Jax, you say? What business do you have with him?"

"I'd love to discuss it with you," Yolken said. "But not here."

Leanne walked over to Yolken and said quietly, "So you have business with Jax?"

Yolken nodded.

Leanne looked at Yolken for a moment then snorted. She walked to the end of the bar, retrieved a key from a pegboard, and returned. She slid it across the bar and said, "Here."

Yolken scooped it up.

"Room 310," Leanne said. "Now, sit down and have something to eat."

Yolken didn't argue. He just hoped the offer of food included some ale. Draego knew he needed it.

CHAPTER 18

Yolken jumped to his feet when the pub door opened and three familiar faces filed through it. Jax immediately caught sight of him standing at the table on the far side of the dimly lit room and walked over to him. Jax and Deanna stopped on the far side of the table, but Deborah came around and embraced him with a hug.

Deborah ended the hug and grabbed both of Yolken's hands. "We've searched every town we passed through looking for you," she said. "Please tell me Kaylan's with you."

Yolken shook his head.

Deborah embraced him again and cried into his shoulder.

Yolken wrapped his arms around Deborah and hugged her back. Holding Kaylan's mother brought emotions he hadn't known he'd buried to the surface, and he began to cry as well. "I tried," he sobbed quietly.

"I know you did," Deborah said between sobs. "I'm just glad you're safe."

Yolken held Deborah until she eventually let go and took a step back.

Jax stepped closer and clapped Yolken on the shoulder. "It's good to see you, lad. Do you have a room?"

Yolken nodded.

Jax shoved Yolken's rolled-up cloak and satchel into his hands and said, "Good." Jax finished Yolken's half-empty glass of ale, then said, "Let's go."

Yolken scowled at Jax, but led them to the stairs and up to the third floor.

The room was small and cramped with four people in it. Yolken stood next to the bed, which Deborah sat on. Jax leaned against a rickety dresser, and Deanna peered out the window overlooking the mountains to the south of the village.

A moment of silence hung over the room before Jax broke it by saying, "What you did was foolish."

Yolken immediately felt his temper rising. Jax had responded the same way when he protected Kaylan from the bandits.

"Jax," Deborah said, "We decided that—"

"No," Jax said. "It needs to be said. It was an obvious trap and running back after Kaylan put our entire mission at risk."

"What was I supposed to do?" Yolken asked. "Let them take her?"

"Sometimes," Jax said, "being a member of the Order requires us to make difficult decisions."

"I'm *not* a member of the Order!" Yolken shouted.

Jax looked at the door, then tersely said, "Watch your voice. Maybe not officially, but whether you like it or not, you are integral to the Order's purpose. We must carefully consider every decision we make. The Order has not survived this long by acting hastily."

Yolken transferred Energy from his bones into his Core, then formed a fist. He thought about punching Jax in the jaw but knew he'd probably break it. He returned the Energy to his bones and said, "I don't regret what I did."

"Neither do I," Deborah said. "I just wish you'd found her."

"I already said I tried," Yolken said.

"I know, dear."

"There were just too many of them."

"I'm not blaming you."

A moment of silence hung over the cramped room.

"I've spent two weeks trying to figure out how they knew we would be there," Jax said, "and I can't make any sense of it. What happened back there was planned. They knew exactly when we would be going through Onta."

"I still think it was Urgil," Deborah said.

"That's the only thing that makes sense," Deanna added without looking away from the window.

"No," Jax said with a look toward Deanna.

"How can you be so sure?" Deborah said.

"Because he was a man of ambition. If he thought I offered him even the slightest chance of becoming the captain of Devin's ship, he wouldn't have betrayed us," Jax said. "No, something else tipped the Regency off."

Guilt flooded into Yolken when he realized that just as losing Javen in Lonely Oak was his fault, losing Kaylan was as well. "I think I might know," he said.

Deanna looked over at him.

Jax glared at him. "What?"

"You remember that corner outside the wall in Onta? By the docks with all the beggars?"

"Yes?"

"When you went down to get a boat, Deborah went to buy food. I told her Kaylan and I were going for a walk."

Jax clenched his jaw. "What did you do?"

"So many of them were suffering…"

"What did you do?"

"Some of them had deformities. Most of them had this horrible skin affliction."

"*What* did you *do*?" Jax said.

Yolken looked Jax in the eye, afraid to admit what he had done. But he knew it was his fault, so he needed to own it. "I healed them," he said.

Jax clenched both hands into fists, then slammed his left hand on the top of the dresser.

"I couldn't help it," Yolken said. "When we passed by the square, I was drawn to their need. I knew I could heal them, so I did. I… I was careful. I looked around to make sure nobody was around before I did anything."

"You were *careful?*" Jax said. "Did I not warn you, when you pulled the stunt with the bandits, not to openly Synthesize?"

"I didn't!" Yolken exclaimed. "I didn't draw Energy from the sun. I used the Harachin sword."

"You Synthesized," Jax said, taking a step toward Yolken, "in the middle of Onta, a city crawling with regents *and* Watchers."

"I was careful," Yolken said. "I followed your instructions. Nobody was around!"

"Nobody was *around?* People talk, Yolken!" The last bit, Jax shouted.

"Jax…" Deborah said.

"I'm sorry if you're mad," Yolken said. "But I'm not sorry for what I did. Healing those people was the right thing to do. I mean, what's the point of being Blessed and not using the gift Draego gave me?"

"He has a point," Deanna said.

Jax pointed sharply at Yolken and said, "This is your fault!"

"Jax!" Deborah shouted. Yolken was taken aback. He didn't know if he'd ever heard Deborah raise her voice in his entire life. "There's no point in getting mad about something that can't be undone."

"Don't get mad?" Jax asked. He pointed at Yolken and said, "It is because of *his* inability to control himself that your daughter is now *also* a prisoner of the Regency."

"I don't blame Yolken," Deborah said.

Jax's anger at him made Yolken's temper rise again. He once again transferred Energy from his bones to his Core. When he didn't immediately do anything, beads of sweat started forming on his head.

"Oh, no no no no," Jax said, pointing a finger at Yolken. "I may have sworn an oath to protect you, but don't let that fool you into thinking I wouldn't crush you if you even *attempt* to use Synthesis against me!"

"Jax!" Deborah shouted. She jumped to her feet and positioned herself between Yolken and Jax.

Yolken snorted as he transferred the Energy back into his bones. Jax was so mad right now that he hadn't even noticed Yolken had accessed Energy without the aid of a dragon bone.

"You think this is funny?" Jax said around Deborah.

Yolken simply shook his head. If Jax hadn't noticed, he wasn't going to tell him. "I didn't mean for this to happen," he said instead.

"Well…?"

"Well, what? What do you want me to say? You want me to apologize to you? I'm not going to."

"None of it matters now," Deanna interjected without looking away from the window. "What's done is done."

A silence hung in the air.

"That still doesn't explain how they knew when we would be returning to Onta," Deborah eventually said. "The only person who knew that was Urgil."

Deanna turned from the window and said, "Yolken, tell us as much as you can about what happened when you reentered the city."

"Start with how you Synthesized after leaving your sword behind," Jax said.

So he did *know*, Yolken thought. No point in hiding it any longer. "Somehow, after I visited Deth, I was able to store Energy in my bones."

"So you had Energy stored in your bones the whole time?" Jax said.

Yolken nodded.

"And you didn't think to tell us?"

Yolken shrugged.

"Why wouldn't you?"

"I didn't feel like it." Saying it gave him a smug sense of satisfaction.

"You didn't *feel* like it?" Jax asked. "Yolken, you shouldn't keep secrets from us."

Yolken laughed.

"You think this is funny?"

"Considering you've been lying to me since the start... yes." Jax rolled his eyes.

"You lied about who my father was—"

"I told you who he was," Jax said defensively.

"You said he was a *descendant* of Drae."

"He was."

"He was his son!"

"Technically a descendant. And we've been over this."

"You lied about the fact that you knew Anivera wasn't just a fable..."

"Technically Anivera *is* a fable. She doesn't exist," Jax said. "She was just someone made up to cover who Deanna really was."

Growing frustrated that Jax didn't seem to think his lies were a big deal, Yolken added, "Well, you also lied about the fact that the reason you dragged me all the way to the island of Kvorga was to get Deanna to help the Order and *not* to help me find Javen."

"Technically, that wasn't a lie."

"Yes it was."

"Why couldn't both be true?" Jax asked.

"You lied about the fact that the sun was dying..." Yolken was still having a hard time coming to terms with what that meant.

"As I already said, I couldn't tell you."

"Jax," Deborah said. "He has a point, and you know it. We withheld information from him."

Jax snorted. "Secrets of the Order that we weren't at liberty to share."

"Not only did you lie to me, but you also used me," Yolken said. "The Council had no intention of helping me rescue Javen. They just wanted to use me to get to Deanna."

"And now you've lost Kaylan," Jax said.

Yolken clenched his hand into a fist again. Despite Jax's biting words, he resisted the urge to transfer Energy into his Core. He wasn't about to let Jax have the satisfaction of once again proving he didn't have any self-control.

Awkward silence descended over the cramped room. Jax ran his fingers over the grain of the dresser, and Deborah sat back down on the bed.

"But how?" Deborah eventually said.

"How what?" Yolken said tersely. He regretted the tone of his voice the moment he said it. He wasn't mad with Deborah.

"How can you suddenly store Energy? I didn't think the dragon did anything to you."

"It's because he's the Blessed of the Dragon," Deanna said.

"So you could do that all along?" Deborah asked.

"I think so, but I only figured it out after visiting Deth," Yolken said.

"What happened after you entered the city?" Deanna said.

Yolken glanced over at Jax, who had become conspicuously quiet. He was leaning against the dresser and looking out the window. It reminded Yolken of Jax's bad mood after the Regency found them in the Mindons. *Is he pouting again?* He shook his head, then took the next several minutes to recount everything that had happened from the moment he slipped through the closing gate. He told them as much as he could remember from his conversation with Devin. Deanna and Deborah stared at him intently as he spoke, making him feel self-conscious. When he described the dragon's rescue, Jax finally looked over at him. He seemed to pay close attention as Yolken recounted his conversation with Deth in the meadow. Jax sighed and visibly slouched when Yolken finished by saying that Deth flew away. Yolken suspected Jax was jealous of him for getting to meet the dragon—twice now.

"So, the *dragon* just left you in the mountains?" Jax asked.

The way Jax emphasized the word 'dragon' confirmed for Yolken that Jax *was* jealous. But rather than pointing that out and further perturbing Jax, he simply nodded.

"Anyway," Yolken added, as the others all looked like they were thinking about what he'd said, "I remembered this village from when we stayed here on our way to Onta. I came here and settled in to wait, figuring you'd likely head back toward Croff. You owe Leanne, by the way."

"What do you mean?" Jax asked.

"I didn't have any money, and I remembered Leanne looking at you like she knew you when we were here before. I figured she was a part of the Order or something, so I used your name to get lodging while I waited."

"That was risky, don't you think?"

"Apparently, I don't think things through," Yolken said wryly.

Another silence fell over the room.

Yolken couldn't stand it. He knew logically that there was no way of rescuing Kaylan and Javen, but the more time he'd had to think about it, the less he could simply turn his back on them and leave. "We need to go back," he said.

"Absolutely not!" Jax said. "Even you should know better than to return to a hornets' nest after kicking it."

"I can't leave her. I love her."

"I know you do, dear," Deborah said, "but Jax is right. I've cried my way here, each step taking me farther from my daughter, but us returning is exactly what they would want. Especially now that they know Deanna is with us."

"They'll be extra careful—and diligent—now that they know I'm alive," Deanna said. "As much as I hate the idea, Yolken, we must move forward."

"Meaning forget about Kaylan and Javen and restore balance to the sun? Whatever that's supposed to mean..."

"If we don't stop the sun from dying, what will be the point of rescuing Kaylan or Javen?"

"I don't suppose you know how to do that? Or even what restoring balance means?"

"I do not," Deanna admitted.

"What about igniting the flame Deth said was in me?"

Deanna shook her head. "I had no idea dragons could create Energy until you just told that story about hatchlings."

"Even after all the time you spent with him?" Yolken asked.

"I thought Deth was just storing it, same as you."

"Deth seemed to think it obvious that he couldn't store enough to last four hundred years."

"It wasn't obvious," Deanna said. "He wasn't always in the cavern when I went to visit. I figured he was out hunting or refilling his bones."

"If we aren't going back to Onta, what *are* we going to do?" Yolken said.

"I don't know," Deanna said.

"We return to Croff," Jax said, "and report to the Council."

"I don't want to leave Kaylan behind," Yolken said.

"You know it's necessary," Jax said.

Yolken sank heavily onto the bed. He leaned forward, resting his elbows on his knees, and buried his face in his hands. Deborah put her arm around his shoulders.

"They're expecting us to return," Deanna said.

"I know," Yolken said into his hands.

"Then you know we'll be playing directly into their hands."

Yolken looked up and wiped tears from his eyes. "I-I know," he said. He took a deep, shuddering breath and said, "To Croff, then."

Deborah rubbed Yolken's back and said, "To Croff."

"To Croff," Jax repeated.

CHAPTER 19

Unless anyone objects," Jax said as they made their way down the stairs of the inn, "I suggest we travel as expeditiously as possible. There's no sense in hiding anymore."

"What do you have in mind?" Deanna said.

"Horses."

In the pub, Jax walked over to where Leanne was cleaning the bartop with a rag. He set a bag of gold on the counter and said, "This should cover the lad's expenses."

Leanne scooped the bag up, placed it under the bar, and continued wiping without a word.

Jax led the way out of the inn. He stopped in the middle of the road and looked in both directions. With purpose in his step, he walked to a stable down to the right. He stopped in front of a dirty boy sitting on a barrel with his back against the wall. His eyes were closed, and his jaw hung open. A raspy snore accompanied each breath he took. Jax swatted the boy's foot, startling him awake.

"I'm finished with the stalls, Gorin!" the boy shouted as he came to his senses.

"Relax, lad," Jax said. "Gorin's not about."

The boy rubbed his eyes, then said, "Wha… what'd ya want, Mistah?"

"I need four horses."

"For what?"

"To buy."

"None of 'em are for sale."

"None of them?"

"Nah. There's two that belong to someone staying at the inn, and the rest belong to Gorin."

"I'm guessing by your reaction when I woke you that Gorin owns this stable?"

"Yessir."

Jax reached into an inner pocket of his coat and said, "And you don't think Gorin would be willing to part with any of his horses?"

"No, sir."

Jax pulled out a bag of gold and jingled it. "Not even for gold?"

The boy's eyes grew wide.

"Would four drakes per horse be enough?"

"Y-yessir!" the boy exclaimed without hesitation.

"Good," Jax said. "Saddle them and bring them out."

"Yessir." The stable boy hopped off the barrel and scurried into the stable.

"How long will it take to get to Croff?" Yolken asked while they waited. Vividly remembering their slow and arduous journey from Croff to Onta, he was not looking forward to repeating it any time soon.

"As I said," Jax said, "as expeditiously as possible."

Yolken wasn't about to point out that that didn't answer his question. Jax was still sore with him, so he didn't want to irk him any further for the time being.

"You mean by Synthesizing?" Deborah said.

Jax's lack of response was response enough.

"You sure this is wise?" Deborah said. "Moments ago, you were angry with Yolken for Synthesizing. In fact, I can tell by your demeanor that you're *still* angry."

"I think it's necessary," Jax said.

"How was going after Kaylan not necessary?" Yolken said. He was beside himself at Jax's remark.

Jax glared at Yolken. "It's necessary now because *you* gave us away. Now, are your bones charged?"

Jax was unbelievable. Yolken turned and walked off. He waited on the far side of the stable entrance from the rest of the group. When the groom finally returned with four saddled horses, Yolken watched Jax hand the groom the bag of gold. The boy counted them then looked at Jax, confused. "Remember," he heard Jax say, "you sold them for four drakes a piece." The boy grinned broadly as he ran off.

Jax walked a horse over to him and, handing him the reins, said, "Try to keep up."

Jax mounted his horse, then urged it into motion. Yolken did likewise, and fell in line with Deanna and Deborah. Jax rode just a little ahead of them.

"What's the plan?" Yolken asked as they rode out of town at a walk.

"You remember when you ran from the Mindon Falls to Croff with Jax?" Deborah said.

"Yeah." Yolken thought about his and Jax's sprint to Croff. They'd used Energy to both increase their stamina and strengthen their legs so they could run faster.

"The process is the same on a horse as it was on yourself. When we're clear of town, give Deanna her sword, and give me the Harachin sword." Yolken nodded. "When Jax gives the signal, we'll use the sun to boost the horses' stamina for as long as it's up. After it sets, we'll use the bones."

About half a league out of town, Jax increased the speed of his horse to a trot. Yolken unbundled his cloak and handed Deanna the Aliza sword, and gave his sword to Deborah. Jax took off at a gallop before Yolken finished fastening his cloak around his neck, and Deborah and Deanna urged their own horses into a gallop. Yolken situated his cloak, then urged his horse into a run. He leaned over in the saddle and opened himself to the warmth of the sun. He reached into the horse with a tendril of Energy and felt for its Core. When he found it, it felt dormant, unused. Yolken directed the tendril into its Core. The horse surged forward, forcing Yolken to hold on tightly as it raced to catch the others.

With a steady stream of Energy, the horse's gallop never faltered. They ran continuously at speeds the horses would otherwise only be able to maintain for a short while. When the sun set, Yolken began drawing Energy from his bones. With the amount of Energy he had stored, he knew he could easily keep his horse running through the night. Based on his experience fleeing from Lonely Oak, he knew Deborah and Deanna wouldn't have a problem running out of Energy either. The Harachin sword had great capacity, far more than any dragon bone of similar size. The Aliza sword was made from the same dragon bone, so it would have a similar capacity. The only one he wondered about was Jax, but Jax didn't seem to be worried when he'd told them the plan, and Yolken wasn't interested in asking him about it. He would simply run and let Jax wallow in his self-pity.

They ran through the night, not stopping except to let the horses drink.

"Keep the Energy flowing," Deborah instructed the first time they stopped. "If you don't, the horse will collapse in exhaustion. And no amount of Energy will convince it to get back up."

"We're killing them, then?" Yolken said.

"No, they'll just be extremely fatigued when we're finished with them," Deborah said. "Just like when you Synthesized for the first time. And we have people in Croff to help them recover when we get there."

While the horses drank, the four Synthesizers ate some dried meat that Deborah had thought to buy from Leanne. Jax stood apart from the group. Yolken made sure not to let go of his connection with the horse.

When they all finished eating, they resumed their race toward Croff. Under cover of night and the light of the moon, they ran without inhibition.

"If we can maintain our pace, it should take us no more than a few days to reach Croff," Jax said the next time they stopped to let the horses drink and graze. The horses' coats shone in the early morning light. "Now," Jax said, "let's see what these horses are really capable of."

"Haven't they proven themselves already?" Deborah asked wearily. "We've run them straight for half a day and a night."

"The sooner we reach Croff, the sooner we can put a plan together. The Regency knows we're up to something, so if it's at all possible, we need to try and stay ahead of them." Jax mounted his horse, then said, "I fear events will soon come to a head. We need to be prepared when they do."

CHAPTER 20

From his perch above the Engine Car, Javen watched as the Train descended into the valley. Below them sprawled the largest city he had ever seen. Enormous snow-capped peaks rose behind the towering buildings, creating a wall as far as the eye could see. A league from the capital of the empire, the Train descended underground into a tunnel similar to the one they had started in when they'd left Onta. With nothing else to see, he climbed down the spiral staircase and walked slowly back to his quarters.

As he passed the door leading into the dining room, Devin shouted from within, "Javen!"

Javen entered the dining room, which was illuminated by several lamps. Drenan was present, and he and Devin both wore their finely cut blue suits.

"I don't know what's going to happen when we arrive," Devin said, "but things will likely move quickly."

"What do you mean?" Javen glanced over at Drenan. He was tracing the scars on the back of his hand with the fingers of the other.

"Well, to be honest, nothing like this has ever happened before. No one has openly defied the emperor, so I don't know how he's going to react. Well, I have an idea…"

"I don't under—"

"The Train will soon arrive at the Grand Station, so go retrieve your woman and put on your suit. When the Train stops, be ready to exit."

Javen nodded, wondering what the Grand Station was, then made his way to his quarters. He hesitated at the door, but then turned the handle and opened it. The room was empty, as he had expected it would be. Kaylan hadn't left the bedroom since they'd begun their journey except to retrieve the food he left for her. He took a deep breath and crossed the room, then, without hesitation, he opened the door leading into the bedroom. It was almost completely dark, so he turned the knob on the lamp hanging by the door. As the room lit up, he saw Kaylan lying on her side on the bed with her back to the door. She didn't move.

"Kaylan," he said. When she still didn't move, he said her name again.

Kaylan rolled onto her back and looked at Javen.

"We'll be arriving soon."

Kaylan turned her head and rolled back onto her side.

"Lie there if you wish," Javen said, "but when the Train stops, we're getting off… together." He stood by the door and looked at her back for a moment, but then he walked over to the large armoire and opened it. There were several changes of clothes for them to wear while traveling, and a blue suit, finer than anything he had ever owned. It was even finer than Brall, the owner of the Oak's, new suit. An elegant dress hung in the armoire as well, the same shade of blue as the suit.

Javen looked over his shoulder at Kaylan lying on the bed. He thought about changing right there—it was his room, after all—but decided to change in the sitting room. He took the suit with him, then shrugged out of his sweaty shirt and pushed his pants to the floor. Oshie had filled the washbasin with hot water, and he used this to clean off. Then he unbuttoned the three buttons on the suit coat, revealing the shirt and pants underneath. He pulled the pants from the hanger and put them on. He followed with the shirt, then the coat. There was also a short tie similar in style to the ones the servants wore, but he had no idea how to fasten it. Instead, he folded it carefully and put it in one of the inner pockets of the coat.

When he was fully dressed, Javen peeked back into the room. Kaylan was in the exact same position.

"There's a blue dress in here for you to wear," he said. "Please put it on."

Javen sat on a couch to await their arrival at the Grand Station. He sat there for several minutes before he felt the Train begin to slow. As it slowed, it began to grow lighter outside. Because of the slowing of the Train, Javen didn't feel comfortable standing up and walking over to the window, but from his position on the couch, he saw they had entered a large cavern. It was much larger than the cavern they'd started in back in Onta. As the Train continued to slow, they passed several long buildings, some passing close to the Train and some farther away. Rising out of the buildings were diagonal structures extending up to the high arching ceiling.

When the Train finally came to a stop, Javen went and knocked on the door to the bedroom. When Kaylan didn't answer, he slowly opened the door and looked in. She sat on the edge of the bed in the blue dress. "We're here," he said. Silently, she stood and walked over to him. Javen reached out and took her by the hand. For the first time since their journey began, he led her out of the bedroom.

Together, they walked out into the hallway. Through the window, Javen saw that the Train had stopped in front of a long building similar to the ones they'd passed as the Train entered the cavern. Javen led Kaylan to the next carriage. Everyone else except Lannary and Leena had already gathered by the door leading out to the stairs.

"Welcome to Kyinth," Devin said when Javen and Kaylan stopped next to them, "the capital of the United Realms."

"Where's your tie?" Karina said.

"I don't know how to put it on," Javen admitted.

"Do you have it?"

Javen pulled it out of his coat pocket.

Karina took the tie from Javen and set to tying it around his neck. She tucked it under his shirt collar, cinched it into place, and adjusted it so it hung straight down to the middle of his stomach. "You look nice," she said, grabbing the lapel of Javen's coat lightly with her fingers when she finished with the tie.

"Thank you," Javen said. "Aren't Lannary and Leena coming with us?"

"Why would they?" Drenan said.

"I thought…" Javen started, but then stopped, not knowing what to say.

"They're of no consequence to me," Drenan said. "They were merely entertainment for the journey."

"You mean like Astora?" Javen said. He still hated to think about how Dorlan had taken her from her family and bedded her until he no longer wanted her.

Drenan took a step toward Javen.

"Did you kill them as well?" Javen asked.

"You are not regent yet, *get*, so unless you want to hang alongside Reago, I'd be careful were I you."

"Gentlemen," Karina said, "let's not spoil our arrival at the capital by bickering. This is a momentous occasion for Javen."

Devin gestured toward the door leading out of the Train and said, "Shall we?"

A servant opened the door. Karina slipped her arm into Devin's, and Devin stepped out onto the marble platform. Drenan followed them, then Javen held his arm out for Kaylan as Devin had done for Karina. Kaylan reluctantly slid her arm into Javen's, and he followed Drenan down the steps. The remainder of the servants were lined up on the platform, dressed in their sharp black and white clothing. They nodded their heads slightly as each regent walked by. They even nodded for Javen and Kaylan.

As Javen walked past the Engine Car, the operator, Norin, placed his hand on Javen's arm. Javen stopped and looked at the bearded servant. Norin leaned in and said, "Never forget who you are, son of Danavin."

Javen looked him in the eyes until Norin bowed his head. Javen continued to stare at him, feeling as though Norin was warning him about something. He felt a tug on his arm.

"We're falling behind," Kaylan said.

Javen wanted to talk to Norin, to find out why he felt it his prerogative to say anything to him, let alone attempt to give him advice. He had yet to acclimate to the master-servant relationship, but he knew enough to know that Norin was speaking out of place. And if he was willing to take that risk…

But Javen didn't have the time.

He turned from Norin, putting him out of his mind, and took in the immenseness of the Grand Station. Small, shimmery tiles covered the walls and ceiling. There were five more sets of tracks, each leading to a long building such as the one they were about to walk into. Diagonal structures rose from each building to the high ceiling above. At each end of the cavern, the tracks disappeared into tunnels. The Train they had arrived in was the only one in the immense underground building.

Devin led the way through the entry of the building. They followed a walkway and passed two dozen small shacks all lined up in a row. "These are called ticket booths. When Trains were still in use, travelers bought tickets to ride the Trains from attendants who manned each shack."

Each booth had a door on one side and a large window on the other. Waist-high fences made from metal posts connected each building. There was an opening in the fence by each window. Behind the ticket booths, the small fences continued in a back and forth pattern, creating a series of paths leading to and from the booths.

After they passed the last ticket booth, they turned and walked along the fenced paths to a tiled wall. They followed the wall into a tunnel, which led to two very long sets of metal stairs.

"When this station was still in use," Devin said. "Energy powered these stairs. They moved up and down, carrying people to and from the surface."

"Draego's Fire," Javen whispered as he looked up at the stairs in amazement.

"They haven't run in a very long time," Devin added.

When Devin, Karina, and Drenan started up the metal stairs, Javen placed his hand on the handrail and followed. He started counting his steps as they climbed, wondering how far underground they were, but lost count when he thought about what Norin had said. It didn't bother him that Norin knew who he was; most of the servants probably did. What bothered him was Norin had referred to him by his father's real name. He doubted regents talked about dead rebels to servants, but perhaps Norin had simply overheard a conversation while doing his job. The question was, why did Norin use *that* name? Why say anything to Javen at all? Neither was normal. As they climbed the stairs, he considered whether he should say something. He didn't mind servants talking to him—in fact, he preferred that they did—but he didn't like that Norin was secretive about it.

The group entered a wide foyer at the top of the metal stairs. On the far side stood four tall columns extending from the tiled ground to the domed ceiling. The dome curved down to meet each column. It arched between them, creating five entryways to the Grand Station. A group of men wearing gray armor stood in a long row just this side of the columns. One man separated himself from the group and met them in the middle of the foyer with a bow. He wore the same gray armor as the guards in Onta. The two differences were that his sword sheath was gilded, and the left breastpiece of his armor was white. The rest of the guards, Javen noticed, didn't have the white breastpiece on their armor.

"Greetings, Your Majesty," the guard said, bowing toward Devin. He repeated his greeting to Drenan.

"Did you see where the chancellor went?" Devin asked.

"Yes, Your Majesty. He was in a hurry."

"I didn't ask whether he was in a hurry or whether he looked as if he were on a leisurely stroll. I asked if you saw where he went."

"Sorry, Your Majesty. His Highness is on his way to the West Tower."

"Thank you," Devin said.

"And Your Majesty…"

"Yes?"

"His Blessed Highness wishes to speak with you."

"I imagine he does," Devin said wryly.

The captain of the guard turned around and the line of soldiers behind him moved to create two rows of guards, ten on either side. When they were in place, the captain led the group between them. They passed under the center arch and out of the station.

Drenan separated himself from the group and walked off to the left.

"Where are you going?" Devin said.

"I have some loose ends that need tying up," Drenan said over his shoulder.

Javen stepped through the archway and stopped. Across a wide paved road towered a building that dwarfed the palace in Onta. The building began as six rectangular tiers, one on top of the other, each one a little smaller than the one below. On top of the highest tier rose a tall, squared tower. It tapered to a point at the very top. Each tier had several rows of windows. The tower also had rows of windows, all the way up to where the tower began to taper. Many of the windows had individual balconies, and at the very top, a balcony stretched the entire length of the tower and wrapped around the sides.

"What is that?" Kaylan asked.

"It's gotta be the emperor's palace," Javen said.

"That it is," Devin said. "Come."

The two rows of guards spaced themselves out across the width of the road, blocking it in both directions. Devin and Karina started across the road, and Javen and Kaylan followed. When they were across, the captain led them up the marble steps.

"This thing is the size of a mountain," Kaylan said.

"I know," Javen said. Kaylan speaking made him smile. "It's incredible."

Javen looked up, but a bout of vertigo from the dizzying height of the building forced him to look back down at the steps.

"How did news of our coming sit with His Blessed Highness?" Javen heard Devin say to the captain.

"Not well," the captain said.

"Good," Devin said.

The two rows of guards stopped when the forward-most guards reached the top of the stairs. They remained outside as the captain led Devin and the others through the tall wooden doors banded with metal. A gilded statue of the emperor greeted them in the enormous entryway. The emperor's head tilted down, his eyes focused on the doors. When Javen looked up into the statue's eyes, he felt very small. He couldn't help but look down at his feet in subservience.

Devin strode across the entryway, which was lined on both sides with several hallways. Their arched ceilings were half as high as the entryway's. Karina sauntered along on his arm. Javen had been so fascinated with the Grand Station and the palace that he hadn't even noticed the servants were following behind them until they moved off toward a door to the left. Turning to look, he noticed Norin was not among them.

Javen and Kaylan continued to follow Devin and Karina around the statue. There were six metal doors lined up on the far wall. There was also another hallway between them with an arched ceiling equally as high as the entryway's.

Instead of walking down the hallway, as Javen half-expected Devin to do, Devin turned and walked past the metal doors. A guard opened a door at the end of a shorter hallway revealing a small room. Devin gestured for them to enter. "I'll meet you upstairs in a bit," he said. He kissed Karina on the cheek then waited for them to enter.

Karina pulled Javen and Kaylan by Javen's free hand through the door and into a stairwell, which Karina immediately started up.

They passed a door each time they made a complete circle.

"Where do those metal doors go?" Javen asked after several turns around the stairs.

"They're called Lifts," Karina said.

"*Lifts?*"

"Similar to the stairs leading out of the Grand Station," Karina said, "they were Energy-powered Machines that took you up or down levels in the palace. As I'm sure you noticed, the palace is quite large. Moving about has become quite laborious since the emperor banned their use. The only one that's still in operation is the one leading up to his quarters."

"Really?" Javen said in wonder. The idea of such a Machine fascinated him. The very thought of them didn't seem real. Hopefully, he could see one in operation.

After passing several more doors, Karina finally exited the stairwell. They walked down a hallway, passed another set of the metal doors, and turned down a wider, more ornate hallway. Tapestries depicting landscapes from around the empire lined the walls. A tapestry of the Mindon Falls made Javen smile and think of home.

Karina stopped at a door and said with a wink, "This is your suite, regent."

"I'm not a—"

"You will be soon. Now, go on in and make yourself comfortable."

A servant dressed all in white stood next to the door and opened it with a bow.

"Where's Oshie?" Javen said.

"She'll be along in a bit."

Kaylan slid her arm out of Javen's and walked through the door. Javen hesitated a moment and watched Karina as she walked back up the hall. When she turned the corner he entered his suite.

The room was exquisitely decorated with fine furniture, tapestries, and paintings. However, Javen hardly noticed any of it. His eyes locked almost immediately on the blue dragon armor waiting on a rack in the center of the room.

CHAPTER 21

Drakonias looked down at the Grand Station from his balcony atop the palace. The guards crossing the road from the palace to the station looked like ants. He gripped the marble railing with both hands and fought the urge to crush the marble with Synthesis. Anger roiled in him that Reago would travel to Kyinth in the Train he had graciously permitted him to keep after he'd banned the use of Machines. He didn't know what angered him more: that Reago used his Train, or that he hadn't bothered to tell him he was coming.

He waited several minutes after the guards went into the station. A solitary person was the first to emerge from the station on the left side. He watched as the individual turned and walked south. Shortly after that, the guards reemerged. Another individual separated from the group as the guards formed two columns across the road, blocking the traffic, and headed in the other direction. Once they were in place, a small group crossed the road.

He forced himself to remove his hands from the railing and clasped them behind his back.

* * *

Devin walked down the long hallway alongside the captain of the guard. With his mind occupied by exactly what he was going to say to the emperor, he ignored all the relics on display as he passed them, except for one. He stopped briefly before the display case containing the Dragon King's golden armor. *Has Reago truly come to believe that Drakonias was at fault in causing the war?*

At the end of the hall, before the gold-plated doors that led into the throne room, the captain of the palace guard turned left. He walked down another hall to another door guarded by two guards. Unlike the rest of the palace guards, these two wore Glasses. When they approached Devin, he held his arms straight out to his sides. They patted him down—searching for dragon bones, he knew—then returned to their places.

The captain opened the door and entered the small room. The only thing in the room was the door to the emperor's private Lift. The captain pushed the small illuminated circle, a button, to the side of the door, and the door slid open. Devin followed the captain inside. The captain then pushed the single button on the inside, and the door closed. They rode silently as the Lift ascended to the top of the palace. When the door slid open, Devin stepped out.

He crossed the short distance from the door of the Lift to the ornately-carved wooden doors leading into the emperor's private quarters. Two more guards wearing Glasses patted Devin down again, then opened the doors. He walked through the first few rooms then poked his head into Drakonias' library to see if he was in there. He saw Angania—the woman Drakonias was bedding, and the reason there were rumors the emperor was taking a wife for the first time in centuries— lounging on a chaise couch by a fireplace.

"He's out on the balcony," Angania said.

"Thank you," Devin said with a nod. He hesitated a moment, looking at the woman wearing a white robe and drinking a glass of wine, wondering what was so special about her. She was beautiful, but her beauty alone didn't explain why the emperor would consider marrying her. He shook his head and proceeded out onto the balcony.

The emperor stood by the rail with his hands clasped behind his back.

"Your Blessed Highness," Devin said. He knelt with his right knee on the ground. He rested his arms on his left knee and bowed.

"Rise," Drakonias said without turning around.

Devin stood back up and joined his father at the railing. Looking over at the emperor, he saw that Drakonias was looking down at the Grand Station.

"You know," Drakonias began, "Watchers could see the Train coming for leagues."

"It wasn't my idea," Devin said. "I tried talking Reago out of it."

"And what was so important that Reago felt compelled to come here unannounced, and in such *fashion*?"

"A dragon attacked Onta."

Drakonias' head turned sharply to look at Devin. "A *what*?"

"We learned that Danavin's rogue son passed through Onta in the company of some rebels—one of whom was the rebel who nearly killed Drenan—and would be returning. We set a trap for him, but before we could apprehend him, the dragon rescued him."

Drakonias' eyes narrowed. "A dragon *helped* him?"

Devin knew what the emperor was thinking: Dragons did not concern themselves in the affairs of humans. Even when they'd begun killing the dragons, the dragons never fought back. They'd fled from attacks, but never defended themselves. To have a dragon help a human was most unusual.

"Yes, Your Highness."

Drakonias snorted and returned his gaze over the balcony. "That can't be accurate."

"I was there, Your Highness. I saw it with my own eyes." Devin hesitated a moment, trying to assess his father's reaction, then continued. "There's more…"

Drakonias turned his head toward him again.

"Danavin's son was able to Synthesize without dragon bones."

Drakonias' eyes narrowed again. "That's impossible. He had to be using the sun."

"It had already set."

"Then he had it in his Core."

Devin shook his head. "No one can hold the amount of Energy he used in their Core for so long."

"Hmm…"

"We gave him the opportunity to surrender, but he refused. And, before he attacked us, he said Deanna was with him."

"*Deanna!*" Drakonias said, turning toward Devin abruptly. "Danavin's son finds a dragon *and* Deanna? Something we haven't been able to do for four hundred years?"

Devin took a step back. "Yes, Your Highness. From what we could ascertain, she was hiding on Kvorga."

Drakonias stared at Devin intently for several moments then turned back toward the balcony. "Reago could have conveyed all this by condor."

"There's this as well," Devin said, reaching into his pocket. He pulled out the letter Reago had instructed him to give the emperor.

"What's this?" Drakonias said.

"It's from Reago."

Drakonias held his hand out, and Devin gave him the letter. "He couldn't deliver it himself?"

Devin shook his head.

"Is he even here?"

"Yes, Your Highness. He said he'd be along shortly."

"I see," Drakonias said. He used his thumb to break the wax seal, pulled the sheet of parchment out, and unfolded it.

Devin watched his father's eyes, trying to judge his reaction. He knew Drakonias would be furious. The words written on the letter were treasonous. He doubted they were true; it all sounded like the talk of someone half-crazed, but speaking them was still treasonous. And if they were true, his own life was in danger. His only real solace was that Reago had, as he said in the letter, supposedly sent similar letters to Dorlan, Sheal, and Thena. He didn't know for sure, though, because he hadn't seen him do it. But if what Reago said *was* true... he couldn't bring himself to think it.

Drakonias lowered the parchment and crumpled it in his fists. He made no other move that Devin could read. The emperor simply stared over the balcony.

"So," Devin said, deciding to test the waters. "Is it true?"

"Is what true?"

Devin could hardly believe he was about to ask the emperor if he himself had committed treason against the empire. "What Reago said about Drashon."

Drakonias snorted. "Of course not."

"What could be his motivation for making such accusations then?" Devin asked.

"You, of all people, should know Reago has been delusional for some time. Perhaps it stems from his sympathies toward the rebels. I don't know... but it's time for me to take action. It's past time." Drakonias paused and looked over at Devin. "Did you bring the second son of Danavin?"

"Yes, Your Highness."

"Are his sympathies in the proper place?"

"They are."

"Are you sure?"

"He has been most receptive to your promises. And he refused to help or go with his brother when he had the chance."

"Good," Drakonias said. "Then I shall deal the rebels a blow that rivals the killing of Danavin."

Devin waited patiently for the emperor to finish his thought.

"Do you think he's up to the task of governing Onta?"

"*Onta?*" Devin said, his voice elevated in pitch.

"My brother is no longer fit to rule."

A smile grew on Devin's face. He fought to keep it from

growing too big, not wanting to betray the immense pleasure growing within him.

"On the morrow, I will name you chancellor," Drakonias said. "However, if I am to do that, I will need to replace you as the Regent of Onta. What I need to know is if the boy is capable of governing Onta."

"He is untried, Your Highness," Devin said. Not wanting his father to change his mind and ruin his chances of becoming chancellor, he added, "But, with my tutelage, he will become an excellent ruler."

"Present him in the throne room at dawn."

"Yes, Your Highness," Devin said. "And what of Reago?"

"I have already dealt with him."

Devin looked over at his father, wondering what he meant. He couldn't have killed him already, could he? He suddenly wondered if what Reago said about Drashon *was* true. If he could kill his brother, was he also capable of killing his son? Now was not the time to ask. Not now—not ever.

He bowed to his father, then left. Thoughts of at last becoming Chancellor of the Western Realm, and not just Reago's proxy, swirled in Devin's mind as he walked back inside. He was not going to ruin it by pressing his father's patience.

CHAPTER 22

Nera poured herself a cup of tea. To avoid thinking about what she had just ordered done at the behest of the emperor, she stared out the window and thought about her journey to Mount Mazam. She never grew bored with looking at the snow-capped mountains north of the city. The majority of the peaks rose thousands of feet into the air, some almost a league tall. They made the towering buildings look like sticks a child had stuck into the mud.

Mazam was the tallest. It was a league and a half tall. Not visible from the city, it took several days of hiking into the frigid mountains just to get to the range surrounding it. She had done it once, with a group of worshippers of the Great Dragon, but only because she was able to use Synthesis to stave off the cold. She had no idea how the zealots did it and survived. They said Draego's Fire burned within them, but she knew that wasn't true. Only the Blessed had a spark of his fire.

She clearly remembered the view from the top of the frontal range surrounding Mazam. The terrain dropped sharply into a deep, forested valley where the snow melted in the summer months. It was in that relatively temperate area where the worshipers rested and gathered the strength for the next phase of their journey. From the valley encircling the entire mountain, it rose majestically into the sky. Those who worshipped Draego—she didn't worship him, but she counted herself among those who believed he existed and was the source of their gift—believed that when he descended from the ribbons of existence into Dradonia, he alit atop Mazam.

She spent several days in the valley with the worshippers while they rested. It then took them five days to climb the mountain to their destination: a large cave. She remembered her surprise after passing two large bonfires just within the entrance of the cave to find a small village nestled inside. She hadn't needed to Synthesize anymore, as the inside of the cave was quite warm.

Paintings and carvings of dragons, illuminated by several torches, decorated the walls of the cave. She made her way through the simple wooden structures—one a dining hall, the rest filled with mats for sleeping—to the end of the cave. A life-size carving of a dragon adorned the wall. Seeing it had evoked in her the memory of the actual beasts that once soared high in the skies.

The cave was as high as the worshippers could go. Any higher and they would be unable to breathe. She didn't linger long with them, though; she was uninterested in their pious ministrations. With the aid of Synthesis, she filled her lungs with the thin air and continued up the mountain. The climb up the ice-covered rock was arduous, but she was glad she'd made the effort. A view like none possible anywhere else in the empire greeted her. She walked around the peak, looking in all directions. Looking down at the peaks she had looked *up* at from the window of her study was almost humorous. She never did find an answer to what the six pillars sticking up out of the ice were.

Nera drank half the cup, refilled it, then returned to her desk. Darek kept putting a bug in the emperor's ear about the growing severity of the rebellions in his province—Turnig—which the emperor passed on to her. Officially, the rebellion hadn't escalated beyond Reago's authority, but given the history in Turnig, Darek was trying to keep on top of things. She pored through piles of reports but had yet to find evidence the Order was involved, which meant she had no reason to get the Sodality involved. She had reported as much to Drakonias, but he insisted she look again. It surprised her that the emperor was more concerned with a harmless rebellion than the troubling weather conditions in the south, but she wasn't about to bring it up—it wasn't her place.

Another batch of reports had arrived by condor, so she settled in to review them. Despite their almost daily arrivals, she saw nothing new. Either the Order was not involved this time, or they were being more careful than normal.

Nera lowered the report she was reading when the door opened. She opened her mouth to scold her servant, who knew better than to enter without knocking, but froze when Drenan strode in. Her servant was on his heels and skirted around him, bowing and saying, "I'm sorry, Your Ladyship, he wouldn't wait."

"It's all right," Nera said. "Shut the door."

"Yes, Your Ladyship," the servant said with another bow.

Nera waited until the servant stepped out of her study and shut the door, then said, "Drenan. What brings you back to Kyinth so soon?"

"I trust you received my message?" Drenan said.

"I did."

"I never heard back from you."

"So you came all the way here to speak to me in person? I figured my silence would be answer enough." His vendetta against Danavin was not her problem.

"I am not in the habit of leaving loose ends unaddressed."

She was as surprised as the emperor had been when Dorlan sent a condor a few months ago to inform him of the events that had transpired in the Croff province. The only reason she knew about it was that he had come and asked her about it. She'd shown him all the information she had regarding the mission to kill Danavin. "As I told His Blessed Highness, I knew nothing about them. I can show you the reports from the mission if you wish."

"You may not have known about them, but they are *your* problem. And now, one of them has attacked Onta, and His Blessed Highness is about to make the other a regent."

"What are you doing here, Drenan? I have a lot of work to do."

"I'm here because I want you to take care of the loose ends you left behind."

"I already told you, I knew nothing of them, so they are *not* my problem. Besides, if His Blessed Highness has chosen to make one of them a regent, I'm not about to interfere. Doing so without his express permission would be nothing short of treason."

"You've already committed treason, *aunt*."

Nera set the parchment down on her desk. She looked sternly at Drenan. "What are you talking about?"

"I'm talking about Turnig."

"Turnig? What about it?"

"You had the opportunity to kill Danavin, and you didn't."

"Drenan, the Sodality was after Danavin for hundreds of years, and there were dozens of failed attempts to kill him before we finally succeeded."

"Turnig was different."

"How so?"

Drenan approached Nera's desk. He made fists and braced his weight on them as he leaned down.

Nera looked at the scars on the backs of his hands.

"Because you *intentionally* let him go," Drenan said.

Nera looked up into Drenan's icy eyes.

"Oh, yes, aunt. I know all about Relan."

"So I had a lover. The emperor has a lover. Even you did, at one point. You have a bastard if I recall."

"You're right. But *your* lover was a rebel. One whom you sabotaged a mission of the group you oversee to save. A mission that would have succeeded in killing Danavin *before* he fathered children."

Nera stared at Drenan. "What do you want," she finally said.

"I want the Sodality to do its job. I don't expect it to be done before Danavin's get is made regent, but I want it done."

"You want me to kill a regent? To commit treason?"

"You've already committed treason."

"And if I don't?"

"Then His Blessed Highness will learn of your... indiscretions."

"Get out of my study," Nera said. When Drenan didn't move, she shouted, "Get out!"

Drenan stood erect. "*Both* of Danavin's get," he said.

Nera held Drenan's gaze until Drenan turned and walked out of her study, leaving the door open.

Nera's servant peeked his head in. She waved him away, and he shut the door. She stood up, siphoning Energy from the edge of the desk where she had rested her arm the entire time Drenan was in her study. With no other outlet available to vent, she picked up her teacup and threw it across the room, strengthening her arm in the process. The cup smashed against the door into thousands of tiny shards.

CHAPTER 23

Outside of the Grand Station, Reago turned right and walked along the side of the building. He fully intended to meet with the emperor to discuss his reason for coming to the capital in a Train, but he would do it on his terms. He wanted to give Dorlan and Sheal time to respond to his message. The more people he could convince to join him, the better his chances of swaying the emperor. And while he waited, he would wait in his residence, not in the palace. He knew the truth of what had happened to Drashon; the palace wouldn't be safe.

He made his way toward one of four identical buildings. The West Tower was his home in Kyinth, the center of western business in the capital. Each realm had an identical tower, with only minor variations representative of the respective realms. The only building taller than the four towers was the palace at the center of the city—the epicenter of the empire. The four towers surrounded the palace, about halfway from the palace to the city wall, one in each city quadrant. The majority of the commerce in each quadrant was directly related to its realm. As it was, the eastern quadrant of the city had been largely dormant since contact with the east had been lost.

He walked down the street bustling with activity. Not dressed in orange, the color of his station, he was almost unrecognizable. If he *had* worn orange, he'd have been an easy target for the assassins that were almost certain to be after him, which was why he was going to his residence—the staff there were his own. Still, he would have to inspect them individually when he arrived, just to be safe.

It was one league from the palace to the West Tower. And as he crossed street after street, he kept a watchful eye. Even dressed as he was, he received an occasional side glance or look of recognition.

The street curved right around a round-faced building and merged with a roundabout. Reago ignored the statue of the emperor in the middle of the roundabout as he followed the flow of traffic. On the other side, he started up the steps of the West Tower. The guards at the top, standing on each side of the set of double doors, recognized him—he could tell by the shocked looks on their faces. They hurried to open the doors and bowed deeply as he approached.

Reago walked through the open doors and stopped. Norin was sitting on a bench, picking at his nails. "What are you doing here? And how'd you get here so fast?"

"Four assassins were waiting in your room," Norin said without looking up.

He wasn't surprised. He expected to have to do a thorough sweep of the tower. "*Four?*" He said, feigning. "If I remember correctly, that's two more than they sent to kill Danavin."

Norin looked up at Reago. "Huh… I wouldn't know."

CHAPTER 24

Javen didn't know what he was more amazed about: the fact that he was staring out the window of the Emperor of the United Realm's palace, or the view out the window. He'd seen paintings of Kyinth before, but the needle-like towering buildings never seemed real. Even now, looking out the window at those structures, they still didn't seem real. How could anything be so big?

The buildings spread out all around. There were hundreds of them. None of them were taller than the palace, though. They varied in height and shape as well: some were square, some rectangular, some circular; some were wide at the base like the palace and grew thinner toward the top, and others were of uniform size from top to bottom. Each of them was unique in its own way. It was opposite the design of the buildings in most of the towns he'd been in. Even the majority of the white-marble buildings in Onta were the same. They were pristine, but they were identical.

Kaylan didn't share his enthusiasm about being in Kyinth or the view their suite had to offer—almost immediately after arriving, she'd locked herself in a small bedroom. He couldn't tear himself away from it, though. The servant attending to them brought him some food and set it on a table by the window. He ate it while standing and admiring the view.

From the floor-to-ceiling windows at the end of the main room of his suite, he had a northern view. Seeing the mountains in person made the paintings seem like an understatement. Their size made the Mindons feel as small as the hills surrounding Lonely Oak.

When the sun began to set, he went into the master bedroom, where he had a western view. He watched as the sun slowly dipped below the buildings, turning them into towering silhouettes.

A knock on the door pulled him out of his reverie.

"Come in," he called.

"Master Javen," Oshie said from behind him, "sorry to interrupt you."

"It's all right," he said. "Did they get you acclimated?"

"They did, Master. I've been here for a while, but I didn't want to disturb you. His Majesty Devin is here to see you."

"Thanks." He left the view behind and followed Oshie out of the bedroom. Devin lounged on a couch near the armor rack, one leg crossed over the other, a glass of wine in his hands.

"Have a seat," Devin said. He gestured toward the couch opposite him.

"Would you care for some wine, Master Javen?" Oshie asked Javen when he was seated.

"Yes, please," Javen said.

Oshie poured Javen a glass of wine from a bottle on a nearby table and handed it to him. She brought the bottle with her and refilled Devin's glass.

"Leave us," Devin said.

Oshie bowed to Devin and returned the bottle to the table, then left through a side door in the front corner of the long entry room.

"The emperor asked me if you were ready to lead," Devin said.

Javen's heart began to race. "What did you tell him?"

"That with the right tutelage, you will make a fine regent. So, tomorrow at sunrise, His Blessed Highness will name you Regent of Onta."

Javen choked on his wine. "*Onta?* What about... what about you?"

"I will become Chancellor of the Western Realm."

Javen didn't know what to say. He knew Reago was reclusive, but to have him removed as chancellor? Was it because of what had happened in Onta? He knew that wasn't Reago's fault—it had been Devin and Drenan who organized the trap. He wanted to know more but was afraid to ask.

"I can tell by the way you're looking at me that you want to know why the emperor is making me chancellor, and don't worry, you will. All the regents in the Regency will be brought up to speed, beginning with those in the west. For now, let's get through tomorrow."

"All right," Javen said. Regent of Onta! The very thought was incredible. There were many lower positions within the Regency that he figured he'd be assigned to as a way of acclimating him to being in a position of authority. Never had he imagined the emperor would choose to place him directly in the second most prestigious position in the western realm.

"The ceremony itself is straightforward—the emperor is not one for pomp. But after... after will be a celebration you will likely not soon forget."

Javen thought about the festival that had been thrown in honor of Dorlan when he visited Lonely Oak. That had been a celebration he would never have forgotten. His heart raced at the thought of being made a regent. "What do I need to do between now and then?"

"Just try to get some sleep if you can. Your servant will ensure you're up and dressed," Devin said. He upended his glass, downing the remainder of his wine, then stood. "Now, Regent of Onta, go bed that woman of yours; it'll release some tension and help you get some sleep."

Javen stood and bowed as Devin turned to leave. Once he was gone, Javen sat back down on the couch and took a sip of wine. He truly wished he could do exactly that. He wished, in this moment of personal triumph, that Kaylan was willingly by his side. But based on the fact that she had immediately shut herself away, she wasn't.

Regardless of how she felt, he intended on bedding someone. And if she wasn't willing…

He finished his wine, then went over to the wall and pushed the illuminated button the palace servant had shown him upon his arrival. Less than a minute later, Oshie appeared through the same door she'd exited through when Devin dismissed her.

"Yes, Master Javen?"

He waved her closer as he looked at the room Kaylan hid in. When she was near, he said quietly, "Is it possible to get someone into my bedroom discreetly?"

"Yes, Master Javen. Is there someone in particular you had in mind?"

"Yes," Javen said, thinking about what Drenan said when they'd left the Train. "Do you know what happened to Lannary?"

"I believe she and Leena are in the servants' quarters here at the palace."

"Good. Send her up, please. Discreetly."

"Yes, Master Javen," Oshie said with a bow. She disappeared again through the door in the corner.

Javen poured himself another glass of wine then went to his bedroom. He shut the door and went back to the window to wait. At sunrise, he was going to be a regent. He intended to celebrate.

CHAPTER 25

Hadie sat in the corner, watching her patrons come and go. It had been twenty days since she had spoken with her father. She didn't know what she'd expected to happen after she talked to him, but so far, it had been nothing. Sheena's notoriety was ever as much as Sonja's had been, and her girls were regularly called to pleasure the Blessed and other Silks, but she had yet to hear about or be invited to an event where she could put her plan to action. At least her father hadn't turned her in. Every time the door opened, a part of her expected it to be the Regency coming to arrest her.

Another part of her expected to see her mother walk through the door. Her mother had been heartbroken when Hadie had announced that she was leaving Hantlo. Her grief-stricken face was still clear in Hadie's mind. Ever since the night she spoke to her father, she'd wondered if he would tell her mother that she was back, and whether she would try to make her come home. She feared that if she looked her mother in the eyes, she would lose her resolve for what she was planning to do.

She had been studying the faces of the Silks who visited, looking for some clue—a look or nod in her direction— indicating her father was doing what she wanted him to. A rebellion wouldn't be successful if there wasn't something to replace the Regency. Overthrowing the Regency would cause chaos in what remained of the south, and she wanted to mitigate that as much as possible. But nothing. Not a single indication any preparation was being made.

The hour grew late—or early, rather—and all the patrons who would visit the brothel for the night had already been serviced or were presently with a whore. Sitting in the dark, in a half-drunk stupor, Hadie began to nod off. A touch on the arm and an accompanying, "Madam," woke her. She opened her eyes to see Ursella lit by the dim wall sconces.

"Yes," Hadie said.

"Edill has returned."

Edill had gone to Drenan's palace to visit Boralin, she remembered. On occasion, he abused the whores she sent to him. Boralin wouldn't be among those killed during their attack, being just a local administrator, but he was part of the reason she needed her father to make preparations. She didn't want people like Boralin to assume control. "Is she all right?"

"Yes, Madam."

Hadie looked curiously at Ursella. She seemed excited. Edill had regular appointments at both Dorlan's and Drenan's palaces, and Ursella had never made it a point to report her comings and goings unless she came back bruised. "What is it, Ursella?"

"She has news, Madam."

Hadie fought her stupor and rose to her feet. "Where is she?"

"In your room, Madam."

Hadie looked at Ursella for a moment before she hurried off to her room. Ursella wasn't even trying to hide her feelings. They had all been waiting patiently for news of any sort, and even though they didn't yet know what Edill had to report, Ursella's obvious excitement was indicative of how she felt.

Hadie hurried down the hallway, up the stairs to the top floor, and to her room. She pushed the door at the end of the hallway open. Edill stood in the corner by the mirror. When she saw Hadie, she fidgeted excitedly. Hadie walked over to her and inspected her for fresh bruises, despite what Ursella had said. Finding her unharmed, she said, "Ursella tells me you have news?"

"Yes, Madam."

"Well," Hadie said when Edill said nothing more, "out with it!"

"Boralin let slip that the chancellor has called a meeting."

"A meeting?"

"Yes, Madam. With *all* the regents. And… it's to be preceded by a gala."

"A gala?" Hadie said. "With every regent in the south attending?"

"Yes, Madam," Edill said.

"Thank you." Hadie tried her best not to betray her emotion. "You may go."

Edill curtseyed, then moved toward the door.

Just before she opened it, Hadie said, "Edill…"

"Yes, Madam?" Edill said, turning back around.

"Keep everything you earned tonight."

"All of it?"

Hadie nodded.

"Thank you, Madam." Edill curtseyed again and left.

Hadie sat on the bed to think while she waited for Ursella to come to prepare her for bed. Even if she didn't yet know when the gala was going to be, or if her brothel would be invited, the news was most welcome. Nothing was certain yet, but she decided she would tell the girls at the morning meeting. She didn't know if they'd been losing heart like she had been, but she knew that even though most of them were enjoying the additional money they were making, they wanted out of whoring as much as she wanted to free the south from the Regency.

Hadie rose from the bed and walked over to the mirror when Ursella entered her room. She stood quietly while Ursella undressed her and slipped her thin nightgown over her head. Next, she sat on the cushioned chair so Ursella could brush her hair. While Ursella worked rhythmically with the brush, Hadie said, "I want there to be wine at the meeting tomorrow."

"Yes, Madam."

CHAPTER 26

Your Majesty, the Regent of Onta, Javen thought as Oshie undressed him in front of the blue armor. He liked the sound of that. While Oshie worked to get him into the scaled leggings, he couldn't help but wonder why the emperor was elevating him to such a height. There were lesser positions within the Regency he could fill to gain some experience. He'd never ruled or been in charge of anything in his life. He grew up with Selena and Yolken always telling him what to do. And now he was becoming the Regent of Onta! He held his arms forward as Oshie slid the breastplate on.

When Oshie finished, she handed Javen matching gloves. Just like the leggings and breastplate, fine wool lined the insides. As he slid them onto his pale hands, he looked at the palms. They lacked scales. Instead, they were lined with soft leather. He flexed his hands into fists. The scales covering the backs of the hands and fingers flexed easily.

He walked over to an old brass-framed mirror. The dragons molded into the frame caught his eye, and he leaned in and inspected them closely. The dragons on the sides and bottom had folded wings, but the dragon on top had its wings extended up and above the frame. All of them had flames coming out of their mouths. The detail of their scales was amazing.

He stepped back and inspected himself in the mirror. He looked regal. Smiling, he turned to Kaylan, who had been sitting quietly on a couch while Oshie dressed him, and said, "What do you think?"

"You look like one of them," Kaylan said.

Javen frowned. He had hoped she would like what she saw. He turned back to the mirror and looked at himself again. He could hardly believe he was wearing dragon armor! Never in his life had he ever imagined he would wear something like this.

"Javen," Kaylan said.

He looked past his reflection at Kaylan sitting behind him and said, "Yeah?"

"Are you sure you want to do this?"

"What?"

"This," Kaylan said. "Become one of them."

"Why wouldn't I? I'm becoming a regent, Kaylan! I'm… *we* are Blessed! People will worship us."

"I don't want to be worshiped, Javen. And deep down, I don't think you do either. Besides, you can't ignore what they've done to your family."

"Yes, I *do* want to do this. I'm *going* to do this. Nothing would have happened to my family if they hadn't betrayed the emperor."

"Javen… this isn't you."

"Yes. It is."

"No," Kaylan pleaded. "You aren't one of them." She rose to her feet and took a couple of steps toward Javen. "Please, let's leave and go find Yolken. I don't want to be here."

"No," Javen said. "I'm doing this. And whether you like it or not, you're going to be right there next to me when I do."

Kaylan shook her head, returned to the couch, and plopped back down.

Javen turned his gaze back to his reflection. He looked himself over again.

"You still have a few minutes before we must leave," Oshie

said.

"Excellent," Javen said. "Would you please pour me a glass of wine? Pour the lady a glass as well."

While Oshie prepared their drinks, Javen went and sat on the couch next to Kaylan. The servant brought the glasses over to them and handed one to Javen. She tried to hand the other glass to Kaylan, but Kaylan just stared blankly past her. Javen took the glass from Oshie and thanked her, then held the glass in front of Kaylan and said, "Here." When Kaylan didn't move to take the glass, he added, "Take it."

Kaylan took the glass from him without looking at him.

Javen held his glass up before them and said, "To the future. To *our* future!" Kaylan didn't respond, so Javen reached over, clinked his glass on hers, and took a drink. "Kaylan," he said, "would you *please* just give me a chance?"

"I don't love you, Javen. I love Yolken. I've told you that. Nothing you say or do will change my mind about how I feel."

"Fine," Javen said tersely. He wasn't going to let Kaylan ruin this experience for him. He stood and strode over toward the floor-to-ceiling windows overlooking the city. The sky was just beginning to show hints of dawn.

A knock on the door caused him to turn. Oshie hurried over and opened the door. She bowed deeply when Devin walked in. He wore blue armor as well.

"You ready?" Devin asked.

A sudden bout of nervousness washed over Javen, but he took a deep breath and said, "I am." He walked back to where Kaylan sat and held his arm out for her. She silently stood and slipped her arm into Javen's. Oshie took their wine glasses.

Javen accepted Kaylan's compliance. He knew he had a long life ahead of him, so there was plenty of time for her to come around. He hoped she came around sooner rather than later, but he was willing to wait if she made him.

Devin led them out of the room. Karina was waiting by the Lifts. She greeted Devin and Javen with a kiss. She tried to kiss

Kaylan as well, but Kaylan turned her head. Karina hugged her instead. Kaylan kept her arms stiffly at her side. Devin turned and walked down the narrow hallway to the stairs at the end.

As they started down, Javen's stomach started to roil. He reached out and placed a hand on the railing to steady himself as he descended in slow circles. He'd been thinking about standing before the emperor and becoming a regent since he had woken up on Devin's ship, but now he was actually doing it. He was *actually* on his way to meet the emperor. Right now.

When Javen was growing up, the emperor had been almost as much a figure of fantasy as dragons. Nobody ever imagined they were any more likely to see him in their lifetime than they were to see a dragon. For most residents of Lonely Oak, it was a big deal whenever Dalia, the provincial regent, came down from Croff. She was usually just passing through on her way to Matis, but people flocked out to get a glimpse of her. Javen still remembered how excited he had been mere months ago when he'd learned the Chancellor of the Southern Realm was going to be spending the night in Lonely Oak. It had been all he could do to get the opportunity to see him. And now, here he was, on his way to stand before the *emperor*. He felt like vomiting.

When they reached the bottom and Devin opened the door, Javen let out a deep, shuddering breath.

Karina placed a caring hand on his arm and said, "Don't be nervous."

"I'm n-not," Javen lied.

Devin led them past the metal doors to the abandoned Lifts, then down the long hallway that ran opposite the entrance to the palace.

Tapestries adorned the walls. Each of them was beautifully woven and depicted scenes of curious locations. As he passed each one, he wondered where it might be in the empire. Javen stopped as they passed the first glass display. He looked closely at a broken sword made from bone. "What's this?" he asked.

"It's Lio Drake's sword. He was one of the emperor's

brothers who fought against him during the war. Like all those who survived the war, he went into hiding after the Dragon King surrendered. The Mattath sword, as it is known, was recovered when the Synod finally found him."

"Why's it broken?"

"Because he resisted the Sodality." Devin turned from the display and continued down the hallway.

Javen followed him. As they made their way down the ornate hallway, known as the Hall of Relics, they passed several more displays. He looked at each of them with great interest as they passed, and looked forward to coming back and taking the time to learn about every one of them. However, after passing a closed set of double doors, he stopped at a display protecting dark yellow armor. Next to it, on a small, round table, sat a gold crown fashioned in the shape of a dragon. *Draeko's armor and crown,* he thought to himself.

"Come, Javen," Devin said. "We mustn't be late."

Overwhelmed with everything he had been feeling, Javen took another deep breath and turned from the display. They walked the rest of the way down the long hallway and stopped in front of two large, gold-plated doors. Javen stared at the dragon emblems emblazoned on them.

A pair of guards grabbed large metal rings on the doors and pulled them open. With Kaylan walking beside him, Javen followed Devin and Karina into a small foyer. Karina took Kaylan by the hand and led her to a set of stairs to their left. Javen looked after them with confusion.

"They'll watch from the viewing balcony," Devin said.

After the guards pulled the gilded doors closed behind them, they walked around Devin and Javen and opened another set of doors. They bowed deeply as Devin led Javen through the doors and into the throne room. Flickering torches illuminated the large chamber. It looked like it was big enough to accommodate a multitude of envoys from around the empire. The floors and walls were made of marble like the rest of the palace.

"Just follow my lead," Devin said.

Javen kept to Devin's right as they walked the length of the throne room. Armored men wearing gray, blue, and violet crowded the floor of the room, leaving a clear aisle to a dais at the opposite end. A gold throne sat at the top, empty. Two dragon statues perched high above the throne. They appeared to be looking intently at Javen as he walked forward. He looked up at the balcony to his left and saw Karina wave at him. Kaylan stared blankly down. Dozens of other spectators had gathered up there as well. As they progressed, he looked up in awe at the glass ceiling that arched over the long room, making the pre-dawn sky visible overhead. They reached the foot of the dais and stopped. A din filled the chamber as all those gathered talked amongst themselves while they waited for the ceremony to begin. Wanting to appear dignified, Javen clenched his hands into fists to prevent himself from fidgeting.

A loud, rumbling noise from overhead took Javen by surprise. Metal covers began moving slowly up the sides of the glass ceiling. After several minutes, they joined at the top and clanged to a stop, leaving only a small opening behind the throne.

After a couple of minutes, sunlight began shining through the hole and illuminated the throne.

A trumpet pealed, and Javen heard a wave of motion behind him. He turned to look and saw that everyone had fallen to their knees, including Devin. He felt foolish and quickly lowered himself to his knees as well. He glanced over at Devin and saw that his head was bowed, so Javen imitated him. He waited in this position for what seemed like an eternity.

Javen heard some rustling from above, and then a sonorous voice said, "Rise."

Another rustle filled the throne room, and Javen glanced over at Devin, who was pushing himself to his feet. He followed Devin to his feet then looked up at the throne. It was no longer empty. A man sat on the throne, the red armor he wore shimmered brightly in the sun. In his right hand, he gripped a large, golden scepter nearly six feet long. A carved dragon twined its way up it. A dozen men wearing white armor and full-face helmets cascaded down the steps, six on each side, each gripping a tall spear.

"You may approach the throne, son of Danavin," the emperor said.

Javen looked over at Devin, and Devin gestured with a quick motion of his head for him to go. He looked back up at the dais and hesitantly began to climb the steps. Alone. His legs felt unsteady as he climbed. On the last step, with a white-armored man on either side of him, he stopped. Ahead of him, mere paces away, sat the Emperor of the United Realms. He could hardly believe he was standing so close to Drakonias Draeko Arvarin Drake, a man who had lived for thousands of years. He didn't know what to do, so he knelt and bowed his head.

"You may stand, son of Danavin," Drakonias said.

Javen stood back up and looked at the emperor. Until this point, he'd been nervous about meeting him, but hearing his father's name spoken was somehow calming, even if he was a rebel.

"I must confess that the fate your father met saddened me greatly," Drakonias said. "For centuries, I had hoped he would choose to put his foolishness behind him and pledge his allegiance to me. I am not an unforgiving man. I was willing to put behind us all that he had done. In the end, however, he refused. The fact that you now stand before me testifies that the actions of one's father have no bearing on how I feel about those he sires. After all, we were all once loyal to the Dragon King," Drakonias said with a chuckle. "A mere four months ago, I had been unaware that Danavin even had children." After a brief pause, he said, "Devin tells me that you are ready to swear allegiance to me?"

Javen bowed and said, "I am, Your Blessed Highness."

"Then you need not fear me, son of Danavin, or be ashamed

of who you are. You are a Drake. The blood that flows in your veins is that of the Blessed." Drakonias looked at Javen pensively, which, despite what Drakonias had just said, made Javen nervous. "I am told that the same is not true of your brother?"

"No, Your Highness."

"When I first heard about the two of you from Dorlan, I had great hope, as I did with your father, that your loyalties would fall in the proper place. I saw in the two of you the opportunity to redeem the line of Drae, who died a traitor of the realm. Each man must decide for himself the path he will follow. Your brother has aligned himself with rebels, but you have the opportunity to right the wrong done against me by your father and by his father." The emperor paused, then added, "Are you willing to right that wrong? Are you willing to redeem the lineage of my brother?"

"Yes, Your Highness."

"Then kneel, son of Danavin."

Javen knelt.

The emperor rose to his feet and stepped toward Javen. He held the large golden scepter up in front of himself and said, "Son of Danavin, do you pledge your life to me?"

"Yes, Your Highness."

"Are you willing to lay it down on my behalf should the need ever arise?"

"Yes, Your Highness."

"Then I, Drakonias Draeko Arvarin Drake, Emperor of the United Realms, True Blessed of the Dragon, place under your authority all the lands and riches contained within the province of Onta." After a pause, the emperor said, "Rise, Regent of Onta."

Javen stood.

A din overtook the chamber.

The emperor stepped down to stand next to him and directed Javen to turn around. Javen turned and looked down at all those gathered below. He looked up at the balcony as well. His eyes settled on Devin, who stood at the base of the dais. The emperor held up his hand, and the chamber went quiet. "I present to you Javen Danavin Dairion Drake, Regent of Onta."

The crowd erupted in applause.

When the applause died down, Drakonias gestured with his left hand for Javen to descend the steps.

Javen bowed to the emperor then quickly made his way to the bottom. As he approached the last few steps, he locked eyes with Devin. Devin winked at him. As soon as his foot hit the marble floor, he heard the emperor say from behind him, "Approach, Devin Drakonias Metra Drake." Javen turned and watched as Devin ascended the steps.

At the top, Devin knelt before the emperor. Drakonias turned and sat upon the throne, leaving Devin kneeling on the top step. "It grieves me," Drakonias said, "to name my brother, Reago Draeko Yarin Drake, a traitor." Another din overtook the chamber. The emperor waited until it quieted down, then said, "I hereby strip him of his authority over the Western Realm." The emperor once again rose to his feet and approached the still-kneeling Devin. He held the Dragon Scepter up as he had done when Javen knelt before him, and said, "From this day forward, I, Drakonias Draeko Arvarin Drake, Emperor of the United Realms, True Blessed of the Dragon, place under your authority all the lands and riches contained within the Western Realm." After another pause, he said, "Rise, Chancellor of the Western Realm." Devin rose, and, as Javen had done, turned to face the crowd. "I present to you Devin Drakonias Metra Drake, Chancellor of the Western Realm."

The throne room erupted in another round of applause. Javen joined with everyone else and clapped vigorously.

CHAPTER 27

Javen shook hands with countless people. Some of them introduced themselves, and others told him how lucky he was to become Regent of Onta, the most desired of all provinces. Everyone who spoke to him and shook his hand congratulated him.

Javen was talking with Melina, a regent wearing violet armor, when Devin approached. Melina bowed and said, "Chancellor." She held out her hand.

Devin took it in his and kissed it.

"I should be kissing *your* hand, Your Highness," Melina said.

"There'll be time enough for that later," Devin said.

"Will that be appropriate now?"

"I'm the chancellor, so I get to decide what's appropriate."

Melina smiled. "Yes, Your Highness."

"If you don't mind," Devin said, "I'd like a private word with the Regent of Onta."

"I look forward to getting to know you better, Javen," Melina said. She reached out, took his hand, and kissed the back of it, looking up into his eyes the whole time.

"We'll see you at the gala," Devin said. Then, to Javen, he said, "Come with me."

Javen followed Devin across the throne room. He already

knew who Melina was—his aunt had ensured he and Yolken knew who the rulers were. She was the regent of the Arinin province located south of Kyinth in the Western Realm, nestled between the west and north ranges of the Ontalis. The province extended north, its borders the North and Kyinth Rivers. Arinin was only a few days' ride south of Kyinth. Situated on the Kyinth River, he remembered from paintings he'd seen, it had a picturesque view of the west Ontalis.

Devin ushered Javen through a side door into a room lined with shelves laden with dragon bones. A servant stood next to a set of orange armor hanging on a rack. When Devin shut the door, the servant walked over to him and began unbuckling the blue breastpiece he wore.

"We'll have an official briefing with the regents from the west in Kyinth after the gala," Devin said, "but I wanted to have a private word with you beforehand."

The servant removed Devin's breastpiece, revealing his muscular torso. Devin sat in a chair, and she started unlacing his boots.

"You are the Regent of Onta now, so there are some things you need to know. First off is that Reago was a traitor, and has been dealt with accordingly."

"Meaning…?"

"The emperor has no patience for treason and executes swift punishment for those guilty of it."

"They don't get a trial?"

"When there is a question, yes, but Reago's behavior has been questionable for centuries, and acting in direct violation of an edict by using a Train sealed his fate," Devin said. After the servant removed Devin's boots, he stood, and the servant unbuckled his leggings. She slid them down, and he stepped out of them. "Three of his children are regents in the west."

Javen nodded, knowing from his childhood education who they were: Kendra, Hanlog, and Ceesa.

"Two of their provinces are close to Turnig, where there is

currently a small rebellion," Devin said. He stepped into new orange leggings, then sat. The servant started putting on matching boots. "It's been going on for about four months but remains relatively small. Its impact has thus far been negligible and is only ongoing because of the skilled elusiveness of the rebels. However, with Reago removed from power, we will need to keep a close eye on his children. If Kendra and Hanlog rebelled, the three provinces together could cause trouble."

"Aren't they loyal to the emperor?"

"They are," Devin said. "But one can never be sure how a child will react when their father is executed for treason."

"Are rebellions normal?" Javen asked. Stories were told over ale of uprisings, but they were just that—stories.

"Early on after the war ended, yes. But not anymore," Devin said.

"What about in Croff?" Javen asked, remembering a rumor he'd heard the morning of the festival in Lonely Oak.

"Why do you ask?"

"I remember hearing that the mayor of Croff got arrested and that he was a rebel."

Devin stood and permitted the servant to slip on his breastpiece. "Although the Northern Realm is not your concern, yes. We suspected he was a rebel, but the Synod is still investigating."

Javen nodded thoughtfully. "What about in Onta?"

"Onta is very quiet. My… *your* citizens are far too happy drinking wine and bedding to concern themselves with lost causes. The province hadn't seen anything close to what happened with your brother in over two hundred years."

The servant finished buckling Devin's breastpiece.

"Now, let's get to the celebration," Devin said. "I'll fill you in on the intricacies of the Onta province later."

"All right," Javen agreed.

The servant opened the door to the throne room for them.

"One thing I *will* tell you, though," Devin said, stopping in the doorway, "is that it was not by chance that the Regent of Arinin was just showing so much interest in you."

Javen looked at Drenan, confused. "What do you mean?"

"Regents tend to bicker and feud with each other as they all try to maneuver themselves within the Regency, but the two provinces have maintained a close relationship. I'd appreciate you keeping it that way."

They reentered the throne room, which was, except for a few small groups of people chatting, now largely empty.

Devin led Javen out the doors at the back of the throne room and down the Hall of Relics. The doors halfway down, next to the Dragon King's relic display, were now open. Devin walked right in, and Javen followed.

The room had high arching ceilings that curved down to two marble columns in the center of the room, spaced equally from the walls and each other. Dozens of wall-mounted oil lamps, as well as six crystal chandeliers, brightly illuminated the room. People milled about everywhere.

Devin led them into the cavernous room. When those milling nearby noticed his new armor, they started clapping and cheering. Soon, the attention of everyone in the room was on Devin—and, consequently, Javen, who stood next to him. The greeting lasted for several minutes, then attentions began to return to their previous engagements.

A servant wearing a trim black and white uniform approached, a tray bearing several glasses held up next to his shoulder. With a bow of the head, he said, "Might I offer His Highness some of Onta's finest?"

Devin nodded.

The servant reached up with his other hand, retrieved a glass, and handed it to Devin. Turning toward Javen, he said, "And for His Majesty?"

Javen nodded as well. He took a sip of the wine and smiled. It was the first time anyone had referred to him by his new honorific since he'd officially become Regent of Onta.

Karina walked up to them and said, "You look stunning." She kissed Devin and said, "Orange suits you much better."

Javen looked up from his glass and blushed. She wore a very revealing orange dress that clung tightly to her body.

"And you look stunning as well," Karina said. She stepped close to Javen and kissed him.

"Thank you," Javen said with a smile. After looking behind Karina, he asked, "Where's Kaylan?"

"She said she wasn't feeling well and had a servant take her back to your suite."

Javen pursed his lips and furrowed his brow.

"Don't let her *delicacy* ruin your celebration," Karina said. "This is, after all, your celebration—both yours and the chancellor's."

"She's right," Devin said. "Mill about. Meet people. We'll stay here for a spell then go up to the emperor's."

"The emperor's?" Javen asked as a bout of nervousness washed over him.

"Yes. There'll be a more intimate celebration upstairs after a bit." Karina slipped her arm into Devin's, and Devin added, "I'll come get you when it's time." They moved off and left Javen standing alone.

He looked around the large room, not sure what to do or where to go. Eventually, with glass in hand, he started wandering. He found a table off to the side piled with food, and headed toward it.

He picked up a plate at the end of the long table and made his way down the table, looking each dish over carefully. When he found something that looked interesting or that he was familiar with, he pointed at it, and a servant standing on the other side dished it onto his plate. When his plate was full, he turned and looked for somewhere to sit.

"You have to eat standing up, Your Majesty," a familiar voice said.

Javen turned and smiled when he saw Lannary. "There aren't

any tables?"

"It's a gala," Lannary said. "There never are."

"Well, that's annoying."

"You're the Regent of Onta now," Lannary said with a wink, "so when you host galas of your own, you can change it if you wish."

"You look stunning," Javen said, noticing her outfit. It was very elegant, and not nearly as revealing as her clothing tended to be. Her unusual modesty was, itself, oddly attractive.

"Why, thank you, Your Majesty," Lannary said with a curtsy.

Javen couldn't help but stare at her.

"What is it?"

"It's just... you look beautiful, is all."

Lannary smiled. "Come, we're in the way."

Javen hadn't even realized people were lining up behind him.

Lannary took him by the arm and led him toward the nearest column. There, she stood by his side while he ate.

"Where's that little dove of yours?" Lannary said.

Between mouthfuls, Javen said, "Karina said she wasn't feeling well."

"That's a shame. She's missing out."

When Javen finished eating, a servant swooped in and took his plate. He also exchanged Javen's nearly empty wine glass for a full one.

"Come," Lannary said. "Let's socialize."

Javen spent the next couple of hours with Lannary on his arm as he wandered the ballroom. Lannary explained that there were four ballrooms in all, one for each of the realms under the emperor's rule, and they were in the West Ballroom. The artwork adorning the walls reflected scenes from around the west. There were paintings of mountains, beaches, rivers, and cities. He recognized a huge tapestry depicting Onta with its gleaming white walls, tall spire, and surrounding vineyards. His city.

Javen met more people than he could keep track of. There were regents from around the empire wearing blue, green, and violet armor. Those he knew. It was the plethora of other people wearing equally fine suits of various colors and cuts, as well as exotic dresses of varying shapes and size, that confused him. "Who are all these people?" Javen finally asked Lannary when they stood alone.

"The Suits, Silks, and Reds. There's even a few Pearls milling about. There's one over there," Lannary said, pointing.

Javen looked where she was pointing and saw a very old man standing in the corner.

"They're getting so old you hardly see them anymore," Lannary said.

An empty-handed servant approached and, after bowing, said, "Would you care to change, Your Majesty?"

"Change?" Javen said.

"The dancing is about to begin," Lannary answered for the servant. "I know your armor is supple, but it's not suitable for dancing. Yes, he would like to change."

"Follow me, if you will, Your Majesty," the servant said.

Javen followed the servant into a small side room. Several suits hung on racks. The servant sifted through them and selected a blue one. He changed Javen out of his armor, hanging it on an empty rack, and into his suit.

When Javen emerged from the side room, Lannary took him by the hand and led him to the center of the ballroom. The area had been cleared out and was now occupied by a small platform with musicians on it, playing instruments that gleamed in a way they never did in Lonely Oak. People were already dancing.

Lannary spun to face Javen and took him by both hands. They began to move in a way unfamiliar to Javen. It took him a few songs to catch the rhythm and learn the moves, but he soon began to flow as confidently as he did when he danced back home.

One surprising difference was that he remained with Lannary. They danced until someone tapped Javen on the shoulder. He stopped and saw Devin flick his head sideways.

"Might I await you in your room, Your Majesty?" Lannary said, batting her eyes.

"Please," Javen said. He bent down and kissed her, then turned and followed Devin.

They left the ballroom and turned down the Hall of Relics toward the throne room. At the gilded doors, they turned left and proceeded down another hallway. Two guards awaited them, standing on either side of a door at the end.

"They're going to search us before we go up," Devin said.

"Really?" Javen said.

"His Blessed Highness is very cautious."

The two guards stepped away from the wall and simultaneously searched Javen and Devin for hidden weapons. When they finished, they returned to their spots, and one of them opened the door.

Devin led Javen into a small room. "The only operating Lift in the palace," Devin said when the door closed behind them. He pushed a round, illuminated button, and the doors slid open.

Javen followed Devin in. There was another door opposite the one they entered through.

The door closed, and Devin pushed another illuminated button. "The other Lifts used to take you to all the floors except His Highness', but this one is his personal Lift. It makes only one stop."

The Lift lurched into motion, and Javen grabbed the polished railing on the side. A feeling of vertigo overcame him as he sensed they were moving. The feeling was very unsettling, not unlike what he felt when he'd woken up on Devin's ship. At least then, he could look outside and see that he was moving, but now, he was in a small room which his mind told him should be stationary. He started to feel as though he was going to vomit, but then the sensation stopped, and the second door slid open.

Javen followed Devin through the door into a high-ceilinged room. Two staircases rose in the center of the room, spiraling around each other and climbing through an opening in the ceiling.

Even though the room was large, the gathering was much more intimate. Every guest wore either blue, green, or violet. Devin was the only person wearing orange. Although everyone present was a member of the Regency, there were still Watchers positioned in the corners.

"Let's go pay our respects, and then we'll be free to socialize," Devin said. He led Javen to the center of the room, to the space underneath the staircases where there was a large red semicircular couch. Javen felt an odd sensation as they walked through the opening. Devin knelt before the man sitting on the opposite side wearing a red suit and said, "Your Blessed Highness."

Javen knelt next to Devin and echoed him. "Your Blessed Highness."

"Please, sit," Drakonias said. "The time for formalities is past."

Devin and Javen rose. Devin sat to Drakonias' left and gestured for Javen to sit on his right.

"So," Drakonias said in his deep, sonorous voice, "what do you think so far?"

"It's all a bit overwhelming," Javen said.

"How so?"

"Everything that's happened over the last few months. I just never thought I'd be here."

"Well, get used to it. You are a regent now. A person of power and influence."

Javen nodded.

"Listen to Devin. He will ensure your transition from peasant to ruler goes smoothly once you return to Onta. Until then, while you're in the capital, enjoy yourself."

"Yes, Your Highness," Javen said.

"Now, go enjoy yourself and permit me to speak privately with the chancellor," Drakonias said.

Javen stood and bowed toward the emperor. He felt the odd

sensation again as he walked through the opening in the couch.

* * *

"The Sodality failed," Drakonias said.

"Have we need to worry?" Devin said.

"What can he do? He's alone in the city, and we have an army of Synthesizers at our disposal. He may be foolish, but he's not *that* foolish. And he wouldn't dare set foot in the palace because he knows I've instructed everyone to kill him on sight. If he has even half of his wits remaining, he'll leave Kyinth."

"But wouldn't he be more dangerous that way? Send the Sodality in again."

"He's expecting them now. And what's he going to do? His closest ally is Sheal, and Sheal has already sent word—he wants nothing to do with Reago's foolish ideas. That leaves the *Order of the Dragon*." Drakonias chuckled.

"They could unite around him," Devin said.

"And do what?"

"I'm not trying to disagree, Your Highness, I'm just thinking aloud."

"As you should, Chancellor. Just see to it that his get doesn't unite with Turnig, and we won't have any problems."

"Do you want me to replace them?" Devin said.

"Call them to Onta and meet with them. I trust you to use your best judgment."

"Yes, Your Highness."

* * *

A woman wearing a violet sequin dress approached Javen as soon as he stepped past the couch. "Hello, Your Majesty," the woman said with a slight bow.

Javen tried not to stare at Melina's chest as she bowed, but it was hard. She offered her hand to him, and he took it gently in his and kissed it. "Hello, uh…"

"Your Ladyship," Melina said.

"Your Ladyship," Javen repeated. "You look stunning."

"Have you eaten?"

"I have."

"Something to drink, then?"

Javen nodded.

They walked to the corner of the room, where there were two long tables laden with food and drinks.

"May I offer you something from my province?" Melina said.

"Sure," Javen said.

Melina gestured to a crystal decanter with a brown liquid in it. The waiter behind the table turned over two short crystal glasses and filled them both half full with the liquid. After stoppering the decanter, he lifted both glasses and held them out toward Melina. Melina took them and offered one to Javen.

"Thanks," Javen said, taking the glass from Melina. He stuck his nose in the glass and smelled it, pulling back when the strong smell of alcohol burned his nostrils.

"Not a fan of whiskey?" Melina said.

"I'm just used to ale, that's all," Javen said. He sipped the whiskey delicately. "It was available in limited quantities back in Lonely Oak, but I preferred ale. It's much cheaper."

"Yes," Melina said, walking toward some open doors leading outside, "most of the empire's whiskey was imported from the east. There are, of course, several varieties from the north and south, but of much inferior quality. My province is the only one that produces anything near the same quality as that which came from the east. Maybe it has to do with the minerals in the water flowing down from the Ontalis, I don't know, but I prefer it to wine."

"It's good," Javen said. "I'm just not used to something so strong."

They walked through the open doors out onto a balcony. A few other regents were gathered, but the balcony was largely unoccupied.

"Over this way," Melina said, turning to the right. She walked the length of the balcony as it wrapped around the palace. She crossed over to the railing.

Javen stared wide-eyed at the range of snow-capped mountains visible in the distance. The North River was visible beyond the city wall and disappeared into the range. It was one of the most serene things he had ever seen.

He leaned over the railing and looked down, but immediately leaned back. The distance down to the ground was unbelievable.

"The tallest building in the empire," Melina said.

"It's incredible," Javen said. "How high we are, *and* the view."

"More incredible than this?"

When Javen looked at Melina, she was toying with the deep neckline of her dress. He blushed, realizing what Devin had meant earlier when he said the Onta and Arinin provinces had maintained a close relationship. "Your dress sort of reminds me of tiny dragon scales."

"That's not really what I was looking for."

Javen looked at Melina in a new light. "Of course you're more beautiful!"

"That's better," Melina said. She sipped her whiskey, then said, "So, what exactly is the nature of your relationship with that woman?"

"Lannary?" Javen asked.

"No," Melina said, "I know she's not much more than a whore. I'm talking about the woman in your quarters."

"I… we grew up together."

"You love her?"

"I thought I did… I mean, I do… but she doesn't love me," Javen said. "She refuses to even try. And ever since Onta, all she's done is hide from me."

Melina stepped closer to Javen and said, "So long as she doesn't interfere with my plans for tonight."

Javen swallowed a lump in his throat. "Tonight?"

"You are the Lover of… I mean Regent of Onta now, Your Majesty," Melina said slyly.

"I-I'd already planned on spending the night with—"

"Lannary. I know." Melina upended her glass, finishing off

her whiskey. "I know you've already met with His Blessed Highness…"

Javen nodded.

"Then finish off that whiskey and let's go."

Javen upended his glass. He choked back a cough and followed Melina as she sauntered ahead.

* * *

From against the wall at the back, Drenan watched as Devin and Javen knelt before the emperor. He was annoyed that the emperor had chosen to ignore his petition to have the boy executed. He was beside himself that Drakonias continued with what he considered to be foolishness, though he would never say such to His Highness' face.

He upended Melina's whiskey and closed his eyes as it burned going down his throat. He flexed the scars on his free hand then opened his eyes again. He held the glass up, and a waiter standing nearby took it and exchanged it for a full one.

He watched Javen rise from the couch and leave. He watched as Melina walked up and greeted him. When they walked over to the tables in the corner, he turned his attention back to the emperor and Devin. *What are they discussing?* He hated being excluded from the conversation. And not knowing why the emperor had chosen to remove Reago from power—an unprecedented event—was being excluded. He had a mind to return to Hantlo, but the thought of dealing with the mess there was too much. He wanted to know what was going on here. Whatever it was, in his opinion, it was much bigger.

The emperor had a vacuum set up around the couch, so no one could hear what they were talking about, even if Drenan could Synthesize, which he couldn't. He looked around the room and didn't see anyone he cared to speak with, so he snatched a second glass from the waiter standing next to him and walked through the open balcony doors just to his left.

He stepped out onto the balcony overlooking the mountains to the north and saw Javen and Melina. He rolled his eyes and went a different direction. Seeing Nera standing in the corner by herself, he headed for her.

Drenan strolled over to her, set his second glass on the ledge, and sipped from the first. He looked over at his aunt, who didn't acknowledge his presence. "Not interested in socializing today?" he said.

Nera didn't respond.

Drenan sipped from his drink and looked over at Nera again. "Something bothering you?"

"No," Nera said with a small shake of her head.

"Ah, come now, aunt. I can tell something's the matter." Drenan slid the second glass over in front of her. "Care for a drink?"

Nera looked down at the glass but otherwise ignored it. "What do you want, Drenan?"

"Nothing," Drenan said. "I'm celebrating the new chancellor and Regent of Onta, just as you should be."

"You're not celebrating anything, and you know it."

"You're right. And since you don't seem to be either, I'll cut the banter."

"The assignment has been made, if that's what you're wondering."

"When?" Drenan said.

"Soon."

"Today?"

Nera looked over at him for the first time. "No, not today. But soon enough."

"Drink the whiskey, aunt. You wouldn't want to give His Blessed Highness the impression you aren't enjoying yourself." Drenan left the second glass of whiskey in front of Nera and walked away.

He certainly wasn't enjoying himself, but he was good at pretending. What he needed was someone to vent his dissatisfaction to. He was beside himself at the inanity of Danavin's get having acquired the most coveted province in the empire.

He went in search of Lannary.

CHAPTER 28

Yolken trotted his horse into Croff next to Jax. It had taken Jax a couple of days, but he finally seemed to have forgiven Yolken—even though Yolken never admitted to doing anything wrong and did not apologize to Jax. Deanna and Deborah rode slightly behind them. Yolken patted the horse on the side of its neck and whispered, "Good job, Ollie." He didn't know if he would ever see the horse again after today, but since he'd made it perform an impossible task, he thought it deserved a name. And since Jax hadn't bothered to ask the boy what the horses' names were, he decided it would be Ollie. With his own body suffering from the fatigue of riding in a saddle for days without sleep, he couldn't imagine how Ollie must be feeling. "That was truly incredible," he added. He looked over at Jax and said, "What do we do with the horses?"

"There's a stable prepared to take care of them. This isn't the first time we've used horses like this."

Yolken didn't press the matter further, not now that they were within range of prying ears. They'd already switched to using Energy from the bones they carried rather than drawing it from the sun, to prevent attracting unwanted attention.

With an ample amount of gold from Jax's seemingly never-ending supply, they left their horses in the care of a stablemaster at a stable only a few streets away from the house they'd stayed at when they were last in Croff. As instructed, Yolken didn't withdraw his flow of Energy from the horse until it was safely in a stall. The moment he ended the flow, Ollie collapsed to the ground. "Are you sure he's going to be okay?" he asked the stablemaster.

"Aye, lad. With our care and proper rest, he'll be fine."

Yolken nodded, then hesitantly followed the others out of the stable, still unsure about Ollie's well-being.

Jax shrugged out of his coat and said, "I have a few errands to run, so I'll meet you at the house."

"You should rest first," Deborah said. "We all need to rest."

"I will after." He handed his coat to Deborah and said, "Will you take this to the house for me?"

Deborah took the coat from Jax as he strode off, then she said to Yolken and Deanna, "This way." She started off in the opposite direction. When the door closed behind them in the familiar house, she said, "Anyone care for some tea?"

"That would be excellent," Deanna said, "lest I fall asleep right here on this couch. It looks more comfortable than anything I've slept on in centuries."

Deborah snickered. "What about you, dear?"

"No thanks," Yolken said. He had something entirely different in mind. Ale. *His* ale. He moved into the kitchen and drew himself a mug from the barrel in the corner and took a deep drink. When the liquid concoction made by his own hand hit his lips, nostalgia flooded into him. He gulped down half the mug, then refilled it. He took the mug back to the couch and plopped down on it, accidentally sloshing a little ale out. He slurped it up from the sides of the mug, then propped his feet on the table and settled back.

As he reclined on the couch, he let the familiar-tasting ale guide his thoughts back to when things were simpler. Since the night Kaylan had been stolen from him, all he could think about was getting her back. Every step taken by the muscular horse he'd ridden had brought him further from the woman he loved and closer to an unknown fate. Now that he was back in Croff, that still-unknown fate loomed over him like a dark cloud, close enough to almost touch. However, until Jax returned, he decided to let his ale carry him back to Lonely Oak.

He imagined how events might have unfolded after the night the Chancellor of the Southern Realm visited, had he not healed Issa. He imagined his relationship with Kaylan blossoming after the festival, and them quickly becoming betrothed. Selena would have taken over the day-to-day at the tavern—except for brewing, which he would still do—so he could finally build the home his father always intended to. In his daydream, both he and Selena knew it would be tough running the tavern without him, especially since Javen continued to be flighty, so they finally hired help. As soon as he finished their home, he and Kaylan married. Kaylan moved out of the bakery, and together they moved into their new home. Yolken returned to work in the tavern, and, with the additional help, the tavern finally began to grow. He entered into an agreement with Norin, and he began shipping his ale throughout the province. Kaylan continued to help her mother in the bakery until she gave birth to their first child. Their daily walks to and from town quickly became some of their favorite moments together.

As Yolken finished the ale, he wondered if any of it would ever be. Even with everything that had happened, he remained fixed in his intent to marry Kaylan, but he wondered if they would ever be able to return to the lives they'd once lived in Lonely Oak. Even though he knew it was not likely, deep down, he clung to that hope.

CHAPTER 29

Jax navigated the winding streets leading to the center of the city. Most of the city had been built with foresight—the roads lined up east to west and north to south—but the streets in the oldest part of the city followed the curve of the Croff River slicing the city in two. Dalia's mansion sat on a rise on the south side of the river, which caused the river to curve around it to the north. It overlooked the majority of the city, which was situated on the north side.

He joined with a narrow, curved street. One row of buildings was all that separated the street from the river. He walked down it as it slowly curved left, past an old, weather-worn stone bridge, then entered an alley wedged between two buildings. At the end of the alley, he climbed an iron staircase and opened the door at the top.

"Master Jorgan is not—" a voice said, then stopped. "Oh, Master Jorgan, when did you get back?"

"Hello, Neil," Jax said, looking at the boy sitting behind a rickety desk. He was old enough to have a few whiskers on his chin and upper lip, but not old enough for them to grow into anything. "Just arrived. Any news?"

"Yes, yes. Lots of messages have come in your absence."

"Anything significant?"

"There have been several updates on the rebellion in Turnig," Neil said. "I forwarded those to Tabitha, as you instructed."

"Anything else?"

"There's also been several from your informant in the south. Those are on your desk."

"Thanks, Neil." Jax stepped around Neil's desk, holding out his hand. As he passed, Neil placed a key in it. He inserted the key into the door on the other side of the small room.

"Do you require anything?"

"No thank you. I won't be long," Jax said before closing the door.

He stopped in front of the desk, which shined from several coats of lacquer. There was a pile of rolled-up parchments with unbroken seals. He walked around the desk, looked out the window at the mansion across the river, then sat in his cushioned seat. He sorted the messages by the dates scrawled on them, then broke the seal on the first one. It was dated a few days after he'd met with Sethlan in Croff.

> *CS changed plans. Will be taking respite in LO rather than Edis.*

What Sethlan hadn't known was that after Jax met with him in Croff, the Council had finally approved Jax's plan, and he'd left Croff several days after Dorlan's caravan to inform Deborah and Selena. Even taking a wide berth of the caravan, he'd still managed to arrive in Lonely Oak the evening before Dorlan. He still wondered what Dorlan was doing in Lonely Oak. His presence had ended up completely fouling his plan, which was to take both Yolken and Javen safely under the Order's protective wing—that, and to take them to Kvorga. The latter portion had ended up working out, though not without considerable trouble. He hoped Javen and Kaylan were safe. Jax set the parchment aside and opened the next one.

Well, that helped a little. He'd guessed it was because Lonely Oak had been growing. But a part of him worried that they'd somehow learned Orwyn had children. Thinking back on it now, it had been incredibly stupid of him to let Yolken and Javen out of the tavern the night of the festival. But in the moment, he knew he was about to upend their lives by forcing them to leave Lonely Oak behind, and he'd wanted them to enjoy the time they had left. In the end, none of it mattered. The Regency had found out about them the next day, even if they hadn't known before. He opened the next message.

Jax knew all this, of course—but he would still pay Sethlan. The informant couldn't have known that Jax had gone to Lonely Oak and had already learned this from Yolken and Deborah. He opened message after message, feeling the smooth lacquered arm of his chair with his hand, looking for something he didn't already know. *Dorlan training boy. Boy so far unable to use gift. Drenan killed girl from LO named Astora, forcing boy to use his gift? Boy sent to Onta with Devin.* If only they'd known.

Should he tell Yolken about the lass? No, it was better he didn't know. He'd lied to Yolken enough already—he was glad he didn't have to lie about Javen's whereabouts as well. They were going to Kvorga whether they knew where Javen was or not. And knowing about the lass would only distract Yolken more than he already was.

He opened the last message and read it with great interest. The girl Javen was bedding is plotting to overthrow the Regency in the Southern Realm. *I believe she has the means to do it,* Sethlan had written. Jax set the last parchment on his desk. He tapped the wooden arm with his left hand and ran the fingers of his right through his beard.

That last message was time-sensitive. Sethlan had only managed to intercept it because Dorlan had just received news from the west—Sethlan didn't know what, but he figured it had something to do with their recent trip through Onta. It was only a matter of time before news of the girl's plans reached the chancellor.

Jax leaned forward and opened a drawer, pulled out a piece of parchment, and scribbled a quick message:

> *Ensuring her success reaps great reward.*

Jax rolled the message tightly, selected one of two dozen seals in another drawer, and sealed it. He wrote another brief message and folded it in half. Then, he pushed his chair back, stepped over to the closet, and slid the thin wooden door open. He changed into matching tan clothes and walked out of the room with the message in hand.

"Please dispose of the messages on my desk," he said as he walked around Neil's desk. He set the folded message in front of Neil and said, "After the messages on my desk are gone, take this to Enif." He opened the door and walked out.

Jax made his way up the alley then down the curved street to the stone bridge. He started up the arching span; Dalia's mansion was visible atop the hill on the far side. On the opposite side, the street continued straight toward the hill, as well as splitting both left and right. He continued straight.

The buildings ended at a gate at the base of the hill. Jax got in line with other couriers lined up to the right of the gate. When it was his turn, Jax placed the message in the hand of an armored guard. The guard inspected the wax seal. This particular time he had gone with Ronld Shar, a wealthy man owning vast tracts of land to the north of the city—he probably wouldn't be too happy if and when someone went to investigate why he'd used a condor to send a message to Hantlo.

The guard handed the message back to Jax and permitted him through a small side gate. He followed the small walking path to the side of the larger brick path, lined on both sides with manicured hedges, leading up to the mansion.

At the top, the main path looped around a bronze statue then up to a set of four ornate doors. The walking path Jax followed went straight to a side door. The door was split in half horizontally, with the top half being open. The bottom half had a small counter on it.

He waited until it was his turn, then reached into his pocket. He grabbed hold of five drakes first, then the rolled-up parchment. He set the coins and the parchment on the counter and said, "An urgent message for the Chancellor of the Southern Realm."

The attendant swiped the message and the coins with one hand.

Jax turned and started back down the path. It was a risky enterprise he conducted; the attendant would likely be questioned about who had authorized the use of a condor, which was why he used them only for the most urgent of matters. The opportunity to ignite a rebellion of a magnitude the empire had never seen was, he'd concluded, of sufficient urgency.

He returned to the small office where he conducted his business and changed back into his travel-soiled clothes. The messages on his desk were gone, and the fireplace in the corner had fresh ash still smoldering in it. Neil had not yet returned, though. There was no reason for him to loiter, so he made his way to meet the others at the house. He hoped it wouldn't take long for the Council to convene. With news of Deanna's presence, he didn't think it would.

CHAPTER 30

Care for another?" Jax said after walking into the house.

Yolken looked down at his empty mug and said, "I've already had two."

"Well, we aren't going anywhere for a while, lad," Jax said. "At least not until we hear from the Council. It's doubtful a meeting will happen today."

"Then sure," Yolken said. He started to stand but stopped when Jax held out his hand.

"I'll get it," Jax said.

Jax went into the kitchen, where Deborah and Deanna chatted over tea, and retrieved a second mug.

"So?" Deborah asked while Jax filled the mugs.

"Nothing to do but wait," Jax said. "Come join us. I have some interesting news to share." He walked back to where Yolken reclined on the couch and handed him the mug while Deborah and Deanna joined them with their tea. "I went and caught myself up on what's been happening while we've been gone. Turns out when we left for Kvorga, we just missed receiving information from my contact embedded in Dorlan's caravan."

"What did he have to say?" Deborah said.

"That Javen left Dorlan's caravan in Portstown."

"And went to Onta," Yolken said. It pained him to think about his conversation with Javen at the steps of the palace in Onta. "I still can't believe he was there this whole time."

"Would it have changed anything?" Deborah said.

"I was standing face to face with him. He *chose* to stay. After all we've been through trying to find him, and he never intended to leave."

"I refuse to believe he's willingly joined with the Regency," Deborah said.

"He certainly didn't look like a prisoner to me," Yolken said.

"There has to be some other explanation."

Jax raised his mug to his mouth and took a drink. From over the rim, he said, "Devin never intended to let either of you walk out of Onta." He took another drink, then set the mug down. "So it's probably better we didn't know he was there."

"You don't think he had anything to do with what happened with Kaylan, do you?" Yolken said.

"There's really no way to know that."

Yolken sat back in his chair and looked blankly at his ale. Shaking his head, he lifted the mug and took a drink.

"What else did you learn?" Deborah said.

"There's a rebellion brewing in the south."

"*Really?* Well, with the way things are down there, I can't say I'm not surprised. Especially since the Regency isn't doing anything about it."

"Neither am I," Jax said. "And what else is surprising is who's behind it."

"Who?" Yolken said.

"A lass who knows your brother."

Yolken looked at Jax, confused. "Who?"

"Does the name Hadie ring a bell?"

Yolken shook his head.

"Well, my contact indicates that she's the daughter of a very powerful Silk."

"What's a Silk?" Yolken asked.

"The southern version of a Suit. Turns out she's hatching a plan to overthrow the entire Regency."

"That's ambitious," Deborah said. "Should we mention it to the Council when they call on us?"

"I've already seen to it that she has the help she needs to succeed," Jax said.

"Well, that was presumptuous."

"You don't think the Council would have approved simultaneous rebellions in both the west and the south?"

"No, I think they would. It's just it's not your decision to make."

"If we ran every decision that needs to be made past the Council, our efforts would become even less effective than they already are."

Deborah pursed her lips, then took a sip of her tea. "So what exactly should we expect from the Council?"

Jax looked from Yolken to Deanna as he took a drink of ale. "I don't know for sure. We were sent to find Deanna, but I don't know whether they thought we would succeed, or what their intentions would be if we did. Plus, they will not be expecting news of our encounters with a dragon or what he revealed to Yolken."

"I have to tell you right now," Deanna said, "just so there are no surprises later, I do *not* intend on becoming a pawn of the Order."

Jax swallowed his ale and said, "I shouldn't think so."

"I haven't remained hidden from Drakonias for as long as I have simply to immerse myself back in it again. I don't care about your rebellions, or whether my brother remains in power or not. If the Council's plans are not consistent with my own, then I will not be a part of it."

"Meaning if you had the opportunity to remove your brother from power, you wouldn't?"

"You think that I can do anything about that?"

"If anyone can, it's you."

"I couldn't stop him from taking power, so what makes you think I can remove him?"

After another sip of ale, Jax said, "That was a different era."

"Meaning that things are different now? That somehow one person can now do what many were previously unable to prevent in the first place?"

"You never know," Jax said.

Yolken had finished his third mug of ale. His head was starting to spin, and he was becoming acutely aware of his fatigue. "I'm going to bed," he said.

"Good idea, lad," Jax said. "You should be well-rested when it's time to go before the Council."

As Yolken stood, someone started pounding on the front door. He exchanged a questioning look with Jax.

"Are we expecting someone?" Deborah said.

"No," Jax said.

The pounding on the door repeated.

Jax strode to the door, unlocked it, and cracked it open. He peered out, then opened the door wider. Someone outside handed him a folded parchment. Jax shut and locked the door, then unfolded the parchment.

"What's it say?" Deborah said.

The parchment fell from Jax's fingers.

"What?" Deborah said.

"A proclamation has been sent out from Kyinth."

"Jax…"

"Javen was named Regent of Onta."

CHAPTER 31

Yolken's mind reeled as he followed silently behind Jax, Deborah, and Deanna. They made their way to the warehouse under which the Order of the Dragon's headquarters hid. The clipped manner in which the others moved told him they were as anxious to get answers as he was.

Javen was in Kyinth. How did he get there so fast? He was the Regent of Onta, and Devin the Chancellor of the Western Realm? Reago, a traitor of the empire?

Javen's betrayal was complete. He'd officially joined the Regency—the entity responsible for killing their parents, their aunt. *How could he?* When he'd faced Devin in Onta, Devin had said Javen was going to go pledge his allegiance to the emperor, and he had. *Why?* Yolken didn't understand what would make Javen join with those who had caused so much pain for their family. Yolken felt like someone punched him in the stomach with Synthesis-fueled strength.

Yolken wiped tears from his eyes as he stifled a yawn. After hearing the devastating news, he didn't think he would be able to sleep, but his exhaustion eventually won. Even so, he'd slept fitfully.

Jax knocked on the side door of the whitewashed building when they arrived. While they waited for the guard to unlock the door, Jax turned to Yolken and said, "Why do you think it happened the way it did?"

Jax's question pulled Yolken out of his quiet contemplation. "Why what happened?"

The door opened. Deborah and Deanna entered the warehouse.

"The more I think about it, the more I think Devin was specifically after you in Onta."

"Why would he be?" Yolken knew where Jax was going with this, but he refused to believe it.

Javen became a regent. He betrayed me.

"Are you coming in or not?" said the portly man who sat by the door on a rickety stool.

Jax stepped through the door, and Yolken followed. The guard shut and bolted the door when they were all inside, and the stool groaned when he sat back down on it. Jax led them through the warehouse toward the crate that hid the entrance to the underground headquarters.

"Think about it," Jax said.

Yolken didn't want to think about it. Javen said he wasn't going to leave Onta, so what had he thought was going to happen?

"They took Kaylan," Jax said.

"So?"

"Causing what to happen?"

"I went after her."

"Separating you from us. The whole thing was well orchestrated." Jax paused for a moment. "Why would they want to separate you from us, if they weren't specifically after you?"

"I don't know," Yolken said.

"More importantly, how would they know that taking Kaylan would make you react the way you did?"

"They wouldn't."

"But they did, didn't they? Did Javen know about you and Kaylan?"

"I don't know," Yolken said. "Kaylan and I only got together for the first time the night of Dorlan's stay in Lonely Oak."

"Did you ever talk about her to him?"

"No, but he told me that day that he wanted to spend the festival with her."

"Perhaps he somehow knew, and perhaps he didn't. Maybe he wanted her for himself. But if he *did* know," Jax said, "and he told them, then he—"

"Betrayed me!" Yolken exclaimed, stopping. The others stopped along with him. "Is that what you want me to admit?"

"What's the point of this, Jax?" Deborah said.

"He needs to understand exactly what's happened," Jax said.

"*We* don't know what's happened, so how do you expect him to?"

Jax clenched his jaw. "Come on, they're expecting us."

When they arrived at the large crate hiding the stairs leading belowground, two men pushed the crate aside.

Yolken's heart sank. Not only had Javen refused to leave Onta with him, but he'd betrayed him. His own brother. His family. He'd never felt so hurt in his life. He and Javen had had their differences, and Javen was certainly less responsible than Yolken would have liked him to be, but he would never have betrayed Javen for anyone. But Javen had. He'd traded family for—what? The Regency? *Can he even Synthesize?*

"Yolken?" Jax said from below.

Yolken looked down at the others; he hadn't realized they had gone ahead. He followed them down the stairs and trailed behind as Jax led them to the Council Chamber.

"Don't let it consume you, Yolken," Jax said.

Yolken looked at him in disbelief. How could Jax be so nonchalant? Javen had betrayed him!

"No matter what happens, we won't leave your brother in their hands. All right?"

Yolken nodded, but he didn't believe Jax anymore. The Order wasn't going to help him. If he was going to rescue Javen and Kaylan from the Regency, he would have to do it himself.

The chamber door opened, and a young girl wearing a white cassock ushered them in. Yolken recognized her from the first time he was here.

Just as before, the chamber was empty. The girl shut the door behind them, then crossed the room, exiting through the side door. The group stood silently while they waited for the Council members to arrive.

Shifting nervously, Yolken's eyes drifted from the raised platform where the Council would soon be sitting to the dais behind it. He looked at the chair sitting at the top. The throne of the Dragon King. He looked over at Deanna. She stood with poise and had an air of confidence about her. He thought she'd be nervous about meeting with the leaders of the Order, but then he wondered what she had to be nervous about. She was Deanna Aliza Drake, the eldest surviving loyal descendant of the Dragon King. She had every right to take control of the Order. She was his daughter, next in line for the Dragon Throne behind Drakonias. She was… he struggled to remember the antiquated term… a princess.

The side door opened again, and men and women wearing yellow cassocks filed into the chamber.

The Council.

Yolken breathed deeply. For the second time, he stood before those who controlled his fate. In the time since he was last here, he'd memorized their names. He watched Sherya Mernn, the first in line, step up onto the platform. Behind her followed Onig Frell, Jerle Sage, Aleena Harrin, then Enif Maldon, the High Councilman. Behind him came Rheena Drew, Dannl Kand, Corin Foler, and lastly, Tabora Alon. As they took their places, he looked at the green embroidery on the thick band of darker yellow cloth encircling their necks. Dragons. At one point in his life, he'd thought they were mere creatures of fantasy. When he stood before the Council last, he'd thought them extinct. Now he knew one survived. Deth.

Yolken studied the group as they settled into their seats. Every one of them appeared nervous. Sweat beaded on Enif's bald head. *They're afraid*, Yolken realized. He looked again at Deanna.

The side door opened again, and two individuals walked in—the young girl wearing the white cassock, and a boy dressed the same. They walked toward the group of four and waited.

"If you don't mind," Enif started with a shaky voice that betrayed how he felt, confirming Yolken's suspicion, "we will check you for bones."

"You're going to search us?" Jax protested. "Deborah and I are members of the Order!"

"The Council has decided it necessary," Enif said.

"Necessary for what?"

"Our safety."

"Your *safety*?"

"The last time the boy was here, he brought the Harachin sword with him," Enif said. "I do not intend to put the Council at such risk again."

"Fine," Jax said.

Enif gestured with his hand to the two acolytes. The young boy proceeded first to Yolken and the young girl to Deborah. They searched their clothing and their bodies carefully for any hint of hidden bones. When they finished with Yolken and Deborah, the boy moved on to Jax and the girl to Deanna. Finding nothing on any of them, the young boy and girl retreated through the side door.

"We have much to discuss," Enif said, beginning their meeting. "And let me start by saying what an honor it is to meet you, Deanna."

Deanna gave a small nod of her head.

"In these perilous times, we are most fortunate to count you amongst us."

"I count myself amongst no one," Deanna said.

Enif looked to Yolken like a chastised child.

"I am here to help undo the damage Drakonias' war caused," Deanna said. "Nothing more."

"Whatever aid you might lend in this matter would be both needed and appreciated," Enif said. "Now, before we proceed any further, I think it appropriate to discuss last night's proclamation."

Whispers rose among the other Council members.

"The news of young Javen…" Enif said, speaking over the murmur, "is most tragic. I spent all night trying to figure out what motive Drakonias would have in making such a decision."

"He has named Reago a traitor, and Devin replaced him as chancellor," Corin said, stroking his beard. Yolken thought it looked odd that he had a beard but no mustache. "So he needed a replacement."

"Yes," Enif said, "but why Javen? There are better options to replace Devin as Regent of Onta than the untried son of a rebel."

"And why proclaim Reago a traitor?" Sherya said. She wore her hair in a bun. "What has he done?"

"You know as well as I," Enif said, "that the proclamation didn't say."

"The emperor need not explain himself," Jerle said. The way he was stroking his long goatee suggested that he was being sarcastic.

"Yes, well, replacing Reago with Devin makes perfect sense," Enif said. "But replacing Devin with Javen does not. Has he even used his gift?"

"He has," Jax interjected.

"He has?" Yolken said, looking over at Jax.

"Yes. My sources in Hantlo tell me that he was given…" Jax looked over at Yolken, then back toward Enif, "…lessons."

"*Lessons?*" Enif scoffed. "The Regency does *not* give lessons in Synthesis to rebels."

"No, they do not," Tabora agreed. Her green eyes pierced Yolken's heart. They reminded him of Kaylan.

"Unless..." Jax said.

Enif looked down at him tersely. "Unless what?"

"It makes perfect sense."

"How so?"

"You said you spent all night wondering why Drakonias would name Javen as Devin's replacement—well, I did the same thing."

"And?"

"They're using him," Jax said.

"Draego's Fire," Deborah said, covering her mouth. "Oh, Javen..."

"You mean he doesn't actually want to be there?" Yolken said hopefully.

"No," Jax said. "He very much wants to be there. Drakonias would never make such a move unless he was sure he had Javen's loyalty."

Yolken's heart sank anew.

"Why use Javen?" Enif said. "What could Drakonias possibly hope to accomplish by replacing Devin with him? A move such as this has to anger most of the other regents. Regent of Onta! It's the most coveted province. To give it to the son of a rebel would anger even the most loyal of the regents. Remember what happened with Sheal? It doesn't make sense."

"It does, actually," Jax said. "Drakonias is not an idiot. But neither are we."

"He's hoping it will demoralize us," Dannl said.

"Exactly."

"It's devastating!" Rheena shouted.

"Rheena..." Enif said.

"Orwyn would be devastated if he knew his son had joined the Regency, let alone become a regent!" Her curly black hair shook as she spoke.

"It's only devastating if we allow it to be," Enif said.

"How can we not!"

"Javen's loyalty to Drakonias is real, I'm sure," Jax said, "but

I think we can all agree that this is nothing more than a ploy to demoralize us."

"Agreed," Tabora said. "We mustn't let this detract us from our purpose."

Purpose. Yolken stared past the Council at the throne. His mind swirled with Javen's betrayal, but Deth's words crept in: *Your fight is not with the humans, Dragon King.*

"We have more pressing matters that need to be addressed," Enif said. He directed his attention back to Deanna. "There were several reasons the Council sent Jax and Deborah to find you."

Yolken looked down from the throne to Enif. The top of his head glistened.

"Since Danavin's death, the Council has had to face a rather unfortunate predicament."

Yolken glanced over at Deanna. She stood rigid, staring straight ahead at Enif.

"You see, Danavin was the only individual in the Order who had both the strength and knowledge to…" Enif paused, making Yolken wonder if he was afraid to say what he wanted from her. Finally, Enif said, "Regenerate."

Jax gasped. "You lied!" he shouted. "That was *not* part of the plan! You promised if we—"

"I did *not* lie!" Enif shouted back.

Deanna laughed.

"The Order of the Dragon *is* indeed in need of Deanna's help to fix whatever is happening to the sun," Enif said. "We are fully aware of the threat we face."

"Why didn't you tell me you *also* wanted her to restore your youth?" Jax said.

"I am the High Councilman," Enif said, "and it is my decision what to tell the subjects and what not to tell them."

"*Subjects?*" Jax said. "The members of the Order are *not* subjects! Perhaps you've occupied that seat too long."

The Council members sitting on either side of Enif shifted uncomfortably.

"Remove me at the next election if you can," Enif said. He redirected his attention to Deanna. "The needs of the Council are many. It's no easy task to lead a group constantly under threat of attack. Especially with what's happening now. Our bodies and wits must remain sharp. The fact is that the Regency remains young, and the Order grows old."

Yolken realized that the only reason the Council had sent him to Kvorga was to use him. They'd sent him to that cursed island under the guise of helping him rescue Javen, but had no intention of doing anything of the sort. And now Javen was being used by Drakonias. The same way the Council was using him. Well, he wasn't going to let the Council use him anymore.

"No," Deanna said.

"No?"

"Four hundred years ago, I decided to permanently remove myself from my brother's doings. It was not until these three came," Deanna said, pointing at Jax, Deborah, and Yolken, "that I finally realized the full ramifications of the war. And at their behest, I have agreed to return and help fix what I helped cause." Deanna took a few steps toward the platform. "And now you're telling me that what you really want from me is Regeneration?"

"As I said, it is necessary—"

"I'm *not* here to fight the Regency," Deanna said.

"You lied to me," Yolken said.

No one seemed to have heard him, as Deanna and Enif continued to argue.

"All this time you were just using me," he said.

Deanna's and Enif's words grew distant.

Yolken looked past Enif again, who was moving with great animation, back up to the throne sitting atop the dais. The situation was spiraling out of control. He knew the Council was dangerously close to losing Deanna's help. The Order needed her, not for Regeneration, or even to rein in Drakonias. He understood that she wanted nothing to do with her brother. At that moment, Yolken finally realized what he needed to do.

Before Yolken could convince himself to change his mind—
this was *not* what he wanted; he wanted to just get Kaylan and
Javen and go home—he strode around the side of the platform.
Everyone's attention was fixed on Deanna and Enif, so they
didn't notice—or didn't care. Behind the platform, he climbed
the steps of the dais and stood in front of the throne. The back
had two dragons carved into it. They sat on their haunches,
heads tilted up, and spewed fire out of their mouths. It reminded
him of the gates of the Dragon Shrine. He touched a lacquered
arm with one hand, then turned around to face the Council
below.

Tabora glanced up at him. "Enif," she said.

Enif and Deanna continued with their verbal confrontation.

"Enif!" she shouted.

Enif turned angrily toward Tabora and said, "*What?*"

Tabora pointed up at the throne.

Enif turned in his seat and looked over his shoulder. "What
in Draego's Fire are you doing? Get down from there."

Yolken looked down at the Council, all of whom had turned
in their seats to look up at him. He looked past the Council at
Jax, Deborah, and Deanna. They were looking at him with as
much concern as the Council.

Shifting his gaze back to Enif, Yolken said, "I hereby
dissolve this Council."

Audible gasps reverberated around the room.

Enif jumped to his feet. "Just who do you think you are?"

"I am Yolken Danavin Dairion Drake, firstborn of Danavin
Drae Hippolyte Drake."

"You think because you're Orwyn's son, you have the right
to dissolve the Council?"

Yolken shook his head.

"Then on whose auth—"

"On my own authority," Yolken averred.

"And what authority might that be?" Enif scoffed.

Yolken looked down at the nine individuals dressed in

yellow robes. He knew the life he'd imagined while sitting on the couch drinking ale made by his own hand would never come to be. He knew that the Great Dragon had chosen a much different fate for him. Like his father, the life he truly wanted to live would forever elude him. Knowing he could not avoid it, at that moment, he embraced it and sat.

"The Dragon King."

CHAPTER 32

A re you mad?" Enif shouted.

Yolken drew Energy from his bones and gathered air from around him.

"The Dragon King has been dea—"

He used the air to plug Enif's mouth.

Enif's eyes went wide with shock.

Some of the Council members reached underneath the platform, and Yolken wrapped them with air as well. He stood and said, "Anyone else wish to oppose me?"

"How are you doing this?" Tabora said.

"I am the Dragon King."

"That doesn't make sense. You Synthesize with no dragon bones. Not even Draeko did that."

"He speaks the truth," Deanna interjected. All eyes turned toward her. "My father required either the sun or dragon bones to Synthesize, just as we all do. But not so with him!"

"How?" Tabora asked.

"Ask him," Deanna said.

All eyes turned back toward Yolken.

Yolken looked down at the robed individuals. "This isn't how I want this to go," he said. "I'm going to release those of you I have restrained so that we can talk. All right?"

Those who were not restrained nodded, and Tabora said, "Yes."

Yolken let the air he had used to restrain Enif and the others move freely with the air in the room. "Please, sit," he said.

Enif obeyed.

Yolken sat once again upon the throne. He waited to see if any of the Council would protest further, then said, "Deanna, Jax, Deborah, please join us."

Enif furrowed his brow as the three of them walked around the side of the platform. They stood at the end, next to Tabora.

"From now on," Yolken said, "these three have equal status as the rest of you."

"You can't just undo centuries of protocol," Onig said.

"On what authority do you speak?" Yolken asked. "I've dissolved the Council."

Onig did not reply. He just stared with his mouth slightly open.

"You certainly have a different air about you," Enif said.

"I am not the same person who came before you two and a half months ago."

"Meaning?" Enif said.

Yolken looked over at his three friends. Deanna nodded at him. He turned back to Enif and said, "You sent me to Kvorga to find Anivera. What none of you expected when you sent us there, regardless of what your true motivations might have been, was that she would help me in a way that neither I nor you could ever have imagined."

"She gave you the ability to Synthesize without aid?" Enif said.

"No," Yolken said. "The ability was always within me. I just didn't know it."

"That's not possible. Not even your father could—"

"And yet it was," Yolken said.

"How did you find out you had this… ability?"

"A dragon helped me figure it out."

Enif stared at Yolken wide-eyed, and he heard gasps around the room.

"A… a dragon?" Enif said.

A din overtook the room as the Council members began talking amongst themselves.

Yolken waited patiently, as he knew the news of a living dragon was not something they would have expected him to proclaim. When the room quieted down, he answered Enif. "Yes. The same dragon that gave Draeko the gift of Synthesis."

The stares Yolken received were those of disbelief.

"What do you mean a dragon gave Draeko the gift?" Enif said. "Was not Draeko blessed by the Great Dragon?"

"That's what I was taught as a child," Yolken said. "It's what's taught in shrines throughout the empire. But it isn't true. Draeko was no more Blessed of the Dragon than the average citizen of Dradonia." After a pause, Yolken added. "But I am."

"*You?*" Enif said incredulously.

"Draeko received his gift from a dragon named Dethoicrinth."

"Dethoi…" Enif tried the name out on his tongue.

"And Dethoicrinth broke the laws of the dragons that date back to the advent of man."

"What laws?"

"Dragons were forbidden to meddle in our affairs," Yolken said. "Unlike us, they lived in peace. From the very beginning, they always did. And they couldn't understand why we weren't able to live peacefully as well. They were weary of our constant wars but could do nothing about them, as they were forbidden to ever interfere. Countless wars were fought, kingdoms rose and fell, until one dragon had had enough."

"But Draeko was the Dragon King," Corin protested.

"It was a name he bestowed upon himself."

"As you're doing now."

"I didn't want—" Yolken began. Then he shook his head, deciding against further elaborating his feelings to these people he didn't know. Instead, he continued with his explanation. "The *sole* Blessed of the Dragon, and one *true* Dragon King, was Dimras."

"And who was that?" Enif said.

"The first of the dragons. He was their king. He was the sole recipient of the Great Dragon's blessing. And now, for reasons I still don't understand, the Great Dragon has chosen to bless me." Yolken paused for a moment, then added, "When I stood before Dethoicrinth, he acknowledged me as the Blessed of the Dragon. He acknowledged me as king. The Dragon King."

Quiet fell over the room. The way the Council was staring up at Yolken was making him nervous. For once, he wished someone would say something. But they just stared, each of them presumably trying to piece together what he'd just told them. He wished they would talk amongst themselves again; at least then they wouldn't all be staring at him. He tried his best not to fidget.

Finally, Enif spoke. "What was Deanna's role in this?"

"She took me to meet with the dragon."

"*Deanna* was friends with a dragon?" Enif asked with a side look at Deanna.

"I wouldn't necessarily say we're friends," Deanna said with a smirk. "More… companions in death."

"This is all too much," Enif said. "This tale you spin—"

"Is the truth," Yolken said.

"I didn't think there were any dragons left."

"Neither did I," Deanna said. "By the time the war ended, we thought all the dragons were gone. It was a belief I maintained until the day I met Deth deep in the mountains of Kvorga."

"Where is… Deth?" said Aleena, the woman sitting to the left of Enif. "Is he nearby?"

As far as Yolken knew, none of them had ever seen a dragon, let alone met one. If they were anything like Jax, then they were probably giddy with excitement as well as jealous that he'd met a dragon while they, the leaders of the Order of the Dragon, had not.

"Where Deth is presently is not important," Yolken said. They didn't need to know that he didn't know where Deth was or that he'd practically begged Deth to help him. "What *is* important is what else Deth told me."

"You mean there's more to this tale?" Enif said.

With the help of Jax, Deanna, and Deborah, Yolken spent the next couple of hours retelling all that had occurred to them since they'd left Croff in search of the fabled Anivera. The Council listened intently, interrupting only occasionally to ask for clarification when needed. Yolken finished by saying, "Our task is not to bicker about who sits on the Council or who the rightful ruler is. I have no desire to overthrow the Regency and—"

"And yet you declare yourself Dragon King," Enif said.

"Permit me to finish, please." Yolken waited a moment, then continued. "As I said, I have no desire to overthrow the Regency and establish my own empire as though that would somehow be better. I'm not here to declare myself the ruler of anything. I'm here only to restore the balance lost during Drakonias' war."

"We've been trying to figure out how to do that ever since we learned of the astronomer's studies."

"Deth told me I need to replace what was taken."

"And did Deth also tell you how we're supposed to do that?" Enif asked.

"Not *we*," Yolken said. "Me."

"*You?*"

"Deth told me that *I* must replace what was lost."

"And how do you propose doing that?" Enif said. "You said yourself that all the Synthesizers in the world combined couldn't ignite the flame within you."

Yolken was starting to get annoyed with Enif. He was beginning to sound insolent. Figuring that Enif wasn't used to not being in charge, he decided to ignore it. For now. "If what

Deth says is true, you're right. According to Deth, it took the entire Assembly to ignite a flame within a hatchling. Even if Deth added his strength to that of every Synthesizer, we still wouldn't have enough."

"That doesn't answer my question," Enif said. "What is it that you propose?"

"I must figure out how to ignite the flame within myself," Yolken said.

Enif snorted. "You think you're stronger than the Assembly of dragons?"

"No," Yolken said. "I don't possess that kind of strength. But Draego gave me the task of restoring balance to the sun, so there must be another way."

"Such as?"

"I'm not exactly sure," Yolken said, "but I think it may somehow involve the sun."

"You think the sun might be the answer?" Deanna asked.

Deanna's unsolicited input resulted in a sidelong glare from Enif. Yolken saw it and said, "If we're going to succeed, we must for once work together." Turning to Deanna, he said, "Yes. I don't know exactly how, but I think that somehow the sun might provide the Energy I need to ignite the flame within me."

"That doesn't make any sense," Corin said.

"You're right, Corin," Yolken said. "It doesn't. I don't have it completely figured out yet, but I think when I *do* figure it out, it will directly involve the sun in some way. In the meantime, let's talk about our other problem."

"What other problem?" Enif said.

"As I said before, I don't care about removing Drakonias from power, but something needs to be done about him."

Javen's in Kyinth…

"What do you think we've been trying to do?"

"The Order works to undermine the Regency, I know," Yolken said. *I'm not leaving Javen in the Regency. And if he's in Kyinth…* "And even though I now believe that Drakonias' rule needs to come to an end, that's a second-kettle worry."

"A what?"

"Second-kettle," Yolken said. "It's a brewing phrase."

"Meaning…?"

"It's not as important as the first kettle."

"I don't—"

"What I'm trying to say is, whereas removing Drakonias from power would be beneficial to Dradonia, there are more pressing matters." *Is Kaylan with him? Or is she still in Onta?* "What's in the second kettle is important, but not if we don't get the first kettle right."

"You mean the sun," Tabora said.

Yolken glanced over at her. "Yes. Any continued effort to remove Drakonias from power is moot if we don't figure out how to restore balance to the sun. What we need right now, more than ending Drakonias' rule, is to have him on our side."

"What is it exactly that you're proposing?" Enif said.

Yolken looked back at Enif. "I'm not *proposing* anything."

Enif furrowed his brow.

"I'm telling you that it's time the Order and Drakonias put aside their differences and, at last, come together for the greater good."

"The emperor will never agree to—"

"It is up to *us* to convince him," Yolken said. "The Order's efforts to undermine Drakonias have not worked, and it needs to end."

"You can't just—"

"It ends *now*," Yolken said as firmly as he could.

Enif sighed. He took a deep breath, exhaled slowly, then said, "What do you suggest we do?"

Yolken looked intently down at the group, as Selena used to do when he or Javen had done something wrong as lads. He knew they wouldn't like what he was about to suggest, but he also knew that it was time the Order shifted tactics. "I intend to go to Kyinth and offer Drakonias a truce."

"He'll never go for it," Enif said.

"Not a permanent truce," Yolken said. "As I said, I'm not interested in ruling anything. I'm only proposing a truce until we resolve the problem with the sun. If we do nothing, then we're all doomed. Until we restore balance, we *must* work together. After that, you can go back to killing each other if you wish."

"It is not we who wish to kill the other."

"Do you think you're any better than they are?"

"Careful, lad," Enif warned.

Yolken jumped to his feet. "I will *not* be careful! And you will address me by my title!"

"I-I'm… yes, er… what are we to call you?"

Yolken looked over at his friends.

Jax shrugged his shoulders and said, "Highness?"

"Yes," Yolken said with a nod. He turned back to Enif and said, "You may address me as Your Highness."

"Yes, Your Highness," Enif said.

Yolken sat. He took a deep breath and wished he was back in Lonely Oak, where his biggest concern was getting Javen out of bed early enough to tend the bar so he could brew. "The Regency wants us all dead, I know. But is what you desire any better? Do you not wish to simply replace them with yourselves? And if you succeed in taking power, what will you do with them? Let them go?" He paused to let his words sink in. "The only possible resolution—at least for now—is to come together peacefully."

A moment of silence hung over the room.

"So you would go petition the emperor for a truce?" Enif asked. "As what? The Dragon King?"

"Yes."

"And you think he'll be amenable to someone using his father's title?"

"It was not his title."

"Nevertheless, it was the title he used while he subjugated the world. *And* the title he used while he ruled. Claiming it for yourself will not come without certain… implications."

"I'm not claiming it for myself. I just want to go home, make ale, and marry Kaylan—but it seems that Draego has different plans for me."

"You would go alone?" Enif said.

"No. As the head of a delegation."

Enif looked from left to right at the Council members sitting on both sides of him. "Might we have some time to discuss privately what you propose?" Enif said.

Yolken nodded. "But know this: A delegation *is* going to Kyinth. I stand by my decision to dissolve the Council. If you don't wish to be a part of my plan, then I will choose for myself who it will be."

Enif looked at Yolken momentarily, then rose to his feet. When he did, the other Council members stood as well. Enif gestured toward the door, and the Council filed slowly by Deanna, Jax, and Deborah.

When the door closed behind them, Jax said, "Well, I must say, I didn't expect that."

"What?" Yolken asked.

"For you to take control like that. Were you planning that the whole time?"

"No," Yolken said. "It just came to me, and I knew what I needed to do. What do you think?"

"About what?"

"My plan."

"I'm not sure."

"Honestly," Deborah said, "it's as good as any I've heard."

"*Really?*" Jax said.

"When was the last time anyone has suggested a peaceful resolution?"

"I… I can't remember," Jax said.

"That's because it hasn't happened in your lifetime."

"Deanna?" Yolken said, "I would, of course, want you to be a part of the delegation."

Deanna stared at her feet.

"Deanna? If the Council agrees to participate, would you be willing to join me in a delegation to talk to your brother?"

Deanna looked up at Yolken and said, "What exactly would be my purpose?"

"We must convince Drakonias to confront the problem. And nobody knows him as well as you. Everything I've been told indicates that he still refuses to accept what's happening, let alone do anything about it. Maybe it's because he doesn't know what *to* do. But if we all come together, maybe we can find a solution. If the Council agrees to a delegation, will you join me?"

Deanna studied Yolken pensively. "Whether the Council agrees or not," she said at last, "I will join you." Then she bowed.

CHAPTER 33

The side door opened, and the Council filed back into the chamber. Yolken eagerly watched them climb the steps of the raised platform, hoping that they had decided to cooperate with his plan. He was going to Kyinth to confront Drakonias whether they agreed to cooperate or not, but having the support of more people than just Jax, Deanna, and Deborah would be immensely helpful. Everyone except Enif took their seats. He remained standing, looking up at Yolken.

"Well?" Yolken said.

"We have decided to submit to your plan," Enif said.

Yolken stopped himself from breathing a sigh of relief. "Good," he said.

"However," Enif continued, "we want something in return."

"I'm not here to barter."

"Maybe not. But you need our help; else you would have gone straight to Kyinth instead of coming here. And help does not come without a price."

"He's right," Jax said. "Everything has its price."

Yolken wondered if that was true. One of Jax's main assets to the Order was that he gathered valuable information from his network of spies, and that information cost lots of money—he still wondered how Jax always seemed to have the right amount of gold about his person at the right time. But was the same true for Drakonias? Did he barter with the members of his Regency?

"Even for the king?" Yolken asked.

"*Especially* the king," Enif said. "Please, at least hear us out."

Yolken glanced over at Jax, Deanna, and Deborah. In unison, they nodded. He looked back at Enif and said, "All right. What is it that you want?"

"We will help you convince Drakonias to join with us in figuring out how to restore balance to the sun. However, we will not go to Kyinth as delegates representing the Order of the Dragon, but rather as delegates of the Dragon King."

"Delegates," Yolken said thoughtfully.

"The Order of the Dragon exists because we reject the legitimacy of Drakonias' rule. The throne upon which you sit is there to remind us why we risk our lives daily. It is no accident that you presently sit on the throne and have declared yourself Dragon King," Enif said.

"What do you mean?" Yolken asked.

"You are the king we've spent centuries dreaming about— the king we've fought for, the king we've died for. We will not help the lad Yolken Thornhill from Lonely Oak. However, we will help our king, Yolken Danavin Dairion Drake. To him, we will pledge all that we are and have. To him, we will pledge our lives."

"You want me to be your king?" Yolken asked. When he'd decided to ascend the dais and sit on the throne, he didn't think they would want him to actually *be* their king. He had only claimed the title and throne because he wanted to get the Order to focus on his goal. He was still resolved *not* to overthrow Drakonias. He was intent on doing what Deth sent him to do and then going home to Lonely Oak.

"Not just our king," Enif said. "We want you to reclaim the throne that rightly belongs to the Dragon King. If you promise to us that when this is done, when balance has been restored, that you will lay claim to the Dragon Throne, then we will do whatever you ask of us."

Yolken gripped the arms of the throne he sat upon. He looked down at the wood, considering what the throne represented. The arms were carved with intricate patterns. The lacquer made the wood shine in the light. He wondered if the carvings were the same as the actual Dragon Throne in Kyinth. He didn't want to *actually* be king. *I just want to restore balance to the sun and go home,* he repeated to himself. "Why?" he said.

"Why what?"

"Why me?" He didn't know the first thing about ruling.

"Because Drakonias is a usurper. He stole the Dragon Throne from its rightful owner."

Yolken's mind raced through all the lessons Selena had made him sit through as a child. "But I'm not the rightful ruler." Drae was his grandfather, but of all those who remained loyal to Draeko, Drae wasn't the next in the line of succession. He looked over at Deanna. If the throne belonged to anyone, it belonged to her.

Deanna met his gaze. She bowed her head and said, "The throne is yours, Yolken."

"But…"

"I know what you're thinking, but the Great Dragon has chosen you. The Great Dragon never meant for my father to follow the same patterns as the kings and queens he replaced."

"The Great Dragon didn't choose him to—"

"But he has chosen you," Deanna said. "*You* are the rightful king. The Dragon Throne belongs to you, and no one but you."

Deep down, Yolken knew this to be true. And deep down, he had known that the moment he sat on the throne that he would never get to go home. As much as he hated the thought, he knew that where Draeko had failed to stop Drakonias, he must succeed. He wanted people across Dradonia to experience the peace of the dragons. And to do that, he would need help.

"Fine," he said. "But know this: I do so not because I want to be king, but because I want peace. If the dragons could live in peace, then so can we." He thought about all the loss Deth had suffered for trying to help. "I don't want Deth's efforts to be for naught."

"Peace is all we've ever wanted," Enif said.

Yolken knew what he needed to do next. He felt foolish, but it needed to be done. He took a deep breath, knowing that once he stood and spoke, he would never be able to turn back. He looked at his friends standing to his right. Jax nodded, silently telling him he was doing the right thing.

Yolken closed his eyes and thought about Kaylan. He wondered if she would approve of who he was about to become. He hoped that she would but, at the same time, he would understand if she didn't. She wanted the same thing as him—to get married and raise a family in Lonely Oak. If he proceeded with what he was about to do, that wouldn't be possible. Would she still want to marry him? Doing so would make her—what? A queen?

What would Javen think? If he was still in Kyinth when Yolken arrived, what would he do? Yolken hoped he was still there, would still be there. He needed another chance to talk to him.

Taking another deep breath, Yolken stood. He transferred a small amount of Energy from his bones into his Core to help soothe his nervousness. How silly would it be if, in the middle of declaring himself the rightful ruler of Dradonia, he vomited?

With as steady a voice as he could muster, he said, "I am Yolken Danavin Dairion Drake"—he didn't like dropping his last name, but he wasn't a Thornhill anymore—"true Blessed of the Dragon, chosen ruler of Dradonia, Dragon King. Come, those who are willing, forsake your previous allegiances, and swear fealty to me."

He had never imagined he would be saying anything like this, so he had no idea how the words came so readily. They were just there.

Enif was the first to move. He climbed the steps and

stopped one from the top. "I have been the High Councilman of the Order of the Dragon for one hundred and eighteen years. I relinquish all the authority I have over the Order to you, Yolken Danavin Dairion Drake." He removed the dragon-embroidered stole from around his neck and knelt before Yolken. He laid the stole at Yolken's feet. "To you, I, Enif Maldon, pledge my life and loyalty." After a moment, Enif looked up at Yolken and whispered, "This is where you accept my offer."

"I acc… accept," Yolken said.

Enif smiled at him, then rose to his feet. He bowed at the waist and said, "Your Blessed Highness," then turned and descended the steps.

When Enif sat in his chair, Tabora rose to her feet. She ascended the steps and removed the dragon-embroidered stole from around her neck as well. She knelt before Yolken and, with a small variation appropriate to her seat on the Council, repeated the words that Enif had spoken. After she returned to her seat, the remainder of the Council followed one by one.

After the ninth Council member came Deanna. "The last time I swore fealty to anyone," she said, "it was to my father. That was fifteen hundred years ago, Yolken. And, for fifteen hundred years, I have lived a lie. I believed my father when he told me that the Great Dragon had blessed him. I followed him through countless campaigns while he slowly took control of, and brought under his rule, every kingdom on Dradonia. I married the man he told me to marry to help him secure his empire. I followed my father as he fought back against Drakonias, and those whom Drakonias convinced to betray him. I stood by his side as we slowly marched toward destruction we didn't even know we were causing. I wept bitterly when I stood by and watched my father surrender, forfeiting all that he had created. I did all that because I thought he was the Blessed of the Dragon. I thought that if we brought all the kingdoms of the world under his dominion, we could bring peace to a war-torn world. I was wrong.

"For the last four hundred years, I have hidden from the many wrongs we caused. In isolation, those wrongs have haunted me. That changed when I first saw you. In you, I saw hope. I saw in you an answer."

Why? Yolken wondered. He was just a brewer. How could she have thought any of that about him? He felt his eyes begin to glisten.

Deanna smiled at him. "An answer to what, exactly, I wasn't sure—at least not until I had the opportunity to speak with Jax and Deborah. Even then, I pushed back against what I knew must be. I wanted to restore the balance I'd helped disrupt, but I wanted nothing more to do with my brother. Now I know that is not what needs to be. He needs to be stopped. I now know that the answer to the problem that has existed since Deth first gave the gift of Synthesis to my father is you." Deanna climbed the last step and knelt. "To you, Yolken Danavin Dairion Drake, I, Deanna Aliza Drake, pledge my life and loyalty."

Jax ascended the dais next. "Your father and I were friends for a very long time. He was the one who discovered I had the gift and brought me into the Order. When you were born, he made me swear an oath that if anything ever happened to him, I would protect you. At the time, I never thought I would have to keep that oath; I never once thought anything would happen to your father. He was the infamous Danavin Drake! But after tragedy struck that fateful night in the tavern, I kept my oath. I've spent every day since then doing just that—and I extended that oath to your brother as well. Your father was one of the few people whom I was willing to do anything for. The efforts I made to retrieve his sword testify to the truth of what I say."

Jax paused for a moment, then continued, "You are your father's son, Yolken. And to you, Yolken Danavin Dairion Drake, I gladly pledge my allegiance." Jax knelt and bowed before Yolken. Standing back up, he added, "Your parents would be proud of who you have become."

Yolken blinked, and a tear fell. "Does this mean you're done giving me a hard time?" he said with a tearful laugh.

Jax smirked. "Yes, Your Highness." Bowing again, he turned and descended the dais.

Deborah was the last in the room to climb the steps and pledge her allegiance to Yolken. After she spoke the words and stood back up, Yolken asked, "Do you think Kaylan would approve?"

Deborah smiled, her own eyes glistening. "Dear, I don't think any sane person would voluntarily do what you're doing. You act not out of self-interest but out of selflessness. For that, I know with all my heart that Kaylan's love for you will do nothing but grow."

Yolken choked back a sob. Feeling tears run down his cheeks, he nodded, unable to speak.

"We're all proud of you, Yolken," Deborah said. She hugged him, then returned to her place with Jax and Deanna.

Yolken wiped his eyes, then said, "I never imagined I would ever travel more than fifty leagues from my home, let alone be sitting here. I never imagined I'd be the king of anything.

"I've often wondered," he continued, "whether or not things would have been different had I stayed in Lonely Oak the day I healed Issa. Would Selena still be alive? Would Javen have been taken prisoner? Most of what has occurred—to me and to those I love—has been a direct result of my fleeing from Lonely Oak." He paused. "As much as what's happened to them pains me, I have come to believe that Draego calls each of us to a specific purpose. Selena died protecting me from the Regency. Perhaps, in doing so, she fulfilled her purpose. I hate the idea that my brother is in the control of those who would do him harm, but perhaps he is there for a reason still unknown to us. Had I stayed in Lonely Oak, I probably would have been killed. I think that everything that has happened, has happened for a purpose.

"As your king," Yolken said, "I intend to fulfill the calling that Draego has placed upon me." Pausing again, he added, "But

I will need your help. You have centuries of knowledge and experience that I would be a fool to cast aside. If, or when, the day comes that I move against Drakonias, I will be unsuccessful if I attempt to go it alone." Yolken looked down at those below him intently. "I name each of you Advisors of the Dragon King. If you accept this role, come and retrieve your stoles."

Without hesitation, the Council members climbed the dais and retrieved their stoles.

When they finished, Yolken said, "We need three more for Deanna, Jax, and Deborah."

"Uh, yes," Enif said. "Tabora, would you go retrieve—"

"Actually," Yolken interjected, "I would like you to do it."

"Me?"

"You are all on equal footing now, Enif."

"Yes… Your Highness." Enif bowed his head slightly then moved quickly to the side door. He returned after a few moments with three stoles and presented them to Deanna, Jax, and Deborah. Yolken was pleased to see that Enif had also exchanged the stole he'd previously worn for one that matched the others.

"Now that that is behind us," Yolken said, his stomach and bowels no longer threatening unpleasantness, "I need something to eat."

CHAPTER 34

Whoever heard of a brewer turned king, anyway?" Jax said as he walked alongside Yolken. Deanna, Deborah, and the rest of Yolken's new advisors trailed behind.

"So you've just exchanged harassing me about Synthesizing for harassing me about being a brewer?" Yolken said.

"I've got to keep things light, you know. Can't always be serious about everything."

"You know, as your king, I could just send you away."

"You wouldn't dare. I swore an oath, remember."

"Don't you think you've fulfilled that oath?"

"I think you'll need my protection now more than ever."

"You think I need protecting?" Yolken asked.

"You are, without a doubt, stronger than me in Synthesis," Jax said. "But there's still much for you to learn."

Jax opened the door to the lounge room for Yolken and gave him a slight bow as he walked through. Deanna and Deborah followed. Jax went to shut the door but stopped when Enif said, "Hold on now."

"What?" Jax said.

"There should be some sort of rule in place about who gets to be alone with the lad… I mean with the king."

"What are you talking about?" Yolken said.

"I mean… it's just… we've had… the Council has had certain authority for centuries. I don't think we should be cut out of proceedings all of a sudden."

"What proceedings?" Yolken asked. "I'm hungry. I'm just getting something to eat."

"But," Enif said, "undoubtedly there will be a discussion about where to go from here. Your friends will no doubt have certain… um… influence."

"Are you asking if you can join me?"

"I… yes, very much so. Uh, Your Highness."

"Fine," Yolken said with a nod.

Enif tentatively stepped through the door then waved the other advisors off.

Jax shut the door, then directed his attention to the food table.

"Have a seat, Your Highness," Enif said, "and we'll see to your needs."

Yolken hesitated, but Enif motioned toward a couch, so he went and sat. When Enif brought him a plate, he ate voraciously.

He watched as Jax peered into every decanter. "Isn't there any proper drink in this place?" Jax said.

"We have Ontan wine right here," Enif said, pointing toward one of the decanters Jax already looked into.

Jax furrowed his brow, wrinkled his nose, and shook his head.

"You and your *ale*," Enif said, as though the word tasted bad. "Sorry, but you're the only one who drinks the stuff, and you're hardly around, so we don't—"

"Make it a habit of having it available," Jax finished for him. "Yeah, yeah, I know. And we go through this every time I *am* here." He poured wine into a glass and said, "We'll have to see about changing that." He took a sip and made another face. "Not for me. For the king," he said with a wink toward Yolken.

Everybody gathered around Yolken, sitting where they could on couches, and ate.

"Start getting used to it, lad," Jax said.

"To what?" Yolken said.

"People waiting on you."

"What if I don't want them to?"

"You don't have a choice."

"Why not?"

"It's just the way things are." Jax took a drink of wine and, after shaking his head, said, "Now, let's talk about this delegation."

Yolken nodded. "Who else do you think should come?"

"Before we talk about who *should* come, let's talk about who shouldn't."

Yolken looked sternly at Jax. "I know what you're going to say."

"Kings don't do their own work, lad."

"I'm going."

"They make others do it for them."

"If there's any chance of this working, it has to be me."

"Sorry, lad. I won't allow it."

"Won't *allow* it?" Yolken said tersely.

"My father did it," Deanna said.

Everyone looked at her.

"Did what?" Yolken said.

"He didn't come to rule Dradonia overnight," she said. "And kings and queens didn't give up their kingdoms peacefully."

"No," Jax said. "It's not going to happen."

"He led every campaign," Deanna continued.

"I swore to protect him."

"Then go with him. But the time for treating him like a child who needs protecting is past."

"I'm going," Yolken averred.

Jax snorted and gulped the red liquid he could barely tolerate.

"Before you go to Kyinth," Enif said, "I think there's something else you should do first."

"What?" Yolken said.

"When you go to Kyinth, you want to do so from a position of power."

"Meaning?"

"You should send Drakonias a message that shows him exactly who you are."

"Such as?"

"Croff is the headquarters of the Order. Until we remove Drakonias from the Dragon Throne, you will need a capital. I say we take Croff."

Yolken shook his head.

"It'll give legitimacy to your claim and show Drakonias who he's contending with."

"No," Yolken said.

"But—"

"My answer is no."

"Your Highness, if you—"

"If you wish to remain an advisor," Yolken said sternly, "you'll let it go. Taking Croff forcefully—which is what would happen, as I'm sure Dalia won't hand the city over freely—will undoubtedly result in people dying. I've already said I don't want this—any of this—and I certainly don't want to be someone who starts wars."

"As soon as word gets out about you," Enif said, "people *will* die."

"Then we don't let word get out," Yolken said, "at least not until we're ready. Now, enough talk. Let me eat, and then we'll reconvene our discussion about the delegation."

After that, the group ate in silence. When everyone finished, they returned to the Council chamber, or as it was now, Yolken's throne room.

"In the interest of keeping you a secret," Enif started after everyone was once again assembled, "we need to limit the size of the delegation."

"I agree," Deborah said. "Sending too large a group would

be alarming."

Yolken nodded his agreement. "How many do you suggest?"

"I propose that you send a maximum of six," Enif said. "A group of that size shouldn't attract attention while you travel to Kyinth."

"Six it is," Yolken said.

"But I must assert that if you insist on going to the capital and announcing yourself as the Dragon King, Drakonias will see it as a provocation."

"I understand."

"The emperor will *not* respond amicably."

"If you're trying to suggest that I not go or that I cancel the trip altogether, that's not going to happen."

"Understood," Enif said with a bow. "Then who do you wish to be in your delegation?"

"Myself, Deanna, Jax, Deborah, and whomever else you choose."

Enif turned to his left and looked past Rheena. He gestured at the next two sitting next to her. Corin and Tabora. "They've volunteered to go with you."

Yolken nodded. He looked toward Tabora and Corin and said, "I know what I'm doing is dangerous, but I'm guessing that when you volunteered, you already knew this?"

"Yes, Your Highness," Tabora said with a bow.

"And you willingly accept this risk?"

She nodded.

"And what about you?" Yolken asked Corin.

"I do, Your Highness," Corin said.

"And you?" Yolken asked, looking toward his friends.

"You are our king," Jax said. "We'll do whatever you ask."

Deborah and Deanna nodded their agreement.

"Even permit me to put myself in danger?"

Jax smiled and let out a little snort. "Yes, Your Highness."

"And what of the rest of you?" Yolken said. "What will you be doing in our absence?"

"We will begin to lay the groundwork for your rule, Your Highness," Enif said.

Yolken looked down at him and said, "Good. Then let us make preparations. I intend to be on the road by morning."

CHAPTER 35

It had been a few days shy of a month since Hadie had met with her father, and four days since she'd first heard the rumor about an upcoming event at the chancellor's palace. The excitement she and the girls felt after Edill brought word of the event had died down. She'd expected to receive an invitation, but thus far had not. She worried a little more each day that it wouldn't come. Now she could hardly sit still in her seat as she oversaw business in the lobby.

A man Hadie didn't recognize entered the brothel. He wore a finely tailored suit, as fine as any Silk in Hantlo. Even growing up as the privileged daughter of one, she didn't know them all. She'd received a few new clients in the time she had been running the brothel, so she wasn't surprised to see a new face. The more business the brothel conducted, the more money the girls would have when this was all over.

She rose to her feet to greet him as he started in her direction. "How may I help you?" she said. She knew he didn't have an appointment, as all the girls were presently with clients.

"Madam Sheena, I presume," the man said. He held a hand out toward her.

"I am," she said.

She reached out her hand, and he took it into his and kissed the back of it. "Might I have a word in private?"

Hadie looked at him suspiciously. "May I ask what about?"

"Certainly. I wish to speak to you about your father."

Hadie's breath caught, and a spike of fear shot up her spine. "Right this way," she said.

She led him toward the beaded curtain and through the brothel. She closed the door to her room behind the man and waited expectantly. She fingered the bottom of her corset, where the knife was hidden. She was ready if he made a move toward her.

The man walked farther into her room. He brushed his fingers along the top of her desk before turning to face her.

"You have news from my father?" Hadie said.

"Not per se," the man said. "Let me start by introducing myself. My name is Sethlan, and I am His Highness' personal servant."

Hadie's eyes widened, and her mind raced. What could he possibly want? And why was he dressed in a suit? *That* was certainly not typical servants' clothing.

She reached for her knife but stopped when Sethlan said, "Fear not, lass." He sat in one of two matching chairs on the back side of Hadie's desk, then said, "Your secret is safe with me."

"My secret?" Hadie said. She walked around the desk.

"Yes. Your father. Please sit," Sethlan said, gesturing at her chair.

Hadie tentatively sat, keeping her back straight.

"He came to see the chancellor. Fortunately—for you—His Highness was a bit preoccupied at the moment and was not taking visitors."

"Wh-what did he want?"

Sethlan reached into an inner pocket in his suit and pulled out an envelope. He held it out over the desk toward Hadie and said, "To give him this."

Hadie took the envelope, which was open, and pulled out a

letter. She unfolded it and read. Her stomach started to roil. When she finished, she said, "Has the chancellor seen this?"

"He has not."

Hadie breathed a mental sigh of relief. She sat back in her chair, still clutching the letter in one hand, and rested both her arms on the armrests.

"It seems your father was not inclined to take you up on your offer," Sethlan said. "In fact, it seems he was *so* against it that he was willing to turn his own daughter in… which would have ended only one way."

"I'd have been hanged," Hadie said. She studied the well-dressed man sitting across from her.

"You're quite fortunate His Highness was preoccupied when your father came to see him."

"I was?"

"It enabled me to intercept his letter."

"And you didn't give it to him?"

"I did not."

"Why?"

"Wine."

"Wine? Why would you do that for—" Hadie said, thoroughly confused.

"Do you have any wine?" Sethlan said.

"Oh," Hadie said. "Yes, over there."

Sethlan pushed himself to his feet and went to the table in the corner where Hadie gestured. He poured two glasses of wine then returned, setting one in front of Hadie. After sitting, he took a sip from his glass and said, "I am a man who collects information."

Hadie sipped from hers and waited for him to continue.

"I'm paid quite well to listen and collect bits of information that might be of value."

"For whom?" Hadie asked.

"My true employer."

"You're a spy."

Sethlan nodded.

"Who do you work for?"

"A man named Jorgan," Sethlan said. "Know him?"

Hadie shook her head.

"I suppose you wouldn't; why would you?" Sethlan sipped his wine. "Unless…"

"Unless what?"

"You're a rebel and would, therefore, lie about your association."

"I said I don't know him, and I'm not a rebel."

"Well, he knows you."

"He does?"

"I told him about you, anyhow."

"Why would you do that?"

Sethlan drank from his wine. "It's not every day that the Blessed give lessons to a rogue Synthesizer."

"*Javen…*" Hadie said quietly.

"So I naturally took an interest in him. You knew him, didn't you."

Hadie nodded, fighting back tears.

"Of course you did. You were bedding him. Question is, do you really *know* him? I mean, who he really is."

Hadie studied Sethlan, not sure how to respond. For all she knew, he was trying to pry information out of her.

"Do you know who his father is?"

"He told me his mother and father died in a fire when he was young."

"But do you know who he was? Or what the brother of this lover of yours has done?"

Hadie sipped her wine and said, "You tell me. Better yet, tell me why you told your employer about me."

"Because I was, admittedly, a bit surprised when the father of the lass bedding someone of interest to my employer showed up to turn her in for plotting a rebellion."

"Why would your employer be interested in Javen?"

"Because of who Javen is. Who Javen and his brother are."

"Who?"

"Blessed. Only they aren't. They're rebels."

"Javen wasn't a rebel," Hadie said.

"Perhaps not. But his father was."

"What interest does your employer have with rebels?" Hadie regretted the question the moment she asked it. She knew the answer. "Oh."

"Yes. And now, the lad's lover is attempting something that my employer would be *most* interested in."

"Which is why you told him about me."

"Exactly." Sethlan sipped his wine.

Hadie did the same. Sethlan's employer must have sent him here, else why had he come? "And?"

Sethlan fished a small piece of parchment from a pocket inside his suit coat. He handed it to Hadie and said, "He sent me this."

Hadie took it from him and read, *"Ensuring her success reaps great reward."* She lowered the rolled parchment and said, "He wants you to help me?"

"It's the only reason that pretty neck of yours hasn't seen a noose."

Hadie gently touched her neck with the fingers of one hand. She took a sip of wine and considered what Sethlan said. Truthfully, she felt small. Insignificant. She'd taken a lot of risks since returning to Hantlo, and it had always worked out. But this time… she couldn't believe her father had betrayed her. She *had* threatened him, but she was his daughter. Should she follow through with her threat now that she knew he wouldn't help?

"I've been pondering why you would tell your father your plans," Sethlan said. "And I have to say, it makes sense."

"What does?"

"The Silks. They're every bit as greedy as the Blessed—some of them *are* Blessed, albeit the lessers."

Hadie hadn't thought of that. The regents weren't the only

ones who were Blessed. They had children and grandchildren of their own, all of them richer than anyone else in the realm.

"I can tell by the look on your face I've uncovered a flaw in your plan," Sethlan said.

"I don't know how it's possible I forgot about them."

"Don't worry about them."

"I don't want to do this only to have more Blessed take over."

"They won't."

"How can you be sure?"

"Your mother."

"My mother?"

"You'd be surprised how much influence she has with the Silks, and I have several of my own contacts. But we're going to have to work fast. Dorlan is hosting his regents in six days, and I've added your brothel to the list of invited guests." Sethlan finished his wine and said, "Your father will be away tomorrow, so go talk with your mother. Then, be ready. Your invitation will soon arrive."

"Will Drenan be there?" Hadie said. The reign of the Blessed needed to end, so the path she was on was one of necessity, but Drenan... he was the only one that she *wanted* to kill.

"Unfortunately, no. He went to Onta and is now wrapped up in the Reago business that has His Highness upset."

"What business is that?" She tried her best not to betray her disappointment.

"Never mind that," Sethlan said, rising to his feet. "Point is, he's powerless to stop what's about to happen. Go see your mother."

Hadie nodded, then Sethlan turned to leave.

Hadie didn't know who she wanted to see less: Drenan or her mother. She knew that by leaving her parents behind, she had likely broken her mother's heart. She hadn't wanted to hurt her mother, but at the same time, she couldn't stay in the south any longer. And now, she didn't want to go to her mother, to face the hurt she caused her, but her endeavor wasn't going to succeed without the help of the Silks. There was no one else she could turn to. She picked up her glass and went over to the table to refill it. She upended it, drinking down the content in three big gulps, then filled it anew.

CHAPTER 36

Hadie's head pounded, and she'd hardly slept. She'd had Ursella make her tea extra strong when the servant had come to wake her from what little sleep she *did* get, but she still fought to stifle her incessant yawning as the attendant led her down the long entryway to the home she grew up in.

Hadie stopped at the top of the porch steps—made from the same brown slate the majority of the city was made from—and said, "I'll wait out here."

"Yes, ma'am," the attendant said. "I'll go let Lady Tara know you're here."

"Thank you." Hadie walked down the covered porch, looking at the potted flowers as she went. She stopped at a bench near where the porch curved around the side of the house. The heat was stifling, and here there was a slight breeze. She tried her best not to fidget.

After several minutes, a middle-aged woman with her hair in a bun emerged from the front door. Hadie rose to her feet. When her mother saw her, she covered her mouth with her hand and walked briskly toward Hadie.

Tara wrapped Hadie in a hug and said, "I thought I'd never see you again."

Hadie hugged her back, and let her mother hold her for as

long as she wanted. When she finally let go, Hadie said, "I wish you and Pap would have come with me."

Tara sat on the bench. "You know we couldn't leave, Hadie."

Hadie sat next to her.

"I wish you had stayed," Tara said. "But now you're back. For good, I hope?"

Hadie shook her head. A silence hung in the air. Hadie tried her best to meet her mother's expectant gaze.

"What are you doing here, then?"

"There's something I need to talk to you about," Hadie said.

"Yes, dear?"

"Something is about to happen that you need to know about…"

"What?"

"But first, I need to tell you something about Pap," Hadie said.

Her mother's eyes narrowed.

"I've been back in Hantlo for a while now, and—"

"And you're just now finding the time to come see me?"

"I've been running a brothel."

"A *brothel?* Why would you ever want to get into whoring? You have all you could ever want right here—"

"I didn't have…" Hadie started. "Never mind. That's not why I'm here. Have you ever heard of Sonja?"

Her mother nodded.

"Well, she left Hantlo, and I took over her brothel."

"Sonja's? Why?"

"Because I'm using it to do what I came back to Hantlo for."

"Which is what? Spit it out, Hadie. You're taking longer than it takes a dragon's egg to hatch."

Dragons were creatures of fable—except the Great Dragon, of course—but her mother was fond of the saying. She'd always wondered how long it took a dragon's egg to hatch. But her mother was right; she was avoiding saying what she came here to say, so she just blurted it out. "I'm going to overthrow the

Regency."

Tara just stared at her. She looked deep in thought. Eventually, she said, "And what does this have to do with your father?"

"He came to the brothel shortly after I started running it," Hadie said. "Turns out, he was a regular."

"Erig!" Tara called.

The attendant emerged from the front door of the house and walked over to them. "Yes, ma'am?"

"Bring us some wine, please."

"Yes, ma'am," Erig said.

"Something from the cellar," Tara called just before he disappeared through the door. "How far did you make it before you came back?"

"A little over halfway to Croff," Hadie said.

"Why did you come back?"

"Do you really want to know?"

"I wouldn't have asked if I didn't."

"I met someone."

"Someone from Hantlo?"

"No, Ma. He was from a little town called Lonely Oak."

"Where's that?"

"In the north."

Tara looked confused.

"There was a festival celebrating the presence of Dorlan, of all things, and I met Javen there."

"And how did Javen end up here?"

"He didn't." Seeing the confused look on her mother's face, Hadie said, "It's a long story."

"Well, Erig *is* bringing wine."

Hadie smirked.

They sat in awkward silence until Erig returned with an open bottle and two wine glasses. He handed a glass to Hadie's mother and the other to Hadie, then filled them both with wine.

"Leave the bottle," Tara said.

Erig set the bottle between them, then excused himself.

Not really wanting to talk to her mother about her father's sexual proclivities, Hadie talked through the bottle about her trip north, meeting Javen, and how she'd ended up back in Hantlo. The wine made her headache go away and emboldened her to say what she needed to say. So, when the conversation died back down, she said, "I'm planning on starting a rebellion. Here. In Hantlo."

"You've said. How?"

"By killing Dorlan and his regents."

Tara stared down into her glass of wine.

"Ma?"

"Are you insane, Hadie?" Tara looked back up at her, her eyes intense.

"It was you who gave me the idea."

"Me?"

"Remember what you always used to say about how beautiful I was?"

"That your beauty diminished that of the setting sun."

"It *is* beautiful. I love how it turns this red color as it approaches the horizon."

"The Blood River," Tara said.

"Exactly."

"Tell me how you plan to do something nobody has ever successfully done."

"Sonja had this poisoned hairpin. I was going to use it to kill Drenan, but he got called away before I could. I was this close, Ma," Hadie said, gesturing with her index finger and thumb. "This close. I was standing in his quarters. So, when I started wondering if I could kill them all, I wondered if I could get more of those pins."

"And?"

"I found out who made them. They're made from those flowers you have along your entryway," Hadie said. She turned and looked over the railing and pointed at the potted yellow flowers.

"Those?" Tara asked. "Erig says they're from the north."

"They are, and the oils are deadly to humans." Hadie spent the next few minutes explaining her plan to her mother and finished by saying, "But it won't work without the support of the Silks."

"Which is where your father comes in?"

Forced to return to the subject she wanted to avoid discussing with her mother, Hadie said, "Pap was a regular at Sonja's. After I started the brothel back up, he returned. I knew I needed something in place if I killed Dorlan, so I turned to Pap. I told him if he didn't help me, I'd come to you about his… indiscretions."

"You know he doesn't respond well to threats, dear."

"I know. And he didn't. He went to Dorlan."

"Phen turned his *own* daughter over to the Regency?" Tara said. She sounded exasperated.

Hadie nodded.

"But then… how are you still alive?"

"Only because Dorlan's servant is sympathetic to the rebels, the Order of the—"

"Dragon," Tara finished. "So Dorlan's servant—"

"Intercepted Pap's message to Dorlan and then came to see me. He said his contact in the Order instructed him to help me." Hadie sipped from what was left in her glass and said, "Ma, I don't know about you, but I hate the Regency; I hate the stranglehold it's had on the empire. There has to be another way; a way without—"

"They're the Blessed of the Dragon."

"They still die, just like you and me. They may use their gift to live longer than us, but they still die. And what are they doing to help the south? The realm is imploding, and they're not doing anything about it."

"And what are we supposed to do?" Tara said.

"I don't know. I just know it's time for someone else to have a shot at ruling."

"You mean me?"

"Yes, you. Who else is better fit to usher the south into the next era—an era without the Regency?"

"Your father would never go for it. He's already demonstrated that by—"

"He is only a Silk because of you, Ma. You hold the power—and the others know it."

Tara sipped her wine. "People are going to die, you know."

"I know," Hadie acknowledged.

"The emperor won't just let one of his realms withdraw from the empire."

"He didn't do anything about the east."

"That wasn't because someone killed a bunch of Blessed." Tara looked thoughtfully at Hadie. "Why are you doing this?"

"I grew up privileged," Hadie said. "I had things that most people don't. I think it's largely due to the way the Regency has things set up. I think everyone deserves the opportunity to live like us, and I think you do, too. I can tell by how you treat those who work for you."

"That's not enough. Tell me why."

"I want the Regency gone because I know how they really are. Sure, on the surface, they seem benevolent, but underneath they're cruel and evil. I experienced what they are capable of firsthand when Javen and I were trapped in Dorlan's caravan."

"What if they find you out before you have the chance to poison them?"

"It's a risk I'm willing to take," Hadie said. She watched her mother stare pensively into her glass. "I'm doing this, Ma, whether you're willing to help or not. But I *need* your help. It'll be much better—for everyone—if you're there to lead the rebellion."

Tara twisted on the bench and looked over her shoulder at the yellow flowers lining the manicured entryway. "You think this will work?"

"I do," Hadie said. "They're rebelling in the west. Why not here?"

"From what I understand, they're not having much success."

"Maybe not. But I'm at least willing to try."

"Then," Tara said, turning and looking directly at Hadie, "let's make the blood river flow."

CHAPTER 37

Yolken rode out of Croff on horseback, surrounded by his delegation. He had wanted to take Ollie, but the horse was still recovering from his efforts to bring Yolken to Croff. Yolken was, however, glad to see that Ollie was recovering well—despite Jax's assertions, he had worried that they'd run the horses to death.

The season had now turned to fall, but it was hot out under the sun. The summer heat didn't typically start abating until weeks after the fall moon festival, but he knew all of Dradonia was getting progressively hotter. He'd noticed it the last few years with poor snowpack up in the Mindons. Whereas he was accustomed to having to watch the Little Mindon closely in the spring for potential flooding—his tavern sat right next to the creek, and he relied on its waters for his brewing—flooding hadn't been a concern the last few years. And now he knew why.

The sun's oppressiveness caused Yolken to look up at it. He shielded his eyes after a second, unable to look directly at it longer. He scoured his mind, trying to find a clue in his conversations with Deth as to how he was supposed to restore the sun's balance. *What was taken must be replaced.* It was impossible.

Solarian.

Yolken reflected on the lessons taught in the Dragon Shrine, even though it had been ages since he had last been. The sun sustained life on Dradonia. But the sun itself was sustained by Draego. From the Ether, Draego breathed its power into the sun, and the sun in turn gave that power—Energy, he now knew—to Dradonia. *If the sun is out of balance, why doesn't Draego fix it?* Yolken wondered. Was Draego punishing Dradonia for what Drakonias did? But either way, Yolken was *not* Draego, so he didn't know why Deth believed he had the ability to replace the Energy that had been taken. He squinted, forcing himself to look at the sun again. He almost thought he saw Deth circling before he was forced to look down. Just his imagination, he knew, as Deth had abandoned him in the Ontalis.

They traveled in plain clothing and had their dragon bones—the Harachin and Aliza swords, as well as the best bones the Order possessed for the others—wrapped in bundles and stored in saddlebags or on the back of the saddle. Jax had his coat, which, despite his ingrained habit, he had rolled up on the back of his saddle. Yolken still couldn't believe Jax wore that thing even in the hot summer months. But now that he knew Jax had tiny bones woven throughout the hems, it made perfect sense.

They traveled considerably more slowly than they had on their way back from the west. Yolken wanted to arrive in Kyinth quickly, but at the same time he heeded the caution that they would prematurely alert the emperor if they weren't careful. They didn't travel at a completely normal pace, though. They alternated between boosting the horses' stamina and riding at normal paces used for long-distance journeys. At times their progress was excruciatingly slow.

Over the course of several days, Yolken sank progressively into pensiveness. He tried to remain optimistic and confident about his plan to petition Drakonias for peace, but as his mood inevitably began to change, he drifted to the back of the group and rode alone. He didn't want to be the king of anything, and his new advisors were already talking about him laying claim to the Dragon Throne when they met with the emperor. But he didn't want that. He didn't want to rule. He simply wanted a truce long enough for them to figure out how to restore balance to the sun, and then to return home. And the thought that that was never going to happen dragged his spirits down.

Deanna dropped back from the others and joined Yolken. "How's it going?"

Yolken shook his head.

"Want to talk about it?"

"I know we're doing what we have to," Yolken said, "but going before the emperor—something I never thought I'd *ever* do in my life—claiming to be a king is starting to sound insane."

"It's normal for rulers to have doubt."

"It is?"

"I don't know what my father thought when he first came into power—I don't even know what his life was like before he became king because he never talked about it—but I do know that just like you, he often doubted."

"He did?"

"He doubted himself—what he was doing—almost daily. And, despite what history might say, my father was not insane, or a tyrant. Even though he kept the truth from his children, I know his heart and intentions were in the right place. He wanted nothing more than what every sane person wants: peace. Like you, he didn't want to rule, but he did it because he knew it needed doing," Deanna said.

"Just like me," Yolken repeated.

"And even though he had doubts, he succeeded," Deanna continued. "For the first time in the history of humanity, my father established worldwide peace. But remember, he didn't want to rule—he did so only because he knew he needed to."

"Deanna?"

"Hmm?"

"I've been wondering… what exactly was it that made

Drakonias want to betray your father?"

"Well, I don't think there's ever a simple answer for questions like that. But I think in part it was our father's vision of returning power to those he ruled. He shared this vision with his children, and some of them were against it."

"Why?"

"You have to understand, Yolken, we lived as gods likened unto Draego himself. Just as people worshiped the Great Dragon who guarded over the night, many had come to worship the Blessed as well."

"And Drakonias didn't want to give that up?"

"No, he did not. He didn't betray our father at first. He bided his time. Our father put his plan on hold, hoping to win the unanimous support of all his children before he acted. He was naïve, though. While he worked to convince us to all go along with his plan, Drakonias plotted to overthrow him. Once he had enough support, he acted."

"So Draeko wanted to give his power away?"

"Mmm-hmm."

"Do you think that's what I should do?"

"I'm not saying that. What I am saying is that when circumstances force you into a position you'd rather not be in, you'll do what you know is the right thing. Just as you're doing now. Just as I believe you will successfully restore balance to the sun, I have complete confidence in you to do what needs doing. Whatever that might be."

"Thanks."

"I wouldn't be here if I thought otherwise," Deanna said. "You'll do just fine, son of Danavin."

* * *

Deanna spurred her horse and brought herself back up alongside Deborah and Jax, leaving Yolken to once again ride alone.

"And how is our young king?" Jax said.

"As good as can be expected for someone going to openly defy the emperor," Deanna said.

Jax looked over his shoulder at Yolken.

"He sure has come a long way, hasn't he," Deanna said. "Even in the short time that I've known him. He reminds me of his father."

"Me too. A little *too* much. And I hardly recognize the lad who fled his home mere months ago. I knew he was special, but I never imagined this would be his future. You know," Jax said, looking over at Deanna, "if we fail, it's likely we won't leave Kyinth alive."

"I know. But if he fails, it won't matter."

"Do you believe it's up to him?"

"It has to be."

"Why?"

"Because it's impossible. Think about what it is he's supposed to do. Nobody can do that. The very thought is insanity. So it has to be."

"And you have no idea what he's supposed to do?"

"No," Deanna admitted.

"Do you think your brother does?"

"I don't know. That's why we're going to Kyinth, isn't it? To find out?"

"I suppose."

They rode along in silence for a while. Deanna tried not to think about the fact that she was riding to confront her brother. She hadn't seen him since he had executed their father. She worried that her presence was going to have a negative influence on Yolken's efforts. She knew that when Drakonias laid eyes on her, he was as likely to attack her as not. But Yolken insisted. And he was her king. She'd sworn her allegiance to him, so she continued.

After a while, she said, "I lied."

Jax turned to look at her. "About what?"

"When we first met, I told you that I hadn't met Deth until after Yolken's father came to see me. Truth is, I already knew Deth, and I took Danavin to see him."

Jax looked at her, his eyes wide. "*And?*"

"I don't know what Deth said to Danavin. But you know

what's interesting?"

"What?"

"Danavin told me that at some point his son would come to see me as well."

Jax stared over at Deanna as though he didn't know what to say. Eventually, he was able to stammer, "Orwyn knew—what... three hundred years ago?—that he would have a son who would also come to see you?"

Deanna nodded. "And that I was supposed to take him to see Deth as well."

"How could he possibly have known that Yolken would... Orwyn's death precipitated our entire trip to find you!"

"I don't know what to tell you, Jax. All I know is that Danavin said it would happen."

"And you didn't tell us, *why*?"

"Yolken couldn't know."

"You could've at least told me!"

"I couldn't risk him finding out."

"Finding out what?"

Deanna shook her head. "He just had to arrive at the path he was destined to take on his own. If he ever found out that his father had also visited Deth, it would have led to too many questions which, if answered, would have affected his decisions."

Jax looked back over his shoulder at Yolken again. Then he turned back to Deanna and said, "It still would have been nice to know."

Deanna shrugged.

"What is that?" Jax said. "Some sort of an apology?"

"No. I'm not sorry."

"No, apparently you're not."

"You're right, I'm not. And you can't tell him."

Jax snorted then pulled back on his reins to slow his horse. When he fell behind her, she turned in her saddle and looked as crossly at him as she could.

"No telling him," she said.

"I won't."

CHAPTER 38

Why so glum, Your Highness?"

Yolken looked down from the sun at Jax, who was riding next to him. "Just thinking."

"About what?"

He wasn't about to tell Jax that his mind was playing games with him. He wasn't going to tell him that he had the nagging feeling that Deth was following him. He'd specifically asked Deth to help him—he'd even asked Deth to take him to Kyinth, but Deth had refused. So why would he be following him? Yolken knew it was silly and just the heat playing with his imagination. "Do I really have to spell it out for you?"

"Have I ever told you about the day your father died?"

Yolken perked up. Jax had always refused to talk about the night his parents died, despite Yolken's efforts to get him to. Now he shook his head. "You've managed to avoid telling me every time I've asked."

"Well, I'm going to tell you now."

"*Really?*"

"I suppose if you ordered me to."

"Huh?"

"I don't particularly enjoy remembering that night…"

"No, you don't."

"But if you were to order me to, then as your loyal subject, I would be obligated to, wouldn't I?"

Yolken stared blankly at Jax.

"Just order me to, lad."

"I… uh… order you to tell me about the night my parents died," Yolken said. Remembering the first conversation he'd had with the Council, Enif had said it had something to do with someone named… what was her name? Dentra? He remembered asking about her after the meeting, and just as Deborah had been about to tell Yolken who she was, Jax had cut her off. He'd always meant to ask him about it, but Jax had eluded his every effort. "It had something to do with Dentra's death, didn't it?"

"Detron," Jax said.

"Detron," Yolken repeated. Maybe she was a he. It was so long ago, and much of the meeting with the Council was so blurry that he couldn't really remember. "Who was he?"

"Not he. It."

Yolken looked at Jax, confused. "What?"

"You know I don't like talking about this, right?"

"Yes, you just said that."

"Well, aside from my feelings for your parents, there were reasons I couldn't tell you. Nobody outside of the Order could know what happened. Not to your father, but to Detron."

"Okay…"

"But now that you know the real threat we—all of Dradonia—face, there's no sense in keeping it from you any longer."

"You said reasons. Plural," Yolken said.

"I did."

"Why else?"

"Because it's all my fault."

"Detron's death, you mean?"

"No," Jax said. "It wasn't the Council's fault the Regency found your father that day; it was mine."

Yolken looked over at Jax again. Jax rode stiffly, staring straight ahead. He looked... sad.

"Sharing responsibility for your father's—and mother's—deaths is something I've had to live with every day."

"I'm sure it wasn't your fault," Yolken said to console Jax.

"Judge for yourself," Jax said. "The events that led up to that fateful night began long before you were born. It all started in 295."

"When Drakonias issued the edict?" It was a date Yolken was now well familiar with.

"That was when he finally understood what was happening to the sun. However, about fifty years before that, he issued another edict banning an art known as Astronomy."

"What's that?"

"It was the art of studying the stars. Drakonias banned it, then commissioned a solitary astronomer to study the sun. The Order, thanks to your father, managed to learn about the astronomer's work just before he reported his findings to the emperor. And, for the right price, the astronomer was willing to betray the emperor."

"He told you what he found?" Yolken said.

"He gave your father a copy of his report. And the astronomer's report made certain predictions. The day the Council met your father in Lonely Oak was the day one of those predictions occurred."

* * *

"You're sure today's the day?" your father said as he walked down the dusty road in the middle of Lonely Oak.

"Yes," I said.

The meeting was at the Haven, so that was where we were headed. The lobby was empty, which wasn't entirely uncommon in the middle of the afternoon, so I pulled the hood of my cloak off my head. And yes, before you offer some sort of snide remark, I had a cloak back then. I led your father to the stairs and up to the second floor.

"How can you be sure?" Orwyn said.

"Didn't you read the report?"

"My job was to procure it," Orwyn said, "not read it. Besides, I couldn't understand all the symbols the astronomer used."

"They *are* strange until you learn what they mean."

"Were you able to find a bone that'll fit the Telescope?"

"Yes," I said. "But it's not charged."

Orwyn let out an audible sigh. "That's to be expected, I suppose. Was it too much for me to expect you to charge it on the way here?"

"In broad daylight?" I said, even though I knew he was right. I should have risked it. And now, instead of charging it slowly over time, we were going to charge it quickly, and in the middle of town.

"It's going to put us at considerable risk, you know."

"I know."

"All the more reason that you must be certain of the day."

"Today is the day."

"The Telescope's assembled?"

"Yes."

Orwyn nodded determinedly. I led him down the hallway to the last room on the left. When I knocked on the door, it cracked open. Peering eyes assessed us, then opened the door fully.

Six faces greeted us: three men and three women. Two of the women sat on the bed, and the others were standing, looking impatient. The Telescope—an Energy-powered Machine long ago banned by the emperor—was mounted on a stand and angled toward the window in the room.

"Welcome, Orwyn," Corin said.

"Corin," Orwyn said, nodding at the man. He greeted the others—Tabora, Rheena, Dannl, and Jerle—solemnly, but smiled when he saw Selena. I had been able to convince the Council to let her come, even though she wasn't a member of the Council.

"Where's Enif?" Orwyn said.

＊ ＊ ＊

"Wait!" Yolken interrupted. "If Selena wasn't on the Council, what was she doing there?"

"I just said it was because I'd convinced them to let her come," Jax said.

"Yes, but why?" He'd long suspected—no, *knew*—that Jax and his aunt Selena had once loved each other. But like the story Jax was now telling, it was a subject he always avoided.

"Because… do you want me to tell this story or not?"

Yolken had half a mind to *order* Jax to tell him, but something told him if he did that, Jax would get into one of his huffs and not speak to Yolken for the remainder of the journey. He sighed. "Fine."

＊ ＊ ＊

As I was saying, your father asked where Enif was.

"He didn't think it prudent for the head of the Council to be present at such a risky endeavor," Tabora said.

"But of course not," Orwyn said sarcastically.

I pulled a dark piece of glass from a pocket in my cloak and handed it to Orwyn. "This lens will protect your eyes from the sun."

"*My* eyes?" Orwyn said, looking at it.

"You're the only one who can quickly charge the bone, so it should be you who first witnesses the event. Plus you're the one who risked yourself to get the report from Vashon."

"I still don't understand why this had to be done here," Rheena said. "It would have been much easier, logistically, in Croff."

I opened a small chest sitting on the table and pulled out the dragon bone. It was a little over a foot in length and had red ribbons in it. I held it up and said, "Because it would have been much riskier charging a bone this big in Croff. As it is, I should have tried charging it on our way here."

"You know we couldn't take that risk out in the open," Rheena said.

At this point, it didn't matter. It wasn't charged, and we hadn't even tried on the trip down from Croff. But if we were going to verify the veracity of the astronomer's report, it needed to be charged. I held the bone out in Orwyn's direction, but Orwyn didn't take it.

"Even here, we are not free from risk," Orwyn said.

"But you've said yourself that Dalia rarely ever comes to Lonely Oak," Tabora said.

"Which is why I came here. But just because I've left the Order doesn't mean the Regency has given up on me." Orwyn paused and looked at those surrounding him. "If I charge this bone, I could very well be putting every one of us in danger. You all know the Regency has eyes and ears everywhere… possibly even here in Lonely Oak. I will do this only if everyone here is willing to accept the risk."

"Verifying the astronomer's assertions are worth the risk," Tabora said. "At least then we'll have a better idea of how to move forward."

After the others all nodded their assent, Orwyn reluctantly held out his hand and accepted the dragon bone from me. He moved to stand beside the window, out of view from the street below, but in view of the afternoon sun.

I watched my long-time friend take a deep breath. I couldn't see Orwyn absorbing Energy—I don't think you appreciate how much the Order has wanted to get hold of a few pairs of Glasses—but knew he'd begun charging the bone. After a few tense minutes, during which we half-expected regents to come bursting through the door, Orwyn turned from the window and handed the bone to me. The time it had taken him was a fraction of what anyone else in the Order would have been capable of.

I took the bone and slid it into the slot at the end of the Telescope, made specifically for a bone of that exact size. I screwed the cap into place over the slot and asked Orwyn for the piece of glass. He gave it back to me, and I screwed it onto the eyepiece. Then, I pressed a series of buttons on a panel on the side of the Telescope. The Telescope whirred to life. I pushed a few more buttons, and the Telescope began to move on its own. When it pointed directly at the sun, I peered into the eyepiece to check my calibration. With the filter installed, I was able to look directly at the sun without harming my eyes.

The sun consumed the entire view. At this magnification, the movement of the sun's fiery surface was visible. A black circle was in the very center—Detron, a small planet much closer to the sun than Dradonia.

* * *

"Detron was a planet?" Yolken exclaimed.

"Yes," Jax said.

"And it died? How is that even possible? Planets aren't alive. Are they?"

"Can I finish my story?"

"Sorry," Yolken said.

* * *

Satisfied with the calibration of the Telescope, I stepped back and said, "There. Now the Telescope will adjust itself automatically." I gestured that it was ready for Orwyn.

Orwyn moved over to the eyepiece and looked into the Telescope.

"I've set it to track Detron," I said. "If you look directly at the middle of the viewfinder, you'll see it."

"I see it," Orwyn said.

"As Detron slowly orbits the sun, the Telescope will track it so it remains stationary in the center."

Orwyn looked into the viewfinder for several minutes.

A timepiece clicked, and Tabora said, "It's time."

"Nothing's happening…" Orwyn said. Then, a moment later, he exclaimed, "It caught fire! The whole thing just burst into flame!"

Orwyn stared, transfixed, for several more minutes. Then, he stepped away from the Telescope. The others took turns looking into the Telescope to witness Detron's destruction as well. By the time it was my turn, Detron was no longer the silhouetted ball it had been when I'd looked at it moments ago. It was now a fiery ball leaving a trail of fire streaming behind it, similar to that of a comet.

"It'll burn like this for some time," I said, without pulling my eye away from the viewfinder. "Fortunately, Detron's proximity to the sun will shield its fiery death from view."

"Imagine the mayhem that would ensue should news of this get out," Jerle chimed in.

"I imagine that's why the astronomer met the fate he did," Orwyn said. "Drakonias was trying to prevent the total collapse of the empire."

"Drashon as well," Tabora added. "Drakonias has become quite nefarious in his efforts to keep this knowledge secret."

"Today was worth the risk," Tabora said. "What we've witnessed today undeniably confirms the astronomer's predictions."

"Now," Corin said, "we must act!"

"But what can we possibly do?" Tabora exclaimed. "Drakonias has responded to all of our efforts with nothing but ruthlessness."

"We must do something," I said coolly. "If we do nothing, then our fate will be the same as Detron's. Maybe not our generation, or the next, but it *will* happen."

* * *

"You think they found my father when he charged the bone?" Yolken said when Jax stopped talking.

"I do. I shouldn't have waited; I should have charged it on the way to Lonely Oak," Jax said. "I don't know why I waited."

"If they *did* see him charge the bone, there must have been a Watcher nearby, right?"

"Yes. And I know what you're going to say, 'If there was already a Watcher in Lonely Oak, they already knew where he was.' The only problem with that is, if they already knew where he was, why hadn't they killed him yet? And besides, it doesn't excuse my showing up with an uncharged bone."

They rode in silence for a few minutes.

Trying to process what Jax had just told him, Yolken asked, "So Detron… died. Why? I don't understand what happened."

"Drakonias must have realized something was wrong with the sun, that it was changing somehow, which would explain why he banned astronomy. And he didn't just *ban* astronomy; he killed every known astronomer and had all of their equipment destroyed. It was conceivable that someone had already discovered what he suspected, and he couldn't risk whatever it was getting out. He spared the life of one astronomer—his name was Vashon—and commissioned him to study the sun. And Vashon's study revealed exactly what he feared. The sun *was* changing. I don't understand exactly how it works, but the sun was out of balance. It was… growing, or expanding. I'm not sure what the right description is for what was taking place. Vashon predicted that the growth—or expansion—of the sun would consume Detron, and that expansion would one day do the same thing to Dradonia."

Yolken started getting a mental picture of what was transpiring. In a sense, it already was. The climate had been slowly warming. The south was experiencing the effects with its droughts and fires. The East Sea as well. The cyclones that used to seasonally plague the sea, making crossings dangerous, now plagued the sea year-round, making crossing impossible.

"And Drakonias killed Vashon?" Yolken asked.

"Yes."

"What about Drashon?"

"Drashon was the Chancellor—"

"—of the Western Realm," Yolken finished for Jax.

"And Vashon lived in Tieger. So Drakonias put Drashon in charge of the astronomer and oversaw his work. And Drakonias couldn't risk even the chancellor knowing what Vashon discovered, so he killed him as well."

"His own son," Yolken said.

"Does this surprise you?" Jax said.

"Sort of."

"He started a war, Yolken… against his own family! And in the process, doomed the entire world!"

"I know. It's all still hard to understand sometimes."

"At any rate, we stayed the night in Lonely Oak then returned to Croff the next day."

"If my father wasn't part of the Order, why'd you go there in the first place? If it was to go somewhere where you could safely charge the bone, you could have gone almost anywhere."

"We owed it to him. If it wasn't for him, the Order wouldn't have even known Detron existed, let alone that the sun was dying. He did all the work acquiring the astronomer's report, so it was only right that he be present when Detron died. Anyway, I had a feeling something was going to happen after that day. I even tried convincing your father to leave Lonely Oak, but he refused. So I used every source I had available within the Regency to try and stay ahead of them.

"It's nearly impossible to find out what the Sodality is up to, but somehow, we lucked out. The moment I found out, I left straight for Lonely Oak. I was *not* going to let them win. The only question was whether I could beat them there."

CHAPTER 39

Three months after Detron met its fiery fate, I found myself racing back to Lonely Oak. I stayed clear of the busy highway and took advantage of the rolling grassy hills to safely Synthesize. I ran without inhibition, using the Energy stored in the bones woven into my cloak until I crested a final rise and the little clump of buildings surrounding the solitary oak came into view.

I scanned the road in the distance to my right and it was clear, so I gripped the tattered cuff of my cloak and covered the remaining distance quickly. When I approached the edge of town, I let go of the bone protruding from my cuff and slowed to a normal walk.

Children were playing under the tree, and the framework of two more floors at the Oak was under construction. It was my idea for Brall to expand, you know.

I navigated through town and crossed the Little Mindon to where your parents' tavern still stood by itself. Except for their tavern, Lonely Oak had yet to expand beyond the creek. I remember looking up at the two-story building and thinking how crazy your father was when he said what he wanted to do was build an inn and have a family. It was his dream come true. Well, except for the part about building a separate home down in the maple grove. The tavern had become so popular he never had the chance to build the home, and instead lived upstairs. He let out the other rooms from time to time, but it never became the inn he imagined it being.

There was smoke coming from the stone chimney, but I half-expected to find either the building abandoned or everyone dead inside. So, when I pushed open the front door and saw the boisterous crowd of people having their evening meals, I breathed a sigh of relief and walked in.

The pervasive aroma made me want to march into the kitchen and dive into whatever was cooking. The only person whose cooking came close to Selena's was your mother's—and Selena wouldn't cook for me anymore, no matter how hard I tried. "That was my previous self," she always said. I desperately wanted to eat one of your mother's famous hot meals, but the urgency that filled me prevented me.

Orwyn stood behind the bar with his back to me, filling mugs with ale, so I walked over to the only empty stool at the bar and waited.

"What'll it be?" Orwyn said over his shoulder.

When I didn't answer him, he turned around. He looked surprised to see me.

"We need to talk," I said.

"Sit," Orwyn said. "I'll get you something to eat."

The coolness with which he responded to seeing me was almost eerie. There was only one reason I would return to Lonely Oak so quickly, and he knew it. Yet he acted with complete nonchalance. He set two mugs down in front of a couple of patrons sitting a few stools down from me, then turned to fill another. Your father approached and set the mug in front of me, so I said, "We *really* need to talk."

"First, you eat," Orwyn said. He walked over to the little window dividing the tavern from the kitchen and hollered back an order for food. Moments later, a thin woman emerged from the kitchen with a steaming bowl of stew and a hunk of warm bread. She set them both down in front of me with a smile.

I should tell you that I originally objected to your father marrying that comely woman he met while on a mission in Tieger. Primarily it was because I knew what would happen if Orwyn got married: His priorities would change. And I was right. As soon as Orwyn came to Lonely Oak with Elen and started his little venture, he had essentially retired. I couldn't blame him, though, beautiful as she was. Her brilliant blue eyes and sparkling smile would win the heart of any man—especially a man who had lived a long life and was ready to experience that which he'd never had before... a family.

I begrudgingly ate, and Orwyn continued with his work until I finished. As soon as I sopped up the last vestiges of the stew with the final piece of bread, he hung his apron on a peg and stepped into the kitchen. I dropped some coins on the bar and left the tavern the way I'd entered. I followed the cart path between the tavern and the creek around to the back, then reentered the tavern into the kitchen.

"What news do you have?" Orwyn said the moment I stepped through the door.

"Now, I was hoping to pay my compliments to the cook," I said, noticing that Elen wasn't in the kitchen.

"*Jax.*"

Sensing that Orwyn wasn't in the mood for jesting, I got to the point. "The Synod knows where you are—they're going to assassinate you, Orwyn." I watched from across the long wooden table occupying the center of the kitchen as Orwyn furrowed his brow. "But we couldn't figure out when. What I *do* know is that you need to leave. You, Elen, *and* the boys. *Now.* Before it's too late."

I had expected him to rush into action, but Orwyn just stood there and stared vacantly at me.

"Orwyn… we need to leave."

"No."

"No?" I exclaimed with exasperation. That was *not* what I

expected to hear. "Orwyn, you know how these things work."

"I do. And my answer is no."

"Orwyn—"

"Listen, Jax. If we're ever going to put a stop to what's happening to Dradonia, my answer must, at last, be 'No.' I refuse to live out the rest of my life in hiding. If I run and don't face what's coming, then I'll be unable to create the life I want for my family. I—we—must, at last, begin to take a stand, to fight back."

"But, Orwyn, if you don't leave, they *will* kill you."

"Maybe. Maybe not. We're rarely able to determine the plans of the Synod. As such, we don't typically have forewarning about these things. Maybe we can use this to our advantage." A grin blossomed on his face. "Plus, I have you!"

I groaned.

"How long did you say we had?"

"We don't know. But if I had to guess, I'd say a day, maybe two. Word arrived by condor that the Synod—"

"*Condor?*" Orwyn said.

"We're aware of the risk. But the Order doesn't want to lose you. They can't afford to."

Orwyn snorted. "It's so kind of them to care."

"*Now* you want to be funny?"

"Relax, Jax."

"How can I relax? The Sodality is coming, Orwyn!"

"All right. Tell me, when did the condor arrive?"

"A few days ago. I left Croff immediately and came here as fast as I could," I said. I peered across the table at your father. I could tell he was thinking, and it wasn't about getting you, your mother, and Javen to safety. "If you're going to insist on this foolishness—"

"I am," Orwyn said without looking at me.

"Then, if I'm to be of any use to you, I need to recharge my bones. And rest."

"Go upstairs and rest. I'll make arrangements for Elen and

the lads to stay with Deborah until this is over."

"Orwyn…" Finally, he looked at me. "Are you sure about this?"

"My mind's made up, Jax."

"Fine."

I left the tavern and walked east of town. There was a rise not too far away, out past the few farms peppering the valley, where I could safely charge my dragon bones with the sunlight that remained.

I sat in the tall grass, facing west, and watched the sun inch closer to the horizon. As I recharged the bones in my cloak, I thought about how foolish your father was being. I knew he had survived several attempts by the Regency to kill him, but he'd never had a family before. He was being foolish.

I wasn't able to get the bones fully charged before the sun set, which was disappointing. Even with your father at my side— or rather, it'd be more accurate to say that I was at his side—I didn't like the idea of starting this foolishness at less than full strength. But there was nothing to be done.

I made my way back to the tavern, feeling the fatigue of prolonged Synthesizing. I went straight to the stairs at the back of the room and went up. There were six rooms plus a washroom on the second floor. You shared one with your brother, and your parents occupied another. I entered the room opposite your parents' room and lay down, fully clothed. You know how tiring Synthesizing can be—sleep didn't delay in consuming me.

* * *

"I don't understand why my father refused to leave," Yolken said.

With a shake of the head, Jax said, "Neither did I."

"Why didn't you make him?"

"What was I to do? No one could ever make your father do something he didn't want to. Not me, not the Council. And I wasn't in a position to force him to."

"But if he'd left, then maybe—"

"Don't."

"What?"

"I know what you were going to say, and you can't do that to yourself," Jax said. "I know. I've been doing it every day since then." Jax opened a water flask and took a drink. He handed it to Yolken, and Yolken did the same. After screwing the cap back on, he said, "My rest that night would be short-lived."

* * *

I woke with a start and jumped to my feet. Unease overwhelmed me. It took only a moment to gather my wits and remember where I was. The light that had remained when I lay down was now gone. I crept over to the door, which had a thin line of light under it, and opened it. I peered cautiously out. It was quiet except for movement in the washroom at the end of the hall. I tapped on the door, and Orwyn opened it, bare-chested and drying his bristly face with a towel.

"What is it?" he said.

"Where are the lads?"

"Deborah's."

"Elen?"

"She's in the kitchen. Said she had a few things to finish up before coming to bed."

"Why isn't she with the lads?"

"She insisted on staying with me. Jax?" A concerned look crossed Orwyn's face. "What's the matter?"

"I don't know... I woke with this feeling—something isn't right."

Orwyn grabbed a shirt hanging on the back of the door and slipped it on. He went into his bedroom and came out with the Harachin sword in hand. Together, we headed for the stairs, me gripping the protruding bone in the cuff of my cloak.

At the bottom of the stairs, I saw a glint of metal reflect light from the fire in the hearth. I drew Energy from the bone I held between my fingers and thumb and used it to deflect the object that was flying toward us. A blade thudded in the wall next to Orwyn's head. Several more blades flew, from two different locations. This time Orwyn deflected them, and they thudded harmlessly into the wall as well.

"What do you have for us now?" Orwyn said when no more blades followed. The assassins didn't respond, and he shouted, "Are you prepared to confront Danavin Drake face to face?"

"Your wife is dead," one of the shadowed men calmly said.

Orwyn's gaze shifted toward the kitchen door.

The shadowed men pulled thin swords from sheaths strapped to their backs and attacked. But they had only taken a few steps before they froze in the air, mid-leap, with their swords held out before them.

Orwyn's gaze turned back toward the assassins. He casually walked up to them and looked them in the eyes. As they hung helplessly in the air, they involuntarily moved their swords up to their necks. I watched the assassins' eyes widen as their blades cut into their own throats. As blood drained from their wounds, the bodies fell to the floor.

I joined Orwyn beside the dying men, who wore matte-black leathers. "Black Sodality," I said. Fear began to well up inside me as I realized the full gravity of what was happening. I looked over at Orwyn, who was staring down at the bodies, holding his black sword at his side. "Orwyn, what's the pla—"

I recoiled as the tavern exploded in heat. I instinctively lifted my arms to shield my face. After the initial wave of heat abated, I lowered my arms and saw that the entire front wall of the tavern was now in flames. The fear that pooled inside me turned to panic when the flames began creeping eerily across the floor.

Draego's Fire.

"Jax, quickly, go check the back door," Orwyn said.

I eyed the flames warily then darted for the kitchen. I stopped short at the sight of… of Elen lying in a pool of blood. I covered my mouth with a hand and choked back vomit. I had to force myself to walk around her corpse and push on the door.

It was jammed.

Without looking down at Elen again, I rejoined Orwyn in the tavern. "The door's jammed. A trap?"

Orwyn nodded. "They have us boxed in."

"Then let's fight our way out!"

"Jax, you know as well as I that the Sodality is out there in force. And they do not underestimate those they're sent to eliminate. The moment we attempt to force that door"—Orwyn's gaze left the unnatural flames moving toward us, and shifted to the kitchen door—"they will attack us with everything they have. We wouldn't make it two steps out of this building, and you know it."

"What do you suggest, then? That we stay here and die?"

"Our only hope is that they don't know you're here as well."

I instantly knew what your father was about to suggest. "I'm not leaving you here, Orwyn."

"It's our only option, Jax. I'm getting you out of here."

"No!" I exclaimed.

"There's no other choice."

"We should've left when we had the chance."

"I know," Orwyn acknowledged. "But I'm tired of hiding."

"Orwyn, no matter what, we're in this together. I'm not abandoning you here."

He turned from the assassins and looked intently at me. "If you stay here, we're both dead. And I won't permit it."

"Then I'll stay."

"No. You know they're here for me."

"Orwyn, if I had brought you—"

"Jax!" Orwyn shouted. "This isn't about that! The Regency's wanted me dead since the war. Now, listen to me. *Please.* Go upstairs and position yourself by the window in my room. I'll create a distraction to draw them in. Wait until I strike. When you see them close in on the back door, flee out the window."

"Orwyn—"

"I'll catch up with you in the Mindons."

I hesitated. Stroking my beard, I looked at the man standing beside me. I put a hand on your father's—my friend's—shoulder and squeezed it tightly. "See you in the Mindons."

I turned from your father and made for the stairs.

Smoke from the fire had found its way to the stairwell. It was filling the hallway on the top floor in a dense cloud. I hunched down as I made my way down the hall and pushed open the door to Orwyn and Elen's bedroom. I closed the door to stop the smoke from following me in.

I moved carefully in the dark room and crept along the wall to the window, then crouched in the corner and waited.

The light of the moon made visible dark figures milling around outside—dozens of them. I hated to admit it, but Orwyn was right. We were seriously outnumbered. But was it more than Orwyn could handle? He'd foiled their plans to kill him before.

I waited for only a moment before the figures moved toward the kitchen door. *He must have sprung the trap.* As the shadowy figures drew closer to the building, an explosion sent rubble flying into the night. Debris knocked most of the dark figures to the ground.

I forced myself to wait. The ground outside the window was still, but then additional shapes emerged from the night and converged on the rear entrance and went inside. When I didn't see any more movement, I climbed out the window and jumped down onto the roof of the adjoining shed where Orwyn brewed his ales. I crept silently along the roof and, glancing over my shoulder, saw that the back side of the kitchen was almost completely gone. I continued to the end of the shed and slid to the ground.

And then I ran away. The single biggest moment of shame in my life. I left my friend and ran to safety. I knew I should have returned and helped your father, but I obeyed him. The farther I got from the tavern, the stronger my desire grew to disobey. But deep down, I knew Orwyn had likely given his life to ensure I escaped, so I forced myself to continue. If he'd sacrificed himself for me—even though it didn't make sense; he was much more of an asset to the Order than I was—I couldn't let it go to waste.

CHAPTER 40

That doesn't make any sense," Yolken said.

"You're right. It doesn't," Jax said.

"Why would he make you leave like that?"

"We were seriously outnumbered, so he probably figured—"

"Even if you were outnumbered, why would he suddenly change his mind?"

"I've been trying to figure that out myself, Yolken," Jax said. "I thought he was invincible—many of us in the Order did, and probably took advantage of him because of it."

"But he never showed up…"

"No. I waited at the rendezvous point, but he never showed."

They rode in silence for a few minutes. The gravity of the moment hung over Yolken like low-hanging early morning clouds. Yolken's eyes fixated on his horse's twitching ears. He knew his mother and father had died in a fire, but until recently, he'd never known that it wasn't an accident, that they had been murdered. And now Jax had revealed that, in the process, he had been selfless enough to give his life for Jax, to provide a way for him to escape. It made him miss his father in a way he never had before. Made him wish he'd had the chance to know him personally. But all he had were the wisps of memories from when he was very young.

He turned back to his father's bearded friend and said, "What happened after that?"

"You sure you want to know?" Jax asked.

Yolken nodded. "I've spent my whole life not knowing."

* * *

I waited at the rendezvous point in the foothills of the Mindons. I was tired. And as sleep gnawed at me, threatened to drag me into the ether, I fought it by clinging to the hope that Orwyn had somehow escaped. But when the sun arrived and Orwyn did not, I knew he hadn't.

From my vantage point, a dark plume of smoke was visible on the southern side of town, climbing into the sky. I watched it, struggling to process what had just occurred. The emotional side of me refused to accept it, but the rational side knew it was true. I sat there, continuing to wait, continuing to hope, the two sides fighting for control.

I wrestled with the things you just mentioned. How could Orwyn go so quickly from being determined to fight to resigning himself to death? The force that I'd seen outside was indeed strong, but I would rather have stayed and died alongside your father than to have left him behind. But he wouldn't have it any other way.

As I looked down on Lonely Oak, I couldn't help but feel that Orwyn and Elen's deaths were a waste. It could have been avoided. If only your father had heeded my warning. It never crossed my mind when I arrived in Lonely Oak to warn him that he might choose to stay.

I remained at the rendezvous point until the sun reached its zenith, at which point I descended from the foothills and returned to Lonely Oak, to the remains of the tavern… to my friends.

It might seem hasty to you, but I wasn't worried. Your father's efforts to help me escape wouldn't be wasted by my returning to the tavern. The Sodality, I knew, would be long gone. It was how they operated—get in, get out, leave no evidence behind.

As I walked under the heat of the sun, I slowly charged the dragon bones woven within my cloak until they were full. Was there an irony in the fact that they were now full? When I knew I wouldn't need them?

A crowd gathered around what remained of the kitchen wall. I stopped before I reached them and looked at the burned ruins. Its demise had been inevitable the moment it went up in flames. A town as small as Lonely Oak didn't have the means to do much when it came to combating structure fires. I remembered hearing the bell ringing as I fled, but I wasn't surprised to find the structure burned throughout. All that remained were the walls of the stone kitchen and some of the thicker timber, blackened and protruding like the ribs of a burned-out carcass. A trail of smoke still streamed into the sky. I watched it rise and listened to voices in the crowd.

"What happened?"

"Only Draego knows."

"Did you hear the explosion?"

"Yes."

"Us too!"

"We heard it all the way out at our farm!"

"But what could have caused an explosion like that?"

I forced my grief down and looked from the smoke to the gathered crowd in search of Deborah and you lads. I was thankful when I didn't find you; you were too small to have to be witnesses to this.

I pushed myself to the front of the crowd, where blankets covered two bulges.

Corpses.

Tears welled in my eyes. Try as I might, I wasn't able to hold my grief back any longer. At last, I gave in and let them fall.

All evidence of the Sodality's presence was gone, everything except the hole in the wall. There were no bodies to attest to the nefarious deed that had been done. Just the hole, which probably perturbed Drenan, who had likely been the Overseer in charge of the mission. The hole represented loose ends, and Drenan hated loose ends. I, of course, knew what had happened, but I couldn't tell them. The locals would forever consider it an unfortunate accident.

I looked from the unburned kitchen back to the corpses. Elen's body was burned, although she'd been in the kitchen, not in the fire—part of the Sodality's clean-up. Duty compelled me to investigate further, to see how thorough they'd been.

I entered the kitchen through the large hole. The kitchen was largely unscathed. Elen's blood was gone from the spot where I'd seen her lying on the floor. The wooden wall separating the kitchen from the tavern mostly gone. From my vantage, standing where I knew Elen had actually died, the blackened remains of the tavern were visible. The remnants of the wooden bar and tables still smoldered. I hesitated to move into the tavern; I didn't know how much integrity remained in the structure. Sections of the ceiling rafters remained intact, but a few of them angled from the ceiling to the ground. The second floor was visible in several places through gaping burned-out holes. The whole thing could have come crashing down at any moment, but I felt obligated to see if the Sodality had overlooked your father's sword during their mop-up. Losing it, I hate to admit, would have been almost as tragic as losing your father.

I forced myself into the charred ruins and sifted through ashes and smoking piles of wood with my boot, not wanting any area to remain overlooked.

"Draego's Fire!" I swore when I realized the sword was gone.

Also missing from the debris, I noticed, were the remains of the would-be assassins—and their weapons. That didn't surprise me, though. The Sodality had done their job well. Likely, the assassins' corpses had been disposed of in the same manner as those who'd littered the ground outside.

Wood cracked overhead, causing me to give up any further

inspection.

When I stepped back out of the hole in the kitchen wall, the crowd was looking at me like I was insane. "Will someone help me bury them?" I said.

"I will," someone said.

I locked eyes with a familiar face.

Relan.

"I have a cart around front," said a man standing next to Relan, dressed in tattered brown overalls.

"Thank you," I said.

"I'll bring it around."

I nodded.

The chatter of the crowd picked back up when the man who had volunteered to help walked around the side of the ruins.

"Such a tragedy."

"Indeed."

"Didn't they have children?"

"I'm not sure."

"I think so. Two lads, I believe."

"What's to happen to them?"

Relan stepped close to me and said, "It was them scales, weren't it?"

I nodded sharply.

"Cursed scales," Relan said through clenched teeth.

The man returned on the path between the tavern and the creek, leading a horse pulling a cart.

"What's your name, sir?" I asked.

"Rett."

"You from around here?"

"Ya. I have a farm just over the hill there," Rett said, pointing toward the hills to the east. "Them was good folk, they was. Surely didn't deserve to die like that. I can ask the missus if we can bury 'em under one of the oaks at the farm if they have nowhere else to rest."

"I already have a place in mind. There's a clump of maples

by the creek southeast of town. They wanted to build a house there."

"I know the spot," Rett said. "It's just down from our farm. Come then, let's get 'em loaded."

The cart was full of dry goods, but there was room at the back for both bodies to lay side by side. Relan helped me load Orwyn and Elen into the wagon, then Rett led the horse by the reins back around the tavern to the road. Relan and I followed behind. We walked a little farther down the road to a cart path that split off to the left, and followed it through the wild grass. As we crested the first rise, a few farms peppering the landscape came into view.

"You know you can never speak about what happened here, right?" I said.

"Aye," Relan said. "How'd you know they were coming?"

I looked over at Relan and raised an eyebrow. He nodded his understanding.

That was all we said to each other. We walked the rest of the way in silence.

As we approached Rett's farm, the path split, and a new one led to the farm. Rett stopped the horse in front of the farmhouse, which was surrounded by half a dozen mature oak trees. A woman with her hair in a bun and wearing a dirty apron around her thick waist came out the door and stood on the porch.

"What'd you learn about the smoke, hun?" the woman said.

"Thornhill Tavern burned up," Rett said. "Took both 'em good people with it."

"The fire get all four of 'em?"

"No, just Orwyn and his wife."

"What's become of the lads?"

"Dunno," Rett said. He looked at me in question.

"The Thornhills were close with the Brownings," I said.

"The bakers?" Rett said.

"You know that, you big oaf!" his wife retorted.

"I believe they're with them at the moment," I said. "What will become of them, though, is anyone's guess."

Rett's wife shook her head and said, "That's a shame. And who exactly are you?" Her eyes shifted to Relan and me in an accusatory fashion.

"We're friends of theirs," I said.

"I told him I'd help bury 'em. Come," Rett said, "let's be about puttin' 'em in the ground."

"That's good of you," Rett's wife said. "Where you plannin' on laying 'em?"

"Over on that plot they was wantin' to build on."

Rett led the horse over to the barn, where he retrieved three shovels. Then we continued past the farm and toward the small maple grove in the distance. As we drew near, I began to hear the Little Mindon. We found a spot beneath one of the trees on the eastern edge of the grove with a picturesque view of the Mindons and set to digging one large grave. We labored in silence. When we finished, Rett said, "I'll see about getting 'em proper markers."

"We're forever indebted to you," I said.

"Think nothin' of it."

* * *

"Relan knew what happened?" Yolken said when Jax let his story trail off.

"He did."

"Is he a member of the Order?"

"Not exactly."

"What does that mean?"

"It means he was a friend of your father's."

"Huh," Yolken said. "I never knew that." It made sense, though, and explained why Relan spent so much time at the tavern. He was one of Yolken's most loyal patrons. "I always wondered who buried them. Selena said it was the locals who looked after them."

"That was to protect our identities," Jax said. "If you knew

Deborah and I were connected to your parents, it would have undermined your father's wish for you to not know about the Order."

"What happened next?" Yolken asked.

"I got drunk," Jax said.

* * *

Relan and I parted ways with Rett after we finished burying your parents, and walked back to Lonely Oak. The last glimpse of the sun shone in our eyes as we walked. My arms and back ached, and I thought about numbing the pain with Energy until I fell asleep, but I had other plans.

We made our way to the square and straight to the Oak. I found an empty stool at the bar and sat heavily. Relan sat next to me. When Brall saw us sitting there, he went straight to a barrel, drew out two tankards, and placed them before us.

"Some of Orwyn's," Brall said.

I drank the tankard down, savoring the taste. "How'd you come by this?"

"'Tis a shame. We were workin' on an agreement: He makes it, I sell it. This here is the only barrel I got before—" Brall cut himself off. "Anyway, I'll leave you be."

I sat quietly next to Relan. The other patrons left us alone. Every sip I drank reminded me of your father, and made me wonder how we'd ended up where we were. Brall ensured our tankards didn't remain empty. I have no idea how much I drank. I don't even know if I settled with Brall before I left. I barely remember stumbling across the square toward Deborah's. I also remember hoping you and Javen were abed because I didn't want any more reminders of Orwyn that night.

* * *

"What happened next?" Yolken asked when Jax stopped talking.

"I don't remember," Jax said. "Deborah had to fill me in the next afternoon when I finally woke."

"What did she say?"

"Ask her."

"Really?"

Jax scratched at his throat. "My throat's dry. I'm done talking."

Seeing that Jax was serious and didn't intend to say any more, Yolken urged his horse into a trot. When he reined it in next to Deborah, opposite Deanna, they stopped talking.

"What is it, dear?" Deborah said.

"Jax has been telling me about the night my parents died," Yolken said.

"Oh?" She looked over her shoulder at Jax.

"He says he doesn't remember going to your bakery the night after."

"That's because he was drunk," Deborah said. "Very drunk." She took a drink from her water flask, then said, "Those were a few very difficult days. For starters, I was with child—"

"I forgot that Kaylan wasn't born yet," Yolken said. "I was young when they died and can barely remember them. She never got to meet them."

"Maybe not on the outside, but she heard them from the womb. I'm sure their voices are in her heart."

Yolken nodded. "What happened after?"

"As I said," Deborah continued, "those were a difficult few days. It was all I could do to control the emotions welling in me. When Orwyn brought you and Javen to the bakery, I knew there was trouble. The next thing I knew, I heard the fire bell. Morning came with no word from either of your parents, or from Jax. Naturally, I feared the worst. Then you and Javen woke, confused about where your parents were. I had no answers, so I tried my best to distract you with breakfast. You kept asking when you could go home, and Javen kept repeating that he missed his mama and papa. He... he was so little. I tried to be strong, to hide my tears. But Kaylan kicked and squirmed in my belly, making it nearly impossible. I knew I needed to be strong for the two of you, to hide the pain I felt for you, the fear of what your futures might hold... my own worries of being less than a month away from bringing a baby into this dying world." Deborah wiped tears from her eyes. "I always knew what might happen when I was given the assignment, but nothing could have prepared me for the time when possibilities became realities."

Yolken wished he could hug Deborah. "I can't imagine how you must have felt."

"You already have," Deborah said. Her eyes glistened. "You felt it when that rider took Kaylan from you."

Yolken choked back tears.

"We'll get her back," Deborah said. "Of this, I am certain."

Yolken wiped his eyes on the sleeve of his shirt and said, "But Onta is so far away. And it's getting farther with every step we take."

"Dradonia is a lot smaller when you're a Synthesizer," Jax said.

The group rode in silence for several minutes. The only sound was the clopping of the horses' hooves on the dirt road.

"It wasn't until after dark that I found myself hustling to the front door as best as I could," Deborah eventually said. "I'd only just managed to get both of you to sleep and was mentally cursing whoever it was that was rapping on my door. I remember tersely whispering, 'What in Draego's Fire…' as I unbolted the door. The smell of drink hit me like a false contraction. Jax swayed as he stood in the doorway. 'What happened?' I asked him. When he didn't answer, I took him by the hand and led him around the counter and into the kitchen.

"He slumped into one of the twin chairs at the table and laid his head down. I got him a glass of water and set it on the table in front of him, but he ignored it. I told him I'd been worrying all day and that I'd heard the alarm. I could see the smoke from the front door but couldn't tell what it was that was burning. All he did was lift his head off the table long enough to nod. That told me everything I needed to know.

"When I asked him what happened, he said, 'They're dead.'

And when I asked how, all he said at first was, 'The Black took 'em.' Then he let out a flurry of slurred words about how he didn't know what happened; how Orwyn had wanted to stay and fight, but he'd tried to talk him out of it. He said something about how Orwyn insisted it was necessary to stay, and then all of a sudden changed his mind. Then he shouted at me, 'I ran, Acca! And Orwyn died!'

"Jax never uses my real name…

"He went on about how many there were, and I urged him to keep his voice down; you and your brother were sleeping upstairs. Then he started whispering over and over that he should have stayed and that it should have been Orwyn who ran because Orwyn's life was worth a hundred of his. And then I made tea. I forced him to drink it because I knew if he didn't, the morrow would be worse than it was already going to be.

"We drank in silence. I finally succeeded in getting him to drink a few mugs of water before he stood to leave. I asked him to stay, and he grudgingly agreed. I led him to the couch upstairs and covered him with a blanket. He asked me, 'What's to become of the boys?', but how was I supposed to know? It didn't matter anyhow; he was asleep before I could reply."

"What *did* happen?" Yolken asked. "I mean, how did Selena end up in Lonely Oak when she wasn't our aunt?"

"If you'll remember," Jax said, "she was in Lonely Oak when we met to witness the, uh… event. Well, she'd barely returned to her assignment in Tieger when she was summoned back to Croff. They hadn't even bothered to tell her why she was there. She was shocked when I told her what had happened. She was even more surprised when she eventually learned she was being reassigned to raise you, and that she'd do it in Lonely Oak. She was from Tieger and did wonderful work for the Order there, so it didn't make sense to her—to any of us—at the time, why the Council chose to keep you in Lonely Oak."

"Why *did* they keep us there?" Yolken asked. "And how did the tavern get rebuilt?"

"Selena arrived in Lonely Oak about three months after the death of your parents," Deborah said. "And the very first thing she saw when she arrived was Orwyn's eldest son fighting with other children under the oak tree."

"*What?*" Yolken said, looking over at Deborah, surprised.

"Of course, she didn't know it was you at the time; she was just breaking up a fight. But when she arrived at the bakery, one of the little fisticuffers was sitting at my table."

"I don't remember that."

"You were young. Anyway, she came with plenty of gold and instructions from the Council to rebuild the tavern. The fact that the two of you had survived that night was proof the Synod didn't know you existed. The Order isn't in the habit of returning to hideouts the Regency infiltrates, so they thought the perfect place for you to grow up was in a location the Regency now knew about. They'd never expect it. And they didn't."

"I'd almost give up my gift to have seen Drenan's face when he first learned Orwyn had children," Jax said, "and that they'd been raised in the very town he was sent to assassinate him in. The very tavern. He is *not* a fan of loose ends. He must have been furious."

"Do you think that's why he killed Selena?" Yolken said.

"Hmm," Jax said. "I hadn't thought of that."

With everything that had been happening, Yolken hadn't thought of Selena in a while. His thoughts had been so consumed by what transpired in Onta, and his meeting in Croff, not to mention the onus Deth had bestowed upon him. He felt bad that she'd slipped to the wayside.

"If there's one person in the Regency I wouldn't mind killing," Yolken said, "it'd be him."

"Aye," Jax agreed. "I had my chance, and I blew it."

Yolken saw Jax's eyes begin to glisten before he turned and stared into the distance.

CHAPTER 41

The invitation to Dorlan's gala arrived four days after Hadie met with her mother. A mixture of emotions flooded into her the moment she broke the wax seal stamped with the chancellor's insignia. She buried them, knowing she had only one day to prepare herself and the girls.

The first thing she did was sit down one-on-one with each of them and talk to them about what they were about to do. Society looked down on what they did, and a whore was aware of her place in society. However, it was one thing to be a whore, as morally decrepit as the profession was, but it was an entirely different thing to be a killer. Hadie had come to peace with the idea of taking someone else's life when she'd attempted to kill Drenan, and she wanted to make sure each girl who would be accompanying her to Dorlan's gala had done the same. She invited each girl to her quarters, starting with Ursella.

In addition to making sure each one fully understood what they were volunteering to do, she wanted to assess whether they could actually do it. She expected some of them to back out now that the day was almost upon them, and she was surprised when none of them did.

After the last girl left, she went and stood in front of the mirror and asked herself the same question.

"Yes," she said to her reflection.

She took over Ursella's nightly tasks and sent her to make the final preparations for the gala, which included picking up the new orange corsets she'd had made to match the chancellor's armor, as well as attending to each girl's gold. She wanted them to be adequately prepared to fit into whatever society arose in the aftermath.

She didn't sleep that night, and hoped the tea she drank while Ursella did her hair would be enough to keep her wits. She tried not to fidget, and found herself fighting the temptation to brush the tops of her breasts with the tips of her fingers like Sonja used to do. When Ursella finished, she opened the drawer on her desk and removed a long wooden box. She carried it level in front of herself as she and Ursella descended the stairs to the lobby. Ursella held the beads aside for her, and she joined the others. She watched them as they chatted and fidgeted. Their nervousness hung in the air, as oppressive as the wet air. She did her best to exude confidence, and hoped her demeanor would influence them. The din died down as, one by one, they noticed her presence.

She set the box on an end table and opened it, revealing the neatly lined-up rows of hairpins. Each of them had a small flower made from tiny yellow and red gems. She sat on the couch, and Ursella took one of the pins and placed it in her hair, right above her left ear. She stood and invited each girl to come, sit, and receive her pin. Ursella placed each one in the same location. Lastly, Ursella sat, and Hadie placed her pin for her.

After that, Hadie sat in her chair, and the girls loitered in the lobby. Some of them sat on the couches while others stood.

When Ursella said, "The carriages are here, Madam," Hadie rose from her chair with a fluid motion and walked to the center of the room. Every eye in the room was on her. She looked around the room at each of them individually, all dressed as she was, in a new orange corset and wearing their hair in similar dos.

"Please, sit," she started. She waited for those standing to find a space on the couches then continued, "Well, this is it. Tonight, Draego has seen fit to bless us with the opportunity to right a great injustice." She paused, looking around the room again. She didn't know if her statement about the Great Dragon was true—it likely wasn't, she thought, since she didn't even believe the Great Dragon existed. However, many of the girls did, and if they believed Draego was on their side and had blessed their actions, then they would believe in their success. "I want you all to know that I need each of you to come with me if we are going to be successful. There will be twenty-two regents plus the chancellor at the gala tonight, and there are twenty-two of us. Plans are in place to deal with Dreanna, the sole woman. I wish I didn't have to rely on someone else's help tonight, but the truth is we are but one spoke in a larger wheel that will start turning tonight. That, and despite the esteem you have worked so hard over the years to build, Dreanna is just *not* that into you." The girls all nervously chuckled. "However, before we leave this brothel, I want to give each of you one more opportunity to back out. Once we load up into the carriages waiting outside, the opportunity to leave will be gone. If we do not *each*," she continued, looking around the room, "do the task that I'm asking of you, then it will be us who dies tonight and not them. If even one of you falters, we will all be through. I say this not to scare you, but because I need to be absolutely sure that you are all with me." Hadie paused, then said, "If you are, then stand."

Every girl in the room stood without hesitation.

The bottled-up emotion in Hadie nearly escaped. She felt her eyes began to glisten. "Good." She gestured to Ursella, who opened the door.

The girls filed out of the brothel for what Hadie hoped would be the last time. No… it *was* the last time. No matter what happened tonight, they would not be returning. And if they succeeded, each of them would be rich enough that they'd never have to whore again. She smiled as each girl walked through the door, knowing that they would never walk through it again.

When the last girl exited and only Ursella remained, Hadie moved to exit the brothel herself.

Even though she had never whored herself, the brothel now represented the unpleasant road that had brought her back to Hantlo. It represented her love for Javen, which Drenan had ripped from her before it had the opportunity to blossom. She didn't know if she would ever see Javen again, so she tried to take what comfort she could through knowing that in one night she was going to rid the world of almost two dozen vile rulers. She wished desperately that Drenan were in Hantlo, but she took solace in knowing that when he returned, what remained of the southern realm would be gone.

She stepped through the door, and Ursella closed it behind her.

They descended the steps together and climbed into the carriage at the front of the line. Three other girls huddled together inside.

"Are you ready, Edill?" Hadie asked the girl sitting in the middle of the three.

"Yes, Madam," Edill said.

The city was bedding down for the night, so the carriage ride was quick. Still, to Hadie, it seemed to take an eternity. They were riding toward either liberation or death. Hadie breathed a sigh of relief when the carriage pulled up in front of the chancellor's palace—not because she was anxious about getting on with the business, but because she was anxious to finish it.

The carriage door opened and Hadie took the initiative to lead the others out. She took the coachman's hand, stepped down onto the smooth pavement, and waited for the rest of the girls to climb out of their carriages.

A palace guard greeted them and led them to the entrance. The walkway was lined on both sides by old-growth trees, creating a canopy illuminated by torches. The night was cool for a southern night, but the wet air still made Hadie's skirt cling uncomfortably to her thighs.

When they entered the palace, the guard led them through back corridors and up several flights of stairs. He opened a door, and Hadie paused, looking into a ballroom full of finely dressed people. When she eventually stepped through the door, her girls followed. Once inside, she turned to address them. "Just do what you do best, and tonight will be a night that will never be forgotten."

She turned around and strode confidently into the room, looking for the nearest regent to talk with. The girls spread out behind her and began to mingle with the chancellor's guests as well.

It would be hours yet before the regents were ready to do any bedding, so in the meantime, it was the girls' responsibility to ensure their appetites were as wet as the air.

* * *

From the doorway at the top of the stairs, Sethlan watched the servants' door open on the far side of the ballroom. Nearly two dozen women wearing stunning orange corsets filed through. They looked around hesitantly. He watched Hadie turn and face the huddled girls, then they dispersed.

He fidgeted with a gem-encrusted pin protruding from the cuff of his shirt while he watched them mingle. He'd gotten the idea from his true employer. All the servants, including himself, were dressed for the occasion—the men wore black suits with white shirts, and the women wore black skirts with low-cut, frilly, white shirts. He originally thought to put the pin on the lapel of his suit jacket, but he figured it would be too conspicuous. Jorgan was always fiddling with his cuffs, so it had given Sethlan the idea to hide the pin there.

Dorlan's mood was sour. He wanted to be alone and had yet to emerge from his quarters. So Sethlan stayed at the top of the stairs and waited. He wanted to talk to Hadie, but at the same time, he didn't want to draw unnecessary attention to her. There was nothing to be said anyway. All that was left was for her to do her job and for him to do his.

Hadie moved around the room and conversed with many people. Several regents, as well as quite a few Silks, complimented her on maintaining Sonja's reputation after her retirement. She caught the eye of her father, working his way toward her, and turned her attention back to the regent talking to her. She silently hoped he was not coming to talk to her, but knew she wasn't going to be so lucky. He had obeyed her command to not return to the brothel, but he let her know he wasn't pleased she had gone to see her mother.

She glanced to her left and saw him standing nearby. She continued talking with the regent, but eventually, he excused himself with a kiss on the hand and telling her he was looking forward to later in the evening. She feigned her best smile and bowed as he walked away.

A hand grabbed her by the arm and pulled her roughly aside. "I don't know how you convinced her," her father said, "but what you're doing is foolish."

Hadie pulled away and said, "Let go of me." When her father let go, she took a step away from him and looked around. No one was paying attention to them.

"No one cares about you or how you're treated," Phenor said. "You're a whore, and that's all you'll ever be."

He stormed away, leaving Hadie staring after him.

"It's all right, dear," a familiar female voice said.

Hadie turned from her father to find her mother standing next to her.

"Don't worry about him," Tara said. She wore an elegant red dress. "He has fallen in line and will do as he's told."

"I can't imagine he's happy about taking orders from you."

"You're right; he's not. He's been cross since the day you came to visit." Tara took a sip of the wine she was holding and said, "Are you ready for this?"

Hadie nodded and said, "I am. Are you?"

"Except for your father, the Silks present tonight are your

allies. Including the Blessed ones. Do your thing, and all will go well after."

Hadie nodded again. "I love you, Ma."

"I love you too, Hadie." Tara turned away and immediately entered into conversation with a regent.

Hadie watched her smile and talk jovially. The regent looked in her direction and smiled at her. She smiled back and began mingling again. She glimpsed a red-headed servant wearing a black suit and holding a tray of wine on the far side of the room. She walked over to him and said, "Might I have a glass, please?"

Lyoll smiled as he lifted a glass off the tray. He handed it to her and said, "Anything for you, Madam."

"What are you doing here?" she asked.

"I'm working, Madam."

Hadie narrowed her eyes. Teamsters weren't servants, so she wondered how he had finagled his way into the palace. She knew better than to ask, though. Instead, she smiled at him and walked away, feeling a sense of relief that he was here.

Hadie made her way to the balcony. Three sets of double doors were all open, and the chancellor's guests moved freely in and out. The palace sat on the edge of the cliff that dropped down to the Kvorgan Sea, and its height above the water provided a majestic view. Some considered it the best view in the realm. However, it was dark, so when she stopped at the railing, there was nothing to see except blackness.

She mingled with Silks and regents on the balcony, enjoying the fresh sea breeze, as the night slowly grew late. She sipped her wine so her judgment wouldn't get clouded. Her girls were under the same instruction. The regents, however, consumed it freely. The later the hour grew, the more hints she heard about the nature of the big meeting the following day. There was lots of speculation—largely about the deteriorating state of the realm—but no one knew for sure. She only caught tidbits of information; each time she she approached a group, they changed the subject as soon as they noticed her.

The concern she detected among them as their inhibitions lowered throughout the night gave her pause. She knew the realm was in trouble—it was why she'd left in the first place. And they were the only ones with the power to do anything. They didn't seem to be able to fix whatever it was that was causing the weather to get so bad, but they were able to use their gift to help restore the city and villages after they were devastated by a cyclone. Without them, the people's ability to recover would be greatly diminished. She balked, suddenly wondering about the soundness of her plan.

A tap on her shoulder caused her to jump.

"Madam," Sethlan said, "it's time."

* * *

Sethlan stood in his place as the night progressed. He checked in periodically on the chancellor, but his mood hadn't changed. He simply sat on the couch in front of the panoramic windows that overlooked the sea, wearing an orange silk robe and drinking wine.

Before the guests arrived, Sethlan had repositioned couches from along the wall next to the chancellor's couch. The chancellor was so absorbed in thought he didn't even ask why.

Sethlan checked on the status of the wine bottle sitting on the table at the end of the couch and retrieved another when he found it empty. The chancellor ignored him; his gaze was fixed on the windows that now reflected the light in the room. Sethlan set the bottle on the table and returned to his spot at the top of the stairs.

With his hands clasped together below his navel, he could feel the gem flower pin in his cuff. It was just a matter of time.

After several hours and several trips in to check on the chancellor, the door behind him opened, and the chancellor appeared. The knot that had cinched his robe closed was undone and his robe hung open.

"Send the whores in," Dorlan said.

Sethlan nodded, and the door closed.

"Gather the whores and proceed up the stairs," Sethlan said.

Hadie nodded.

She scanned the balcony and saw three of them, so she walked over to them and, after politely interrupting their conversations, instructed them to follow her inside. She pointed for them to head over to the stairs on the side of the ballroom then went around the room, gathering the rest. The regents moved toward the stairs as well and went through the open doors at the top. The Silks continued to socialize where they were. This was how southern galas went, she knew: The Silks and the regents intermingled for a while, then the regents retired to a more intimate gathering.

By the time she had all the girls together, Sethlan waited for them at the top of the stairs. He gestured for them to ascend the steps, then ushered them through the doors. She'd seen her father go up these stairs on a few occasions, but she had never been up to Dorlan's private rooms herself.

The regents mingled in groups in the smaller, but equally lavish, ballroom. Hadie took one quick look at the large windows and gasped, wondering how amazing the view must be during the day. She gestured for the girls to go mingle with the regents—all of whom were in the room. All of them, that is, except Dreanna. Sethlan led her by the arm to the couches lined up in front of the windows, then he turned and walked away.

Hadie stood frozen a moment, looking at the chancellor sitting on the couch with his robe open, half exposed. When he looked at her, she stepped close and bowed deeply, showing him plenty of cleavage. She danced provocatively in front of him, applying everything Ursella had taught her.

"Take the corset off," the chancellor said when she leaned in close.

"Patience, Your Highness," Hadie cooed. She stepped back from the chancellor and called out, "Ladies!"

Sonja's whores—*her* whores—each took a regent by the

hand and led them over to the couches. When they were all seated, each whore faced a regent. Hadie stood in front of Dorlan.

For Hadie's plan to work, she needed them all to work as one. If the regents didn't all fall at precisely the same moment, their plan would fail. It was Edill who had come up with the idea of how to accomplish this. She said she'd seen something similar done once at another brothel she worked at before joining Sonja's. However, this time it would not end with bedding.

Hadie stood before Dorlan, about two paces away, with her whores lined up on both sides of her. As a single unit, they began to move in a synchronized dance. Each girl took the same steps. They all bent in the same direction and lifted the same legs. Unlike when Drenan had forced Hadie's clothes off in the carriage she'd once shared with Javen, Hadie voluntarily began to remove her clothes before the chancellor and regents.

They followed the same progression that Sonja had engrained in Hadie's head when she'd prepared Hadie to visit Drenan. First, their skirts came off, revealing the smallclothes that scarcely covered their bottoms. Next, their left legs went up onto the cushions of the seats as they untied the lace holding their stockings in place. Once they were free, in unison, they pushed the stocking down to their ankles and freed their feet. They repeated the process with their right legs, then stepped back.

They danced around provocatively again, then set to slowly loosening the lace that kept their corsets cinched tight. Hadie didn't want to bare her body before these vile men, but she knew it was necessary. She let her corset fall to the ground. With girls to her left and right, clad in only their small silk bottoms, Hadie stepped closer to Dorlan. The girls followed. In her peripheral vision, Hadie saw two dozen servants slipping into the room. Lyoll was among them. They stood back so their images wouldn't reflect on the glass.

Hadie stopped half a pace from Dorlan and began slowly

removing pins from her hair. One by one the pins fell to the floor. As they worked at pulling them out, they turned and twisted, bent and moved, and counted.

* * *

Sethlan opened the servants' door and ushered the chosen servants in. Whores danced in front of the regents and the chancellor on the far side of the room. He instructed the servants to line up and wait, but to stand back until the deed had been done.

Quickly, he made his way around the periphery of the room to the main entrance. He cracked the door open and pulled it shut after slipping through it. He took a quick look around the room, located his target, then descended the stairs. He had but moments to get into position.

"Your Ladyship," he said with a bow in front of Dreanna.

She stopped talking to the Silk she was conversing with—Hadie's father—and looked in Sethlan's direction.

"Might I have a word?"

"Excuse me a moment," Dreanna said.

Phenor shook his head and said, "No worries, Your Ladyship."

"What is it?" Dreanna said when they stood alone.

"There's something in His Highness' quarters I think you should see," Sethlan said.

"I'm not interested in whores."

"Your Ladyship," Sethlan said with a small bow. "Please?"

Dreanna let out a sigh but started toward the stairs.

Sethlan followed and took a deep breath. He'd had some close calls when meeting with Jorgan or performing a task Jorgan had asked him to do, but this… the timing of what was about to take place would have to be impeccable.

* * *

Dorlan watched Sheena pull another hairpin from her hair and drop it to the floor. She stepped toward him, and he saw the girls on either side of him move in as well. He stared at Sheena's breasts. The whores all leaned in. Sheena placed her right hand on the back of the couch, next to his head, then pressed her bare chest close to his face. He resisted the urge to lean forward and take a breast into his mouth. She reached up and pulled another pin from her hair. She leaned closer, her breath hot on his ear, and whispered, "The blood river runs red tonight."

Pain pierced his neck.

Sheena stood erect and stepped back.

He reached up and felt a pin protruding from the side of his neck. He pulled it out and looked at the bejeweled yellow and red flower. He looked up at her, his eyes going hot with rage.

His arms and legs suddenly felt weak. He attempted to push himself to his feet, but thick arms slipped around his neck and held him in place. He struggled to rise, the desire to strangle the whore standing before him coursing through him. But he was powerless. Without dragon bones, they were all powerless.

The poison worked quickly, and Dorlan was soon unable to move, his body paralyzed.

The whore standing in front of him blinked tears from her eyes. He watched as they streamed freely.

The room closed in around him, and he heard an exclamation, but the words he didn't understand.

Everything went black.

* * *

Sethlan held the door open for Dreanna. When she stepped through, he followed behind her while pulling the pin from his cuff.

"What in Draego's Fire!" Dreanna exclaimed.

Sethlan took a quick look over at the couches. A row of servants stood behind the regents and chancellor, holding them in place. They were barely struggling. Naked women stood between them and the panoramic window.

He stepped close to Dreanna and grabbed her around the neck. He held her head frozen in place and buried the pin in her neck.

She struggled for only a few moments before he supported her full weight with his arm.

He loosened his grip, and she fell to the ground.

* * *

Hadie looked away from Dorlan when she heard the exclamation. With tears freely running down her cheeks, she watched as Sethlan ended Dreanna's life. She looked at Lyoll, who was holding Dorlan in place with his thick arms. The struggle was over. Dorlan was dead. They were all dead.

She became acutely aware of her nakedness but resisted the urge to cover her breasts. As calmly as she could, she bent down and picked up her corset. Emotions flooded out of her as she cinched it back into place. She couldn't stop herself from crying any longer.

Lyoll hurried around the couch and embraced her in a hug. She collapsed into his embrace and cried.

She cried for all those who had needlessly lost their lives to the Blessed. She cried for Astora. She cried for Javen. She cried for herself.

CHAPTER 42

The growing ruckus caused Hadie to step back from Lyoll. Silks were pouring into Dorlan's chamber as fast as they could shove through the door. Her mother hurried over to her and wrapped a cloak around her shoulders and said, "We must hurry before any of them get power hungry."

Tara wrapped an arm around Hadie's waist and guided her away from Lyoll. She led Hadie around the couches where Dorlan and the regents slumped, through the Silks, who tentatively inched closer to the dead rulers, toward the door Sethlan held open.

Hadie looked down at Dreanna's body as they passed it.

"We must hurry," Sethlan said.

"Don't you think I know that," Tara said.

Sethlan hurried to clear a path through those still gathered in the ballroom. He guided them through the exit, out into a hallway. Halfway down the hallway, Sethlan and Tara turned down another hallway. Hadie breathed a sigh of relief when she saw Lyoll was following close behind.

"Where are we going?" Hadie asked.

"To get you ready," Tara said.

"For what?"

"Your coronation."

Hadie pulled her arm free from her mother's grip and stopped. When her mother turned around, she said, "My *what?*"

"Coronation," Tara said. "You're going to be Queen of the South."

"*What?* What's that?"

"Over the years, I've learned many interesting things from my true employer," Sethlan said. "Such as in the Previous Era, the time before the Dragon King, rulers were known as Kings and Queens."

"Wait," Hadie said, looking from Sethlan to her mother to Lyoll. "You want *me* to be in charge?"

"Yes, dear," Tara said. "But not just be in charge. We want you to rule."

"But I don't know the first thing about ruling."

"None of us do, dear."

"But... but I didn't do this so I could rule. I did it so *you* could—"

"It's not up to you," Tara said.

"What do you mean it's not up to me?"

"The decision's been made."

"By who?"

"Me, Sethlan, Sethlan's employer, Lyoll. Others as well."

Hadie looked at Lyoll tersely. He smiled sheepishly. "You knew about this?"

"Sorry, lass," Lyoll said. "After you went to visit your mother, she came to see me."

Hadie looked from Lyoll to her mother. "You know each other?"

"How else do you think I got those flowers for my garden?" Tara said.

"At first, your mother was mad at Ganip for being so careless in his... enterprise," Lyoll said, "but when she found out I knew you, she started asking me what I thought about you."

"*Me?* Except for the time in the caravan and our trip to Onta," Hadie said, "what could you possible know about me?"

"Please," Tara said, "this is not the time or the place."

"Agreed," Sethlan said. "We must hurry."

"Why hurry?" Hadie said. "If I'm to be... queen,"—the word sounded strange on her tongue—"I want answers." Hadie glared at her mother and said, "Why aren't you going to be queen?"

"I'll explain it to you in due time," Tara said.

"No. You'll explain it to me right *now*." Hadie stomped her foot as she said 'now'.

"Now, you see, you're going to be a fine ruler."

"*You* were supposed to be the one who led."

"Well... I don't want to be queen."

Hadie snorted. "What makes you think I do?"

"It doesn't matter. You wanted this. And besides—"

"I did *not* want this."

"The Silks will trust you."

"*Me?*"

"More importantly, the people will trust you."

"Why wouldn't the Silks trust you?" Hadie said. "You *are* one."

"No. Your father is. And they don't trust him."

"Why not?"

"Look, Hadie, we can go into as much detail about this as you want later, but right now you need to take command before one of the Silks works up the courage to do it themselves. You certainly don't want one who's Blessed to, else we'd be right back where we were."

"If they don't trust Father, why would they trust me? I'm his daughter."

"Who had the courage to do what none of them could. And he betrayed you."

Hadie stared at her mother not knowing what to say.

"Now come," Tara said.

Tara took Hadie by the arm and pulled her forward.

Hadie didn't want to be queen of anything. She just wanted to finally, and permanently, be rid of the Southern Realm. She wanted to go and find the man she loved. She didn't care if he was bedding the most beautiful women in Onta. She should have never left. She should have confronted him… given him the chance to choose. But she didn't resist her mother's pull. She allowed herself to be pulled to an unknown future.

CHAPTER 43

The acrid smell of burning flesh filled Drakonias' nose. The amount of Energy flowing through his Core, down his arms and into the marble railing of his balcony, numbed the pain.

"Your Blessed Highness," a familiar voice, that of his fourth son, said from behind.

Drakonias released his grip on the railing and healed his hands. Continuing to look south, he said, "Who is Phenor Morrigan?"

"Phenor Morrigan?" Drenan repeated.

"Who is he?"

"A Silk, Your Highness. Why?"

"I've just received a message from him."

"From Phenor? Why would he…"

Drakonias stared into the distance for a prolonged minute then said, "To inform me that the chancellor is dead."

"*Dead?* What happened?"

"Along with every last regent in the south."

Silence hung in the air.

"H-how?" Drenan stammered.

Drakonias looked down at his handprints burned into the marble. "Moreover," he began, turning around. Drenan stood next to Devin. "Phenor informs me his *daughter* has been proclaimed *Queen* of the South." His voice was calm and evenly moderated.

"Hadie!" Drenan spat.

"You know her?"

Drenan pounded the marble railing with a clenched fist and said, "I *knew* I should have killed her when I had the chance."

"What are you talking about?" Drakonias said.

"She was mixed up with"—a smile blossomed on Drenan's face—"with Javen."

"*Javen?*" He shifted his gaze from Drenan to Devin.

Devin took a step back.

"Send for him."

"Yes, Your Highness." Devin spun on his heel and hurried inside.

Drakonias turned and looked to the south again. He reached into an inner pocket of his suit jacket and pulled out an open envelope. "There's this as well," he said, holding the envelope out to his side.

Drenan stepped up alongside the emperor and took the envelope. He pulled out a folded parchment and read it. "*Dragon King!*" he exclaimed.

"What's this?" Devin said as he rejoined them.

Drenan handed Devin the parchment, and Devin read it.

"How is it that within the span of a few hours I receive news that the south is in *complete* rebellion—overthrown!—*and* that a man is approaching Kyinth claiming to be the Dragon King?" Drakonias turned to face Devin and Drenan again.

Devin and Drenan stared at him with blank faces.

"Your Highness, we… what should we do?" Devin said.

"Start by telling me what connections Javen had to this… *Queen* of the South," Drakonias said.

"She was just the daughter of a Silk—a loyal Silk," Drenan started. He spent the next several minutes explaining to Drakonias how he'd found Hadie with Javen in Lonely Oak, ending with when they parted ways in Portstown.

"So, you threaten to rape her, and then she returns to Hantlo and somehow manages to kill *everyone*?"

"This… this is *not* my fault!" Drenan exclaimed.

"Perhaps not," Drakonias said. "But the moment I tend to this so-called Dragon King, you *will* return to the south and end this nonsense."

"Yes, Your Highness," Drenan said with a bow.

"What do you intend to do about this 'Dragon King'?" Devin said.

"I will do what I always do to rebels," Drakonias said. "I will crush him." He turned back to the south and stood with his hands clasped behind his back.

He wondered how events could possibly have ended up as they now were. He couldn't imagine how a single whore had succeeded where thousands of others had failed. But if it was true, his empire was now half what it was seventy years ago. *Are they connected?*

He'd resigned himself more than twenty years ago to the fact that he was going to eventually lose the south, and that it would be similar to how it happened to the east. The cyclones that plagued the East Sea used to only threaten sea crossings in the summer and fall, but they'd grown in intensity and frequency to the point that they made it impossible to cross year-round. Officially, the Eastern Realm was still a part of the empire, but Drakonias hadn't heard from Thena in seventy years. When the ships had first stopped crossing the sea, he'd been able to maintain contact with the east by condor, but eventually, even the condors refused to cross.

The first time Dorlan had come to Kyinth with news of dramatically changing weather in the southern provinces of his realm, Drakonias had known the same was about to happen to the south. Dorlan petitioned several times for him to do something, but the unfortunate truth was that there was nothing he *could* do. Dorlan mentioned several times how he used to alter the weather, back when he used to watch the sunrise every morning, but that had been local manipulation only. No one was strong enough to affect the weather of an entire region. Even if he'd had that kind of strength, any changes he made would have had no *lasting* effect—natural patterns took over quickly. What Dorlan wanted was impossible. It was all moot now anyway. Whether or not Drenan was successful in restoring order in the south, it was lost—if not today, in the next decade or century. But he would send him with an army of Synthesizers to restore what order remained. He would not give the rebels a foothold to challenge the control he still maintained.

The road leading toward Croff was visible in the distance. *Is that joke of a Council behind this… this Dragon King?* As he gazed down at the road, he wondered who could be foolish enough to come to the capital of the United Realms claiming the title of his long-dead father. And with a force of only six! Were the two events related? They had to be. And Deanna was at the center of it, he was certain. It was too coincidental that after being in hiding for four hundred years, she had surfaced at the same time an entire realm collapsed *and* someone named himself Dragon King.

He had a few days yet before the delegation arrived. Even if his sister was somehow involved, he was not concerned with six rebels. He would hear them out, then deal with them as he dealt with all rebels.

"Your Blessed Highness," a voice stammered from behind.

Drakonias turned around. Javen was kneeling a few paces away, head bowed low. "Rise, Regent."

Javen stood.

"What connection does Hadie have with the rebels?"

"H… Hadie?" Javen stammered. Drakonias could tell the lad's thoughts were swirling, searching. "I… none that I know of."

"It wouldn't be wise to lie to me, *Regent*," Drakonias said.

"I-I'm not, Your Highness. I only met her the night… that night in Lonely Oak when… when my brother… I didn't even know my aunt was associated with the… If Hadie was somehow associated with them, she never said anything about it the whole time we were together."

Drakonias scrutinized Javen. He seemed to be telling the truth.

"W-why?" Javen asked.

"Because she has killed Dorlan"—the lad's eyes went wide—"and every single regent in the south. *And* she's declared herself Queen of the South."

Javen stared at him, his face blank.

"As soon as I finish this Dragon King business," Drakonias continued, "you will accompany Drenan to Hantlo and attend to this… *queen.*"

Javen's eyes darted over at Drenan, then back to him, and the blank look on his face shifted to one of fear.

CHAPTER 44

Queen of the South? Javen thought as he rode down the Lift from the emperor's quarters. He gripped the rail to steady himself, still not used to the feeling of the Lift's movement. The Machine stopped, and the metal door slid open. He stepped out into the small room and opened the door. The guard waiting on the other side bowed to him as he emerged.

He made his way down the hallway and turned down the Hall of Relics, his mind spinning. The last eleven days had been a whirlwind. He still fondly remembered waking up in bed with Lannary and Melina the morning after he had become a regent. Melina had led him by the hand through the halls to his quarters—not discreetly, as he had instructed Lannary. Even with desire welling in him for what he knew was about to happen, he still secretly hoped Kaylan was hidden in her room so she wouldn't know about it.

"Where are we going?" he'd asked when he realized they weren't going to his suite.

"To your suite, Your Majesty," Melina had said.

"This isn't the right floor," Javen protested. "My suite is down three floors."

"Those aren't your rooms, Your Majesty. Those are guest quarters." Melina stopped in front of a door ornately carved with grapevines and said, "The Regent of Onta's suite is this one."

"Oh," Javen said. He breathed a sigh of relief as he realized he wouldn't have to hide from Kaylan.

The door opened, and a naked Lannary greeted him with a lascivious grin. She took Melina by the hand and quickly proved to Javen that they were already intimately familiar with each other. They kissed each other passionately, then took Javen by the arm, led him into his new suite, and spent the rest of the night helping him catch up with their familiarity.

After waking the next morning and engaging in another round of bedding the two beautiful women, Javen met with Devin again. After their meeting, Devin told him they'd be returning to Onta in about two weeks and that in the meantime, he was free to enjoy himself while they were in Kyinth.

The rest of that day, he kept busy without even leaving the palace. He initially went and checked in on Kaylan. Oshie greeted him warmly when he entered his original suite, but Kaylan had locked herself into her room and refused to talk to him. He asked Oshie to let her know she had the suite to herself, and instructed Oshie to see to any need she might have. Upon returning to his new suite, he was inundated by a dozen invitations from other regents. Melina was gone, but Lannary said, "I've already sorted them for you."

"Thanks," Javen said.

He shared a midday meal with Rebeka, the regent of the Tieger province in the Northern Realm. Then he had afternoon tea with Eran, the regent of the Thena province in the Eastern Realm. He'd been one of the last to successfully cross the Eastern Sea—ironically, he had come to seek help with how to deal with the cyclones. He'd been stuck ever since.

Javen met with two other regents, then attended a dinner party in the Regent of Ronig's suite. There he met several other regents from the western provinces. Even though the names were familiar, his mind swam, trying to keep them straight as he consumed copious amounts of wine. The one solid face in the crowd of rulers was Melina's. She stuck close to his side and escorted him back to his suite when the party ended late in the night—but his night didn't end there. Both Lannary and Melina were hungry to repeat the night before, and Javen didn't protest.

The last person he expected to think about as he fell asleep was Ganip.

* * *

"G'luck!" Ganip called out to Javen as Javen strode up.

Javen stopped and looked at the gangly boy stoking the fire pit back to life. When Hadie wasn't in bed when he woke, he'd assumed she was at the fire pit. But she wasn't.

"Where's Hadie?" he asked Ganip.

Ganip shrugged. "Dunno."

Bile rose in Javen's throat.

"Perhaps tomorrow we'll invite that whore who has been warming your bed."

Drenan's words echoed in his mind.

Fear.

Anger.

Desperation.

Drenan's formula to force him to Synthesize had failed. He'd helplessly watched Astora die.

He'd spent the day sitting across from Hadie in the carriage, unable to tell her what had happened. He couldn't tell her how he had watched Drenan open Astora's throat with a knife, how Drenan had goaded him into healing her. He couldn't tell her that he couldn't save her. He wasn't able to use his gift. He couldn't tell her how Astora's eyes had pleaded with him while Drenan mocked him. He couldn't tell her how Drenan had threatened that she would be next. Dorlan wouldn't allow it, though, he'd convinced himself. He wasn't cruel like Drenan. But Hadie was gone.

"What is it?" Ganip asked.

Javen's heart nearly exploded in his chest. He sprinted across the camp, terrified.

He skidded to a stop in front of Drenan's carriage. The guard standing at the door nodded to him as though everything was perfectly normal. He couldn't make himself take another step.

"Mustn't keep His Majesty waiting," the guard said.

Javen forced himself to climb the steps, each step as heavy as a barrel full of ale. The door was locked. He could see himself doing this exact thing the previous day. It had already happened. Only, when he knocked, he was greeted by Astora's frightened eyes.

He knocked.

He heard screaming within the carriage.

"Hadie!" Javen screamed as he pounded on the door. "Let me in, you monster!"

The door opened.

Hadie answered. But she hung in the air helpless, bound by invisible cords.

"*P-p-please,*" she whispered. "*Javen… h-help.*"

She floated back into the carriage, allowing Javen to step through the door.

"Let her go," he demanded.

"Are you threatening me, get?" Drenan said calmly.

"*Perhaps tomorrow we'll invite that whore who has been warming your bed.*"

"Dorlan won't let you." Javen turned, intending to run to Dorlan's carriage for help, but the door slammed shut.

"Just where do you think you're going?" Drenan's invisible bonds wrapped around Javen and slid him across the floor. They pushed him down onto the couch, and Drenan said, "Sit."

Hadie floated across the air and was forcefully set down in the exact spot where Astora had sat curled up yesterday.

"I don't think I need to repeat everything we discussed yesterday, do I?" Drenan said. "No… I imagine you remember everything we discussed."

Javen icily glared at Drenan. "You're a monster."

"All we need do, then, is wait."

Javen fought against his invisible restraint, but he couldn't move. "Dorlan!" he shouted.

"Will not help you."

"*Please...*" Hadie whispered. Tears streamed down her face.

Tears streamed down Javen's face as well. He looked from Hadie to Drenan.

"Please, let her go."

Drenan strode calmly to the table in the corner and retrieved the long knife he'd used to kill Astora.

The sun inched over the horizon and shone through the open window.

"Ah, there it is," Drenan said. He strode over to Hadie and grabbed her by the hair. Without further word, he tilted her head back and drew the knife across her throat. Blood spurted from the wound. "Now, let's see if she means more to you than that whore from yesterday. What was her name again?"

Javen screamed, startling himself awake. He sat up in bed and looked around the dimly lit room frantically.

"What is it, Your Majesty?"

Javen looked to his side and saw Lannary sitting up beside him. The sheet fell away from her body, and she made no effort to cover herself.

"Yes, what is it, Javen?"

He turned the other way and saw Melina lying next to him.

He put a hand to his forehead.

Lannary placed a hand on his sweaty back. "A dream?"

Javen nodded.

"More like a nightmare, it would seem," Melina said. "Care to talk about it?"

Javen shook his head. "It was just a dream."

"Shall we help you forget it?" Lannary said.

"I... I need a minute." Javen climbed out of bed and stumbled over to the washbasin. He cupped his hands and scooped up water, splashing it on his face. He scrubbed his face with his hands, then used the towel hanging on the rack to pat it dry. Javen returned to the bed, the dream beginning to fade, and said, "I think I'm just stressed."

"Well, let us help you ease some of it," Lannary cooed.

* * *

The next day started with a meeting with the emperor. Javen was nervous at first, still not used to even being in Kyinth, where the emperor resided, let alone to the idea of *meeting* with the emperor. And his dream hadn't completely faded, even with Melina and Lannary's help. But Drakonias put him at ease, and it was during their meeting that Javen finally understood that he was no longer a Thornhill. He was a Drake. Javen Danavin Dairion Drake.

It was at this meeting that he learned for the first time how the Blessed of the Dragon lived so long: Regeneration. "You are young still," Drakonias said, "but when the time comes, if you serve me well, you shall never fear growing old."

As they sat in the emperor's private quarters in the tallest building in the empire, Javen slowly began to respect the man who not only sat atop this building but also sat atop the empire. As they talked, Javen learned that he was more than a figurehead, a worshiped entity, a Blessed. He was a man. Even though many throughout the empire worshiped this man, just like every other person who counted himself or herself a part of the United Realms, he was not without fault. He was a man who, almost daily, made decisions that came with great heartbreak.

Their meeting ended when Drakonias' future wife, Angania, reminded him that he had court. Javen accompanied the emperor down the Lift and sat in the balcony to watch the emperor sit on his throne and hear from petitioners from around the empire. He tried not to let the Dragon Guard, clad in white armor, distract him. He knew that once he returned to Onta, he would be in a similar position, so he wanted to learn as much as he could on how to conduct himself before those he would rule. In Onta, he would be a direct representative of the emperor, and he intended to represent Drakonias well.

After court, he spent the rest of the day with Melina, touring the capital. They dined at a restaurant atop one of the towering buildings. It was the fanciest place he'd ever eaten. Their table had a view of the mountains to the north and the North River that flowed by the city. When they returned to the palace, they had wine with Devin and Karina before retiring back to his suite.

"I have a surprise for you," Melina whispered in his ear the next morning.

Javen stifled a yawn, thankful he hadn't dreamed again—or at least he didn't remember it if he had—and said, "What?"

"After we eat breakfast, we're going to Arinin."

"*Really?* Do you think it'll be okay with Devin if we leave?"

"You're the Regent of Onta, Javen. You don't need his permission." Melina climbed on top of him and said, "But first..." She kissed him passionately. "...I intend to bed you again."

Before they left, Javen invited Kaylan, despite Melina's request that he not. He continued to cling to the hope she would come around, but she said no.

"Make sure she has everything she wants," Javen instructed Oshie.

"Your Majesty," Oshie said, stopping Javen before he disappeared through the door.

Javen turned. "Yes?"

"Might I speak candidly?"

Javen nodded. "Always."

"What she wants," Oshie said, "is to go back to your brother."

"She told you that?"

"Yes," Oshie said. "Whenever I check in on her and ask her if I can get her anything, she always says the same thing."

"That she wants to go back to Yolken?"

"And that she wants you to go with her."

Javen furrowed his brow. Some advised him to punish Kaylan for her disobedience, as regents are often required to do with their subjects, but he refused. He knew that any future chance he might have of her opening her heart to him would vanish if he treated her poorly. Instead, he made sure she had everything she might desire in the hopes of one day breaking down the barrier that divided them.

"You understand why I can't let that happen?" he said.

"It is not my place to understand, Your Majesty," Oshie said with a bow.

Javen left Kaylan's suite, annoyed. But by the time Melina's carriage rolled through the gates of the city walls, Melina and Lannary had remedied it.

The trip to Arinin and back was a blur. It was a beautiful city, lacking in the towering buildings of Kyinth, but it was pleasantly nestled in the woods. Melina's palace, though not towering like the palace in Onta, had many wall-less corridors leading to beautiful gardens.

They toured the distilleries that made the province famous and strolled through the peaceful woods. Though Melina conducted herself modestly during the day and in view of her subjects, unlike Karina in amorous Onta, she was passionate in bedding at night.

And now that he'd returned, he learned of the Queen of the South.

Hadie.

He'd been so distracted by everything that had been taking place that he had barely even thought of her since he'd rescued Kaylan. And now that he did think about her, the feelings he had for her came rushing back.

Now, instead of returning to Onta with Devin, the emperor was sending him to the south. To Hadie. He'd been trying to find Hadie since he first arrived in Onta, but Devin had maintained that he couldn't find her. Now he knew exactly where she was. And he knew exactly what the emperor wanted him to do. And with Drenan—the man he hated more than anything.

His stomach roiled.

He had imagined he would have time to ease into his new role as regent. But before even one month had gone by, before he'd had the opportunity to make even one trivial decision, he was going to have to choose between his loyalty for the emperor and killing someone he loved.

Javen reached his floor and ran to his suite. The moment the door closed behind him, he doubled over and vomited.

CHAPTER 45

Drenan blasted the door open with a burst of Energy and stormed into Nera's office.

Nera lowered her arm from her face and said, "What in Draego's Fire is your problem?"

"You've had plenty of time—"

"Get out of my office, Drenan!" Nera shouted.

Nera's hand moved down toward her desk, but Drenan reached out with a thread of Energy and stopped it. He moved her arm down to her side, then enveloped all but her head with his Energy, freezing her in place. He looked at her with deep pleasure as her eyes widened with fear. "You've had plenty of time," he started over, "to sic your minions on Danavin's miserable *get*. I can understand your reluctance to kill someone His Blessed Highness just made a regent, but I fail to understand why you wouldn't take advantage of his going to Arinin."

"I run the Sodality, Drenan, not you. And I work according to my own volition. You wouldn't want a trail of potential mistakes leading to you, would you?"

"Are you threatening me, Nera?" Drenan spat.

"No, but if you r-rush me, mistakes are inevitable."

Drenan wrapped Energy around Nera's throat and contemplated crushing it. But he resisted the urge. As much as he hated to admit it, he needed her. He squeezed it just enough to make Nera choke. "The emperor has seen fit to have the get accompany me to Hantlo to deal with the rebellion there. But you *will* see to it that he doesn't. Do you understand?"

Nera tried to speak, but she choked instead.

Drenan released his hold on her neck. "Do you understand?" he repeated.

"Y-yes," Nera croaked.

Drenan spun on his heel and walked through the door-less doorway, keeping Nera frozen in place. He walked past the two Watchers guarding the hallway at the entrance to the atrium, neither of them paying any mind to the threads of Energy trailing behind him. He descended the stairs that zig-zagged down each floor of the Synod tower, and only when he walked out the front door did he release his hold on Nera.

As he walked away from the tower, he recharged the bone tucked into his belt.

CHAPTER 46

A lone man on a horse waited in the center of the road.

Jax pulled on his horse's reins and said, "Whoa."

The others brought their horses to a stop as well.

The man standing in the middle of the road ribbed his horse and started toward them.

"Be ready," Jax said.

They were sitting in full sunlight. Even though Yolken's bones were full—he always kept them full now—unlimited Energy was available from the sun should they need it. The man wasn't wearing Glasses, but if Yolken drew more Energy from the sun, he'd have to disperse it because he couldn't fit any more in his bones. So, he transferred Energy from his bones to his Core instead. Even if the man was wearing Glasses, he wouldn't have been able to see what Yolken had done. The man walking his horse toward them had yet to show any sign of posing a threat.

The man stopped his horse about fifty paces away, dismounted, and started walking toward them.

"Draego's Fire," Jax said.

"It's Reago," Deanna said.

Reago stopped ten paces away and knelt. He bowed his head and said, "I am Reago Draeko Yarin Drake. I have come to pledge my loyalty to the Dragon King."

Yolken looked over at Jax. "How does he know?"

"I don't know," Jax said. Jax turned to Deanna.

"Your guess is as good as mine," she said.

"Does it matter how he knows?" Deborah said. "Point is, he knows."

"But why would he be pledging himself to Yolken?" Jax said.

"He *was* branded a traitor," Deanna said. "And because he's always been sympathetic to the rebel cause. He never fully agreed with what Drakonias did, but he begrudgingly went along with it. Maybe he's changed his mind."

"He's the Chancellor of the Western Realm," Corin said.

"*Was* the Chancellor of the Western Realm," Jax said.

"What harm is there in hearing him out?" Tabora asked. "He's alone."

Yolken looked at the surrounding area. They'd been following the North River for some time now, and Jax said they were about a day's ride out from Kyinth. They'd passed several villages since the road came up alongside the river, but presently they were in between two of them. The river was to their left and an open grass field to their right.

"He's likely laid a trap in the next village," Corin said.

"The emperor has named him a traitor," Tabora said, "and he's just pledged loyalty to Yolken."

"To lull him into a false sense of security."

"Might I approach, Your Blessed Highness?" Reago called loudly.

All eyes turned toward Yolken.

"Ultimately, the decision is yours, Your Highness," Tabora said.

"We either see what he wants," Jax said. "Or we kill him."

"If this is some sort of a trap, dear," Deborah said, "it's unlikely he's going to simply let us by."

Yolken looked at the kneeling man. The proclamation Jax had read that night in Croff, which named Javen the Regent of

Onta, had begun by declaring Reago a traitor. If he believed Javen was now a regent, why not also believe Reago was a traitor and no longer the Chancellor of the Western Realm? Yolken didn't see the harm in at least seeing what he wanted. "Approach," he called.

Reago stood and walked toward them.

Jax positioned his horse close to Yolken's left flank, and Deanna positioned herself to his right. Deborah lined up next to Deanna, and Corin and Tabora next to Jax.

"Deanna!" Reago said when he drew near. "What a pleasant surprise!"

"Reago," Deanna said. She sat stiffly in her saddle.

"I haven't seen you since…" Reago started to say, but then he shook his head and said, "There'll be time for reminiscing later. Right now, I suppose you want some sort of explanation."

"That would be nice," Jax said.

"Well, let me start by saying that I'm no longer Chancellor of the Western Realm."

"We heard. Question is, why?"

"For committing treason, of course."

"Then how is it you're standing here and not hanging from a scaffolding?"

"I know what you're thinking," Reago said, "and believe me, he's not pleased that I'm still alive. Four assassins from the Sodality were waiting for me at my tower in Kyinth."

It seemed hard to believe that he had survived four assassins, but then Yolken had recently finished hearing Jax explain how his father had easily overpowered a couple himself. "What happened?" he asked.

"Someone… intervened on my behalf," Reago said.

"What treason did you commit?"

"Well," Reago started, "after your warm welcome in Onta, I used a forbidden Train to travel to Kyinth. I also sent a message to Dorlan, Sheal, and Thena—even though she'll never receive it—to tell them that which I have known since shortly after

Drashon's death."

"Which is what?" Jax said.

"That the sun is dying," Reago said. "And that we—those of us who rebelled against our father—are responsible."

"That'll do it," Jax said. Yolken thought he seemed satisfied with the sincerity of Reago's pledge.

Hearing Reago say the sun was dying out loud made Yolken believe him as well. He knew Drakonias had killed his son to protect that knowledge, so if Reago knew…

"What are you doing here, Reago?" Deanna said.

"I have come to throw my lot in where it rightfully belongs," Reago said.

"Which is where?" Jax said.

"With the Dragon King."

"Why? After all this time?"

"Because, as the empire collapses around us, Drakonias refuses to even admit there's a problem, let alone do anything about it. I have always known what we did was wrong. Drakonias' war should never have been fought."

"And yet you're responsible for killing hundreds of thousands of people," Deanna said. Reago hung his head. "Not to mention you're directly responsible for the murder of two of your brothers."

"No!" Reago said, looking up. "What happened to Eagan and Anshar was *not* what it looked like."

"I was there when Anshar died," Deanna said. "What happened looked pretty clear to me."

Reago looked down at his feet again. "I know how it looked. But I did what I did because I was trying to save Father's life."

"You expect me to believe that?" Deanna said. "I was there when he died."

"You were?"

"Yes. And so were you."

"I went along with Drakonias' rebellion, true, but I did *not* want him to kill Father. And had I not done what I did to Eagan and Anshar, he would have died much sooner. And so would the rest of you."

"Is that why you are so reclusive?" Tabora said.

"Yes," Reago admitted. "What happened has never sat well with me."

"And yet you still killed members of the Order of the Dragon."

"Those lost were only the ones I couldn't save."

"Are you trying to tell us that you worked to *save* members of the Order?" Corin said.

"Yes."

"That's hard to believe. History is rife with members killed in the west—*your* realm—by regents under your direct control."

"I couldn't very well stop every rebel execution," Reago said. "But I assure you, I saved more lives than were lost in my realm."

"And now you want to join with the rebels?" Jax said.

"I have already demonstrated that by pledging my loyalty to the Dragon King." Looking straight at Yolken, Reago added, "Seeing you… You remind me of your father."

"Y-you knew my father?" Yolken stammered.

"I did. And I assure you that I mourned his loss just as much as the Order did."

"Thank you," Yolken said. "So, why are you here? Why have you decided to pledge yourself to me?"

"More importantly," Jax interjected, "how did you know Yolken had declared himself Dragon King?"

"Someone in Croff sent word to Drakonias, and it made its way to me."

"It had to have come from Dalia," Corin said.

"But who would have told her?" Tabora asked.

"It doesn't matter," Deanna said. "Point is that Drakonias knows."

"We'd planned on announcing ourselves soon anyway," Deborah said.

"Why pledge yourself to me?" Yolken said.

"Because we need to stop the emperor," Reago said. "I've been contemplating confronting him for some time, and what happened in Onta was the catalyst I needed to finally act."

"I haven't come to stop Drakonias," Yolken said. "I just want a truce long enough to solve the problem of the sun."

"He will never agree to a truce," Reago said.

"But I intend to try."

Yolken and Reago stared eye to eye.

"Then I will accompany you."

"How do I know you aren't here to kill me?" Yolken said.

Reago reached into a pocket and produced an envelope. He held it out and said, "Because I have this."

No one moved. Jax looked over at Yolken, who nodded. Jax urged his horse forward and closed the gap between himself and Reago. Reago held the envelope out to him, and he took it.

Yolken watched intently as Jax read it. When Jax lowered it, Yolken said, "What does it say?"

"It's the edict from Drakonias to Nera ordering Reago's death," Jax said.

"He didn't even send it to the Synod first," Reago said.

"Because they would never have approved it," Tabora said.

"Exactly," Reago said. "Does that suffice to prove I'm not here to kill you?"

"It could be part of the plan," Corin said.

"It's not," Deanna said. "If what Reago said about traveling to Kyinth in a Train and saying what he did to the other chancellors is true, then Drakonias would react exactly as he did."

"Then it's settled," Yolken said. "I accept your allegiance."

CHAPTER 47

Yolken stared at the approaching wall. It had several evenly spaced flat-topped towers on it. They looked exactly as they'd always looked in paintings he'd seen of the capital, but he'd always thought they looked incomplete. "What's with the walls?" he said.

"You're about to meet with the Emperor of the United Realms, and you're thinking about the walls?" Jax said.

Yolken looked over at Jax, who stared at him as if he were crazy. "What? I've always thought they looked—"

"Incomplete," Deanna finished for him. "That's because they are. Well, they're not so much incomplete as missing something."

"What?" Yolken said.

"Before the war, there weren't walls around the city. My father originally built the wall after the war started. He barely thwarted the first attack on the city, and after pushing Drakonias' forces deep into the Onta Mountains, he ordered the wall's construction. Synthesizers worked day and night to construct it. The flat towers you see now came after we started killing dragons. We naturally thought dragons would begin attacking cities once we started killing them, so we made Machines that sat atop those towers to protect the city."

"What did they do?"

"They launched metal spikes into the sky. The Machines were anchored on a swivel and could be moved left and right, aimed up and down. They would have been an effective deterrent."

"Would have been?" Yolken said.

"My father was wrong," Deanna said. "Dragons never attacked. They fought only in defense. Not once did the dragons initiate an attack on us, even though we were systematically slaughtering them. Instead, we used the Machines to cut down Drakonias' armies when they attacked the city. We... *I*... gruesomely slaughtered helpless people by the tens of thousands."

They pulled their horses to a stop before the closed gates. Yolken looked at them, wondering if Javen was somewhere in the city. He needed to somehow find out, because if he was, Yolken wasn't going to leave him like he had done in Onta.

"Identify yourselves!" a voice boomed.

Putting Javen out of mind for the time being, Yolken looked at Jax, then Deanna. They both nodded. He turned back toward the gate and, using Energy stored in his bones, he amplified his voice and said, "I am Yolken Danavin Dairion Drake, true Blessed of the Dragon, chosen ruler of Dradonia, and Dragon King."

Silence hung in the air.

Yolken and the others sat motionless on their horses and waited.

After a few minutes, several blue-armored men appeared on the balconies of both guard towers.

"Remind you of anything?" Jax asked Deanna quietly.

Deanna nodded. "Let's hope their presence is the only resemblance these towers take to what happened in Onta."

"What is your purpose?" a voice boomed back.

"I request an audience with the Emperor of the United Realms," Yolken said, his voice still amplified.

The armored men disappeared.

Yolken and the others could do nothing but wait. He hoped they would be permitted in, because he didn't want to have to enter the city by force.

"He'll let you in," Reago said after they sat there for another few minutes.

"How can you be sure?" Yolken said.

"Because he would never permit someone at his walls claiming to be the Dragon King to leave of their own accord."

"I hope you're wrong," Yolken said. "About the leaving part, I mean. I don't intend to fight with him."

"No," Jax said, "but remember what we talked about after your confrontation with Crin at the Mindon Falls?"

"Yes," Yolken said. Jax had talked about the periodic need to take someone's life, even if you didn't want to. It was part of being a member of the Order. He wasn't a member of the Order, which was in direct opposition to the emperor's rule—he was more than that, which brought with it the very real possibility of there being the loss of life. "I remember."

The enormous gates lumbered into motion. After they were fully open, Jax urged his horse forward, leading the others. Just before passing through the gates, he waved up at the armored men standing above them on the towers.

"You don't have to mock them," Deborah said.

"I'm not mocking them," Jax said. "Just being friendly."

Yolken had hoped that Javen would be there to greet him when the gates opened, but the streets were deserted. The clopping of the horses' hooves on the paved streets echoed loudly off the tall buildings rising on both sides. Yolken stared ahead, trying not to distract himself. He stole a glance at Deanna; he knew she hadn't been to Kyinth since the end of the war, and he wondered what she was thinking. Her head craned around as she looked at the towering buildings. He occasionally glanced up at them, allowing small trickles of wonder to seep in; each time he did, he caught sight of armored men wearing Glasses standing on balconies. They were ready for them.

"Were they expecting a fight?" Tabora wondered aloud.

"They're certainly prepared for one," Corin said.

"Well," Jax added, "it's not every day that someone declares themselves king and marches into the capital."

CHAPTER 48

Javen spent the next two days largely confined to his quarters. The prospect of traveling to Hantlo with Drenan weighed heavily on him. His appetite was gone, and so was his desire for Melina and Lannary. They visited him several times each day, but each time he ended their visits by sending them away without giving them what they had truly come for.

He tried a couple of times each day to visit with Kaylan, but she proved as uninterested in the problem he was facing with Drenan as she was about him becoming a regent. But when he mentioned the impending meeting with someone claiming to be the Dragon King, she suddenly became interested in what he had to say. He didn't know anything, but each time he visited, she asked him if he'd learned anything new about who it might be.

Now the day had come that the man calling himself the Dragon King was due to arrive. He got word from Oshie that Kaylan had decided to accompany him to the throne room for the meeting. He dressed in his blue armor in his quarters, and when notification came that it was time, he went to Kaylan's quarters to meet her.

On his way, he couldn't help but wonder about why the emperor had decided to break from his long-established rule of never granting audience to rebels. He understood the logic—if the emperor met with a group that was actively rebelling against his rule, then he granted them a measure of legitimacy. Since the end of the war, his rule had been under constant attack by pockets of resistance led by the Order of the Dragon. Early on, Drakonias had established the policy of quickly and mercilessly quashing all resistance groups. Given this longstanding policy, everyone was abuzz as to why the emperor was breaking with protocol. It was all anyone could talk about since he returned from his trip to Arinin. Everyone who was anyone—either in the Regency, or a Silk, Suit, or Red—was attending the meeting.

Javen led Kaylan down the hallway toward the stairs. They joined a crowd gathered at the doorway, slowly filing through. Everyone was speculating about the same thing: What could have made the emperor decide to treat this rebel any different than he always did?

"Does anyone know who this Dragon King is?" Kaylan said.

He shook his head. "Nobody."

When they emerged from the stairwell on the ground floor, a hand grabbed Javen by the arm and pulled him through the crowd. He held onto Kaylan's hand so they wouldn't get separated. "What's going on?" he asked Devin, who was wearing his new orange armor.

"Plans have changed," Devin said. "You're no longer going to be a spectator."

They rounded the corner and proceeded down the Hall of Relics. The gilded doors leading to the throne room were open on the far end, and several dozen armored men were filing in. As they approached the doors, Devin said, "Karina, take Kaylan back to their quarters."

"Yes, Your Highness," Karina said.

"What's going on?" Javen repeated.

"You've been added to the guard detail," Devin said.

"The Dragon Guard's not enough?"

"Not today."

"What changed?"

"My aunt is among the delegation. And so is Reago—but we figured he would be, once he disappeared from the capital."

"Deanna?" Javen wondered aloud. "But if she was in Onta, how did she get here so fast?"

"You're here, aren't you?" Devin replied tersely.

"Yeah, but we came in that Train."

"There are other ways, Javen," Devin said. "Besides, how she got here doesn't matter. The fact that she *is* here compels the emperor to take extra precautions."

Javen followed Devin as he led them down the hallway to the left of the gilded doors. His stomach started churning again. He didn't know anything about guarding anyone. He had only just begun acclimating himself to being in the same city as the emperor, but now he was going to be put in a position of being responsible for his safety? Things were moving too fast.

There were two doors at the end of the hall: one at the end, behind which was the Lift to the emperor's quarters, and another to the right. A guard opened the door on the right when they approached. It was the same room that Devin had brought him into after he was made chancellor, the one with shelves loaded with dragon bones. He counted twelve men wearing white armor—the Dragon Guard. Helmets concealed their faces and each of them carried a tall spear inlaid with dragon bone. There were also a dozen others wearing blue armor, plus two women wearing violet, waiting in the room. Drenan was one of them.

"What's going on, Devin?" Drenan said when the door closed behind Devin and Javen.

"When the delegation of this 'king' approached the gates, we discovered Deanna and Reago were with them," Devin said.

A nervous shuffle spread across the room. Even Drenan seemed on edge.

"His Highness intends to kill them," Devin said. "And he has asked for support in case things get out of hand. You've all been chosen to assist the Dragon Guard should the emperor require help. Arm yourselves with a sword and bone, as well as a pair of Glasses."

Drenan pointed a finger at Javen and said, "I do *not* want him out there!"

"Now's not the time, Drenan," Devin said. "You'll do as you're told."

"With Dorlan dead, I'm Chancellor of the Southern Realm," Drenan shot back. "So I only take orders from the emperor now."

"You are still a regent until the emperor has named you chancellor, so you *will* obey."

Drenan and Devin stared icily at each other for a few tense moments, then Drenan moved to grab a cylindrical bone off a shelf. It was three feet in length and as thick as a man's wrist. It had a grip carved in the middle, and both ends narrowed to sharp points.

Javen strapped on a sword. He knew precious little about Synthesis; he knew even less about swordsmanship. Next, he picked a bone like the others had. He turned it over in his hands and inspected it. Green ribbons in the bone reflected the flickering light of the room.

Javen followed the others as they moved to another shelf. When it was his turn, he picked up a pair of Glasses and slid them over his eyes. The room turned various shades of gray.

Devin was the last to arm himself. As he slid his Glasses on, he turned to the others and said, "Under no circumstances are you to Synthesize unless the emperor needs help. Should I detect even a whiff of one of you preparing to Synthesize, I will kill you myself. Understood?"

"Yes, Your Highness," the regents and Javen repeated in unison.

"Good," Devin said. "Let's go."

The Dragon Guard led the way through the door leading into the throne room. Devin went next, then the regents followed. The Dragon Guard climbed the dais and took their positions on the steps on either side of the throne. Speaking to the rest, Devin pointed to the far side of the chamber and said, "Half of you cover that side. I'm going to greet this *Dragon King* and escort him here. Be ready."

The covers were up on the ceiling, preventing sunlight from entering the throne room. Javen watched where Drenan was going, and, seeing that he had selected a position on the near side of the room, he chose to follow those moving to the far side. He wanted to be as far away from Drenan as possible.

They walked in front of the dais then along the opposite wall, spacing themselves out evenly. Having never done this before, Javen watched the others closely to see how close he should stand from the guard next to him. Since he was the last of those moving to the far side of the chamber, he ended up taking a position against the wall at the foot of the dais.

Once everyone was in place, the metal shields overhead adjusted to permit a stream of sunlight, which through the Glasses looked like a river of color, to illuminate the dais. He looked up through the open portion of the ceiling and became disoriented from the dense streams of colorful Energy flowing overhead.

While he waited, he scanned the balcony on the other side of the chamber. Watchers stood at regular intervals along the railing. He recognized Norin at the back of the chamber. *He's a Watcher?* He supposed that made sense why he was on the Train, then.

Javen's stomach roiled. He hoped this whole business was over quickly, before he lost his bowels.

* * *

Grooms approached Yolken and his delegation when they stopped in front of the palace. While he waited, he took a moment to look up at the towering building. He'd seen the paintings of it, but seeing it with his own eyes surpassed everything he had imagined it would be. The structure was enormous. He felt tiny compared to it—and compared to the man who lived there.

What am I doing?

A groom took the reins from Yolken, and he dismounted along with the others. They gathered at the base of the steps, crowded with hundreds of armored men. A man with orange armor emerged through the palace entrance and began descending the stairs. A dozen gray-armored men flanked him on both sides. Yolken recognized him from Onta: Devin. If he was here, then Javen very well could be as well; Devin had said that Javen was going to pledge his allegiance to the emperor.

"I see I've been replaced," Reago said as Devin approached.

"What did you think would happen when you came here on a Train?" Devin said. His eyes scanned the group, pausing momentarily on Deanna, then stopped on Yolken. "If I had known *you* were the Dragon King, I would have prepared a warmer welcome for you in Onta."

"Don't mock your king," Jax said.

"*My* king?" Devin said, sounding surprised. "He is *not* my king. My allegiance lies with the Emperor of the United Realms."

"Whom I have come to address," Yolken said. He resisted the urge to ask Devin about Javen. Instead, he took a deep breath and said, "If you would kindly show me the way?"

"Straight to the point," Devin said. "Just like in Onta."

"What? No greeting for your aunt?" Jax said.

Devin's eyes narrowed as he looked at Jax. Turning his attention to Deanna, he said, "You think your presence will change how the emperor feels about this... delegation?"

"We shall see," Deanna said.

Devin studied her for a moment then said, "Well, we mustn't keep His Blessed Highness waiting. This way." He spun on his heel and started back up the stairs.

The guards accompanying him put themselves between Devin and Yolken.

Jax led the group as they followed Devin up the steps and into the palace. "At least he didn't make us sit around and wait."

"There is that, I suppose," Deborah said, her voice shaky.

Devin led Yolken and his delegation around the gilded statue of the emperor, down a long hall lined with display cases, to gilded doors at the end. Stopping before the doors, Devin turned and his guards parted, giving Devin an unobstructed view of the delegation. He eyed the sword hanging at Deanna's side and said, "My guards will search you before we proceed in."

Jax pulled open his coat, revealing the Harachin sword hanging at his side. "Today, we will keep our weapons."

"No one is *ever* granted an audience before His Blessed Highness armed," Devin said.

"Well, His Blessed Highness is going to have to make an exception, isn't he," Jax said.

Devin frowned, furrowing his brow. "Wait here," he said. He turned, and one of his guards cracked open the right door, which depicted a flying dragon. Devin slipped through the door, and his guard promptly shut it. He returned a few minutes later and directed his guards to open both doors. Devin gestured through the doors and said, "There are dozens of Watchers in there. Any attempt to Synthesize will be met with a swift death."

Devin led the way into the throne room.

Yolken took a deep breath and followed.

* * *

Javen heard the familiar peal of a trumpet announcing the arrival of the emperor. Along with all the other guards in the throne room, he fell to his knees. He stood when he heard the emperor's booming voice instructing them to rise. Drakonias was sitting upon his throne dressed in his red armor. He was gripping the Dragon Scepter, which was propped point down on the ground to his side.

The doors at the back of the room opened and six individuals made their way forward. Javen's eyes went wide when he saw Yolken. He stared blankly as his brother proceeded forward, flanked by Kaylan's mother, her uncle, Reago, and others he didn't recognize. Their footsteps echoed in the nearly empty throne room. *Reago?* he thought. *So he's joined with the rebels.* He shifted nervously as he slowly pieced together what was happening.

The procession stopped at the foot of the dais and bowed their heads toward the emperor. However, none of them knelt. Javen looked up at Drakonias and fought back the urge to vomit. The emperor was staring icily down at the individuals standing below him. The sound of Jorgan's familiar voice made Javen's gaze shift back to the delegation.

"My name is Jax Karven," Kaylan's uncle said, "To you, Drakonias Draeko Arvarin Drake, Emperor of the United Realms, I present Yolken Danavin Dairion Drake, true Blessed of the Dragon, chosen ruler over Dradonia, and Dragon King."

Javen tasted bile in his mouth and covered it with a gloved hand. He swallowed the small amount of vomit and hoped he didn't completely lose it. As he stared at his brother in complete disbelief, he wished he had something to rinse his mouth with.

* * *

"Danavin's get has named himself Dragon King," Drakonias said with a snort.

Yolken looked up at the metal ceiling hiding the light of the sun from everyone but the emperor. He ignored the emperor's slight. The light reflected brightly off the tall Dragon Scepter which Drakonias held propped against the floor with his right hand. His eyes drifted over the men standing on the steps in two rows, wearing white armor. The full face helmets they wore reminded him of Deth's shiny skin comment. His eyes then settled on the man he'd never imagined he would be standing before, the man he'd grown up believing was the most powerful man in the world. He longed for the weight of the Harachin sword at his side, for the security found in having a trove of Energy available; then he looked inward and sensed the well of Energy stored within himself. He transferred some into his Core and melted away his nerves. As he calmed, he transferred the Energy back. It was not Drakonias who should rightfully sit atop that dais; as much as he hated to admit it, it was him.

"No," he coolly said.

"*What?*" the emperor said.

"I did not name myself Dragon King."

"Who, then?" Drakonias said. "The fools who call themselves the Order of the Dragon?"

"I am here because Draego has named me Dragon King."

"You are as mad as my father!" Drakonias scoffed.

"He wasn't mad," Yolken said.

"He believed the same foolishness as you."

"Huh," Yolken said. Drakonias was all but admitting that what was taught in the Dragon Shrines about the source of their power was a lie. If Drakonias didn't believe their power came from Draego, where *did* he think it came from?

"You question me?"

"No. It's just, I didn't realize Draeko didn't share even with you how he got the gift."

"What are you talking about?"

"Your father got his gift from a dragon that disobeyed the Assembly."

"*Assembly?*"

"You don't know anything, do you?"

"Careful, son of Danavin," Drakonias said

"None of you are *truly* Blessed," Yolken said.

"Aren't we now…" Drakonias said, rapping his fingers on the Dragon Scepter.

"No, you're not."

"And I suppose you are?"

"I didn't want this."

Drakonias continued to drum his fingers on the scepter. "And what is it that you want?"

What he wanted was to go home, but he knew that wasn't going to happen. And even if there was a way that he could go home as though none of this had happened, he wouldn't admit that to Drakonias. "A truce, Your Highness," he said with a small bow.

Drakonias' finger drumming stopped. He gripped the scepter tightly and said, "I don't make peace with rebels. I destroy those who think to question my rule."

"I understand that, Your Highness," Yolken said. "And yet I am here."

"You think I would permit known rebels—and traitors," Drakonias added with a glance at Reago, "to enter this city and live to see the sun rise again?"

"We all understand the risk we've taken by coming here. We must join forces long enough to restore balance."

"Restore balance?" Drakonias said. He shifted slightly on the throne, just enough for Yolken to notice. "To what?"

"All the Order of the Dragon has ever really wanted is to restore the balance lost during your war."

"Excuse me?" Drakonias said.

"All we want is to ensure that we don't suffer the same fate as Detron," Yolken said.

Drakonias' eyes widened. "How could you possibly know about that?"

"You'd be surprised what you can buy with enough gold," Jax said wryly.

Drakonias glared at Jax crossly.

"Your Highness," Jax added with a nod of his head.

"We must confront this evil together, brother," Deanna interjected.

"Yes," Reago added.

"*You,*" Drakonias said, his gaze shifting to Reago, "are a traitor. You both are."

"Whom you tried to kill just as you did Drashon," Reago said. "And for what? To protect that which can no longer be kept hidden."

A murmur rumbled through the throne room.

Drakonias' grip on the Dragon Scepter tightened. "The evil of which you speak exists only in your heads."

"You know that's not true," Deanna said. "The evil we unleashed from our war is as real as is the sun that daily shines from on high! Are you not concerned that you've lost half your empire?"

The murmur increased in intensity.

Drakonias relaxed his grip and once again drummed his fingers on the scepter. He waited until the murmur died down. "You have nerve showing your face here, Deanna," he said. "And have you sworn fealty to this… Dragon King?" Drakonias asked with a gesture toward Yolken.

"I have."

"As have I," Reago said.

"But allegiances are no longer important," Deanna said.

"So for the second time, you have chosen to betray me?" Drakonias said.

"I have always aligned myself with the person I believed rightly belonged on that throne."

Drakonias clenched his jaw. He gripped the Dragon Scepter tightly again and, directing his attention toward Reago, said, "And you. You have always been weak."

"We haven't come here to fight with you, brother," Deanna said. "I gave up all desire to resist you further when you killed our father."

"Recompense befitting a tyrant," Drakonias said.

"He *wasn't* a tyrant, and you know that. It was all a lie to seize power from him."

"The same fate awaits you, Deanna. Both of you."

"I came here," Deanna said, "not to remove you from our father's throne, but to petition you to confront the evil we are *all* responsible f—"

Yolken looked over at Deanna when she abruptly stopped speaking. Her eyes were wide. She grabbed the Aliza sword and attempted to draw it as she fell to her knees.

Reago fell to his knees next to her.

They both screamed.

The movements of everyone around Yolken appeared to slow. He looked up at Drakonias, who sat unmoving on the throne, his hand on the Dragon Scepter.

Yolken closed his eyes.

His heart pounded in his ears, muffling Deanna and Reago's screams.

Yolken's eyes twitched. He opened them and saw two thick streams of colorful light flowing from Drakonias. One poured into Deanna, and the other into Reago.

He transferred Energy from his bones into his Core, then reached out tentatively toward the streams.

The moment Energy left his body, the room exploded into fire.

CHAPTER 49

Through his Glasses, Javen watched as two thick streams of Energy shot down from Drakonias. One hit Deanna in the chest, and the other Reago. He stared, transfixed, as she attempted to draw the sword from the hilt at her side, but she fell to her knees. Reago fell beside her.

His eyes widened when a stream of Energy emerged from Yolken. He knew Yolken could Synthesize, but he wasn't holding any dragon bones—at least none that he could see.

Fire exploded around the throne room, first from the opposite side of the chamber, then from the hands of the Dragon Guard. He threw his arms up to protect his face when it exploded all around him. The inferno came from all directions. He drew Energy from the bone in his hand to protect himself from the sudden heat of the fire, and vomited in the process. Shielding his eyes, he watched as streams of Energy from all directions flowed toward his brother.

Javen watched as Energy, visible only through the Glasses he wore, swirled around Yolken and the other rebels, causing the fire to swirl around them as well. Only the stream from Drakonias to Deanna and Reago continued past the cyclone of fire. The Dragon Guard moved and formed a physical barrier a few steps below the emperor. Their initial assault on the delegation ended as they transitioned to a protective role.

The stream of Energy coming from Yolken pushed and pulled on the streams Drakonias directed into Deanna and Reago. The rest of the delegation huddled around Deanna, Reago, and Yolken. Deanna fell over, curled up into a ball, writhing in pain. She managed to force a hand onto the ground, and smoke immediately started rising. Reago fell forward onto his hands and knees, smoke rising from his hands as well, but fought to stop himself from falling farther. Yolken continued trying to dislodge the Energy into the two traitors.

The regents and guards stepped forward and began moving slowly closer to the huddled group. Javen stepped forward with them but froze when Norin's words popped into his mind.

Never forget who you are, son of Danavin.

Javen remained frozen, unable to coax his body back into motion, conflicted. The individuals at the center of the swirling inferno were his sworn enemies. He watched as his brother tried desperately to sever the deadly stream of Energy from Deanna's writhing body. Reago now joined her on his side, curled up in a ball, both hands futilely tearing at his shirt. Javen had pledged his loyalty to Drakonias, who was now standing, and they opposed him. Yolken opposed him as well. He couldn't fathom why his brother would willingly name himself a king, but he had. The rebels huddling together—which included his brother— deserved death.

The regents tightened their circle around Yolken. Javen stared at his brother, whose shadow he'd spent his entire life under. It wasn't until he left Lonely Oak that he had the freedom to become who he was. The group protecting him was likely pushing back with everything they had to prevent the inferno from devouring them. If he added his own strength to the fire, he knew they would be overcome.

However, looking in, he knew most of them were family. Despite the wrongs he had suffered under Yolken—living in his shadow, stealing Kaylan's heart—he was still family. And so was

Kaylan's mother. Her uncle too. Even if she didn't love him, she was still family.

The words of the bearded servant continued to echo in his mind.

Javen fell to his knees.

He'd made a terrible mistake.

He couldn't bring himself to kill his own brother.

Javen watched as Yolken fought to save his friends.

Never forget who you are, son of Danavin.

He was not someone who could kill his brother.

Or permit him to be killed.

* * *

Yolken struggled to break the connection between Deanna, Reago, and Drakonias. The stream of Energy from the emperor bent and twisted as he pulled on it, but he couldn't stop it from killing them.

He stole a glance over at Jax kneeling nearby, hoping for some help, but Jax's face looked strained. Energy swirled from Jax's hands up and out, pulling air down from above. He sent it spinning around them, trapping the fire flowing toward them. The cyclone carried the fire up and away from them. It looked like he was trying to bend the cyclone back down on the regents, but other streams of Energy repeatedly pushed it away.

Despite Jax's efforts, the air around them burned. People outside their protective cyclone were screaming and falling to the ground with blackened faces and burned scalps.

A scream nearby caused Yolken to turn. Before he could even react, a tendril dragged Corin by the ankle through the cyclone and into the fire.

Other tendrils snaked through the fire into the clearing. One attempted to grab his ankle, but he easily deflected it. Another went for Jax.

"Jax!" he shouted.

Jax looked down, his face covered in sweat, and saw the tendril. It touched the fringes of his coat splayed out around him, and disappeared.

How in the—

Another scream pierced the air.

Yolken turned and saw Deborah sliding away from the circle on her stomach, desperately clawing at the smooth marble floor.

He dove toward her, losing his connection with the Energy killing Deanna and Reago, and grabbed Deborah by the hands. The tendril dragged them slowly across the floor. He barely held onto her, his sweat causing her hand to slip from his.

Deborah screamed as her feet entered the fire.

The cyclone shifted, bulging over Deborah, and pushed the fire back.

Yolken sent Energy into his hands and tightened his grip. Deborah screamed as the bones in her hands broke.

The tendril pulled against Yolken's grip. He reached out with a tendril of his own, but a second tendril whipped out and grabbed Deborah's other foot.

Her hand slid slowly out of his. His fingers curled in a desperate attempt to not lose her.

With an Energy tendril of his own, Yolken yanked one of the tendrils pulling her free, but it immediately joined the other on her other foot.

Yolken locked eyes with Deborah as her hand continued to slip. She mouthed the words, "Find Kaylan."

Their hands separated.

Fire enveloped her.

"No!" Yolken cried.

* * *

Javen watched in horror as Kaylan's mother burned in the fire. His tearful gaze shifted to his brother when Yolken pushed himself to his feet. A thick tendril of Energy shot from him and wrapped around the Dragon Scepter.

Drakonias screamed.

Since leaving Lonely Oak, he'd thought what he wanted most was revenge for all the wrongs done to him. Except for the death of his parents, he blamed his brother for all of it. However, at that moment, he realized that none of it was Yolken's fault. He also realized that in the end, none of it mattered. He let all the animosity he had felt over the last several months for his brother go. He let it burn in the inferno raging around him. The burden he had carried evaporated.

As the fires raged, Javen realized he'd never really wanted revenge. What he wanted was *retribution*. Not for anything that had been done to him. He wanted retribution for wrongs done to the helpless, to the innocent. He wanted retribution for Astora.

Javen looked around the chaos of the throne room for the only man he wanted dead. He found him standing near Devin on the far side of the room. Fire spewed from Drenan's hands toward Yolken.

Javen drew the ceremonial steel sword from the sheath on his belt, and for the first time since the attack on the delegates had begun, Javen moved.

He took two steps, then froze when a booming voice called his name. Thunder clapped, and the steel sword in his hand smashed into his body, shoving him to the side.

Pain erupted in his neck.

The sword was ripped from his grasp, and he fell to his knees.

Javen tried to breathe but choked on something wet. His hand went up to his throat and felt a metal blade. He touched it then looked at his hand. His fingers were red.

Javen looked up at his brother, and tried to yell his name, but coughed up blood instead.

* * *

"Javen!"

At the sound of his brother's name, Yolken paused. A thunderous clap behind him caused him to flinch. The swirling inferno faltered. The attention of those around him turned toward the source of the thunder. The emperor's flow of Energy stopped, and his gaze turned up and back. Yolken turned to see what was happening but froze halfway around when his gaze fell upon a regent on his knees. He had a knife protruding from his neck.

Javen.

A man wearing gray armor was lying near his brother. His throat cut completely open, and his blood was pulsing out. A bloody sword lay next to him.

Yolken's vision narrowed until all he saw was Javen's pleading eyes. His throat was bloody from the protruding blade, but it wasn't flowing as profusely as that of the man next to him. However, Javen choked, and blood spurted from his mouth. With ears ringing from the thunder, he ran to Javen just as Javen fell to his side.

Yolken dropped to his knees next to his brother. Out of the corner of his eye, he saw enormous flows of Energy extend out, so he instinctively looked up. The flows gathered at the back of the throne room, up on the balcony. A bearded man jumped up onto the railing of the balcony and proved to be the focal point of the gathering Energy. The man leaped off the railing and fell rapidly. The Energy swirled toward him into two groups: one slowed his descent to the marble floor, and the other accelerated down and smacked the floor with a deafening crunch. The marble buckled below his fist. Yolken stared transfixed as the man, barely visible over the hundreds of corpses, knelt on the ground for a moment, then stood confidently. Energy swirled toward him.

The room erupted in fire again, so he mimicked the barrier Jax had made to protect himself and Javen. The regents seemed to have forgotten him, the bearded man drawing their attention, so Yolken took advantage of the distraction and turned back to his brother. Javen labored to breathe, but the knife was obstructing his airway. He reached into Javen with Energy and felt his heart still slowly beating. He knew he needed to work quickly, or his brother would die.

He lifted Javen's head with one hand, and reaching around him with the other, he gripped the knife by its hilt. With a quick motion, he yanked it out. Javen's eyes went wide, and he coughed violently. Blood splattered on Yolken's face and chest. Yolken gathered air from around him and sent it down Javen's windpipe, filling his lungs.

Yolken worked instinctively with Energy to stitch Javen's windpipe back together. Next, he moved to Javen's esophagus. When the two passages were whole again, he started on the muscles and nerves, finishing with his skin. Lastly, he used Energy to clear the blood from Javen's airway.

Javen took a breath and looked up at Yolken. Yolken smiled down at him and then, satisfied he would be okay, turned his attention back toward Drakonias. He reached out with a thread of Energy to once again try and take the Dragon Scepter from the emperor, but fell to the ground when the ceiling crashed down around him with a deafening roar.

* * *

Jax stared helplessly at Yolken, kneeling over Javen. He'd failed. He'd promised to protect Orwyn's boys, and he'd failed. He looked down at Deanna and Reago. Neither of them moved. There was a momentary calm in the firestorm while Drakonias and the other Blessed had their attention directed toward the source of the thunder. He picked up the Aliza sword and handed it to Tabora. "Let's go," he said, gesturing toward Yolken and Javen.

"Wait!" Tabora said. "Look."

A bearded man jumped up onto the balcony at the back of the throne room. He hesitated just a moment, then jumped. He disappeared from view behind the ring of regents, but Jax reacted too late to protect his ears from the deafening crunch of marble.

Jax tightened his grip on the Harachin sword. The regents strode away from Jax and Tabora toward whoever was back there.

The firestorm resumed.

Jax resumed his protective barrier of swirling air, and they crouched to the ground. *What is it with the stupid fire?* he thought. There were too many regents and other Synthesizers—the emperor alone being very strong—for them to mount any sort of counter-assault. With Reago and Deanna incapacitated, and Yolken tending to Javen, there was nothing they could do.

The ceiling crashed down around him. He threw himself to the ground and covered his head. He drew as deeply from the Harachin sword as he could, his Core threatening to rip itself apart, and gathered all the air he could down and in. The pressure around him built immensely. He almost lost control when a dragon appeared through the falling glass and metal, but he held tightly.

When the debris crashed down on them, Jax pushed against it with all the air, redirecting the metal to their sides. He covered his head to protect himself from the falling glass. He looked up just in time to see the emperor fall several steps down the dais. The Dragon Scepter was ripped from his hands and flew toward Yolken.

The Dragon Guard scrambled to their feet halfway down the steps and surrounded Drakonias.

The dragon roared, and its tail flicked. Tendrils of smoke rose from its snout.

Jax stood transfixed along with everyone else in the chamber. All eyes were on the dragon.

Movement caused him to look down. Drenan and Devin were running toward a side door.

Jax looked up at the dragon, then over to Yolken. Yolken was looking at him. No, past him. He spun around and saw Drakonias and the Dragon Guard now moving toward the door Drenan and Devin went through.

Yolken stepped past Jax, and the gold dragon enshrouding the scepter started glowing. The gold melted, deformed, smoothed. The rounded base of the scepter elongated and formed into a sharp point. Yolken lifted the scepter over his shoulder like a spear and, with unnatural strength, hurled it at Drakonias. It tore through his armor with ease.

Drakonias fell to his knees with the scepter protruding through his chest.

Flames shot from the dragon's mouth as Drakonias fell forward. The giant lizard-like head turned upward toward the sky and let out another deafening roar.

CHAPTER 50

Jax watched over Yolken, who was kneeling next to Deborah's burned corpse. He looked over his shoulder at the regents standing transfixed behind him. "I'd put down your weapons, were I you," he said.

Swords and dragon bones fell to the floor around the room in a clatter.

"Is that… a dragon?" Javen said with a hoarse voice.

"It is, lad," Jax said. "You all right?"

Javen felt at his throat and nodded. He walked over and knelt beside his brother.

Jax looked over his shoulder again at the regents. None of them moved. He walked toward them and passed between them. One of the gilded doors at the back of the throne room was cracked open. Whoever had jumped from the balcony was gone. "That's disappointing," he said to himself.

He returned to Yolken's side. The boy was still kneeling next to Deborah's burned corpse, repeating over and over, "What am I going to tell Kaylan?"

"It's not your fault, lad," Jax said. He placed his hand on Yolken's shoulder, but Yolken shied away.

"Jax!" Tabora called.

Jax looked up and saw Tabora kneeling next to Deanna's

body. She was gesturing for him to come. "What is it?" he said.

"She has a pulse," Tabora said. "It's faint, but it's there."

"Yolken!" Jax said.

Yolken looked over his shoulder then pushed himself to his feet. He joined Jax, then fell heavily to his knees.

Jax watched as Yolken placed his hand on Deanna's head. While Yolken did his thing, he went over and knelt beside Reago, placing two fingers on Reago's neck to double-check. He didn't feel anything. He closed Reago's vacant eyes then rejoined the others gathered around Yolken and Deanna.

After a few moments, Deanna's eyes opened. She held her hands up and screamed. Her palms were severely burned. Before Jax's eyes, the flesh began to mend.

"You okay?" Yolken said.

Deanna looked at her hands and nodded.

Yolken helped her to her feet. With weariness on his face and exuding from his stance, Jax watched Yolken use Synthesis to pull the Dragon Scepter from Drakonias' corpse. It floated through the air toward Yolken. The bloody bottom clanked onto the marble floor, echoing loudly, when Yolken gripped it.

Yolken turned toward the regents, still standing frozen in place, and said, "Kneel before your king."

Jax, Deanna, and Tabora knelt.

Jax looked over at Javen, who was still standing. Javen was looking Yolken in the eye and, after a moment of hesitation, he knelt.

Yolken shifted his gaze to the regents in the room. They stared at him but otherwise didn't move. "I am Yolken Danavin Dairion Drake. I am the one and true Blessed of the Dragon, and chosen ruler over Dradonia," he said. "If you wish to survive this day, kneel!"

Armored men and women around the chamber began to kneel, one by one.

* * *

Yolken looked around the chamber. Everyone was on their

352 - PATRIK MARTINET

knees. He looked past the Dragon Guard scattered on the dais and up at the throne. He took a deep breath and strode toward it. The deformed scepter clanked loudly with each step he took. *Draego's Fire, it's heavy*. He had to use Synthesis to carry it.

He hesitated at the base—the image of the smaller dais and throne in the underground chamber in Croff came to mind—then slowly started up. When he reached the top, he looked first at the gilded throne, then past it, at the dragon.

Deth returned his gaze.

"Were you following me?" Yolken whispered.

Deth did not respond.

"I know what you are going to say... My fight isn't with them. And you're right. But if I don't do this, someone will replace him, and the fighting will continue. If I do, though, I can end the fighting until I figure out what I'm supposed to do."

Steam emerged from Deth's nostrils.

Yolken turned and faced those kneeling below. He blinked. The colorful flows of Energy from the sun streaming through the broken ceiling became visible. He blinked again, returning his vision to normal, and sat.

He didn't have a clue what he was supposed to do next. He looked down at his subjects, and Jax smiled up at him. He signaled to them to join him. Jax, Deanna, Tabora, and Javen climbed the dais to meet him.

After wary looks toward the dragon and brief congratulations, a debate erupted between Jax and Tabora about what to do with all the Synthesizers in the throne room. The fact that Devin and Drenan were missing from the crowd concerned them, but Yolken could think of nothing but what he was going to tell Kaylan when he saw her.

"We need to lock them up," Tabora said, "until their loyalty can be assured."

"But then Javen would have to join them," Jax said.

"What if we just let them go?" Yolken said.

"Foolishness," Tabora said. "They'll just go join up with

Drenan and Devin."

"Yolken's right," Jax said. "If he's going to successfully rule, he's going to need their support."

"We could just send them to their chambers here in the palace," Deanna said.

"Yes," Yolken said. "That sounds good. But without their armor or dragon bones."

"Surely they have bones in their chambers," Tabora objected.

"We can have Reago's guards search each of their rooms," Jax said.

"Really?" Tabora asked.

"They were loyal to him, and he pledged his loyalty to Yolken. Until we can vet our own Dragon Guard, they're the best we have."

"I agree," Deanna said.

"Your Highness?" Jax said, looking at Yolken.

Yolken nodded. He rose and looked down at the regents standing below. "If you don't want to find yourselves in the dungeon, remove your armor and surrender any dragon bone on your person." Everyone in the crowd below immediately obeyed. When they stood in their smallclothes, he turned to the group before him on the dais and said, "See to the rest of it."

"I'll go get Reago's guards so we can get started on searching their chambers," Jax said.

When Jax left through the gilded doors at the back of the throne room, Yolken explained to the regents what was going to happen. None of them objected. While he waited for Jax to return with Reago's guards, he thought about Devin and Drenan. They were a problem he would have to resolve— especially Drenan. He didn't intend to prosecute the regents in general for their misplaced loyalty, but he wanted to hold Drenan accountable for murdering Selena. There was nothing he could do presently, but in due time, he would ensure the vile man got what he deserved.

With Deth hovering behind him, Yolken's mind inevitably drifted to the problem with the sun. He was no closer to understanding what he was supposed to do than he was when Deth had rescued him in Onta. It was simply impossible. He leaned forward and turned so he could look behind the throne at the dragon behind him. Deth was curled up and looked as though he had fallen asleep. He turned back around and leaned back. *It's impossible.*

His mind drifted from the monumental task and settled on the only thought that rivaled the problem before him: Kaylan. "Javen," he said, turning to his brother. "Do you know where Kaylan is?" Javen looked at him with fear in his eyes. "Someone kidnapped her when we were in Onta." Javen's look made Yolken nervous. "Javen? What is it?"

"She's here."

"In *Kyinth?*"

Javen nodded. "In the palace."

Yolken sprang to his feet. His heart raced. "Take me to her!"

Yolken tilted the scepter toward Tabora and said, "Will you—"

"Yes, Your Highness. Go."

Tabora took hold of the scepter, then Yolken hastily made his way down the dais.

The regents' heads turned as he and Javen crossed the throne room. He made as wide a berth as he could around the corpses littering the ground, and looked down at the hole in the marble floor. He stopped and momentarily considered it, wondering what happened, before exiting through the main doors. A handful of people stood in the long hallway outside, so Yolken looked at every face as they made their way down it. Javen turned when they got to the atrium, passed several metal doors, and proceeded down another hallway. The normal guards at the door were no longer there, so Javen opened the door and held it for Yolken. Javen entered the stairwell after Yolken, then led them up the spiraling stairs, taking them two at a time.

They exited the stairwell, and Javen led them down another hallway. Yolken's heart raced with both excitement and fear. *What am I going to tell her?* he thought as he followed Javen, who turned left and proceeded down a hallway adorned by tapestries. He stopped in front of a door, and Yolken stopped next to him.

"She's in there," Javen said.

Yolken looked at his brother.

"Go on," Javen said. "It's you she loves."

Yolken took a deep breath, then placed his hand on the polished door handle. He turned it and pushed the door open. He looked down a long room. "Kaylan!" he called. Stepping into the room, he called again, "Kaylan!"

A door to his right opened.

Yolken looked over and froze.

Kaylan stared at him through the doorway, her hair disheveled.

"Kaylan…" he whispered.

He purposefully strode toward her and stopped a few feet away.

Kaylan's green eyes were red and puffy. She blinked, sending tears down her cheeks.

Yolken took another step and scooped her up in a hug. He squeezed her tight, breathing the scent of her hair deeply.

"Yolken…" Kaylan whispered into his chest.

"When that rider snatched you, I thought—"

"I tried to convince Javen to go to you but—"

"I ran back through the closing gates, but it was a trap—"

"Javen said they were going to kill—" Kaylan sobbed.

Yolken squeezed Kaylan harder. Neither of them said anything for what felt like a blessed eternity. For the first time since fleeing Lonely Oak, Yolken felt at home. He absorbed the moment, reveling in Kaylan's closeness, warmth, and smell.

He wanted to flee with her, to protect her, but he couldn't. He let her go and took a step back. Tears started flowing from his eyes when she looked up at him. "Kaylan—Missus

Browning… your mother… she…"

Kaylan collapsed into him, burying her head into his chest. An uncontrollable wail escaped from her, muffled by his shirt. Her legs buckled. Yolken supported her, but as tired as he was, he slowly lowered her the ground.

He leaned his forehead against the top of hers and said, "I'm so sorry. I tried everything I could to save her, but…"

"It's not your fault, Yolken," Kaylan said. She looked up at him, forcing him to shift his head. "Yolken…" She pulled his head down, so he looked down at her. "…it's *not* your fault."

"I know, I just wish I could have—"

Kaylan pulled him close and said, "I love you."

"I'm so sorry," he said. He sank into her embrace. "I love you too, Kaylan." They hugged in silence for a while, then Yolken said, "When I thought I'd lost you, I—" Kaylan pulled back from him and looked up at him. She lifted her head and kissed him. Yolken kissed her back as though it was the only kiss they would ever have.

"Kaylan?" Javen said from behind them.

Kaylan and Yolken both looked toward the door. Javen stood in the doorway with his arms folded in front of him.

"I'm sorry," Javen said.

Kaylan waved him over. He stepped into the room tentatively at first, then came and sat on the ground beside them. Kaylan rose to her knees and embraced Javen in a hug. Together, they cried.

INTERIM

Fren cowered in the corner of the empty stall with his knees drawn up to his chest, his hairy calves exposed by his too-short pants. He rocked back and forth, humming the tune of the song his ma always sang to comfort him when he was scared. The deafening roar had ended, but the sound still echoed in his mind. He couldn't bring himself to move.

The stable door groaned open. Fren sighed in relief—Pa was, at last, coming to assure him everything was okay. He crawled across the trampled hay of the dirty stall he was mucking out and peered through the gate's wooden slats. Two sets of scaled leggings, one orange and one blue, walked toward the stall he was in. He ducked low and covered his head with his hands.

"Lad!" a stern voice said.

Fren lifted his head and peered through the slats again. The armored men now stood outside his stall. A breastplate dropped to the floor in front of him, causing him to jump.

"We require horses," the voice said.

Fren hesitantly stood up. At nearly six feet tall, he easily looked over the top of the gate at the two men, now working at removing their leggings. A large satchel sat on the ground next to them. Fren stared at the scars covering the arms and torso of one of the men. The blood drained from his face. The scarred man—the fabled man that his ma and pa used to threaten would come and punish him if he disobeyed—was real. He shied back from the gate. Had the scarred man finally come to punish him for all the times he'd disobeyed?

"Now," the scarred man said.

Fren walked slowly toward the gate and stepped into a pile of horse dung with his bare foot. He unlatched the gate and pushed it open.

The scarred man, clad in only his smallclothes, pointed at two stalls. "Those will do," he said.

Fren looked at the unremarkable mares. His pa ran the finest inn in Kyinth and stabled the horses of the empire's richest. Without questioning the scarred man's choice, he set to work saddling the mares. When he finished, the scarred man transferred the contents of the satchel to the saddlebags then looked at Fren. Fren swallowed nervously.

"Take off your clothes."

Fren hastily pulled his shirt off. The scarred man held out his hand, and Fren handed the shirt to him. Next, he removed his pants, trying his best not to get any of the dung on his foot on the pants as he pulled them off. Unlike the scarred man, he wasn't wearing smallclothes. The pants were wet in the front from losing his bladder during the loud roaring, but the scarred man didn't seem to care.

"Now, go get something for the chancellor to wear," the scarred man said.

"The-the-the..." Fren stammered.

"Go!"

Naked, Fren ran out of the stable.

"What in Draego's Fire..." his ma said as he ran into the house.

Ignoring her, he retrieved another pair of clothes from his room.

"Fren! Get back here right now!" his ma called as he passed her on his way back out.

He ran back into the stable and slowed to a walk when he passed the open doors. With his head down, eyes on the ground, he walked back toward the two men and fell to his knees, holding the clothes out. When the clothes were snatched from his hands, he crawled back into the stable he'd been hiding in.

Through the gap in the wood, he watched the scarred man and the chancellor—of which realm, he didn't know—lead the horses out of the stable, dressed in his clothes. Fren's fear of dying a fiery death at the hands of the scarred man shifted to fear of his ma and pa as the men mounted the horses and rode away. He knew they were never going to believe him when he told them what had just happened.

THE END
of Book Three of
THE BLESSED OF THE DRAGON

DRAKE FAMILY TREE

Previous Era (PE): the era prior to the establishment of the Dragon Throne became known as the Previous Era

Dragon King Era (DKE): the Dragon King Era commenced when Draeko established the Dragon Throne.

United Era (UE): the United Era commenced when Drakonias sat upon the Dragon Throne and proclaimed himself emperor of Dradonia.

Note: Provided below is the first and second generations of the Blessed of the Dragon. A complete genealogy of those loyal to the emperor is maintained at the palace in Kyinth.

(L) indicates those that pledged their loyalty to Drakonias during Drakonias' war.

GENERATION 1

Draeko Dairion Drake (m) (b. unknown d. 1150 DKE)
    Married to:
        Aliza Varias (f) (b 61 PE d. 1148 DKE)
    Children:
        Drakonias Draeko Arvarin Drake (m) (b. 42 PE d.)
        Deanna Aliza Drake (f) (b. 41 PE d. 1150 DKE)
        Eagan Draeko Calavin Drake (m) (b. 39 PE d. 1150 DKE)
        Reago Draeko Yarin Drake (m) (b. 37 PE d.) (L)
        Anshar Draeko Olivar Drake (m) (b. 35 PE d. 1150 DKE)
        Drae Draeko Harachin Drake (m) (b. 34 PE d. 44 UE)
        Reega Aliza Drake (f) (b. 31 PE d. 1150 DKE)
        Orlan Draeko Dairion Drake (m) (b. 29 PE d. 289 UE) (L)
        Thena Aliza Drake (f) (b. 835 DKE d.) (L)
        Nera Aliza Drake (f) (b. 837 DKE d.) (L)
        Lio Draeko Mattath Drake (m) (b. 980 DKE d. 30 UE)
        Atter Draeko Eber Drake (m) (b. 983 DKE d. 1138 DKE) (L)
        Mattha Aliza Drake (f) (b. 984 DKE d. 1150 DKE)
        Sheal Draeko Kena Drake (m) (b. 986 DKE d.) (L)
        Akim Draeko Nash Drake (m) (b. 992 DKE d. 33 UE) (L)
        Bathsheth Aliza Drake (f) (b. 995 DKE d. 80 UE)
        Esli Draeko Elish Drake (m) (b. 1001 DKE d. 19 UE)

GENERATION 2

Drakonias Draeko Arvarin Drake (m) (b. 42 PE d.)
    Married to:
        Mariana Hargen (b. 20 PE d. 1120 DKE)
    Children:
        Drashon Drakonias Irigwin Drake (m) (b 14 DKE d. 295 UE)
        Dorlan Drakonias Irigwin Drake (m) (b 150 DKE d.)
        Devin Drakonias Metra Drake (m) (b. 820 DKE d.)
        Drenan Drakonias Loid Drake (m) (b. 954 DKE d.)
        Darsi Mariana Drake (f) (b. 960 DKE d. 1142 DKE)
        Donlin Drakonias Ronn Drake (m) (b. 980 DKE d. 1128 DKE)
        Dalia Mariana Drake (f) (b. 982 DKE d.)
    Married to:
        Ceena Realag (b. 1101 DKE d. 40 UE)
    Children:
        Darek Drakonias Proogan Drake (m)(b. 1 UE d.)
        Dreanna Ceena Drake (f)(b. 3 UE d.)
        Dunlor Drakonias Metra Drake (m) (b. 3 UE d.)

THE ASTRONOMER
PART I

245 United Era

Drashon's Auto came to a halt and the humming of its motor ceased. The weeklong journey from Tieger to Kyinth was finally over. Travel weary, he looked out the darkened window at the emperor's looming palace. He craned his neck, just able to make out the balcony high above.

While he waited for a guard to descend the palace steps, he reflected on the message from the emperor that arrived by condor seven days ago. He still had no clue what the emperor felt was so urgent that he needed to discuss it in person. It's not like he just sat around all day charging dragon bones for more important people. He was the Chancellor of the Northern Realm. He *was* more important. And he was very busy.

He removed the timepiece from his coat pocket and flipped the lid open. After checking the time, he opened the small latch on the back of the timepiece, revealing the sliver of black bone. He drew Energy into his Core from a bone inlaid in the armrest of the door and transferred it into the tiny bone, replenishing the power that kept the timepiece running. He closed the latch and tucked the timepiece back into his coat.

Guards finally emerged from the palace and started down the marble steps.

About time.

The guards reached the bottom of the grand steps and arranged themselves outside the Auto in two long rows. The gilded sheaths hanging at their hips shimmered in the sun, as did their gray armor. The captain of the guard, identified by the white scale covering the left breast of his armor, walked through the two rows of guards and opened the door. "Chancellor," the captain said with a bow. "His Blessed Highness is awaiting your audience."

Drashon once again removed the timepiece from his coat, flipped it open, and gazed at the time. He flipped the piece closed, returned it to its place, and stepped out of the Auto. Ignoring the captain's bow, he hastily made his way up the steps. The captain rushed to catch up to him and took his place at Drashon's side. The rest of the guard trailed behind in two uniform rows.

"How are things, cousin?" the captain said.

Drashon looked tersely in the captain's direction. He wasn't interested in engaging a cousin so far removed he'd have to refer to the official annals to determine their exact relation.

He entered the palace, briefly taking in the grandeur of the enormous atrium as he walked around the gilded statue of his father. He crossed the atrium with long strides and made his way down the Hall of Relics, directly opposite the entrance. The hallway was uniquely adorned with tapestries reflecting the various cultures under the collective rule of the empire. As he proceeded, he passed relic upon relic on display at interval, all of them protected behind glass casings. The halls were open to the populace, so it was necessary to safeguard against thievery— though he couldn't fathom who would be audacious enough to steal from the emperor.

Drashon paused halfway down the hall at a display case that routinely drew his attention. He looked through the thick glass at the crown and armor of the previous ruler: The Dragon King. His grandfather. The gold crown was fashioned in the shape of a dragon. The front was a dragon's head turned upwards, about the height of a hand. Flames spewed upwards from its mouth, doubling its total height. The dragon's long neck curved down and around, its body wrapping around in a circle, forming the crown. The front legs and claws were situated so that they would extend down over the left ear of whoever wore the crown and the back legs over the right ear. The tail continued around and joined the dragon's upturned neck, finishing off the body of the crown. Intricately carved scales covered the body and individual teeth were visible in the dragon's open mouth. The claws were razor-sharp and looked as though they would slice open the scalp if not placed carefully on the head.

The armor had a dragon emblem on the left breast. It was golden in color, fashioned from the skin of the rarest variety of dragon. As far as he knew, there had only been one yellow dragon. Each of the scales that fashioned this intricate suit shimmered in the light. Anyone wearing this work of art would be truly regal.

"I always thought the crown looked odd without wings," the captain of the guard said.

"Yes," Drashon answered, not taking his eyes off the display. "The design was flawed. Just like the man who wore it."

"Chancellor," the captain said, "I wish we could stand here and discuss the Dragon King's character, but we really must continue. We mustn't keep the emperor waiting."

Drashon turned from the display and followed the captain down the hall. They turned left at the throne room's gilded doors, down to another door at the end of another short hall. He impatiently waited while the guards searched him for dragon bones. They found his timepiece and took it from him. Whatever they thought he could do with such a tiny bone he didn't know. But he was used to it and didn't argue. Then, he followed the captain into the small room with a metal door on the opposite side. The captain pushed the button next to the door. When the door slid open, Drashon stepped into the Lift. The captain followed him in and pushed the button on the inside. The Lift rose quickly, taking Drashon to his father's personal chamber. Thankfully, the captain didn't try to engage him in further banter.

The door slid open and he stepped into the emperor's quarters. He didn't bother searching the chamber but rather, he walked briskly past the pair of spiral staircases leading up to the emperor's bedroom and out to the balcony. He knew where his father would be. He found him standing by the railing looking west, toward the setting sun. Drashon walked over to him and knelt, saying, "I've arrived, Your Blessed Highness."

The emperor did not respond.

Drashon stood back up and joined his father. He looked over at the emperor, who still didn't acknowledge him. Instead, he stared straight ahead, off into the distance, at the sun. He wondered what his father's urgency was since now that he was here, he didn't seem to be in a rush to speak. He didn't want to be impertinent, so he waited.

Drashon shielded his eyes from the setting sun so he could see the city below. It was humming with activity. The streets were rivers flowing with Autos of many different sizes. Trains and Autos were his ideas. Even after more than two hundred years, no achievement had benefited the empire more than Trains and Autos did. It was his to claim. They quickly became integral to the Regency's ability to govern efficiently. Both connected the empire like never before.

"I've made a terrible mistake," Drakonias finally said.

Drashon turned from the river of motorized transportation to his father standing beside him. He was surprised to hear him speak in such a manner. The emperor was still staring directly ahead, not even shielding his eyes from the brightness of the setting sun. When had his father ever admitted being wrong about something? "Mistake?" he said, tentatively.

"Something's happening that I don't understand."

"What do you mean?"

"For a while now, I've been plagued by this feeling that something wasn't right. I've had this… itch. But I could never place my finger on it," Drakonias said. "And then… I finally realized what it was."

Drashon waited patiently for Drakonias to explain himself. However, his father still didn't seem to be in much of a rush. He just stood there, hands clasped behind his back, staring at the sun. He wanted to draw some of the warmth in to burn away his travel weariness, but he didn't dare Synthesize in his father's presence.

When the sun dipped below the horizon, Drakonias lifted a dragon-shaped bone off a stack of parchment sitting on the marble railing. He handed the top piece to Drashon and set the bone back on the remaining piece.

Drashon read it eagerly. But the farther he got the more his eagerness changed to fear and dread.

"What is this? I mean, I know what it is, but I don't understand why."

He didn't have to understand, he knew all he had to do was obey. But this… this *demanded* an explanation.

"The war did something to the sun," Drakonias said, still staring at the horizon.

"What are you talking about?"

"I don't know, but it's changing."

"What do you mean?"

"We must have done something to it."

Drashon looked the parchment over again. "So you're banning astronomy?"

"Yes."

"And ordering the execution of all astronomers?" Drashon again looked at the parchment. He wanted to make sure he'd read it correctly. "*And* their families?"

"And anyone known to be associated with them: friends, priests, it doesn't matter."

"But why?" Drashon said. He was being borderline impertinent, but he didn't care. What the emperor was suggesting… no commanding… was the execution of hundreds, if not thousands of people. And he wanted *him* to be in charge of it. Draego's Fire… if he was going to do this he was going to know why.

"Because news of this *cannot* spread."

"News of what? That's what I don't understand."

Drakonias finally turned to look and him and tersely said,

"Neither do I." He turned back toward the horizon. "But if anyone will, they will."

"So you want me to kill them? *All* of them?"

"Not all of them." Drakonias retrieved the second piece of parchment and handed it to Drashon. He gave Drashon time to read it, then said, "I need you to find out what's happening."

PART II

295 United Era

Vashon sat at his desk, and with frail fingers, put the finishing touches on his life's work. His second life, thanks to the blessed emperor. Despite having lived nearly twice as long as was natural, apprehension and fear gnawed at his senses.

He remembered the day he'd read the edict. He remembered dropping the piece of parchment onto his chart-covered desk and watching it roll back up on itself. He'd stared blankly at it, stupefied, wondering why the emperor would ban astronomy, his trade. It also declared all astronomical implements be surrendered to the Regency. He'd forgone many of life's pleasantries, including that of a wife and children, so that he could fully devote himself to his studies.

He remembered looking across his study at the Telescope positioned next to the window. It had been but one of many that he'd owned. That particular one he'd used for leisure. His other, bigger, Telescopes were at his observatory outside the city. He remembered the feeling of complete meaningless. What was he to do without astronomy? He'd been too old to learn a new trade.

The knock at the door still rang clear in his memory and drew his attention away from his Telescope. As quickly as his frail body permitted, he'd shuffled along the narrow path that wove around stacks of books. He'd gasped in fear when he opened the door just enough to peer out. The door swung open, forcing him to step back. A man wearing orange armor stepped in. Vashon bowed as deeply as the pain in his back allowed and said, "Welcome, Your Highness." He struggled to erect himself, then stepped aside to permit the chancellor entrance.

Two guards wearing gray-scaled armor pushed their way in first, knocking over stacks of books, and took up position just inside the door. The chancellor strolled in with his hands clasped behind his back. Two more guards followed him in and closed the door.

The chancellor walked down the narrow pathway between Vashon's lifetime of accumulated books. He picked one up from a pile, flipped through it as he walked, then set it back down on another pile. He stopped in front of the Telescope and slowly ran his hand down the polished bronze. After inspecting its many parts, he turned to face Vashon, who still cowered by the door.

"The emperor has need of your services," the chancellor said.

"The e-emperor?"

"And with it, comes both riches and immortality."

The fear that held Vashon frozen by the door melted away. Moments ago, Vashon sat at his desk wondering how he was going to survive. But Draego had supplied. He grinned broadly as he silently said a word of thanks.

And all too quickly, fifty years had passed since that fateful day. He sat at his desk in the twilight years of his second life. As he hesitated to put the finishing touches on his work, he reflected on his solitary meeting with the emperor.

The chancellor ushered him to Kyinth on a Train. Along the way, he enjoyed countless pleasantries. The pleasantries increased manifold upon his arrival in the capital of the United Realms. The privilege Vashon felt when he stood before His Blessed Highness was like nothing he'd ever before, or since, experienced. He counted himself as one of a blessed few who stood before the emperor and had the emperor's sole, undivided, attention as the emperor commissioned him for a great work.

He still clearly remembered that wonderful day when, after accepting the task the emperor laid before him, a strange sensation filled his body. Tingles coursed down his spine. Every day since then, he got the same feeling when he thought about the emperor using his gift to reverse times ravages on his body. He remembered the intense burning and the amazement he felt as he watched his withered hands grow smooth again. He remembered the shock he felt when the emperor directed him to an ornate mirror, and he peered once again at his youthful self. He stood amazed, inspecting his reflection. He'd been eighty-five years old, and he stared back in time at his younger self.

After that, he was escorted out of the emperor's presence and out of the royal palace, never to set foot in it again. But his gift was forever tainted when he returned to Tieger and learned of the horror bestowed upon his fellow astronomers and their families. But with time, his greed overshadowed his horror. After all, the emperor was the Blessed of the Dragon—his ways were perfect.

Twice a year, for the last fifty years, the chancellor came to Vashon's study and received an update. And now, once again old and frail, he was about to present his final report to the chancellor. *Did His Blessed Highness remember his promise?* Vashon wondered. Even though he had lived two full lifetimes, fortunate to have been bestowed with such a wonderful gift, he wasn't ready to give it up. He'd grown to love his gift of renewed youth, reveled in every experience he forewent in his first life. But now he sat in his chair, having once again grown old, the end of his life again nigh. With his task completed, would the emperor sweep him aside as a tool whose usefulness was spent? Like he did with the other astronomers?

He imagined he would feel joy and satisfaction after faithfully completing the task given to him, but that didn't turn out to be so. Instead, the apprehension he'd felt when he first read the emperor's edict grew stronger the closer he got to completion.

After much reflection, Vashon picked up a pen and inked his remarks. He set the pen down and sat back, his second life's work now complete. He glanced to his side at the mirror hanging on the wall and gazed at the reflection of the once again frail, gray-bearded man he had, for the second time, become.

Fear accompanied Vashon's apprehension. The chancellor saw that Vashon wanted for nothing. Unlike his first life, he lived his second life in comfort and luxury. The lifestyle had made him greedy and unwilling to give it up. Worried about what would happen to his support after he turned in the report, he'd been considering his need to possibly look after himself, especially since he was old once again. He turned from his reflection in the mirror and contemplated the bag of gold on his desk. It represented half of what was promised should he make a copy of his report and ensure it fell into the right hands. He stared at the bag and weighed the possibility of a painful death against more than enough gold to live comfortably for his remaining years. He turned again to his reflection in the mirror and decided he was likely to die soon either way. With his usefulness spent, he couldn't count on the emperor's gift a second time.

Vashon made up his mind. He turned from his reflection, grabbed a fresh piece of parchment, and began duplicating the report. As he worked, the setting sun began to shine through the window of his study and inched its way across the room. It worked its way up the legs of the desk and onto the surface. When it reached the pale parchment, it reflected brightly, making it difficult to see what he was writing. He set his pen down and rose to draw the shades.

At the window, he paused and gazed at the sun. For fifty years, at the direction of the emperor, he studied it. During that fateful meeting long ago, Vashon listened to the emperor's concerns and had, through careful observation and measurement, confirmed them to be true. The sun was changing. In truth, it was dying. The emperor wouldn't be pleased.

At least, Vashon thought, drawing the shades and turning back to his desk, *I'll be long dead before things get bad.*

PART III

295 United Era

Drashon stood before the gold-plated doors of the throne room. He stared at the dragon emblems emblazoned on each door while he awaited entrance. Huge tapestries hung on either side of the doors featuring the once common dragons soaring among the clouds. He resisted the urge to pull out his timepiece and check the time. He knew it was a nervous tick, and he didn't want to betray his emotions to the guards standing on either side of him.

The captain of the guard emerged from the throne room and, after he closed the heavy door behind him, said, "Chancellor, if you would permit a search of your person."

Drashon unclasped his coat and held out his arms. The captain signaled one of the guards to search him. The guard patted him down and checked the pockets of his coat, inside and out, looking for dragon bones or Energy powered Machines. The guard found the rolled-up parchment in his inner pocket and briefly examined it without breaking the wax seal. There was nothing suspicious about it, so he returned it to its place. The guard then found his timepiece, took it out of its inner pocket, and showed it to the captain.

"I'll need to keep this until you're finished," the captain said.

The guard handed it to the captain and then, finding nothing else, returned to his place at Drashon's side.

"Thank you, Chancellor. You may enter."

The guard to Drashon's left stepped forward and opened the door.

Drashon took a deep breath. Meeting his father here instead of in his personal quarters made him uneasy. He let the breath out and stepped through the gilded doors. He passed through the entryway with stairs on the left leading up to the viewing area, into the throne room.

At the far end of the room, up the stepped dais, his father sat on his throne, illuminated by the sun. Drashon's step faltered when he saw that his father was wearing black armor. The dragon statues perched above the throne looked toward him ominously. He forced himself to approach the dais where his father held the Dragon Scepter. A golden dragon clutched the scepter, its tail winding down the gilded bone. He wished desperately to fill himself with Energy, but he couldn't. The shields over the glass ceiling blocked the sun from reaching him. Even if he had access to Energy, it would be a mistake. Watchers would undoubtedly be keeping an eye on him from the balcony.

When he arrived at the foot of the dais, he knelt on one knee, bowed his head, and waited.

"You may rise," the emperor said.

Drashon stood and clasped his hands behind his back.

"No point in delaying the matter at hand, Chancellor. I've waited fifty years for the astronomer to finish. Do you have his report?"

"Yes, Your Blessed Highness," Drashon said, matching the formality his father chose to utilize. "Though I don't think you'll be pleased with his conclusions."

"Did you take care of the astronomer's… needs?"

"Yes, Your Highness. The astronomer won't be sharing his discovery with anybody. The only person that knows what's contained within his report is me." Drashon reached into his overcoat and drew out the rolled-up parchment sealed with wax. He held it out and said, "May I?"

The emperor gestured with his hand in a sweeping motion toward himself.

Drashon climbed the steps and squinted when the sunlight shined directly into his eyes and handed the parchment over. As he stood in the sun, he briefly considered filling himself with

Energy, but abandoned the thought just as quickly. Instead, he stood helplessly before his father.

The emperor took a few moments to study the report. He looked up and said, "This is much worse than I'd imagined, Drashon."

"Indeed, father," Drashon replied, matching his father's drop in formalities.

"It's been almost three hundred years since I first sat on this throne, Drashon. And it wasn't until now that I finally understand the full ramifications of the war." He paused for a moment and stared blankly at the parchment. "I've often wondered why my father surrendered. We fought for thirty years, neither gaining any significant advantage over the other. And now, I think I might understand why." After another pause, he added, "Perhaps his way would have been better."

Drashon looked at his father, confused, "Father, the war was necessary. What grandfather proposed was—"

"Yes," Drakonias said. "But this," he said, shaking the parchment, "proves our actions weren't worth it."

"It would be treasonous for me to agree…"

"Son," the emperor said, eyeing Drashon pensively. "It seems that everything we fought for was for naught. Unless this problem is remedied—if that's even possible—we're all going to die." Drakonias paused again before continuing. "You understand how vital it is that this information not leak out, don't you?"

Drashon nodded.

"Imagine the wide-spread chaos should this ever escape this room."

"I agree," Drashon said. He hadn't wanted to kill the astronomer, but he understood why it had been necessary.

"I simply cannot allow what's contained within this report to ever get out."

"Word of this will never—" Drashon stopped when he felt a familiar warmth enter his body. He looked at his father, confused. The emperor was directing Energy into him. "Father? I-I'm not due for Regeneration…"

"No," Drakonias said, "you are not." He rose from the throne with the Dragon Scepter in hand and said, "But this is necessary."

Drashon panicked when he realized what his father was doing. He turned and stumbled down the steps of the dais as his body filled with Energy. He'd grown accustomed to the sensation from the many times his father had restored his youth, but this didn't feel quite right. Normally the intense heat dispersed as the Energy wove through his body, undoing the ravages of time, but the heat didn't decrease. It was building. He ran for the doors, pulling the Energy into his Core, but it was building too fast. The heat overcame him, and he stumbled. He fell to the floor a dozen paces short of the exit. He dispersed Energy into the marble floor, but it was too late. The acrid smell of his burning flesh filled his nose.

Drashon writhed in pain. He forced himself to lift his head with the little strength he had left and looked toward his father. He reached out with a hand, pleading for mercy, but screamed as his body burst into flame.

ABOUT THE AUTHOR

Patrik grew up in the southwest and presently lives in Idaho. Earlier in life he almost exclusively read fantasy novels but has since broadened his horizon and enjoys many genres, both fiction and nonfiction. He has wanted to write a book for a long time but never really had any ideas. Then, one random day, when he least expected it, he had an inkling and started writing. In his spare time, he enjoys hanging out with his family and entertaining his exuberant dog Pearl (or the Black Pearl when she is naughty, and yes, she is black). He also enjoys a good beer. He occasionally brews it as well, but he's not nearly as good as Yolken.

www.ingramcontent.com/pod-product-compliance
Lightning Source LLC
Chambersburg PA
CBHW030830110726
47900CB00006B/1819